Praise for Jodi Picoult

'Picoult is a writer of high energy and conviction . . . she forges a finely honed, commanding and cathartic drama.'
– *Booklist*

'[*Plain Truth*] reads like a cross between the Harrison Ford movie *Witness* and Scott Turrow's novel *Presumed Innocent,* with a dose of television's *The Practice* thrown in.'
– *Arizona Republic*

'Picoult writes with a fine touch, a sharp eye for detail, and a firm grasp of the delicacy and complexity of human relationships.'
– *Boston Globe*

'The novelist displays an almost uncanny ability to enter the skins of her troubled young protagonists.'
– *New York Times*

'Picoult has the true storyteller's ability to evoke a world on the page and pull the reader into it.'
– *Woman's Review of Books*

'Engrossing . . . *The Pact* is compelling reading, right up to the stunning courtroom conclusion.'
– *People*

'[*Keeping Faith*] makes you wonder about God. And that is a rare moment, indeed, in modern fiction.'
– *USA Today*

'Part thriller, part courtroom drama and part family portrait, *Perfect Match* is an intriguing "what if".'
– *Sydney Morning Herald*

About the Author

Jodi Picoult received an A.B. in creative writing from Princeton University and a master's degree in education from Harvard. She is the author of ten previous books and lives in New Hampshire with her husband and three children. Read more about her by visiting her website at www.jodipicoult.com.

JODI PICOULT

Plain Truth

FLAME
Hodder & Stoughton

Copyright © 2000 by Jodi Picoult

First published in the United States in 2000 by Pocket Books,
a division of Simon and Schuster
First published in Great Britain in 2004 by Hodder and Stoughton,
a division of Hodder Headline

The right of Jodi Picoult to be identified as the Author of the Work
has been asserted by her in accordance with the
Copyright, Designs and Patents Act 1988.

A Flame paperback

10

A CIP catalogue record for this title is available from the British Library

ISBN 0 340 83547 8

Typeset in Plantin Light by
Palimpsest Book Production Limited,
Polmont, Stirlingshire
Printed and bound in Great Britain by
Mackays of Chatham Ltd, Chatham, Kent

Hodder Headline's policy is to use papers that are natural, renewable
and recyclable products and made from wood grown in sustainable forests.
The logging and manufacturing processes are expected to conform to the
environmental regulations of the country of origin.

Hodder and Stoughton
A division of Hodder Headline
338 Euston Road
London NW1 3BH

For my dad, Myron Picoult, who taught me to be an original.

There are not many men in the world who can sneeze like a duck, spy hales of bay, make very bad puns . . . and cherish their daughters so completely.

I love you.

ACKNOWLEDGMENTS

Once again, I find myself indebted to so many people: Dr Joel Umlas, Dr James Umlas, and Dr David Toub for their medical expertise; Dr Tia Horner and Dr Stuart Anfang for their explanations of forensic psychiatry and clinical interviews; Dr Catherine Lewis and Dr Neil Kaye, for helping me understand neonaticide; my father-in-law, Karl van Leer, who never once blinked when I called and asked about inseminating cows; Kyle van Leer, who saw a 'cookie moon' and let me borrow it; Teresa Farina for the fast transcriptions; Dr Elizabeth Martin, for finding listeria and leading me through autopsies; Steve Marshall, who took me ghost hunting; Brian Laird, for the troll story; Allegra Lubrano, for finding obscure legal statutes whenever I called frantically to ask 'a quick question'; Kiki Keating, attorney extraordinaire, for making the time to come with me to Lancaster and spending all those nights hunched over the tape recorder, brainstorming testimony; and Tim van Leer, for everything. Thanks also to Jane Picoult, who wanted her own sentence this time, for her insight and guiding comments. Thanks to Laura Gross for the same, and for possibly being the only person in the publishing business who wants me to write *faster*. To Emily Bestler and Kip Hakala – here's to the start of a beautiful relationship. And to Camille McDuffie – the third time's a charm. I am indebted to the works of John Hostetler and Donald Kraybill, and to the people I met in Lancaster, Pennsylvania, without whom this book could not have been written: Maribel Kraybill, Lt.

Renee Schuler, and especially Louise Stoltzfus, a wonderful writer herself, whose contributions here were invaluable. Finally, many thanks to the Amish men, women, and children I met, who graciously opened their homes and their hearts and let me into their world for a little while.

I

I must be a Christian child
Gentle, patient, meek and mild;
Must be honest, simple, true
In my words and actions too . . .
Must remember, God can view
All I think, and all I do.
                    – Amish school verse

I

She had often dreamed of her little sister floating dead beneath the surface of the ice, but tonight, for the first time, she envisioned Hannah clawing to get out. She could see Hannah's eyes, wide and milky; could feel Hannah's nails scraping. Then, with a start, she woke. It was not winter – it was July. There was no ice beneath her palms, just the tangled sheets of her bed. But once again, there was someone on the other side, fighting to be free.

As the fist in her belly pulled tighter, she bit her bottom lip. Ignoring the pain that rippled and receded, she tiptoed barefoot into the night.

The barn cat yowled when she stepped inside. She was panting by now, her legs shaking like willow twigs. Lowering herself to the hay in the far corner of the calving pen, she drew up her knees. The swollen cows rolled their blue moon eyes in her direction, then turned away quickly, as if they knew better than to bear witness.

She concentrated on the hides of the Holsteins until their black spots shimmied and swam. She sank her teeth into the rolled hem of her nightgown. There was a funnel of pressure, as if she were being turned inside out; and she remembered how she and Hannah used to squeeze through the hole in the barbed wire fence by the creek's edge, pushing and angled, all knees and grunts and elbows, until by some miracle they'd tumble through.

It was over as suddenly as it had begun. And lying on the matted, stained hay between her legs was a baby.

*   *   *

Aaron Fisher rolled over beneath the bright quilt to stare at the clock beside the bed. There had been nothing, no sound to wake him, but after forty-five years of farming and milking, the smallest things could pull him out of sleep: a footfall in the corn, a change in the pattern of the wind, the rasp of a mother's tongue roughing a newborn calf.

He felt the mattress give as Sarah came up on an elbow behind him, the long braid of her hair curling over her shoulder like a seaman's rope. *'Was ist letz?'* What's the matter?

It was not the animals; there was a full month before the first cow was due to deliver. It was not a robber; there was too little noise. He felt his wife's arm slip around him, hugging his back to her front. *'Nix,'* he murmured. Nothing. But he did not know if he was trying to convince Sarah, or himself.

She knew enough to cut the cord that spiraled purple to the baby's belly. Hands shaking, she managed to reach the old scissors that hung on a peg near the pen's door. They were rusty and coated with bits of hay. The cord severed in two thick snips, and then began spurting blood. Horrified, she pressed her fingers to the ends, pinching it shut, wildly looking around for something to tie it off.

She rummaged in the hay and came up with a small length of baling twine, which she quickly tied around the cord. The bleeding slowed, then stopped. Relieved, she sank back on her elbows – and then the newborn started to cry.

She snatched the baby up and rocked it tightly. With her foot, she kicked at the hay, trying to cover the blood with a clean layer. The baby's mouth opened and closed on the cotton of her nightgown, rooting.

She knew what the baby wanted, needed, but she couldn't do it. It would make this real.

So she gave the baby her pinkie finger instead. She let the small, powerful jaws suckle, while she did what she had been taught to do in times of extreme stress; what she had been doing for months now. 'Lord,' she prayed, 'please make this go away.'

The rustle of chains awakened her. It was still dark out, but the dairy cows' internal schedule had them rising at their individual stalls, their bags hanging blue-veined and round with milk, like full moons caught between their legs. She was sore and tired, but knew she had to get out of the barn before the men arrived to do the milking. Glancing down, she realized that a miracle had come to pass: the blood-soaked hay was fresh now, except for a small stain beneath her own bottom. And the two things she'd been holding when she fell asleep – the scissors and the newborn – were gone.

She pulled herself to her feet and glanced toward the roof, awed and reverent. *'Denke,'* she whispered, and then she ran out of the barn into the shadows.

Like all other sixteen-year-old Amish boys, Levi Esch no longer attended school. He'd gone through the eighth grade and was now in that limbo between being a child and being old enough to be baptized into the Amish faith. In the interim, he was a hired hand for Aaron Fisher, who no longer had a son to help him work his dairy farm. Levi had gotten the job through the recommendation of his older cousin Samuel, who'd been apprenticing with the Fishers now for five years. And since everyone knew that Samuel was probably going to marry the Fishers' daughter soon and set up his own farm, it meant Levi would be getting a promotion.

His workday started at 4:00 A.M., as on all other dairy farms. It was still pitch-dark, and Levi could not see Samuel's buggy approach, but he could hear the faint jingle of tack and traces. He grabbed his flat-brimmed straw hat and ran out the door, then jumped onto the seat beside Samuel.

'Hi,' he said breathlessly.

Samuel nodded at him but didn't turn, didn't speak.

'What's the matter?' Levi teased. 'Katie wouldn't kiss you good-bye last night?'

Samuel scowled and cuffed Levi, sending his hat spinning

into the back of the buggy. 'Why don't you just shut up?' The wind whispered at the ragged edge of the cornfield as they drove on in silence. After a while, Samuel pulled the buggy into the Fishers' front yard. Levi scuffed the toe of his boot into the soft earth and waited for Samuel to put the horse out to pasture before they headed into the barn.

The lights used for milking were powered by a generator, as were the vacuum pumps hooked up to the teats of the cows. Aaron Fisher knelt beside one of the herd, spraying the udders with iodine solution and then wiping them dry with a page ripped from an old phone book. 'Samuel, Levi,' he greeted.

He did not tell them what to do, because by now they already knew. Samuel maneuvered the wheelbarrow beneath a silo and began to mix the feed. Levi shoveled out the manure behind each cow, periodically looking at Samuel and wishing he was already the senior farmhand.

The barn door opened, and Aaron's father ambled in. Elam Fisher lived in the *grossduwdi haus,* a small apartment attached to the main building. Although Elam helped out with the milking, Levi knew the unwritten rules: make sure the old man carried nothing heavy; keep him from taxing himself; and make him believe that Aaron couldn't do without him, although Aaron could have, any day of the week. 'Boys,' Elam boomed, then stopped in his tracks, his nose wrinkled above his long, white beard. 'Why, we've had a calf.'

Puzzled, Aaron stood. 'No. I checked the pen.'

Elam shook his head. 'There's the smell of it, all the same.'

'More like it's Levi, needing a bath,' Samuel joked, emptying a fresh scoop of feed in front of the first cow.

As Samuel passed him with the wheelbarrow, Levi came up swinging and slipped on a slick of manure. He landed on his bottom in the ditch built to catch the refuse and set his jaw at Samuel's burst of laughter.

'Come on now,' Aaron chided, although a grin tugged at his mouth. 'Samuel, leave him be. Levi, I think Sarah left your spare clothes in the tack room.'

Levi scrambled to his feet, his cheeks burning. He walked past Aaron, past the chalkboard with the annotated statistics on the cows due to calve, and turned into the small cubby that housed the blankets and bridles used for the farm's workhorses and mules. Like the rest of the barn, it was neat as a pin. Braided leather reins crossed the wall like spiderwebs, and shelves were stacked with spare horseshoes and jars of liniment.

Levi glanced about but could see no clothing. Then he noticed something bright in the pile of horse blankets. Well, that would make sense. If Sarah Fisher had washed his things, they had probably been done with the other laundry. He lifted the heavy, striped blanket and recognized his spare trousers and jewel green shirt, rolled into a ball. Levi stepped forward, intending to shake it out, and found himself staring down into the tiny, still face of a newborn.

'Aaron!' Levi skidded to a stop, panting. 'Aaron, you've got to come.' He ran toward the tack room. Aaron exchanged a glance with his father, and they both started after the boy, with Samuel trailing.

Levi stood in front of a stool piled high with horse blankets, on top of which rested a sleeping baby wrapped in a boy's shirt. 'I . . . I don't think it's breathing.'

Aaron stepped closer. It had been a long time since he'd been around a baby this small. The soft skin of its face was cold. He knelt and tipped his head, hoping that its breath would fall into the cup of his ear. He flattened his hand against its chest.

Then he turned to Levi. 'Run to the Schuylers and ask to borrow their phone,' he said. 'Call the police.'

'Get out,' Lizzie Munro said to the officer in charge. 'I'm not going to check an unresponsive infant. Send an ambulance.'

'They're already there. They want a detective.'

Lizzie rolled her eyes. Every year that she'd been a detective-sergeant with the East Paradise Township police, the paramedics seemed to get younger. And more stupid. 'It's a medical call, Frank.'

'Well, something's out of kilter down there.' The lieutenant handed her a slip of paper with an address on it.

'Fisher?' Lizzie read, frowning at the surname and the street. 'They're Amish?'

'Think so.'

Lizzie sighed and grabbed her big black purse and her badge. 'You know this is a waste of time.' In the past, Lizzie had occasionally dealt with Old Order Amish teenagers, who'd gather together in some guy's barn to drink and dance and generally disturb the peace. Once or twice she'd been called to take a statement from an Amish businessman who'd been burglarized. But for the most part, the Amish had little contact with the police. Their community existed unobtrusively within the regular world, like a small air bubble impervious to the fluid around it.

'Just take their statements, and I'll make it up to you.' Frank held the door open for her as she left her office. 'I'll find a nice, fat felony for you to sink your teeth into.'

'Don't do me any favors,' Lizzie said, but she was grinning as she got into her car and headed to the Fisher farm.

The Fishers' front yard was crowded with a squad car, an ambulance, and a buggy. Lizzie walked up to the house and knocked on the front door.

No one answered, but a voice behind Lizzie called out a greeting, the cadences of the woman's dialect softening her consonants. A middle-aged Amish woman wearing a lavender dress and a black apron hurried toward Lizzie. 'I am Sarah Fisher. Can I help you?'

'I'm Detective-Sergeant Lizzie Munro.'

Sarah nodded solemnly and led Lizzie into the barn's tack room, where two paramedics knelt over a baby. Lizzie hunkered down beside one EMT. 'What have you got?'

'Newborn, emphasis on the new. No pulse or respirations

when we got here, and we haven't been able to revive him. One of the farmworkers found him wrapped up in that green shirt, underneath a horse blanket. Can't tell if it was stillborn or not, but someone was trying to hide the body all the same. I think one of your guys is around by the milking stalls, he might be able to tell you more.'

'Wait a second – someone gave birth to this baby, and then tried to conceal it?'

'Yeah. About three hours ago,' the paramedic murmured.

Suddenly the simple medical response call was more complicated than Lizzie had expected, and the most likely suspect was standing four feet away. Lizzie glanced up at Sarah Fisher, who wrapped her arms around herself and shivered. 'The baby . . . it's dead?'

'I'm afraid so, Mrs Fisher.'

Lizzie opened her mouth to ask another question, but was distracted by the distant sound of equipment being moved about. 'What's that?'

'The men, finishing up the milking.'

Lizzie's brows shot up. 'The milking?'

'These things . . .' the woman said quietly. 'They still have to be done.'

Suddenly, Lizzie felt profoundly sorry for her. Life never stopped for death; she should know that better than most. She gentled her voice and put her hand on Mrs Fisher's shoulder, not quite certain what sort of psychological state the woman was in. 'I know this must be very difficult for you, but I'm going to have to ask you some questions about your baby.'

Sarah Fisher raised her eyes to meet Lizzie's. 'It's not my baby,' she said. 'I have no idea where it came from.'

A half hour later, Lizzie leaned down beside the crime scene photographer. 'Stick to the barn. The Amish don't like having their pictures taken.' The man nodded, shooting a roll around the tack room, with several close-ups of the infant's corpse.

At least now she understood why she'd been called down. An unidentified dead infant, an unknown mother who'd abandoned it. And all this smack in the middle of an Amish farm.

She had interviewed the neighbors, a Lutheran couple who swore that they'd never heard so much as raised voices from the Fishers, and who couldn't imagine where the baby might have come from. They had two teenage daughters, one of whom sported a nose and navel ring, who had alibis for the previous night. But they had agreed to undergo gynecological exams to rule themselves out as suspects.

Sarah Fisher, on the other hand, had not.

Lizzie considered this as she stood in the milk room, watching Aaron Fisher empty a small hand tank of milk into a larger one. He was tall and dark, his arms thick with ropes of muscle developed by farming. His beard brushed the second button of his shirt. As he finished, he set down the tank and turned to give Lizzie his full attention.

'My wife was not pregnant, Detective,' Aaron said.

'You're certain?'

'Sarah can't have more children. The doctors made it that way, after she almost died birthing our youngest.'

'Your other children, Mr Fisher – where were they when the baby was found?'

A shadow passed over the man's face, disappearing as quickly as Lizzie had marked it. 'My daughter was asleep, upstairs. My other child . . . is gone.'

'Gone, like down the road to her own home?'

'Dead.'

'This daughter who was asleep is how old?'

'Eighteen.'

At that, Lizzie glanced up. Neither Sarah Fisher nor the paramedics had mentioned that there was another woman of childbearing age who lived on the farm. 'Is it possible that she was pregnant, Mr Fisher?'

The man's face turned so red that Lizzie grew worried. 'She isn't even married.'

'It's not a prerequisite, sir.'

Aaron Fisher stared at the detective coldly, clearly. 'It is for us.'

It seemed to take forever to get through milking all forty cows, and it had nothing to do with the arrival of a second battalion of police officers. Samuel closed the pasture gate after letting out the heifers and walked toward the main house. He should go help Levi sweep out the barn one last time for the morning, but this once it would wait.

He didn't bother to knock. Just opened the door, as if the home was already his and the young woman inside at the stove also belonged to him. He stopped for a moment, watching the sun grace her profile and gild her honey hair, her movements quick and efficient as she fixed breakfast.

'Katie,' Samuel said, stepping inside.

She turned quickly, the spoon flying up in the batter bowl as she started. 'Oh, Samuel. I wasn't expecting you yet.' She peered around his shoulder, as if she might see an army behind him. 'Mam said I ought to make enough for everyone.'

Samuel walked forward and took the bowl, setting it on the counter. He reached for her hands. 'You don't look so good.'

She grimaced. 'Thanks for the compliment.'

He drew her closer. 'Are you okay?'

Her eyes, when they met his, were the jewel blue of an ocean he had once seen on the cover of a travel magazine, and – he imagined – just as endlessly deep. They were what had first attracted him to Katie, across a crowded church service. They were what made him believe that, even years from now, he would do anything for this one woman.

She ducked away from him and began to flip the pancakes. 'You know me,' she said breathlessly. 'I get nervous around these *Englischers*.'

'Not so many. Only a handful of policemen.' Samuel frowned at her back in concern. 'They may want to talk to you, though. They seem to want to talk to everyone.'

She set the spatula down and turned slowly. 'What did they find out there?'

'Your mother didn't tell you?'

Katie slowly shook her head, and Samuel hesitated, torn between her trust in him to tell her the truth and the desire to keep her blissfully unaware for as long as possible. He ran his hands through his straw-colored hair, making it stand on end. 'Well, they found a baby. Dead.'

He saw her eyes widen, those incredible eyes, and then she sank down onto one of the kitchen chairs. 'Oh,' she whispered, stunned.

In a moment he was at her side, holding her close and whispering that he would take her away from here, and to heck with the police. He felt her soften against him, and for a moment Samuel was triumphant – after so many days of being rebuffed, to finally come back to this. But Katie stiffened and drew away. 'I don't think this is the time,' she chided. She stood and turned off the stove's gas burners, then folded her arms across her middle. 'Samuel, I think I *would* like you to take me somewhere.'

'Anywhere,' he promised.

'I want you to take me to see this baby.'

'It's blood,' the medical examiner confirmed, kneeling in the calving pen in front of a small, dark stain. 'And placenta. Not a cow's, from the size of it. Someone had a baby recently.'

'Stillborn?'

He hesitated. 'I can't say without doing the autopsy – but my hunch says no.'

'So it just . . . died?'

'I didn't say that, either.'

Lizzie sat back on her heels. 'You're telling me someone intentionally killed this baby?'

The man shrugged. 'I guess that's up to you to find out.'

Lizzie calculated quickly in her mind. Given such a small window between the baby's birth and death, chances were that the perpetrator of the crime was the infant's mother. 'What are we talking? Strangulation?'

'Smothering, more likely. I should have a preliminary autopsy report by tomorrow.'

Lizzie thanked him and wandered away from the scene the patrolmen were now securing. All of a sudden this was no longer an abandonment case, but a potential homicide. There was enough probable cause to get a warrant from a district judge for blood samples, evidence that might point a finger at the woman who had done this.

She stopped walking as the barn door opened. A tall blond man – one of the farm help – stepped into the dim light with a young woman. He nodded at Lizzie. 'This is Katie Fisher.'

She was lovely, in that sturdy Germanic style that always made Lizzie think of fresh cream and springtime. She wore the traditional garb of the Old Order Amish: a long-sleeved dress, covered by a black apron that fell just below her knees. Her feet were bare and callused – it had always amazed Lizzie to see these Amish youth running down gravel roads without their shoes, but that was how they spent the summer. The girl was also so nervous that Lizzie could nearly smell her fear. 'I'm glad you're here, Katie,' Lizzie said gently. 'I've been looking for you, so that I can ask you some questions.'

At that, Katie moved closer to the blond giant beside her. 'Katie was asleep last night,' he said. 'She didn't even know what happened until I told her.'

Lizzie tried to gauge the girl's response, but something had distracted her. She was staring over Lizzie's shoulder into the tack room, where the medical examiner was supervising the removal of the baby's body.

Suddenly the girl wrenched away from Samuel and ran out the barn door, with Lizzie chasing her to the farmhouse porch.

As reactions to death went, this was a violent one. Lizzie watched the girl trying to compose herself, and wondered what had prompted it. Had this been any ordinary teen, Lizzie would have taken such behavior as an indication of guilt – but Katie Fisher was Amish, which required her to filter her thoughts. If you were Amish, you could grow up in Lancaster County without television news broadcasts and R-rated movies, without rape and wife-beating and murder. You could see a dead baby and be honestly, horribly shocked by the sight.

Then again, there had been cases in recent years; teenage mothers who'd hidden their pregnancies and after the birth had tied up the loose ends by getting rid of the newborn. Teenage mothers who were completely unaware of what they'd done. Teenage mothers who came in all shapes, all sizes, all religions.

Katie leaned against a pillar and sobbed into her hands. 'I'm sorry,' the girl said. 'Seeing it – the body – it made me think of my sister.'

'The one who died?'

Katie nodded. 'She drowned when she was seven.'

Lizzie looked toward the fields, a green sea that rippled with the breeze. In the distance, a horse whinnied, and another answered. 'Do you know what happens when you have a baby?' Lizzie asked quietly.

Katie narrowed her eyes. 'I live on a farm.'

'I know. But animals are different from women. And if women do give birth, and don't get medical attention afterward, they may be putting themselves in great danger.' Lizzie hesitated. 'Katie, do you have anything you want to tell me?'

'I didn't have a baby,' Katie answered, looking directly at the detective. 'I didn't.' But Lizzie was staring at the porch floor. There was a small maroon smudge on the painted white planks. And a slow trickle of blood, running down Katie's bare leg.

2

Ellie

My nightmares were full of children. Specifically, six little girls –
two dark-haired, four fair, their knees sticking out beneath the
plaid uniform jumper of St Ambrose's School, their hands
twisting in their laps. I watched them all grow up in an instant,
you see; at the very moment a jury foreman acquitted my client,
the elementary school principal who had molested them.

It was my biggest triumph as a Philadelphia defense attorney;
the verdict that put me on the map and had my phone ringing
off the hook with calls from other well-bred community icons
hoping to dance through the loopholes of the law to keep their
own skeletons in their closets. The night after the verdict came
back, Stephen took me out to Victor's Café for a meal so expensive we could have bought a used car instead. He introduced
me to the maître d' as 'Jeannie Cochran.' He told me that the
two senior partners in his own firm, the most prestigious in the
city, had invited me in to have a talk.

'Stephen,' I said, amazed, 'when I interviewed there five
years ago, you told me you couldn't have a relationship with a
woman that worked at your firm.'

He shrugged. 'Five years ago, Ellie,' he said, 'things were
different.'

He was right. Five years ago, I had still been building my
career. Five years ago, I believed that the main beneficiary of
an acquittal was my client, rather than myself. Five years ago,
I could only dream of an opportunity like the one Stephen was
offering in his firm.

I smiled at him. 'So what time's the meeting?'

Later, I excused myself to go to the bathroom. An attendant

was there, waiting patiently beside a tray of complimentary makeup and hair spray and perfume. I went into a stall and started to cry – for those six little girls, for the evidence I had successfully suppressed, for the attorney I wanted to be years ago when I first graduated from law school – one so full of principle that I would never have taken this case, much less worked so hard to win it.

I came out and ran the water to wash my hands. I hiked up the silk sleeves of my suit jacket and began to scrub, working lather between my fingers, into my nails. At a tap on my shoulder I turned to see the bathroom attendant handing me a linen towel. Her eyes were hard and dark as chestnuts. 'Honey,' she said, 'some stains ain't never gonna come clean.'

There was one more child in my nightmares, but I'd never seen its face. This was the baby I hadn't had, and at the rate things were going, never would. People made fun of biological clocks, but they were inside women like me – although I'd never seen the ticking as a wake-up call, but rather as the prelude to a bomb. Hesitate, hesitate, and then – boom! – you'd blown all your chances.

Did I mention: Stephen and I had lived together for eight years.

The day after the principal of St Ambrose's was acquitted, he sent me two dozen red roses. Stephen walked into the kitchen as I was stuffing them into the trash.

'What did you do that for?'

I turned to him slowly. 'Does it ever bother you? That once you've crossed the line, you can't go back?'

'Holy Christ, you're talking like Confucius again. Just say what you mean, Ellie.'

'I am. I just wanted to know if it gets you. Right here.' I pointed to my heart, still hurting. 'Do you ever look at the people sitting across the courtroom, the ones whose lives were ruined by a person you know is guilty as hell?'

Stephen picked up his coffee mug. 'Someone's got to defend them. That's how our legal system works. If you're such a bleeding heart, go work for the DA.' He pulled a rose out of the trash can, snapped off its stem, and tucked it behind my ear. 'You've got to get your mind off this. What do you say you and I head out to Rehoboth Beach and bodysurf?' Leaning closer, he added, 'Naked.'

'Sex isn't a Band-Aid, Stephen.'

He took a step back. 'Pardon me if I've forgotten. It's been so long.'

'I don't want to have this discussion now.'

'There isn't one to have, El. I've already got a twenty-year-old daughter.'

'But I don't.' The words hung in the air, as delicate and arresting as a soap bubble the instant before it bursts. 'Look, I can understand why you wouldn't want to have the vasectomy reversed. But there are other ways—'

'There aren't. I'm not going to watch you poring over some sperm donor catalog at night. And I don't want a social worker going through everything from my tax records to my underwear drawer trying to decide if I'm worthy enough to raise some Chinese kid who was left on a mountaintop to die of exposure—'

'Stephen, just stop already! You're out of control!'

To my surprise, he quieted immediately. He sat down, tight-lipped and furious. 'That was unnecessary,' he said finally. 'I mean, Ellie, that really hurt.'

'What?'

'What you just said. God – you called me a fucking troll!'

I met his gaze. 'I said you were *out of control.*'

Stephen blinked, then started to laugh. 'Out of control – oh, God! I didn't hear you.'

When was the last time you *did?* I thought, but managed to curb the words before I spoke them.

The law offices of Pfister, Crown and DuPres were located in downtown Philadelphia, sprawled across three floors of a modern

glass-and-steel skyscraper. I spent hours dressing for my appointment with the partners, discarding four suits before I found the
one that I believed made me look most confident. I used extra
antiperspirant. I drank a cup of decaf, afraid that the real stuff
would make my hands tremble. I mentally plotted the route to
the building in my mind, and left nearly an hour for travel time,
although it was only fifteen miles away.

At exactly eleven o'clock I slid behind the wheel of my
Honda. 'Senior partner,' I murmured into the rearview mirror.
'And anything less than $300,000 a year is unacceptable.' Sliding
my sunglasses on, I headed for the highway.

Stephen had left a tape in my car, a mix of what he liked to
call his 'kick-ass' music, which he listened to when he was en
route to litigations. With a small smile, I pushed it in to play,
letting the drums and the backbeat thrum through the car. I
turned it up loud, so loud that when I changed lanes precipitously, I could barely hear the angry horn of the pickup I'd cut
off.

'Oops,' I murmured, flexing my hands on the steering wheel.
Almost immediately, it jumped beneath my touch. I gripped it
harder, but that only seemed to make the car buck like a mustang.
A clear stream of fear pooled from my throat to my stomach,
the quick panic that comes when you realize something has
gone terribly wrong, something that it is simply too late to fix.
In my rearview mirror I saw the truck looming closer, honking
furiously, as my car gave a great shudder and stopped dead in
the middle of sixty-mile-per-hour traffic.

I closed my eyes, bracing for a crash that never came.

I was still trembling thirty minutes later as I stood beside Bob,
the namesake of Bob's Auto Service, while he tried to explain
what had happened to my car. 'Basically, it melted,' he said,
wiping his hands on his coveralls. 'The oil pan cracked, the
engine seized, and the internal parts glommed together.'

'Glommed together,' I repeated slowly. 'So how do you separate them?'

'You don't. You buy a new engine. You're talking five or six thousand.'

'Five or six—' The mechanic started to walk away from me. 'Hey! What am I supposed to do until then?'

Bob glanced at my suit, my briefcase, my heels. 'Get a pair of Reeboks.'

A telephone began to ring. 'Shouldn't you get that?' the mechanic asked, and I realized the sound was coming from the depths of my own briefcase. I groaned at the recollection of my appointment at the law office. I was already fifteen minutes late.

'Where the hell are you?' Stephen barked when I answered the phone.

'My car died. On the middle of the highway. In front of an oncoming truck.'

'For Christ's sake, Ellie, that's why there are taxis!'

I was shocked silent. No 'My God, are you all right?' No 'Do you need me to come help you?' I watched Bob shake his head over the twisted intestines of what used to be my engine and felt a strange peace settle over me. 'I'm not going to be able to make it today,' I said.

Stephen let out a deep sigh. 'Well, I suppose I could convince John and Stanley to reschedule. Let me call you right back.'

The line went dead in my hand. Absentmindedly I clicked it off, and then stepped up to my car again. 'The good news,' Bob said, 'is that after you replace the engine, you pretty much have a brand-new car.'

'I liked my old car.'

He shrugged. 'Then pretend it's your old car. With a brand-new heart.'

I suddenly saw the truck that had been behind me on the highway, swerving and beeping; the other cars that had parted around mine, a stone in a river. I smelled the hot, rippling asphalt that sank beneath my heels as I tiptoed, shaky, across the highway. I was not one to believe in fate, but this had been too close a call, too sure a sign; as if I literally needed to be stopped short before I realized that I'd been running in the wrong direction. After my car had broken down I had called the state police and several service stations, but I had never thought to call Stephen. Somehow, I had known that if I needed to be rescued, I was going to have to do it myself.

The telephone began to ring again. 'Good news,' Stephen said before I'd even given a greeting. 'The Big Guys are willing to see you today at six o'clock.'

That was the moment I knew I would be leaving.

Stephen helped me load my things into the back of my car. 'I completely understand,' he said, although he didn't. 'You want to take some time off before choosing your next big case.'

I wanted to take some time off before choosing whether I ever wanted to take another case, period, but that was beyond Stephen's realm of belief. You didn't go to law school and make *Law Review* and work in the trenches to land the trial of a life-time, only to question your own career choice. But on another level, Stephen couldn't accept that I might be moving away for good. I knew this because I felt the same way. In our eight years together we had not married, but we hadn't separated, either.

'You'll call me when you get there?' Stephen asked, but before I could answer, he kissed me. Our lips separated like a seam being ripped, and then I got into the car and drove away.

I suppose other women in my position – by this I mean heart-broken, at odds, and recently given a large sum of money – might have chosen a different destination. Grand Cayman, Paris, even a soul-searching hike through the Rockies. For me, there was never any question that if I wanted to lick my wounds, I would wind up in Paradise, Pennsylvania. As a child, I'd spent a week there every summer. My great-uncle had a farm there and progressively sold off lots and parcels of land until he died, at which point his son Frank moved into the big house, planted grass where the field corn had been, and opened a woodworking shop. Frank was my father's age, and had been married to Leda long before I was ever born.

I couldn't begin to tell you what I did during those summers in Paradise, but what stayed with me all those years was the calm that pervaded their home, and the smooth efficiency with which things were accomplished. At first, I'd thought it was because Leda and Frank had never had children of their own. Later, I came to understand it was something in Leda herself, something tied to the fact that she had grown up Amish.

You could not summer in Paradise and not come in contact with the Old Order Amish, who were such an intrinsic part of the Lancaster area. The Plain people, as they called themselves, clipped along in their buggies in the thick of automobile traffic; they stood in line at the grocery store in their old-fashioned clothing; they smiled shyly from behind their farm stands where we went to buy fresh vegetables. That was, in fact, how I learned about Leda's past. We were waiting to buy armfuls of sweet corn when Leda struck up a conversation – in Pennsylvania Dutch! – with the woman who was making the sale. I was eleven, and hearing Leda – as American as me – slip into the Germanic dialect was enough to astound me. But then Leda handed me a ten-dollar bill. 'Give this to the lady, Ellie,' she said, even though she was standing right there and could have done it herself.

On the drive home, Leda explained that she had been Plain until she married Frank – who wasn't Plain. By the rules of her religion, she was put under the *bann* – restricted from certain social contact with people who were still Amish. She could talk to Amish friends and family, but couldn't eat at the same table with them. She could sit beside them on the bus, but not offer them a ride in her car. She could buy from them, but needed a third party – me – to transact the sale.

Her parents, her sisters and brothers – they lived less than ten miles away.

'Are you allowed to go see them?' I'd asked.

'Yes, but I hardly ever do,' Leda told me. 'You'll understand one day, Ellie. I'm not keeping my distance because it's uncomfortable for me. I'm keeping my distance because it's uncomfortable for them.'

Leda was waiting when the train pulled into the Strasburg railroad station. As I stepped off, carrying my two bags, she held out her arms. 'Ellie, Ellie,' she sang. She smelled of oranges and Windex; her wide shoulder was the perfect place to rest my head. I was thirty-nine years old, but in Leda's embrace, I was eleven again.

She led me toward the small parking lot. 'You going to tell me what's the matter now?'

'Nothing's the matter. I just wanted to visit you.'

Leda snorted. 'The only time you come to visit is when you're about to have a nervous breakdown. Did something happen with Stephen?' When I didn't answer, she narrowed her eyes. 'Or maybe nothing happened with Stephen – and that's the problem?'

I sighed. 'It's not Stephen. I finished a very trying case, and . . . well, I needed to relax.'

'But you won the case. I saw it on the news.'

'Yeah, well, winning isn't everything.'

To my surprise, she didn't say anything in response. I fell asleep as soon as Leda pulled onto the highway, and woke with a start when she pulled into her driveway. 'I'm sorry,' I said, embarrassed. 'I didn't mean to conk out like that.'

Leda smiled and patted my hand. 'You spend as much time as you need to relaxing here.'

'Oh, it won't be for long.' I took my bags from the backseat and hurried up the porch steps behind Leda.

'Well, we're glad to have you, for two nights or two dozen.' She cocked her head. 'Phone's ringing,' she said, pushing open the door and rushing in to pick up the receiver. 'Hello?'

I set down my suitcases and stretched to work out the kinks in my back. Leda's kitchen was neat as a pin, just like always, and looked exactly the way I had remembered: the stitched sampler on the wall, the cookie jar in the shape of a pig, the black and white squares of linoleum. Closing my eyes, it was easy to pretend I'd never left here, to believe that the most difficult choice I'd have to make that day was whether to curl up in an Adirondack chair out back or on the creaky swing on the screened porch. Across the kitchen, Leda was clearly surprised to hear the voice of whoever it was that had called. 'Sarah, Sarah, sssh,' she soothed. *'Was ist letz?'* I could only make out small snippets of unfamiliar words: *an Kind . . . er hat an Kind gfuna . . . es Kind va dodt.* Sinking down on a counter stool, I waited for Leda to finish the call.

When she hung up, her hand remained on the receiver for a long moment. Then she turned to me, pale and shaken. 'Ellie, I am so sorry, but I have to go somewhere.'

'Do you need me—'

'You stay here,' Leda insisted. 'You're here to rest.'

I watched her pull away in her car. Whatever the problem was, Leda would fix it. She always did. Putting my feet up on a second stool, I smiled. I'd been in Paradise for fifteen minutes, and I felt better already.

3

'*Neh!*' Katie screamed, kicking out at the paramedic who was trying to load her into the ambulance. '*Ich will net gay!*'

Lizzie watched the girl fight. The bottom of her dress, a rich green, was by now stained black with blood. In a tight, shocked semicircle stood the Fishers, Samuel, and Levi. The big blond man stepped forward, his jaw set. 'Let her down,' he said in clear English.

The paramedic turned. 'Buddy, I'm only trying to help her.' He managed to haul Katie into the rear of the ambulance. 'Mr and Mrs Fisher, you're welcome to ride along.'

Sarah Fisher sobbed, clutching at her husband's shirt and pleading with him in a language Lizzie could not understand. He shook his head, then turned and walked away, calling for the men to join him. Sarah gingerly climbed into the ambulance and held her daughter's hand, whispering until Katie calmed. The paramedics closed the double doors; the ambulance began to rumble down the long driveway, kicking up pebbles and clouds of dust.

Lizzie knew she had to get to the hospital and speak to the doctors who would examine Katie, but she didn't move just yet. Instead she watched Samuel – who had not followed Aaron Fisher, but remained rooted to the spot, watching the ambulance disappear from his sight.

The world was rushing by. Overhead, the line of fluorescent lights looked like the dashes in the middle of a paved road, running quick as they did when seen from the back of a buggy. The stretcher she was on came to an abrupt stop and a voice

at her head called, 'On my count – one, two, three!' Then
Katie was being spirited through the air, floating down to a
cold, shining table.

The paramedic was telling everyone her name and, for
goodness sake, that she'd been bleeding *down there*. A woman's
face loomed over hers, assessing. 'Katie? Do you speak
English?'

'*Ja,*' she murmured.

'Katie, are you pregnant?'

'No!'

'Can you tell us when your last period was?'

Katie's cheeks went scarlet, and she turned away in silence.

She could not help but notice the lights and the noises of
this strange hospital. Bright screens were filled with undulating
waves; beeps and whirrs framed her on all sides; scattered voices
called out in an odd synchronicity that reminded her of church
hymns sung in the round. 'BP is eighty over forty,' a nurse
said.

'Heart rate one-thirty.'

'Respiratory rate?'

'It's twenty-eight.'

The doctor turned to Katie's mother. 'Mrs Fisher? Was
your daughter pregnant?' Stunned by the commotion, Sarah
stared mutely at the man. 'Christ,' the doctor muttered. 'Just
get the skirt off her.'

Katie felt their hands tugging at her clothes, pulling at her
privacy. 'It's part of a dress, and I can't find the buttons,' a
nurse complained.

'There are none. It's pinned. What the—'

'Cut it off, if you have to. I want a BSU, a urine hCG, a
CBC, and send a type and screen to the blood bank, all stat.'
The doctor's face floated before Katie again. 'Katie, I'm going
to examine your uterus now. Do you understand? Just relax,
I'm going to be touching you between your legs—'

At the first gentle probe, Katie lashed out with her foot.
'Hold her,' the doctor commanded, and two nurses secured

her ankles in the stirrups. 'Just relax, now. I won't hurt you.' Tears began to roll down Katie's cheeks as the doctor dictated to a nurse with a clipboard. 'In addition to what might be lochia rubia, we've got a boggy, uncontracted uterus, about twenty-four weeks' size. Looks like an open cervical os. Let's get an ultrasound now to see what we're dealing with. How's the bleeding?'

'Still a steady flow.'

'Get an OB/GYN down here now.'

A nurse wrapped a wad of ice in cotton and placed it between Katie's legs. 'This'll make it feel better, honey,' she whispered.

Katie tried to focus on the nurse's face, but by now her vision was shaking as badly as her jellied arms and legs. The nurse, noticing, draped her with another blanket. Katie wished she had the words to thank her, wished she had the words to tell her that what she really needed was someone to hold her together before she broke apart right there on the table, but her thoughts were coming in the language with which she'd grown up.

'You're gonna be okay,' the nurse soothed.

After one sidelong glance at her mother, Katie closed her eyes and blacked out, believing that this might be so.

On the train platform, her mother pressed five twenty-dollar bills into her hand. 'You remember what station you change at?' Katie nodded. 'And if he isn't there to meet you, you call him.' Her mother touched Katie's cheek. 'This time, it's okay to use the telephone if you have to.'

It went without saying that using a telephone would be the least of her sins. For the first time since her brother Jacob had moved out, Katie – only twelve years old – was going to visit him. All the way in State College, where he was going to university.

Her mother looked nervously around at the other passengers waiting to board, hoping to keep out of the sight of other Plain people, who might report back to Aaron that his wife and his daughter had lied to him.

The long, sleek Amtrak ribboned into the station, and Katie hugged her mother tightly. 'You could come with me,' she whispered fiercely.

'You don't need me. You're a big girl.'

It wasn't what Katie meant, and they both knew it. If Sarah went with her daughter to State College, she'd be disobeying her husband, and that wasn't done. As it was, sending Katie as an envoy of her love was walking the very fine tightrope of insubordination. Plus, Katie hadn't been baptized yet in the church. By the rules of the Ordnung, *Sarah would not be able to ride in a car with her excommunicated son; would not be allowed to eat at the same table. 'You go,' she said, smiling hard at her daughter. 'You come back and tell me all about him.'*

On the train Katie sat by herself, closing her eyes against the curious looks and the people who pointed at her clothing and head covering. She folded her hands in her lap and thought of the last time she had seen Jacob, the sun bright as a halo on his copper hair, when he walked out of their house for good.

As the train pulled into State College, Katie pressed her face to the window, searching the sea of English faces for her brother. She was used to folks who were not Plain, of course, but even on the most busy thoroughfares in East Paradise she would see at least one or two others dressed like her, speaking her language. The people waiting on the platform were dressed in a dizzying splash of colors. Some of the women were wearing tiny tops and shorts that left almost all of their bodies bare. With horror, she noticed one young man with a ring in his nose and one in his ear and a chain connecting the two.

She did not see Jacob.

When she stepped off the train, she pivoted in a slow circle, frightened of being swallowed up by so much movement. Suddenly she felt a tap on her shoulder. 'Katie?'

She turned to see her brother, and flushed with surprise. Of course she had overlooked him. She'd been expecting Jacob in his wide-brimmed straw hat, his black trousers with suspenders. This Jacob was clean-shaven, wearing a short-sleeved plaid shirt and khaki pants.

Then she was in his arms, hugging him so tightly that she only now realized how lonely she had been at home without him. 'Mam misses you,' Katie said breathlessly. 'She says I have to tell her every last thing.'

'I miss her too.' Jacob draped his arm around her shoulders and steered Katie through the crowd. 'I think you've grown a foot.' He led his sister to a parking lot, to a small blue car. Katie stopped behind it and stared. 'It's mine,' Jacob said softly. 'Katie, what did you expect?'

The truth is, she hadn't expected anything. Except that the brother she had loved, the one who had turned his back on his religion so that he could study at college, might be living the same life he'd left . . . only somewhere other than East Paradise. This – the strange clothing, the tiny vehicle – made her wonder if her father had not been right all along to believe that Jacob could not continue his schooling and still be Plain in his heart.

Jacob opened the door for her and then got into the car himself. 'Where does Dat think you are today?'

The day that Jacob had been excommunicated by the Amish church was the same day he'd died, in his father's unforgiving eyes. Aaron Fisher would not countenance Katie visiting Jacob any more than he would approve of the letters her mother wrote Jacob and had Katie secretly post. 'Aunt Leda's.'

'Very smart. There's no way he'll stomach talking to her long enough to find out it's a lie.' Jacob smiled wryly. 'We shunned have to stick together, I guess.'

Katie folded her hands in her lap. 'Is it worth it?' she asked quietly. 'Is college everything you wanted?'

Jacob studied her for a long moment. 'It's not everything, because you all aren't here.'

'You could come back, you know. You could come back anytime and make a confession.'

'I could, but I won't.' At Katie's frown, Jacob reached across the console and tugged at the long strings of her kapp. *'Hey. I'm still the guy who pushed you into the pond when we went fishing. Who put a frog in your bed.'*

Katie smiled. *'I guess I wouldn't mind if you changed, come to think of it.'*

'That's my girl,' Jacob laughed. 'I have something for you.' He reached into the backseat and withdrew a bundle wrapped in butcher paper and tied with red ribbon. 'I don't want you to take this the wrong way, but when you come here, I want it to be a holiday for you. An escape. So that maybe you don't have to make the same all-or-nothing choice that I did.' He watched her fingers pick at the bow and open the package to reveal a pair of soft leggings, a bright yellow T-shirt, and a cotton cardigan embroidered with a festival of flowers.

'Oh,' Katie said, drawn in spite of herself. Her fingers traced the fine needlework on the collar of the sweater. 'But I—'

'For while you're here. Walking around in your regular clothes is only going to make it harder on you. Wearing these – well, no one's ever gonna know, Katie. I thought maybe you could pretend for a while, when you visit. Be like me. Here.' He flipped down the visor in front of Katie to reveal a small mirror, then held the cardigan up so that she could see the reflection.

She blushed. 'Jacob, it's beautiful.'

Even Jacob was astounded at how that one awed admission seemed to make his sister look like someone else, like the kind of person he had grown up keeping at a distance. 'Yes,' he said. 'You are.'

Lizzie called the county attorney's office on her car phone, en route to the hospital. 'George Callahan,' the voice on the other end announced brusquely.

'Imagine that. I got the head honcho himself. Where's your secretary?'

George laughed, recognizing her voice. 'I don't know, Lizzie. Taking a powder, I guess. You want to come take over her job?'

'Can't. I'm too busy busting people for the DA to prosecute.'

'Ah, I have you to thank for that. My own little feeder source for job security.'

'Well, consider yourself secure: we found a dead baby in

an Amish barn here, and things aren't adding up. I'm on my way to the hospital to check out a possible suspect – but I wanted to let you know there may be an arraignment in your near future.'

'How old and where was it found?' George asked, all business now.

'Hours old, a newborn. It was underneath a pile of blankets,' Lizzie said. 'And according to everyone we interviewed at the scene, no one had given birth recently.'

'Was the baby stillborn?'

'The ME doesn't think so.'

'Then I'm assuming the mother dropped the kid and left,' George deduced. 'You said you have a lead?'

Lizzie hesitated. 'This is going to sound crazy, George, but the eighteen-year-old Amish girl who lives on the farm, who swore up one side and down another that she wasn't pregnant, is in the hospital right now bleeding out vaginally.'

There was a stunned silence. 'Lizzie, when was the last time you booked an Amish person for a crime?'

'I know, but the physical evidence points to her.'

'So you have proof?'

'Well, I haven't—'

'Get some,' George said flatly. 'And then call me back.'

The physician stood near the triage desk, explaining to the newly arrived OB/GYN what she was likely to find in the ER.

'Sounds like uterine atony, and retained products of conception,' the obstetrician said, glancing at the patient's chart. 'I'll do an exam, and we'll get her up to the OR for a D&C. What's the status of the baby?'

The ER doctor lowered his voice. 'According to the paramedics who brought her in, it didn't survive.'

The obstetrician nodded, then disappeared behind the curtain where Katie Fisher still lay.

From her vantage point in a bank of lackluster plastic chairs, Lizzie came to her feet. If George wanted proof, then she'd get it. She thanked God for plainclothes detectives – no uniformed officer had a snowball's chance in hell of getting confidential information out of a doctor without a subpoena – and approached the physician. 'Excuse me,' she said, worrying her hands in the folds of her shirt. 'Do you know how Katie Fisher's doing?'

The doctor glanced up. 'And you are?'

'I was at the house when she started bleeding.' It wasn't a lie, really. 'I just wanted to know if she's going to be all right.'

The physician nodded, frowning. 'I imagine she'll be just fine – but it would have been considerably safer for her if she'd come to the hospital to have her baby.'

'Doctor,' Lizzie said, smiling, 'I can't tell you what it means to hear you say that.'

Leda pushed open the door to her niece's hospital room. Katie lay still and sleeping on the raised bed. In the corner, motionless and quiet, sat Sarah. As she saw her sister enter the room, Sarah ran into Leda's arms. 'Thank goodness you came,' she cried, hugging Leda tightly.

Leda glanced down at the top of Sarah's head. Years of parting her hair in the middle, pulling it tight, and securing her *kapp* with a straight pin had left a part that widened like a sea with each passing year, a furrow as pink and vulnerable as the scalp of a newborn. Leda kissed the little bald spot, then drew back from Sarah.

Sarah spoke quickly, as if the words had been rising inside her like steam. 'The doctors think that Katie had a baby. She needed medicine to help stop the bleeding. They took her up to operate.'

Leda covered her hand with her mouth. 'Just like you, after you had Hannah.'

'*Ja*, but Katie was wonderful lucky. She'll still be able to have children, not like me.'

'Did you tell the doctor about your hysterectomy?'

Sarah shook her head. 'I did not like this doctor. She wouldn't believe Katie when she said she didn't have a baby.'

'Sarah, these English doctors . . . they have scientific tests for pregnancy. Scientific tests don't lie – but Katie might have.' Leda hesitated, treading gingerly. 'You never noticed her figure changing?'

'No!'

But, Leda knew, that did not mean much. Some women, especially tall ones like Katie, carried in such a way that it could be months before you noticed a pregnancy. Katie would have had her privacy undressing, and underneath the bell of her apron, a swelling stomach would be hard to see. Any thickening of a waistline would go undetected, since the women's garments of the Old Order Amish were held together with straight pins that could easily be adjusted.

'If she got into trouble, she would have told me,' Sarah insisted.

'And what do you think would have happened the minute she did?'

Sarah looked away. 'It would have killed Aaron.'

'Trust me, Aaron's not going to blow over in a strong wind. And he better start dealing with it, because this is only the beginning.'

Sarah sighed. 'Once Katie gets home, she'll have the bishop coming around, that's for sure.' Glancing up at Leda, she added, 'Maybe you could talk to her. About the *Meidung*.'

Dumbfounded, Leda sank down onto a chair beside the hospital bed. 'Shunning? Sarah, I'm not talking about punishment within the church. The police found a dead baby this morning, a dead baby that Katie already lied about having. They're going to think that she's lied about other things, too.'

'It's a crime, to these English, to have a baby out of wedlock?' Sarah asked indignantly.

'It is if you leave it to die. If the police prove that the baby was born alive, Katie is going to be in a lot of trouble.'

Sarah stiffened her spine. 'The Lord will make this work

out. And if He doesn't, then we will accept His will.'

'Are you talking about God's will, or Aaron's? If Katie is arrested, if you listen to Aaron and turn the other cheek and don't get someone to stick up for her in court, then they're going to put her in jail. For years. Maybe forever.' Leda touched her sister's arm. 'How many children are you going to let the world take away from you?'

Sarah sat down on the edge of the bed. She laced Katie's lax fingers through her own and squeezed. Like this, in her hospital gown with her hair loose about her shoulders, Katie did not look Plain. Like this, she looked just like any other young girl.

'Leda,' Sarah whispered, 'I don't know how to move in this world.'

Leda put her hand on her sister's shoulder. 'I do.'

'Detective Munro, you got a minute?'

She didn't, but she nodded at the policeman from the Major Crimes Unit of the state police, which had been scouring the property all afternoon. Once Lizzie had determined that Katie Fisher was going to be hospitalized at least overnight, she had gone to the district judge to secure warrants to search the house and grounds, as well as to get blood from Katie for a DNA match. Her mind buzzing with the million and one things she had left to do, Lizzie tried to turn her attention to the state trooper. 'What have you got?'

'Actually, the scene's fairly clean,' he said.

'Don't sound so surprised,' Lizzie said dryly. 'We may be town cops, but we all graduated from high school.' She hadn't been thrilled about calling in the MCU, because they tended to look down their noses at local law enforcement and had a nasty habit of wresting control of the investigation from the detective in charge. However, the state police's investigative skills were far more advanced than those of the East Paradise police, simply because they'd done it more often. 'Has the father given you any trouble?'

The trooper shrugged. 'Actually, I haven't even seen him.

He took the mules out into the fields about two hours ago.' He handed Lizzie a white cotton nightgown, bloodstained at the bottom, sealed in a plastic evidence bag. 'It was under the girl's bed, all balled up. We also found traces of blood by the pond behind the house.'

'She had the baby, washed off in the pond, hid the nightgown, and went back to bed.'

'Hey, you guys *are* smart. Come over here, I want you to see this.' He led Lizzie into the tack room where the infant's corpse had been found. Crouching, he pointed out what looked like a ripple on the floor, but on closer inspection turned out to be the outline of a footprint. 'It's fresh manure, which means the print wasn't made too long ago.'

'Is it possible to figure out whose it is, the way you do with fingerprints?'

The state trooper shook his head. 'No, but we can determine the size of the foot. That's a women's seven, double E width.' He gestured to a colleague, who handed over another evidence bag containing a pair of unattractive tennis shoes. Slipping on gloves, the trooper withdrew the left one. He lifted the tongue so that Lizzie could read the tag. 'Size seven women's sneakers, extra wide,' he said. 'Found in Katie Fisher's closet.'

Levi was silent during the buggy ride back to his home, something – Samuel knew – that was the result of considerable restraint. Finally, unable to hold it in any longer, Levi turned as the horses drew to a stop. 'What do you think will happen?'

Samuel shrugged. 'I don't know.'

'I hope she's all right,' Levi said earnestly.

'I hope so too.' He heard the catch in his voice and coughed so that Levi would not notice it. The boy stared at his older cousin for a moment, then jumped from the buggy and ran into the house.

Samuel continued to drive down the road, but he did not make the turn that would lead to his own parents' place. By now, they would have heard of Katie and would, of course, have questions for him. He drove into town and tethered his horse at Zimmermann's Hardware. Instead of going into the store, he walked behind the building, into the cornfield that spread north. He ripped off his hat and held it in his hand as he began to run, the stalks chafing his face and torso. He ran until he could hear the roaring music of his own heart; until it was impossible to catch hold of a breath, much less his emotions.

Then he sank down in the field, lying on his back while he gasped. He stared up at the bruised blue of the evening sky and let the tears come.

Ellie was leafing through *Good Housekeeping* when her aunt returned home. 'Everything all right? You took off like you were on fire.' Then she raised her eyes to see Leda – pinched, pale, distracted. 'I guess everything's *not* all right.'

Leda sank into a chair, her pocketbook slipping off her shoulder to thump on the floor. She closed her eyes, silent.

'You're scaring me,' Ellie said with a nervous laugh. 'What's the matter?'

Visibly straightening her spine, Leda got up and began to rummage through the refrigerator. She pulled out cucumbers, lettuce, and carrots and set them on the counter. She washed her hands, withdrew a chopping knife, and began to cut the vegetables into precisely measured bits. 'We'll have salad with dinner,' she said. 'What do you think of that?'

'I think it's only three in the afternoon.' Ellie walked forward, took the knife from Leda's hand, and waited until the older woman met her gaze. 'Talk.'

'My niece is in the hospital.'

'You don't have another – oh!' Understanding dawned as Ellie realized this was the family Leda did not speak of; the ones she left behind. 'Is she . . . sick?'

'She almost died having a baby.'

Ellie didn't know what to say to that. She could think of

nothing more tragic than to give birth, and then not be able to enjoy the miracle.

'She's only eighteen, Ellie.' Leda hesitated, spreading her fingers on the chopping block. 'She isn't married.'

A picture slowly revolved in Ellie's head of a young, unwed girl, trying to rid herself of a fetus. 'It was an abortion, then?'

'No, it was a baby.'

'Well, of course it was,' Ellie hastened to add, thinking that Leda's background would not have made her pro-choice. 'How far along was she?'

'Almost eight months,' Leda said.

Ellie blinked. 'Eight *months*?'

'It turns out that the baby's body was discovered before anyone even knew that Katie was pregnant.'

A small spark rubbed at the base of Ellie's spine, one she told herself to ignore. This was not Philly, after all; this was no crack mother, but an Amish girl. 'Stillborn, then,' Ellie said with sympathy. 'What a shame.'

Leda turned her back on Ellie, silent for a moment. 'I told myself during the drive home that I wasn't going to do this, but I love Katie just as much as I love you.' She took a deep breath. 'There is a chance that the baby wasn't stillborn, Ellie.'

'No.' The word flushed itself from Ellie, low and hot. 'I can't. Don't ask me to do this, Leda.'

'There isn't anyone else. We aren't talking about people comfortable with the law. If this were up to my sister, Katie would go to jail whether she was guilty or not, because it's not in her nature to fight back.' Leda gazed at her, eyes burning. 'They trust me; and I trust you.'

'First of all, she hasn't been formally charged. Second of all, even if she were, Leda, I couldn't defend her. I know nothing about her or her way of life.'

'Do you live on the streets like the drug dealers you've defended? Or in a big Main Line mansion, like that principal you got acquitted?'

'That's different, and you know it.' It did not matter whether

Leda's niece had a right to sound legal counsel. It did not matter that Ellie had defended others charged with equally unpalatable crimes. Drugs and pedophilia and armed robbery did not hit as close to home.

'But she's innocent, Ellie!'

It had been, long ago, the reason Ellie became a defense attorney – for the souls she was going to save. However, Ellie could count on one hand the number of clients she'd gotten acquitted who had truly been wrongfully accused. She now knew that most of her clients were guilty as charged – although every last one of them had an excuse they'd be shouting all the way to the grave. She might not have agreed with her clients' criminal actions, but on some level, she always understood what made them do it. However, at this moment in her life, there was nothing that could make her understand a woman who killed her own child.

Not when there were other women out there who so desperately wanted one.

'I can't take your niece's case,' Ellie said quietly. 'I'd be doing her a disservice.'

'Just promise me you'll think about it.'

'I won't think about it. And I'll forget that you asked me to.' Ellie walked out of the kitchen, fighting her way free of Leda's disappointment.

Samuel's big body filled the doorway of the hospital room, reminding Katie of how she sometimes would stand beside him in an open field and still feel crowded for space. She smiled hesitantly. 'Come in.'

He approached the bed, feeding the brim of his straw hat through his hands like a seam. Then he ducked his head, bright color staining his cheeks. 'You all right?'

'I'm fine,' Katie answered. She bit her lip as Samuel pulled up a chair and sat down beside her.

'Where's your mother?'

'She went home. Aunt Leda called her a taxi, since Mam didn't feel right riding back in her car.'

Samuel nodded, understanding. Amish taxi services, run by local Mennonites, drove Plain folks longer distances, or on highways where buggies couldn't go. As for riding in Leda's car, well, he understood that too. Leda was under the *bann*, and he wouldn't have felt comfortable taking a ride from her, either.

'How . . . how are things at home?'

'Busy,' Samuel said, carefully choosing his words. 'We did the third cutting of hay today.' Hesitating, he added, 'The police, they're still around.' He stared at Katie's fist, small and pink against the polyester blanket. Gently he took it between his own hands, and then slowly brought it up to his jaw.

Katie curved her palm against his cheek; Samuel turned into the caress. Her eyes shining, she opened her mouth to speak again, but Samuel stopped her by putting a finger over her lips. 'Sssh,' he said. 'Not now.'

'But you must have heard things,' Katie whispered. 'I want—'

'I don't listen to what I've heard. I'll only listen to what you have to say.'

Katie swallowed. 'Samuel, I did not have a baby.'

He looked at her for a long moment, then squeezed her hand. 'All right, then.'

Katie's eyes flew to his. 'You believe me?'

Samuel smoothed the blanket over her legs, tucking her in like a child. He stared at the shining fall of her hair and realized that he had not seen it this way, bright and loose, since they were both small. 'I have to,' he said.

The bishop in Elam Fisher's church district happened to be his own cousin. Old Ephram Stoltzfus was such a part of everyday life that even when acting as the congregational leader, he was remarkably accessible – stopping his buggy by the side of the road for a chat, or hopping off his plow in the middle of the field to make a suggestion. When Elam had met him earlier that day with the story of what had happened at the farm, he listened carefully and then said that he needed to speak to some others. Elam had assumed Ephram meant the church district's deacon, or two ministers, but the bishop had shaken his head. 'The businessmen,' he'd said. 'They're the ones who'll know how the English police work.'

Just after suppertime, when Sarah was clearing the table, Bishop Ephram's buggy pulled up. Elam and Aaron glanced at each other, then walked outside to meet him.

'Ephram,' Aaron greeted, shaking the man's hand after he'd tied up his horse.

'Aaron. How is Katie?'

It was slight, but Aaron stiffened visibly. 'I hear she will be fine.'

'You did not go to the hospital?' Ephram asked.

Aaron looked away. *'Neh.'*

The bishop tipped his head, his white beard glowing in the setting sun. 'Walk with me awhile?'

The three men headed toward Sarah's vegetable garden. Elam sank down on a stone slab bench and gestured for Ephram to do the same. But the bishop shook his head and stared over the tall heads of the tomato plants and the climbing vines of beans, around which danced a spray of fireflies. They sparked and tumbled like a handful of stars that had been flung.

'I remember coming here once, years ago, and watching Jacob and Katie chase the lightning bugs,' Ephram said. 'Catching 'em in a jar.' He laughed. 'Jacob said he was making an Amish flashlight. You hear from Jacob these days?'

'No, which is the way I wish it to be,' Aaron said quietly.

Ephram shook his head. 'He was banned from the church, Aaron. Not from your life.'

'They're the same to me.'

'That's the thing I don't understand, you know. Since forgiveness is the very first rule.'

Aaron leveled his gaze on the bishop. 'Did you come here to talk about Jacob?'

'Well, no,' Ephram admitted. 'After you dropped by this morning, Elam, I went to see John Zimmermann and Martin Lapp. It's their understanding that if the police were here all day, they must be thinking Katie's a suspect. It will all hinge for sure on whether the baby was born alive. If it was, she'll be blamed for its death.' He frowned at Aaron. 'They suggested speaking to a lawyer, so that you won't get caught unawares.'

'My Katie doesn't need a lawyer.'

'So I hope,' the bishop said. 'But if she does, the community will stand behind her.' He hesitated, then added, 'She'll have to put herself back, you understand, during this time.'

Elam looked up. 'Just give up communion? She wouldn't be put under the *bann*?'

'I will need to speak to Samuel, of course, and then think on it.' Ephram put his hand on Aaron's shoulder. 'This isn't the first time a young couple has gotten ahead of their wedding night. It's a tragedy, to be sure, that the baby died. But heartache can cement a marriage just as much as happiness. And as for Katie being blamed for the other – well, none of us believes it.'

Aaron turned, shrugging off the bishop's hand. 'Thank you. But we will not hire a lawyer for Katie, and go through the *Englischer* courts. It's not our way.'

'What makes you always draw a line, and challenge people to cross it, Aaron?' Ephram sighed. '*That's* not our way.'

'If you'll excuse me, I have work to do.' Aaron nodded at the bishop and his father and struck off toward the barn.

The two older men watched him in silence. 'You've had this conversation with him once before,' Elam Fisher pointed out.

The bishop smiled sadly. '*Ja*. And I was talking to a stone wall that time, too.'

Katie dreamed she was falling. Out of the sky, like a bird with a wounded wing, the earth rushing up to meet her. Her heart lodged in her throat, holding back the scream, and she realized at the very last second that she was heading toward the barn, the fields, her home. She closed her eyes and crashed, the scenery shattering like an eggshell at impact so that when she looked around, she recognized nothing at all.

Blinking into the darkness, Katie tried to sit up in the bed. Wires and plastic tubes grew from her body like roots. Her belly felt tender; her arms and legs heavy.

A comma of a moon split the sky, and a smattering of stars. Katie let her hands creep beneath the covers to rest on her stomach. *'Ich hab ken Kind kaht,'* she whispered. I did not have a baby.

Tears fell on the blanket. *'Ich hab ken Kind kaht. Ich hab ken Kind kaht,'* she murmured over and over, until the words became a stream running through her veins, an angel's lullaby.

The fax machine in Lizzie's house beeped on just after midnight, while she was running on her treadmill. Adrenaline had kept her awake, anyway, and perfectly suited for a workout that might make her tired enough to catch a few hours of sleep. She shut off the treadmill and walked to the fax, sweating as she waited for the pages to begin rolling out. At the cover page from the medical examiner's office, her heart rate jumped another notch.

Words began to reach at her, tugging at her mind.

Male, 32 weeks. 39.2 cm crown-heel; 26 cm crown-rump. Hydrostatic test . . . dilated alveolar ducts . . . mottled pink to dark red appearance . . . left and right lungs floated, excluding partial and irregular aeration. Air present in the middle ear. Bruising on the upper lip; cotton fibers on gums.

'Good God,' she whispered, shivering. She had met murderers several times – the man who'd stabbed a convenience store owner for a pack of Camels; a boy who'd raped college girls and left them bleeding on the dormitory floor; once, a woman who had shot her abusive husband's face off while he lay sleeping. There was something about these people, something that had always made Lizzie feel that if you cracked them open like Russian nesting dolls, you'd find a hot, smoking coal at their center.

Something that did not fit this Amish girl at all.

Lizzie stripped out of her workout clothes, heading for the shower. Before the girl was no longer free to leave, before she was read Miranda and formally charged, Lizzie wanted to look Katie Fisher in the eye and see what was at the heart of her.

It was four in the morning by the time Lizzie entered the hospital room, but Katie was awake and alone. She turned wide blue eyes to the detective, surprised to see her. 'Hello.'

Lizzie smiled and sat down beside the bed. 'How are you feeling?'

'Better,' Katie said quietly. 'Stronger.'

Lizzie glanced down at Katie's lap, and saw the Bible she'd been reading. 'Samuel brought it for me,' the girl said, confused by the frown on the other woman's face. 'Isn't it allowed in here?'

'Oh, yeah, it's allowed,' Lizzie said. She felt the tower of evidence she'd been neatly stacking for twenty-four hours now start to waver: *She's Amish.* Could that one excuse, that one glaring inconsistency, knock it down? 'Katie, did the doctor tell you what happened to you?'

Katie glanced up. She set her finger in the Bible, closed the book around it with a rustle of pages, and nodded.

'When I saw you yesterday, you told me you hadn't had a baby.' Lizzie took a deep breath. 'I'm wondering why you said that.'

'Because I didn't have a baby.'

Lizzie shook her head in disbelief. 'Why are you bleeding, then?'

A red flush worked its way up from the neckline of Katie's hospital johnny. 'It's my time of the month,' she said softly.

She looked away, composing herself. 'I may be Plain, Detective, but I'm not stupid. Don't you think I'd know if I had a baby?'

The answer was so open, so earnest, that Lizzie mentally stepped back. *What am I doing wrong?* She'd questioned hundreds of people, hundreds of liars – yet Katie Fisher was the only one she could recall getting under her skin. She glanced out the window, at the simmering red of the horizon, and realized what the difference was: This was no act. Katie Fisher believed exactly what she was saying.

Lizzie cleared her throat, manning a different route of attack. 'I'm going to ask you something awkward, Katie . . . Have you ever had sexual relations?'

If at all possible, Katie's cheeks glowed brighter. 'No.'

'Would your blond friend tell me the same thing?'

'Go ask him,' she challenged.

'You saw that baby yesterday morning,' Lizzie said, her voice thick with frustration. 'How did it get there?'

'I have no idea.'

'Right.' Lizzie rubbed her temples. 'It isn't yours.'

A wide smile broke over Katie's face. 'That's what I've been trying to tell you.'

'She's the only suspect,' Lizzie said, watching George stuff a forkful of hash browns into his mouth. They were meeting at a diner halfway between the county attorney's office and East Paradise, one whose sole recommendation, as far as Lizzie could tell, was that they only served items guaranteed to double your cholesterol. 'You're going to give yourself a heart attack if you keep eating like that,' she said, frowning.

George waved away her concern. 'At the first sign of arrhythmia I'll ask God for a continuance.'

Breaking off a small piece of her muffin, Lizzie looked down at her notes. 'We've got a bloody nightgown, a footprint her size, a doctor's statement saying she was primiparous, an ME saying the baby took a breath – plus her blood matches the blood found on the baby's skin.' She popped a bite into her mouth. 'I'll put five hundred bucks down saying that when the DNA test comes back, it links her to the baby, too.'

George blotted his mouth with a napkin. 'That's substantial stuff, Lizzie, but I don't know if it adds up to involuntary manslaughter.'

'I didn't get to the clincher yet,' Lizzie said. 'The ME found bruising on the baby's lips and fibers on the gums and in the throat.'

'Fibers from what?'

'They matched the shirt it was wrapped in. He thinks that the two, together, suggest smothering.'

'Smothering? This isn't some Jersey girl giving birth in the toilet at the Paramus Mall and then going off to finish shopping, Lizzie. The Amish don't even kill flies, I'll bet.'

'We made national headlines last year when two Amish kids were peddling cocaine,' Lizzie countered. 'What's *60 Minutes* going to say to a murder?' She watched a spark come to George's eyes as he weighed his personal feelings about charging an Amish girl against the promise of a high-profile murder case. 'There's a dead baby in an Amish barn, and an Amish kid who gave birth,' she said softly. 'You do the math, George. I wasn't the one who asked for this to happen, but even I can see that we've got to charge her, and we've got to do it soon. She's being released today.'

He meticulously cut his sunny-side-up eggs into bite-size squares, then placed his knife and fork down on the edge of his plate without eating a single one. 'If we can prove smothering, we might be able to charge Murder One. It's willful, premeditated, and deliberate. She hid the pregnancy, had the baby, and did away with it.' George glanced up. 'Did you question her?'

'Yeah.'

'And?'

Lizzie grimaced. 'She still doesn't think she had a baby.'

'What the hell does that mean?'

'She's sticking to her story.'

George frowned. 'Did she look crazy to you?'

There was a big difference between legally crazy and colloquially crazy, but in this case, Lizzie didn't think George was making the distinction. 'She looks like the girl next door. One who happens to read the Bible instead of V. C. Andrews.'

'Oh, yeah,' George sighed. 'This one's gonna go to trial.'

Sarah Fisher pinned her daughter's *kapp* into place. 'There. Now you're ready.'

Katie sank down on the bed, waiting for the candy-striper to appear with a wheelchair and take her down to the lobby. The doctor had discharged her minutes before, giving her mother some pills in case Katie had any more pain. She shifted, folding her arms across her stomach.

Aunt Leda put an arm around her. 'You can stay with me if you're not ready to be at home yet.'

Katie shook her head. '*Denke*. But I ought to get back. I want to get back.' She smiled softly. 'I know that doesn't make any sense.'

Leda squeezed her shoulders. 'It makes more sense to me, probably, than to anyone else.'

As the door swung open, Katie jumped to her feet, eager to be on her way. But instead of the young volunteer she'd been expecting, two uniformed policemen entered. Sarah stepped back, falling into place beside Leda and Katie; a united, frightened front. 'Katie Fisher?'

She could feel her knees shaking beneath her skirts. 'That's me.'

One policeman took her gently by the arm. 'We have a warrant for your arrest. You've been charged with the murder of the baby found in your father's barn.'

The second policeman came up beside her. Katie looked frantically over his shoulder, trying to reach her mother's eyes. 'You have the right to remain silent,' he said. 'Everything you say can and will be used against you in a court of law. You have the right to be represented by an attorney—'

'No!' Sarah screamed, reaching for her daughter as the policemen began to lead Katie through the doorway. She ran after them, ignoring the curious glances of the medical personnel and the cries of her own sister.

Leda finally caught up with Sarah at the entrance of the hospital. Katie was crying, arms stretched toward her mother as the policeman set a hand on her *kapp* and ducked her inside the squad car. 'You can meet us at the district court, ma'am,' he said politely to Sarah, then got into the front seat.

As the car drove away, Leda put her arms around her sister. 'They took my baby,' Sarah sobbed. 'They took my baby.'

Leda knew how uncomfortable Sarah was riding in her car, but pressing circumstances called for compromises. Driving with someone under the *bann* was considerably less threatening than standing in court while one's daughter was arraigned for murder, which Sarah was going to have to face next.

'You wait right here,' she said, pulling into her driveway. 'Let me get Frank.' She left Sarah sitting in the passenger seat and ran into the house.

Frank was in the living room, watching a sitcom rerun. One look at his wife's face had him out of his chair, running his hands over her arms. 'You all right?'

'It's Katie. She's being taken to the district court. They've charged her with murder.' Leda could just manage the last before breaking down, letting go in her husband's embrace as she hadn't let herself go in front of Sarah. 'Ephram Stoltzfus raised twenty thousand dollars from Amish businessmen for Katie's legal defense, but Aaron won't take a penny.'

'She'll get a public defender, honey.'

'No – Aaron expects her to turn the other cheek. And after what he did to Jacob, Katie's not going to disagree with him.' She buried her face in her husband's shirt. 'She can't win this. She didn't do it, and she's going to be put in jail anyway.'

'Think of David and Goliath,' Frank said. With his thumb, he wiped away Leda's tears. 'Where's Sarah?'

'In the car. Waiting.'

He slid an arm around her waist. 'Let's go, then.'

A moment after they left, Ellie walked into the living room, wearing her jogging shorts and tank top. She'd been in the adjoining mud room, lacing up her sneakers for a run, when Leda had come home – and she'd heard every word. Her face impassive, Ellie stepped up to the picture window and watched Leda's car until it disappeared from view.

Katie had to hide her hands beneath the table so that no one would see how much they were trembling. Somehow she had lost the pin to her *kapp* in the police car, and it perched uneasily on her head, slipping whenever she shifted. But she would not take it off – not now, especially – since she was supposed to have her head covered whenever she prayed, and she'd been doing that constantly since the moment the car pulled away from the hospital's entrance.

A man sat at a table just like hers, a little distance away. He looked at her, frowning, although Katie had no idea what she might have done to make him so upset. Another man sat in front of her behind a high desk. He wore a black cape and held a wooden hammer in his hand, which he banged at the moment Katie saw her mother and aunt and uncle slip into the courtroom.

The man with the hammer narrowed his eyes at her. 'Do you speak English?'

'*Ja,*' Katie said, then blushed. 'Yes.'

'You have been charged in the State of Pennsylvania with murder in the first degree, whereby you, Katie Fisher, on the eleventh of July 1998, against the arms and force of the State of Pennsylvania, did willfully, deliberately, and premeditatedly cause the death of Baby Fisher on the Fisher farm in the East Paradise Township of Lancaster County. You are also charged with the lesser included offense of murder in the third degree, whereby you . . .'

The words ran over her like a rain shower, too much English

at once, all the syllables blending. Katie closed her eyes and swayed slightly.

'Do you understand these charges?'

She hadn't understood the first sentence. But the man seemed to be waiting for an answer, and she had learned as a child that *Englischers* liked you to agree with them. 'Yes.'

'Do you have an attorney?'

Katie knew that her parents, like all Amish, did not believe in instigating lawsuits. In rare cases, an Amishman would be subpoenaed and would testify . . . but never by his own choice. She glanced over her shoulder at her mother, sending her *kapp* askew. 'I do not wish to have one,' she said softly.

'Do you know what that means, Miss Fisher? Is this on the advice of your parents?' Katie looked down at her lap. 'This is a very serious charge, young lady, and I believe you should have counsel. If you qualify for a public defender—'

'That won't be necessary.'

Like everyone else in the courtroom, Katie turned toward the confident voice coming from the doorway. A woman with hair as short as a man's, wearing a neatly tailored blue suit and high heels, was briskly walking to her table. Without glancing at Katie, the woman set her briefcase down and nodded at the judge. 'I'm Eleanor Hathaway, counsel for the defendant. Ms Fisher has no need of a public defender. I apologize for being late, Judge Gorman. May I have five minutes with my client?'

The judge waved his assent, and before Katie could follow what was happening, this stranger Eleanor Hathaway dragged her to her feet. Clutching at her *kapp*, Katie hurried beside the attorney down the central aisle of the court. She saw Aunt Leda crying and waving to her, and she raised a hand in response before she realized that this big greeting was meant for Eleanor Hathaway, not for Katie herself.

The attorney steered Katie to a small room filled with office supplies. She closed the door behind her, leaned against it, and folded her arms. 'Sorry for the impromptu introduction, but I'm Ellie Hathaway, and I sure as hell hope that you're Katie. We're going to have a lot of time to talk later, but right now I need to know why you turned down an attorney.'

Katie's mouth opened and closed a few times before she could summon her voice. 'My Dat wouldn't want me to have one.'

Ellie rolled her eyes, clearly unimpressed. 'You'll plead not guilty today, and then we'll chat. Now, looking at these charges, you're not getting bail unless we can get around the "proof and presumption" clause in the statute.'

'I . . . I don't understand.'

Without glancing up from the sheaf of papers she was skimming, Ellie answered, 'It means that if you're charged with murder, and the proof is evident or the presumption great, you don't get bail. You sit in jail for a year until your trial comes up. Get it?' Katie swallowed, nodded. 'So we have to find a loophole here.'

Katie stared at this woman, who had come with her words sharpened like the point of a sword, planning to save her. 'I didn't have a baby.'

'I see. Even though two doctors and a whole hospital, not to mention the local cops, all say otherwise?'

'I didn't have a baby.'

Ellie slowly looked up. 'Well,' she said. 'I see I'm going to be finding that loophole myself.'

Judge Gorman was clipping his fingernails when Ellie and Katie reentered the courtroom. He swept the shavings onto the floor. 'I believe we were just getting to "How do you plead?"'

Ellie stood. 'My client pleads not guilty, Your Honor.'

The judge turned. 'Mr Callahan, is there a bail recommendation from the state?'

George rose smoothly. 'I believe, Your Honor, that the statute in Pennsylvania requires that bail be denied to defendants charged with first degree murder. In this case, the state would recommend this as well.'

'Your Honor,' Ellie argued, 'with all due respect, if you read the wording of the statute it requires bail to be withheld only in the cases where "the proof is evident, or the presumption great." That isn't a blanket statement. Particularly, in this case, the proof is not evident, and the presumption is not great, that this was an act of murder in the first degree. There's some circumstantial evidence that the county attorney has gathered – specifically, medical testimony that Ms Fisher's given birth, and the fact of a dead infant found on the premises of her farm – but there are no eyewitnesses to what happened between the birth and the death of the infant. Until my client gets her fair trial, we aren't going to know how or why this death occurred.'

She smiled tightly at the judge. 'In fact, Your Honor, there are four main reasons bail should be allowed in this case. First, the girl is Amish and being charged with a violent crime, although violence in the Amish community historically does not exist. Second, because she's Amish, she has a much stronger tie to this community than most other defendants. Her religion and her upbringing rule out any risk of flight. Third, she's barely eighteen, and has no financial resources of her own to attempt an escape. And finally, she has no record – this is not only her first arraignment but the first time she's encountered the legal system in any way, shape, or form. I'm proposing, Your Honor, that she be released on stringent bail conditions.'

Judge Gorman nodded thoughtfully. 'Would you like to share those conditions with us?'

Ellie took a deep breath. She'd love to; she just hadn't thought of them yet. She looked swiftly toward Leda and Frank and the Amish woman sitting between them, and suddenly it all came clear. 'We respectfully request bail, Judge, with the following stipulations: that Katie Fisher not be allowed to leave East Paradise Township, but that she be allowed to live at home on her parents' farm. In return, she must be under the supervision of a family member at all times. As for bail – I would think that twenty thousand dollars is a fair amount to ask.'

The prosecutor laughed. 'Your Honor, that's ludicrous. A bail statute is a bail statute; and Murder One is Murder One. It's like that in fancy felony cases in Philadelphia, too, so Ms Hathaway can't plead ignorance. If the proof wasn't evident we wouldn't be charging it this way. Clearly Katie Fisher should not be released on any bail.'

The judge let his gaze touch upon the prosecutor, the defense attorney, and then Katie. 'You know, coming in here this morning, I had no intention of doing what I'm about to do. But if I'm even going to consider your conditions, Ms Hathaway, I need to know that someone agrees to be responsible for Katie Fisher. I want her father's word that she'll be supervised twenty-four/seven.' He turned to the gallery. 'Mr Fisher, would you make yourself known?'

Leda stood up and cleared her throat. 'He's not here, Your Honor.' She pulled hard at her sister's arm, dragging her to a standing position as well. 'This is Katie's mother.'

'All right, Mrs Fisher. Are you willing to accept total legal responsibility for your daughter?'

Sarah looked down at her feet, her words so soft the judge had to strain to hear them. 'No,' she admitted.

Judge Gorman blinked. 'I beg your pardon?'

Sarah raised her face, tears in her eyes. 'I cannot.'

'I can, Your Honor,' Leda said.

'You live with the family?'

She hesitated. 'I could move in.'

Sarah shook her head again, whispering furiously. 'Aaron won't let you!'

The judge impatiently rapped his fingers on the desk. 'Is there any relative of Ms Fisher's here today willing to take responsibility for her round the clock, who doesn't have a problem with the church or her father?'

'I'll do it.'

Judge Gorman turned to Ellie, who seemed just as surprised to have uttered the words as he had been to hear them. 'That's certainly devoted of you, Counsel, but we're looking for a family member.'

'I know,' Ellie said, swallowing hard. 'I'm her cousin.'

4

Ellie

When George Callahan stood up and roared his objection, I had to stop myself from seconding his motion. God, what on earth was I thinking? I came to East Paradise burned out; taking on this girl's case was the last thing I wanted to do – and now I had volunteered myself to be Katie Fisher's warden. Through a haze of disbelief I heard the judge rule against the prosecutor; set bail at $20,000 with provisions, and put me into a prison I'd created for myself.

Suddenly Frank and Leda were standing in front of me, Leda smiling through her tears and Frank staring at me with his solemn dark eyes. 'You sure you're all right with this, Ellie?' he asked.

Leda answered for me. 'Of course she is. Why, she's saving Katie for us.'

I glanced down at the girl beside me, still huddled in her chair. Since our brief interlude in the supply room, she hadn't said a word. She flicked her gaze at me – I saw the bright blaze of resentment. Immediately, my hackles rose. Did she think I was doing this for my own health?

I narrowed my eyes, prepared to give a piece of my mind, but was stopped by a soft touch on my arm. An older, worn version of Katie decked out in full Amish costume waited for my attention. 'My daughter thanks you,' she said haltingly. 'I thank you. But my husband will not want an *Englischer* staying with us.'

Leda turned on her. 'If Bishop Ephram said it's all right to talk to an English lawyer, he's going to say it's all right for that same lawyer to meet the bail conditions. And if the whole community is willing to bend the rules for Katie's welfare, Sarah, couldn't you just once stand with them instead of by your stubborn husband's side?'

In my whole life, I'd never heard Leda raise her voice. Yet here she was, practically yelling at her sister, until the other woman was cowering beneath the words. Leda slipped her arm through mine. 'Come along, Ellie,' she said. 'You'll want to be packing up your things.' She started out of the court-house, stopping once to look over her shoulder at Sarah and her daughter. 'You heard the judge. Katie must be with Ellie at all times. So let's go.'

I let Leda drag me out of the district court, and felt the heat of Katie Fisher's stare burning into my back.

The road to the Fisher farm ran parallel to a creek, which then cut behind their land to form the rear edge of their hundred acres. This world was a kaleidoscope of color: kelly green corn, red silos, and above it all, a sky as wide and as blue as a robin's egg. But what struck me the most was the smell, a mixture of notes as distinctive as any city perfume: the sweat of horses, honeysuckle, the rich tang of overturned earth. If I closed my eyes and breathed deeply, magic happened: I was eleven again and here to spend the summer.

We had dropped off Frank and picked up my suitcases, and now, an hour later, Leda was turning up the long driveway that led to the Fishers' home. Staring out the window, I saw a pair of men driving a team of mules across a field. The animals hauled a tremendous, old-fashioned piece of equip-ment – God only knew what it was. It seemed to be tossing up tufts of hay that were already lying on the ground. At the sound of the car on the gravel, the bigger man looked up, hauled on the reins, and then took off his hat to wipe the sweat from his forehead. He shaded his eyes and glanced toward Leda's car, then handed the reins to the smaller fellow beside him and took off at a dead run for the farmhouse.

He got there ten seconds after the car rolled to a stop. Leda and I stepped out first, then let Katie and Sarah out of the backseat. The man, broad and blond, began speaking words that made no sense to me – the first time I considered that the English Katie had so carefully put before the judge was not her first language, nor that of the people I was going to be moving in with. Sarah answered back, equally unintelligible.

My high heels wobbled on the gravel. I stripped off my suit jacket, uncomfortable in the heat, and studied the man who had come to greet us.

He was too young to be the Father from Hell who had been introduced in absentia in the courtroom. A brother, maybe. But then I caught him staring at Katie with a look that was anything but brotherly. I glanced at Katie, and noticed she was not looking at him the same way.

All of a sudden, in the run of language, there came a word I knew – my own name. Sarah gestured to me, smiled uncomfortably, and then nodded to the blond man. He took my suitcase from the trunk and set it down beside him, then offered me his hand to shake. 'I am Samuel Stoltzfus,' he said. 'Thank you for taking care of my Katie.'

Did he notice the way Katie stiffened at the possessive claim? Did anyone but me?

Hearing the metallic clop of hooves and harness behind me, I turned to see someone leading a horse into the barn. Wiry and muscular, the man had a thick red beard just beginning to sport streaks of gray. Beneath his black trousers he wore a pale blue shirt, the sleeves rolled up to the elbows. He glanced at us, briefly frowning at the sight of Leda's car. Then he continued into the barn, only to reappear a moment later.

Ignoring everyone else, he went straight to Sarah and began to speak quietly but firmly to her in their language. Sarah bowed her head, a willow branch under a wind. But Leda took a step forward and began talking back to him. She pointed to Katie, and to me, and shook her fists. Her eyes snapping with frustration, she set her hands on my shoulders and shoved me forward, into Aaron Fisher's scrutiny.

I had watched men step apart from themselves at the moment they were sentenced to life in prison; I had seen the blankness in a witness's eyes when she recounted the night she was attacked; but never had I seen a detachment like I saw on that man's face. He held himself in check, as if admitting to his pain might crack him into a thousand pieces; as if we were age-old adversaries; as if he knew, deep down, that he'd already been beaten.

I held out my hand. 'It is a pleasure.'

Aaron turned away without touching me. He approached his daughter, and the world fell away, so that when he tipped his forehead against Katie's and whispered to her with tears in his eyes, I ducked my head to offer them privacy. Katie nodded, starting for the house with her father's arm locked around her shoulders.

In a tight knot, Samuel, Sarah, and Leda followed, talking heatedly in their dialect. I stood alone in the driveway, the breeze blowing my silk shell against my back, the sun sugaring new freckles on my shoulders. From the barn came the stamp and whinny of a horse.

I sat down on one suitcase and stared in the direction of the house. 'Yeah,' I said softly. 'It's nice to meet you too.'

To my amazement, the Fisher home was not that much different from the one I'd grown up in. Braided rag rugs were scattered across the hardwood floors, a bright quilt sat folded over the back of a rocking chair, an intricately carved hutch held an assortment of delft china bowls and teacups. I think, in a way, I'd been expecting to step back into *Little House on the Prairie* – these were people, after all, who willingly set aside modern conveniences. But there was an oven, a refrigerator, even a washing machine that looked like one my grandmother had had in the 1950s. My confusion must have shown, because Leda materialized by my elbow. 'They all run on gas. It's not the appliances they don't want; it's the electricity. Getting power from public utility lines – well, it means you're linked to the outside world.' She pointed to a lamp, showing me the thin tubing that piped in the propane from a tank hidden beneath its base. 'Aaron will let you stay here. He doesn't like it, but he's going to do it.'

I grimaced. 'Marvelous.'

'It will be,' Leda said, smiling. 'I think you're going to be surprised.'

The others had remained in the kitchen, leaving me alone with Leda in a living room of sorts. Bookshelves were filled with titles I could not make out – German, I assumed, from the lettering. On the wall was a carefully printed family tree, Leda's name listed just above Sarah's.

No television, no phone, no VCR. No *Wall Street Journal* sprawled across the couch, no jazz CD humming in the background. The house smelled of lemon wax and was warm to the point of suffocation. My heart began to pound in my chest. What had I gotten myself into?

'Leda,' I said firmly, 'I can't do this.'

Without responding, she sat down on the couch, a nondescript brown corduroy with lace antimacassars. When had I last seen *those*?

'You have to take me back with you. We'll figure something out. I can come here from your place every morning. Or I can have an *ex parte* meeting with the judge to find an alternative.'

Leda folded her hands in her lap. 'Are you really so afraid of them,' she asked, 'or is it just that you're afraid of yourself?'

'Don't be ridiculous.'

'Am I? Ellie, you're a perfectionist. You're used to taking charge and turning things to your own advantage. But all of a sudden you're stuck in a place that's as foreign to you as a Calcutta bazaar.'

I sank down beside her and buried my face in my hands. 'At least I've read about Calcutta.'

Leda patted my back. 'Honey, you've dealt with Mafia bosses, even though you aren't part of the Mob.'

'I didn't move in with Jimmy "the Boar" Pisano while I was defending him, Leda.'

Well, she had nothing to say to that. After a moment she sighed. 'It's just a case, Ellie. And you've always been willing to do anything to win a case.'

We both looked into the kitchen, where Katie and Sarah – relatives of mine, once removed – stood side by side at the sink. 'If it was just a case, I wouldn't be here.'

Leda nodded, conceding that I'd gone out of my way – and realizing that she should go out of hers. 'All right. I'll give you some ground rules. Help without being asked; Plain folks put lots of store in what you do, and less in what you say. It won't matter to them that you don't know anything about farming or dairying – what counts is that you're trying to lend a hand.'

'Forget farming – I know nothing about being *Amish*.'

'They won't expect you to. And there's nothing you need to know. They're folks like you and me. Good ones and bad ones, easygoing ones and ones with tempers, some quick to help you out and others who'll turn the other way when they see you coming. Tourists, they see the Amish as saints or as a sideshow. If you want this family to accept you, you just treat them like regular people.'

As if the recollection had hurt her, she stood suddenly. 'I'm going to go,' Leda said. 'As much as Aaron Fisher dislikes having you here, he dislikes having me here even more.'

'You can't leave yet!'

'Ellie,' Leda said gently, 'you'll be fine. *I* survived, didn't I?'

I narrowed my eyes. 'You left.'

'Well, one day you will too. Just keep remembering that, and the day will be here sooner than you think.' She tugged me into the kitchen, where the conversation abruptly stopped. Everyone glanced up, slightly puzzled, it seemed, to find me still there. 'I'm going to take off now,' Leda said. 'Katie, maybe you could show Ellie your room?'

It struck me: this is what children do. When relatives come

to visit, when friends of their own arrive, they take them into their own territory. Show off the dollhouse, the baseball card collection. Reluctantly, Katie forced a smile. 'This way,' she said, starting for the stairs.

I gave Leda a quick, tight hug, and then turned toward Katie. I squared my shoulders and followed her. And no matter how much I wanted to, I did not let myself look back.

As I walked behind Katie, I noticed how heavily she leaned on the banister. She'd just had a baby, after all – most women were still hospitalized, yet here Katie was playing hostess. At the top of the landing, I touched her shoulder. 'Are you . . . feeling okay?'

She stared at me blankly. 'I am fine, thank you.' Turning, she led me to her bedroom. It was clean and neat, but hardly the room of a teenager. No Leonardo posters, no Beanie Babies scattered about, no collection of lip gloss jars littering the dresser. There was nothing, in fact, on the walls; the only individuality in the room came from the rainbow of quilts that covered the two twin beds.

'You can have that bed,' Katie said, and I went to sit down on it before her words registered. She expected me to stay in this room, her room, while I was living on the farm.

Hell, no. It was bad enough that I had to be here at all; if I couldn't even have my privacy at night, all bets were off. I took a deep breath, fighting for a polite way to tell Katie that I would not, under any circumstances, be sharing a bedroom with her. But Katie was wandering around the room, touching the tall neck of the ladderback chair and smoothing her quilt, and then getting down on her hands and knees to look underneath the bed. Finally, she sat back on her heels. 'They took my things,' she said, her voice small.

'Who did?'

'I don't know. Someone came in here and took my things. My nightgown. My shoes.'

'I'm sure that—'

She turned on me. 'You're sure of nothing,' she challenged.

Suddenly I realized that if I stayed in this room, sleeping beside Katie, I wouldn't be the only one incapable of keeping secrets. 'I was going to say that I'm sure the police searched your room. They must have found something to make them feel confident enough to charge you.' Katie sat down on her own bed, her shoulders slumped. 'Look. Why don't we start by having you tell me what happened yesterday morning?'

'I didn't kill any baby. I didn't even have a baby.'

'So you've said.' I sighed. 'Okay. You may not like me being here, and I certainly could find a thousand other things I'd rather be doing, but thanks to Judge Gorman, you and I are going to be stuck with each other for some time. I have a deal with my clients: I won't ask you if you committed the crime, not ever. And in return, you tell me the truth whenever I ask you anything else.' Leaning forward, I caught her gaze. 'You want to tell me you didn't kill that baby? Go right ahead. I couldn't care less if you did or didn't, because I'll still stand up for you in court no matter what and not make a personal judgment. But lying about *having* the baby – something that's been proven a fact – well, Katie, that just makes me angry.'

'I'm not lying.'

'I can count at least three medical experts who've already gone on record saying that your body shows signs of recent delivery. I can wave a blood test in your face that proves the same thing. So how can you sit here and tell me you didn't have the baby?'

As a defense attorney, I already knew the answer – she could sit there and tell me because she believed it, one hundred percent. But before I even contemplated running with an insanity defense, I needed to make sure Katie Fisher wasn't taking me for a ride. Katie didn't act crazy, and she functioned normally. If this kid was insane, then I was Marcia Clark.

'How can you sit there,' Katie said, 'and tell me you're not judging me?'

Her words slapped me with surprise. I, the suave defense attorney, the one with a winning record and a list of credentials as long as my arm, had made the cardinal mistake of mentally convicting a client before the right to a fair trial. A fair trial in which I was supposed to represent her. She had lied about having the baby, and I couldn't push that aside without wondering what else she might be lying about – a mindset that placed me more in line with a prosecutor than a defense attorney.

I had coolly defended the rights of rapists, murderers, and pedophiles. But because this girl had killed her own newborn, an act I simply could not get my head around, I wanted her to be locked away.

I closed my eyes. *Allegedly* killed, I reminded myself.

'Is it that you can't remember?' I asked, deliberately softening my voice.

Katie's eyes met mine, wide and sea blue. 'I went to sleep on Thursday night. I woke up Friday morning and came down to make breakfast. That's all there is to it.'

'You don't remember going into labor. You don't remember walking out to the barn.'

'No.'

'Is there anyone who saw you sleeping all night?' I pressed.

'I don't know. I wasn't awake to see.'

Sighing, I rapped my hands on the mattress I was sitting on. 'What about the person who sleeps here?'

Katie's face drained of color; she seemed far more upset by that question than by anything else I'd asked her. 'No one sleeps there.'

'You don't remember feeling that baby come out of you,' I said, my voice growing thick with frustration. 'You don't remember holding it close, and wrapping it in that shirt.' We both glanced down, where I was cradling an imaginary infant in my arms.

For a long minute, Katie stared at me. 'Have you ever had a baby?'

'This isn't about me,' I said. But one look at her face told me she knew I wasn't telling the truth, either.

There were pegs on the walls, but no closets. Katie's dresses took up three of them, another three were empty on the opposite wall. My suitcase lay open on the bed, stuffed to the gills with jeans and blouses and sundresses. After a moment's consideration, I pulled out a single dress, hung it on the peg, and then zipped the suitcase shut again.

A knock came on the door as I was hauling my luggage to the corner of the room, behind a rocking chair. 'Come on in.'

Sarah Fisher entered, carrying a stack of towels that nearly obliterated her face. She set them down on a dresser. 'You have found everything you need?'

'Yes, thank you. Katie showed me around.'

Sarah nodded stiffly. 'Dinner's at six,' she said, and she turned her back on me.

'Mrs Fisher,' I called out before I could stop myself, 'I know this isn't easy for you.'

The woman stopped in the doorway, her hand braced on the frame. 'My name is Sarah.'

'Sarah, then.' I smiled, a forced smile, but at least one of us was trying. 'If there's anything you'd like to ask me about your daughter's case, please feel free.'

'I do have a question.' She crossed her arms and stared at me. 'Are you secure in your faith?'

'Am I what?'

'Are you Episcopalian? Catholic?'

Speechless, I shook my head. 'How does my religion have anything to do with the fact that I'm representing Katie?'

'We get a lot of people coming through here who think they want to be Plain. As if that's the answer to all the problems in their lives,' Sarah scoffed.

Amazed at her audacity, I said, 'I'm not here to become Amish. In fact, I wouldn't be here at all, except for the fact that I'm keeping your daughter out of jail.'

We stared at each other, a standoff. Finally, Sarah turned away, picking up a quilt on the end of one twin bed and refolding it. 'If you aren't Episcopalian or Catholic, what do you believe in?'

I shrugged. 'Nothing.'

Sarah hugged the quilt to her chest, surprised by my answer. She didn't say a word, but she didn't have to: she was wondering how on earth I could possibly think that it was Katie who needed help.

After my confrontation with Sarah, I changed into shorts and a T-shirt, and then Katie came upstairs for a rest – something, I could tell, that was unprecedented in the household. To give Katie her privacy, I decided to explore the grounds. I stopped in the kitchen, where Sarah was already beginning to cook dinner, to tell her my plans.

The woman couldn't have heard a word I said. She was staring at my arms and legs as if I were walking around naked. Which to her, I guess, I was. Blushing, she whipped back to face the counter. 'Yes,' she said. 'You go on.'

I walked along the raspberry patch, behind the silo, out toward the fields. I ventured into the barn, meeting the lazy eyes of the cows chained at their milking stalls. I gingerly touched the bright crime-scene tape, scouting for clues. And then I wandered until finding the creek, where I'd been ever since.

When I used to stay at Leda and Frank's as a young girl, I'd spend hours lying belly-flat on the shores of their creek, watching the stick bugs skitter over the surface of the water, while pairs of dragonflies gossiped to each other. I'd dip my finger in and watch the water carve a path around it, meeting up on the other side. Time would spin out like sugar, so that I'd be thinking about how I'd just arrived, and in the blink of an eye, it was already sunset.

The Fishers' creek was narrower than the one I'd grown up with. At one end was a tiny waterfall, bogged at the bottom with so many spores and sprigs of hay that I knew it had served as a source of fascination for their children. The other end of the creek widened into a small natural pond, shaded by willow and oak trees.

I dangled a forked twig over the water as if I could dowse for defense strategies. There was always sleepwalking – Katie admitted to not knowing what had happened between the time she went to bed and the time she awakened. It was a designer defense, certainly, but those had had success in recent years – and in a case as sensational as this one was sure to be, it might be my best shot.

Other than that, there were two options. Either Katie did it, or she didn't. Although I hadn't seen discovery from the prosecutor yet, I knew they wouldn't have charged her without evidence to the former. Which meant that I needed to determine whether she was in her right mind at the moment she killed the baby. If she wasn't, I'd have to go with an insanity defense – only a handful of which had ever been acquitted in the state of Pennsylvania.

I sighed. I'd have a better chance proving that the baby had died by itself.

Dropping my twig, I considered that. For any ME the state could put on the stand to say that the baby had been murdered, I could probably find a dueling expert who'd say it had died of exposure, or prematurity, or whatever medical excuses there were for these sorts of things. It was a tragedy that could be pinned on Katie's inexperience and neglect, rather than her intent. A passive involvement in the newborn's death – well, that was something even I could forgive.

I patted my shorts, silently cursing my lack of foresight to bring along a scrap of paper and a pen. I'd have to contact a pathologist, first, and see how reliable the ME's report was likely to be. Maybe I could even put a good OB up on the stand – there was one fellow who'd done wonders for a client of mine during a previous trial. Finally, I'd have to get Katie on the stand, looking suitably distressed about what had accidentally happened.

Which, of course, would require her to admit that it had happened at all.

Groaning, I rolled onto my back and closed my eyes against the sun. Then again, maybe I'd just wait for the discovery, and see what I had to go with.

There was a faint rustling in the distance, and a snippet of song carried on the wind. Frowning, I got to my feet and starting walking along the creek. It was coming from the pond, or somewhere near the pond. 'Hey,' I called out, rounding the bend. 'Who's there?'

There was a flash of black, which disappeared into the cornfield behind the pond before I could see who had vanished. I ran to the edge of the stalks, parting them with my hands, hoping to find the culprit. But all I managed to stir up were field mice, which ran past my sneakers and into the cattails that edged the pond.

I shrugged. I wasn't looking for company anyway. I started back toward the house, but stopped at the sight of a handful of wildflowers, left at the northernmost edge of the pond. Resting just out of reach of the graceful arms of a willow tree, they were neatly tied into a bouquet. Kneeling, I touched the Queen Anne's lace, the lady's slippers, the black-eyed Susans. Then I glanced at the field of corn, wondering for whom they had been left.

'While you're here,' Sarah said, handing me a bowl of peas, 'you'll help out.'

I looked up from the kitchen table and bit back the retort that I was already helping, just by being here. Thanks to my sacrifice, Katie was here with her own bowl of peas, which she was shelling with remarkable industry. I watched her for a moment, then slid my thumbnail into the pod, watching it crack open as neat as a nut, just as it had for her.

'Neh . . . Englische Leit . . . Lus mich gay!'

Aaron's voice, quiet but firm, snaked through the open kitchen window. Wiping her hands on her apron, Sarah glanced out. Drawing in her breath, she hurried toward the door.

Then I heard English being spoken.

Immediately, I turned to Katie. 'You stay here,' I ordered, and walked out. Aaron and Sarah were holding their hands over their faces, cringing away from the small crowd of cameramen and reporters who'd descended on the farm. One news van had the audacity to park right beside the Fisher buggy. There were dozens of questions being shouted out, ranging from queries about Katie's pregnancy to the sex of the dead baby.

Lulled by the quiet and peace of a bucolic farm, I'd forgotten how quickly the media would pick up on the court record of an Amish girl being charged with murder in the first degree.

Suddenly I remembered the summer I fancied myself a photographer, and how I'd pointed my Kodak at an unsuspecting Amishman in a buggy. Leda had covered the camera lens, explaining that the Amish believed the Bible prohibited a graven image, and didn't like to have their pictures taken. 'I could do it anyway,' I had said, stung, and to my surprise Leda nodded – so sadly that I'd put my camera back in its case.

Aaron had given up trying to ask the reporters to go away. It wasn't in his nature to cause a scene, and he'd wisely assumed that if he offered himself as a target, it would keep Katie safe from their prying eyes. Clearing my throat, I marched to the front of the fray. 'Excuse me, you're on private property.'

One of the reporters took in my shorts and top, in direct contrast to Aaron and Sarah's clothes. 'Who are you?'

'Their press secretary,' I said dryly. 'I believe you all are in direct violation of criminal trespassing, which, as a misdemeanor of the third degree, could result in up to a year in jail and a twenty-five-hundred-dollar fine.'

A woman in a tailored pink suit frowned, trying to place me. 'You're the lawyer! The one from Philly!' I glanced at the call letters on her microphone; sure enough, she was from a city-based network affiliate.

'At this time, neither my client nor my client's parents have any comment,' I said. 'As for the incendiary nature of the charge, well' – I smirked, gesturing to the barn, the farmhouse, the quiet lay of the land – 'all I'm going to say is that an Amish farm is no Philadelphia crack house, and that an Amish girl is no hard-core criminal. The rest, I'm afraid, you'll have to hear on the steps of the courthouse at some later date.' I cast a measured look out over the crowd. 'Now – a little free legal advice. I'm strongly recommending that you all leave.'

Reluctantly, they shuffled off in a pack, like the wolves I always pictured them to be. I walked to the end of the driveway, keeping watch until the last of their cars pulled away. Then I started back up the gravel incline, to find Aaron and Sarah standing side by side, waiting for me.

Aaron looked down at the ground as he spoke gruffly. 'Perhaps you would like to see the milking sometime.'

It was the closest he would come to an admission of gratitude. 'Yes,' I said. 'I would.'

Sarah made enough food to feed the whole Amish community, much less her own small household plus one live-in guest. She brought bowl after bowl to the table, chicken with dumplings and vegetables swimming in sauces, and meat that had been cooked to the point where it broke apart at the touch of a fork. There were relishes and breads and spiced, stewed pears. In the center of the table was a blue pitcher of fresh milk. Looking at all the rich choices, I wondered how these people could eat this way, three times a day, and not grow obese.

In addition to the three Fishers I'd met, there was an older man, who did not bother to introduce himself but seemed to know who I was all the same. From his features, I assumed he was Aaron's father, and that he most likely lived in the small apartment attached to the rear of the farmhouse. He bent his head, which caused all the others to bend their heads, a strange kinetic reaction, and began to pray silently over the food. Unsettled – when was the last time I'd said grace? – I waited until they looked up and began to ladle food onto their plates. Katie raised the pitcher of milk and poured some into her glass; then passed it to her right, to me.

I had never been a big fan of milk, but I figured that wasn't the smartest thing to admit on a dairy farm. I poured myself some and handed the pitcher to Aaron Fisher.

The Fishers laughed and talked in their dialect, helping themselves to food when their plates were empty. Finally, Aaron leaned back in his chair and let out a phenomenal belch. My eyes widened at the breach of etiquette, but his wife beamed at him as if that was the grandest compliment he could ever give.

I suddenly saw a string of meals like this one, stretching out for months, with me prominently cast as the outsider. It took me a moment to realize that Aaron was asking me something. In Pennsylvania Dutch.

'The chowchow,' I said in slow, careful English, following his gaze to the particular bowl. 'Is that what you want?'

His chin went up a notch. '*Ja,*' he answered.

I flattened my hands on the table. 'In the future, I'd prefer it if you asked me questions in my own language, Mr Fisher.'

'We don't speak English at the supper table,' Katie answered.

My gaze never left Aaron Fisher's face. 'You do now,' I said.

By nine o'clock, I was ready to climb the walls. I couldn't run out to Blockbuster for a video, and even if I could have, there was no TV or VCR for me to watch it on. An entire shelf of books turned out to be written in German – a children's primer, something called the *Martyr's Mirror*, and a whole host of other titles I could not have pronounced without butchering. Finally I discovered a newspaper written in English – *Die Botschaft* – and settled down to read about horse auctions and grain threshing.

The Fishers filed into the room one by one, as if drawn by

a silent bell. They sat and bowed their heads. Aaron looked at me, a question in his eyes. When I didn't respond, he began to read out loud from a German Bible.

I'd never been very religious; and completely unawares, I'd been tossed into a household that literally structured itself on Christianity. Drawing in my breath, I stared at the newspaper and let the letters swim, trying not to feel like a heathen.

Less than two minutes later, Katie got up and walked over to me. 'I'll be going to bed now,' she announced.

I set aside the paper. 'Then I will too.'

After coming out of the bathroom in my silk pajamas, I watched Katie sit on her bed in her long white nightgown and comb out her hair. Unpinned, it fell nearly to her waist and rippled with every stroke of the brush. I sat cross-legged on my own twin bed, my hand propped on my cheek. 'My mother used to do that for me.'

'Truly?' Katie said, looking up.

'Yeah. Every single night, untangling all my knots. I hated it. I thought it was a form of torture.' I touched my short cap of hair. 'As you can see, I got my revenge.'

Katie smiled. 'We don't have a choice. We don't cut our hair.'

'Ever?'

'Ever.'

Granted, hers was lovely – but what if, like me, she'd had to suffer snarls every day of her life? 'What if you wanted to?'

'Why would I? Then I'd be different from all the others.' Katie set down her brush, effectively ending the conversation, and crawled into bed. Leaning over, she extinguished the gas lamp, pitching the room into total darkness.

'Ellie?'

'Hmm?'

'What is it like where you live?'

I considered for a moment. 'Noisy. There are more cars, and they seem to be right outside the window all night long,

honking and screeching to a stop. There are more people, too –
and I'd be hard pressed to find a cow or chicken, much less
sweet corn, unless you count the kind in the freezer section.
But I don't really live in Philadelphia anymore. I'm sort of in
between residences, just now.'

Katie was quiet for so long I thought she had fallen asleep.
'No, you're not,' she said. 'Now you're with us.'

When I woke up with a start, I thought I'd had the nightmare
again, the one with the little girls from my last trial, but my
sheets were still tucked neatly, and my heartbeat was slow and
steady. I glanced at Katie's bed, at the quilt tossed back to
reveal her missing, and immediately got up. Padding downstairs barefoot, I checked in the kitchen and the living room
before I heard the quiet click of a door and footsteps on the
porch.

She went all the way to the pond where I'd been earlier
that day. I stayed behind, hidden, just close enough to be able
to see and hear her. She sat down on a small wrought-iron
bench set before the big oak tree, and closed her eyes.

Was she sleepwalking again? Or was she meeting someone
here?

Was this where Katie and Samuel had their trysts? Was this
where a baby had been conceived?

'Where are you?' Katie's whisper reached me, and I realized
two things at once: that she was too lucid still to be asleep; and
that I understood her words. 'How come you're hiding?'

Clearly, she knew I had followed her. Who else would she
be talking to in English?

I stepped out from behind the willow and stood in front of
her. 'I'll tell you why I'm hiding, if you tell me why you came
out here in the first place.'

Katie scrambled to her feet, her cheeks flushed with color.
She looked so startled that I took a step back – right into the
edge of the pond, wetting the edge of my pajama bottoms.
'Surprise,' I said flatly.

'Ellie! What are you doing up?'

'I think that's my question, actually. In addition to the following: Who were you expecting to meet here? Samuel, maybe? You two planning to get your story straight, before I corner him for a little interview?'

'There is no story—'

'For God's sake, Katie, give it up! You had a baby. You've been charged with murder. I've been appointed as your legal defense, and you're still sneaking around behind my back, in the middle of the night. You know, I've done this a lot longer than you have, and people don't sneak around unless they have something to hide. Coincidentally, they also don't lie unless they have something to hide. Guess which one of us fails on both counts?' Tears were rolling down Katie's cheeks. Steeling myself, I crossed my arms. 'You'd better start talking.'

She shook her head. 'It's not Samuel. I'm not meeting him.'

'Why should I believe you?'

'Because I'm telling you the truth!'

I snorted. 'Right. You're not meeting Samuel; you just decided you needed a little fresh air. Or is this some midnight Amish custom I need to learn?'

'I didn't come out here because of Samuel.' She looked up at me. 'I couldn't sleep.'

'You were talking to someone. You thought he was hiding.'

Katie ducked her head. 'She.'

'I beg your pardon?'

'*She.* The person I was looking for is a girl.'

'Nice try, Katie, but you're out of luck. I don't see a girl. And I don't see a guy, either, but something tells me if I give it five minutes a big, blond fellow is going to show up.'

'I was looking for my sister. Hannah.' She hesitated. 'You're sleeping in her bed.'

Mentally, I counted everyone I'd met that day. There had been no other young girl; and I found it difficult to believe that Leda would never have mentioned Katie's siblings to me. 'How come Hannah wasn't at dinner? Or praying with you tonight?'

'Because . . . she's dead.'

This time when I stepped back, both feet landed squarely in the pond. 'She's dead.'

'*Ja.*' Katie raised her face to mine. 'She drowned here when she was seven. I was eleven, and I was supposed to be watching her while we went skating, but she fell through the ice.' She wiped her eyes and her nose with the sleeve of her nightgown. 'You . . . you wanted me to tell you everything, to tell you the truth. I come out here to talk to Hannah. Sometimes I see her, even. I didn't tell anyone about her, because seeing ghosts, well, Mam and Dat would think I'm all *ferhoodled*. But she's here, Ellie. She is, I swear it to you.'

'Like you swear you never had that baby?' I murmured.

Katie turned away from me. 'I knew you wouldn't understand. The only person who ever did was—'

'Was who?'

'Nobody,' she said stubbornly.

I spread my arms. 'Well, then, call out for her. Hey, Hannah!' I shouted. 'Come and play.' I waited a moment for good measure, and then shrugged. 'Funny, I don't see anything. Imagine that.'

'She won't come with you here.'

'Isn't that convenient,' I said.

Katie's eyes were dark and militant, filled with conviction. 'I am telling you that I've seen Hannah since she died. I hear her talking, when the wind comes. And I see her skating, right over the top of the pond. She's real.'

'You expect me to fall for this? To think you came out here because you believe in ghosts?'

'I believe in Hannah,' Katie clarified.

I sighed. 'It seems to me you believe a lot of things that may not necessarily be true. Come back to bed, Katie,' I said over my shoulder, and left without waiting to see if she'd follow.

Once Katie was asleep, I tiptoed out of the room with my purse. Outside, on the porch, I withdrew my cell phone.

Ironically, you could get a decent signal in Lancaster County – some of the more progressive Amish farmers had agreed to allow cellular towers on their land, for a fee that negated the need to grow a winter crop. Punching in several numbers, I waited for a familiar, groggy voice.

'Yeah?'

'Coop, it's me.'

I could almost see him sitting up in bed, the sheets falling away. 'Ellie? Jesus! After – what? two years? . . . You call me at . . . good God, is it three in the morning?'

'Two-thirty.' I'd known John Joseph Cooper IV for nearly twenty years, when we were at Penn together. No matter what time it was, he'd growl – but he'd forgive me. 'Look, I need your help.'

'Oh, this isn't just a three A.M. social call?'

'You're not going to believe this, but I'm at an Amish family's home.'

'Ah, I knew it. You never really got over me, and you chucked it all for the simple life.'

I laughed. 'Coop, I got over you a decade ago. Just about the time you got married, actually. I'm here as part of a bail provision for a client, who was charged with murdering her newborn. I want you to evaluate her.'

He exhaled slowly. 'I'm not a forensic psychiatrist, Ellie. Just your run-of-the-mill suburban shrink.'

'I know, but . . . well, I trust you. And I need this off the record, a gut feeling, before I decide how I'm going to get her off.'

'You trust me?'

I drew in my breath, remembering. 'Well. More or less. More, when the issue at hand doesn't involve me.'

Coop hesitated. 'Can you bring her in on Monday?'

'Uh, no. She isn't supposed to leave the farm.'

'I'm making a *house call?*'

'You're making a farm call, if it makes you feel any better.'

I could imagine him closing his eyes, flopping back down

on his pillows. Just say yes, I urged silently. 'I couldn't juggle my schedule until Wednesday at the earliest,' Coop said.

'That's good enough.'

'Think they'll let me milk a cow?'

'I'll see what I can do.'

I could feel his smile, even all these miles away. 'Ellie,' he said, 'you've got yourself a deal.'

5

Aaron hurried into the kitchen and sat down at the table, Sarah turning in perfect choreography to set a cup of coffee in front of him. 'Where is Katie?' he asked, frowning.

'She's asleep, still,' Sarah said. 'I didn't think to wake her yet.'

'Yet? It's *Gemeesunndaag*. We have to leave, or we'll be late.'

Sarah flattened her hands on the counter, as if she might be able to smooth the Formica even further. She squared her shoulders and prepared to contradict Aaron, something she had done so infrequently in her marriage she could count the occasions on a single hand. 'I don't think Katie should be going to church today.'

Aaron set down his mug. 'Of course she'll go to church.'

'She's feeling *grenklich*, Aaron. You saw the look on her face all day yesterday.'

'She's not sick.'

Sarah sank down into the chair across from him. 'People will have heard by now about this baby. And the *Englischer*.'

'The bishop knows what Katie said, and he believes her. If Ephram decides there is a need for Katie to make a confession, he'll come and talk to her here first.'

Sarah bit her lip. 'Ephram believes Katie when she says she didn't kill that baby. But does he believe her when she says it isn't hers?' When Aaron didn't answer, she reached across the table and touched his hand. 'Do you?'

He was silent for a moment. 'I saw it, Sarah, and I touched it. I don't know how it got there.' Grimacing, he admitted, 'I also know that Katie and Samuel would not be the first to get ahead of their wedding vows.'

Blinking back tears, Sarah shook her head. 'That'll mean the *Meidung*, for sure,' she said. 'Even if she confesses and says she's sorry for it, she'll still be under the *bann* for a while.'

'Yes, but then she'll be forgiven and welcomed back.'

'Sometimes,' Sarah said, her mouth tightening, 'that's not the way it goes.' The memory of their oldest son, Jacob, suddenly flared between them, crowding the table so that Aaron pushed back his chair. She had not said Jacob's name, but she had brought up his specter in a household where he was supposed to be long dead. Afraid of Aaron's reaction, Sarah turned away, surprised when her husband's voice came back soft and broken.

'If Katie stays at home today,' he said, 'if she acts sick and don't show her face, people are going to talk. People are going to think she's not coming because she's got something to hide. It'll go better for her, if she makes like it's any other Sunday.'

Overcome with relief, Sarah nodded, only to stiffen as she heard Aaron speak quietly again. 'But if she's put under the *bann*, I'll side with my church before I side with my child.'

Shortly before eight o'clock, Aaron hitched the horse to the buggy. Katie climbed into the back, and then his wife sat down on the wide bench seat beside him. Aaron picked up the reins just as the *Englischer* came running out of the house, into the yard.

She was a sight. Her hair stuck up in little tufts around her head, and the skin of her cheek was still creased with the mark of a pillowcase. At least she was wearing a long cotton dress, though, Aaron thought, instead of the revealing clothes she'd had on yesterday afternoon.

'Hey,' she yelled, frantically waving her arms to keep him from leaving. 'Where do you think you're going?'

'To church,' Aaron said flatly.

Ellie crossed her arms. 'You can't. Well, that is, *you* can. But your daughter can't.'

'My daughter will, just like she has all her life.'

'According to the state of Pennsylvania, Katie's been

remanded into my custody. And she's not going anywhere without me.'

Aaron looked at his wife and shrugged.

There were many misconceptions Ellie had had about the Amish buggies, but the biggest one by far was that they were uncomfortable. There was a sweet, gentle gait to the horse that lulled her senses, and the heat of the July sun was relieved by the wind streaming through the open front and rear window. Tourists in their cars sidled up to the rear of the buggy, then passed with a roar of gears and a racing engine.

A horse moved along at just twelve miles per hour – slow enough that Ellie was able to count the number of calves grazing in a field, to notice the Queen Anne's lace rioting along the edge of the road. The world didn't whiz by; it unrolled. Ellie, who had spent most of her life in a hurry, found herself watching in wonder.

She kept a lookout for the church building. To her surprise, Aaron turned the buggy down a residential driveway. Suddenly they were part of a long line of buggies, a somber parade. There was no chapel, no bell tower, no spire – just a barn and a farmhouse. He pulled to a stop, and Sarah dismounted. Katie nudged her shoulder. 'Let's go,' she whispered. Ellie stumbled from the wagon and then drew herself up short.

She was completely surrounded by the Amish. Numbering well over a hundred, they spilled from their buggies and crossed the yard and gathered to quietly speak and shake hands. Children darted behind their mothers' skirts and around their fathers' legs; a wagon filled with hay became a temporary feed trough for the many horses that had transported the families to church. As soon as Ellie became visible, curious eyes turned in her direction. There was whispering, pointing, a giggle.

Ellie could remember feeling like this only once – years ago, when she'd spent a summer in Africa building a village as part of a college inservice project, she'd never been more aware of the differences between herself and others. She started as someone slipped an arm through hers. 'Come,' Katie said, drawing her across the yard as if nothing was amiss, as if she walked around every day with an *Englischer* by her side.

She was stopped by a tall man with a bushy white beard and eyes as bright as a hawk's. 'Katie,' he said, clasping her hands.

'Bishop Ephram.' Ellie, who was standing close enough to notice, realized that Katie was trembling.

'You must be the lawyer,' he said in English, in a voice loud enough to carry to all the people who were still straining to hear. 'The one who brought Katie home to us.' He extended a hand to Ellie. *'Wilkom.'* Then he moved off toward the barn, where the men were gathering.

'That's a wonderful good thing he did,' Katie whispered. 'Now the people won't all be wondering about you while we worship.'

'Where *do* you worship?' Ellie asked, puzzled. 'Outside?'

'In the house. A different family holds the services every other Sunday.'

Ellie dubiously eyed the small, clapboard farmhouse. 'There's no way all these people are going to fit inside that tiny building.'

Before Katie could answer, she was approached by a pair of girls who held her hands and chattered urgently, concerned about the rumors they'd heard. Katie shook her head and soothed them, and then noticed Ellie standing off to the side, looking distinctly out of place. 'I want you to meet someone,' she said. 'Mary Esch, Rebecca Lapp, this is Ellie Hathaway, my . . .'

Ellie smiled wryly at Katie's hesitation. 'Attorney,' she supplied. 'A pleasure.'

'Attorney?' Rebecca gasped the word, as if Ellie had sworn a blue streak instead of just announcing her profession. 'What would you need with an attorney?'

By now, the women were organizing themselves into a loose line and filing into the house. The young single women walked at the front of the line, but having Ellie there clearly presented a problem. 'They don't know what to do with you,' Katie explained. 'You're a visitor, so you ought to follow the lead person. But you're not baptized.'

'Let me solve this for everyone.' Ellie stepped firmly between Katie and Rebecca. 'There.' An older woman frowned and shook her finger at Ellie, upset at having a nonmember so far up front in the procession. 'Relax,' Ellie muttered. 'Rules were made to be broken.'

She looked up to find Katie staring at her solemnly. 'Not here.'

It was not until Katie began to visit Jacob on a regular basis that she truly understood how people could be seduced by the devil. How easy it was, when Lucifer wielded things like compact disc players and Levi's 501s. It was not that she thought her brother fallen – she just suddenly began to see how one archangel tumbling from heaven might have easily reached out a hand and tugged down another, and another, and another.

One day when she was fifteen, Jacob told her he had a surprise for her. He brought her change of clothes to the train station and waited for her to put them on in the ladies' room, then led her to the parking lot. But instead of approaching his own car, he took her to a big station wagon filled with college kids. 'Hey, Jake,' one of the boys shouted, unrolling the window. 'You didn't tell us your sister was a hottie!'

Automatically, Katie patted her sweatshirt. Warm, maybe . . . Jacob interrupted her thoughts. 'She's fifteen,' he said firmly.

'Jailbait,' called another girl. Then she dragged the boy backward and kissed him full on the mouth.

Katie had never been this close to people kissing in public; she stared until Jacob tugged at her hand. He climbed into the car and shoved aside the others so that there would be room for his sister. He tossed a hurricane of names at her that she forgot the moment she tried to remember them. And then they were off, the car shimmying with the heavy beat of a Stones tape and the muffled movements of two people making out in the back.

Sometime later, the car pulled into a parking lot, and Katie glanced

*up at the mountain and the ski lodge at its base. 'Surprised?' Jacob
asked. 'What do you think?'*

*Katie swallowed. 'That I'll have a hard time explaining a broken
leg to Mam and Dat.'*

'You won't break your leg. I'll teach you.'

*And he did – for about ten minutes. Then he left Katie on the
bunny slope with a ski school full of seven-year-olds and raced up
to the top of the mountain with his college buddies. Katie wedged
her skis into a triangle and snowplowed down the gentle hill, then
let the J-bar tug her up to start all over again. At the bottom, each
time, she shaded her eyes and looked for Jacob, who never came.
The whole world was unfamiliar – slick and white, dotted with
people who cut her a wide berth. This was what it was like, she
thought, to be put under the* bann *forever. You'd lose everyone who
was important to you; you'd be all alone.*

*She glanced up at the chairlift. Unless, of course, you could do
what Jacob had done: turn into someone else entirely. She didn't
know how he could do it so seamlessly, as if he had never had
another life in another place.*

As if this new life was the only one that mattered.

*She was suddenly flushed with anger, that she and her Mam
should work so hard to keep Jacob tucked under their hearts, while
he was off drinking beer and barreling down ski slopes. She snapped
off her rental skis and, leaving them in the snow, marched back to
the lodge.*

*Katie didn't know how long she sat there, staring out the window.
The sun had surely wriggled lower in the sky by the time Jacob stomped
in, his hands clamped around her skis. 'Himmel, Katie!' he shouted,
slipping back into Dietsch. 'You don't just leave skis lying around. Do
you know how much these things cost if you lose them?'*

*Katie turned slowly. 'No, Jacob, I don't. And I don't know
how much they cost if you just rent them for the day. I don't
know how much a case of beer costs, either, come to think of it.
And for sure I don't know why I come out all the way on this
train to visit you!'*

She tried to move past him, but the boots were too big and heavy

*for her to get far enough away before he caught her. 'You're right,'
he said softly. 'I'm with them every day, and you're the one I never
get to see.'*

Katie sank back down on the picnic table bench and propped her
chin on her fists. *'How come you took me here today?'*

*'I wanted to show you something.' As Katie looked down, he held
out his hand. 'Give it one more try. With me. Up the chairlift.'*

'Oh, no.'

'I'll be right with you. I promise.'

She let him lead her outside, where he strapped on her skis and
then towed her to the lift line. He made jokes and teased her and
acted so much like the brother she remembered that she wondered
which personality of his was real now, and which was the act. Then
the lift climbed so high Katie could see the tops of all the trees, the
roads that led away from the ski hill, even the far edge of the university. 'It's beautiful,' she breathed.

*'This is what I wanted you to see,' Jacob said quietly. 'That
Paradise is just a tiny dot on a map.'*

Katie did not answer. She allowed Jacob to help her off the chairlift and followed his directions to slowly make her way down the
hill, but she could not get the image of the world from that mountaintop out of her mind, nor shake the sense that she would feel far
safer when she was once again standing blind at the bottom.

If this were any other Sunday, Ellie thought, she and Stephen
would be reading the *New York Times* in bed, eating bagels and
letting the crumbs fall onto the covers, maybe even putting on
a jazz CD and making love. Instead, she was sandwiched between
two Amish girls, sitting through her first Amish worship service.

Katie was right; they did manage to pack 'em in. Furniture
had been moved to make room for the the long, backless church
benches, which arrived by wagon and could be transported
from home to home. The wide doors and folding room parti-
tions made it possible for nearly everyone to see the center of
the house from his or her seat – the center being where the
ordained men would stand. Women and men sat in the same

room, but on different sides, with the elderly and the married up front. In the kitchen, mothers coddled babies as young as a few weeks; small children sat patiently beside their same-sex parent. Ellie cringed as Rebecca shifted, wedging her closer to Katie. She could smell sweat, soap, and the faint traces of livestock.

Finally, it seemed as though not another person could have been squeezed inside. Ellie waited in the pointed silence for the service to begin. And waited. There was no hurry to start; apparently, she was the only one even remotely concerned by the fact that nothing was happening. She glanced around as a current of whispers volleyed: 'You do it.' 'You . . . no, you.' Finally, an elderly man stood and announced a number. In unison, hundreds of books opened. Katie, who held the *Ausband* on her lap, moved it slightly so that Ellie could see the printed words of the hymnal.

Ellie sighed. When in Rome – or so she had figured. No pun intended, but she didn't have a prayer of sight-reading a musical score that wasn't printed on the page. Only the lyrics were there, and she didn't know the tunes for Amish hymns. Actually, she didn't know the tunes for *any* hymns. One old man began singing in a slow, measured falsetto, and others picked up on his lead. Ellie noticed the ordained men – Bishop Ephram, and the two ministers, and another fellow she had not seen before – leaving their seats to go upstairs. Lucky bastards, she thought.

She thought so, still, thirty minutes later when they finished the first hymn, sat in silence for several minutes, and then launched into the second hymn, the *Loblied*. Ellie closed her eyes, marveling at the stamina of these people who managed to remain upright on the backless benches. She could not recall the last time she attended a church service, but surely that one had finished long before these Amish preachers and the bishop came downstairs again to deliver the introductory sermon.

'*Liebe Bruder und Schwestern . . .*' Dear Brothers and Sisters.

'*Gelobet sei Gott und der Vater unssers Herrn Jesu Christi . . .*' Blessed be the God and Father of our Lord Jesus Christ.

Ellie was nodding off when she felt Katie's soft explanation at her ear. 'He's apologizing for his weakness as a preacher. He doesn't wish to take time away from the Brother who'll bring the main sermon.'

'If he's so bad at this,' Ellie whispered back, 'how come he's a preacher?'

'He's not really bad. He's just showing how he's not proud.'

Ellie nodded, eyeing the older man in a new light. *'Und wann dir einig sin lasset uns bede,'* he said, and as a unit, every single person in the room – except Ellie – fell to their knees.

She glanced at Katie's bowed head, at the bowed heads of the ordained men and the sea of *kapps* and neatly trimmed hair, and very slowly she got down on the floor.

In the middle of the night, Katie's room filled with light. With a rush of anticipation, she sat up in bed, then dressed quickly. Most of the boys kept high-powered flashlights in their courting buggies that they'd shine in a girl's window when they wanted her to sneak down to see them on a Saturday night. She wrapped a shawl around her shoulders – it was February, and freezing outside – and tiptoed down the stairs thinking of John Beiler's eyes, the same warm gold as the leaves on a beech tree in the autumn.

She would scold him, she thought, for dragging her out on a night as cold as this one, but then she'd walk with him and maybe let her shoulder bump up against his now and then to know that she didn't mean it. Her best friend Mary Esch had already let Curly Joe Yoder kiss her on the cheek. She eased the side door open and stepped onto the landing. Katie's eyes were bright, her palms damp. She turned, a smile skimming her lips, and came face to face with her brother.

'Jacob!' she gasped. 'What are you doing here?' Immediately she glanced up at the window of her parents' bedroom. Being found with a beau would be bad enough; but if her father discovered Jacob back in his house, there was no telling what might happen. Putting a finger up to her lips, Jacob reached for his sister's hand and pulled her off the porch, running silently toward the creek.

He stopped at the edge of the pond and used the sleeve of his down jacket to wipe the snow from the small bench there. Then, seeing Katie shiver, he took off the jacket and wrapped it around her shoulders. They both stared at the black ice, smooth as silk, so clear that tangles of marshy grass could be seen frozen beneath it. 'Have you been here yet today?' he asked.

'What do you think?' She had come early this morning, to mark the five years that had passed. Katie held her hands up to her cheeks, blushing to realize that she'd been so full of herself she'd been thinking of John Beiler, when her thoughts should have centered on Hannah. 'I can't believe you came here.'

He scowled at her. 'I come every year. I just never called on you before.'

Stunned, Katie turned to him. 'You come back? Every year?'

'On the day she died.' They both stared toward the pond again, watching the willow branches scratch its surface with each bite of the wind. 'Mam? How's she?'

'Same as every year. She got feeling a little grenklich, *went to bed early.'*

Jacob leaned back and stared at the sky, cracked open wide and carved with stars. 'I used to hear her crying outside on the porch swing, underneath my window. And I'd think that if I hadn't been so chairminded, it wouldn't have happened.'

'Mam said it was the Lord's will. It would have happened whether or not you'd been off reading your books, instead of skating with us.'

'That's the only time, you know, I ever thought twice about wanting so badly to keep up my schooling. As if Hannah drowning was some kind of punishment for that.'

'Why would you be the one punished?' Katie swallowed hard. 'I'm the one Mam told to watch her that day.'

'You were eleven. You couldn't have known what to do.'

Katie closed her eyes and heard the great groan that came from the ice so many years ago, the sound of tectonic plates shifting and deep monsters bellowing at trespass. She saw Hannah, so proud to have tied her skates all alone for the first time, taking off in a streak across the pond, silver blades winking from beneath her green skirts. Watch me, watch me! *Hannah had cried, but Katie never heard, too busy daydreaming of the fancy, glittering costume of an Olympic figure skater that she had seen in the newspaper at the market checkout stand. There was a shriek and a crash. By the time Katie turned, Hannah was already sliding beneath the ice.*

'She was trying to hold on,' *Katie said softly.* 'I kept telling her to hold on, while I got a long branch the way Dat taught us to. But I couldn't reach the branch to break it off, and she kept crying, and every time I turned my back her mittens slipped a little more. And then she was gone. Just like that.' *She lifted her face to Jacob's, too embarrassed to admit to her brother that her thoughts on that day had been worldly, and just as worthy of censure as anything he had done.* 'She would be older now than I was when she died.'

'I miss her too, Katie.'

'It's not the same.' *Fighting tears, she looked into her lap.* 'First Hannah, and then you. How come the people I love the most keep leaving me?'

Jacob's hand crept across the bench to cover hers, and Katie thought that for the first time in many months, she recognized her brother. She could look at him in his puffy red coat, with his clean-shaven face and his short copper hair, and see instead Jacob in his shirt and suspenders, his hat tossed aside, his head bent over a high school English textbook in the hayloft, trying to hide his wildest dreams. Then she felt a stirring in her chest, and her hair stood up on the back of her neck. Lifting her eyes to the pond, she saw a slight figure skimming over it, whistling across the ice and kicking up small clouds of snow. A skater, which would not have been remarkable, except for the fact that Katie could see the cornfield and the willow's greedy arms right through the girl's shawl and skirt and face.

She did not believe in ghosts. She believed, like the rest of her people, that working hard in this life might send you to your greater reward − a sort of wait-and-hope-for-the-best policy that left no room for errant spirits and tortured souls. Heart pounding, Katie got to her feet and inched across the ice to the spot where Hannah was skating. Jacob yelled out, but she could barely hear him. She, who had been taught to believe that God would answer your prayers, realized that it was true: at this moment, both her brother and her sister had come back to her.

She reached out and whispered, 'Hannah?' But she was grabbing at nothing, shivering when Hannah's transparent skirts swirled about her own booted feet.

A strong arm yanked her off the ice to the safety of the pond's bank. 'What the hell are you doing?' Jacob hissed. 'Are you crazy?'

'Don't you see it?' She prayed that he did, prayed that she wasn't losing her mind.

'I don't see anything,' Jacob said, squinting. 'What?'

On the pond, Hannah lifted her arms to the night sky. 'Nothing,' Katie said, her eyes shining. 'It's nothing at all.'

To say that the service lasted forever would not be much of an exaggeration. Ellie was stunned by the behavior of the children, who – having sat through the reading of the Scripture and two hours of the main sermon – barely made a peep. A small bowl of crackers and a glass of water had been passed from room to room for the parents who had little ones curled beside them. Ellie occupied herself by counting the number of times the preacher lifted his white handkerchief and wiped at his brow. In the aisle in front of Ellie, another handkerchief served as entertainment for a little girl, as her big sister folded it into mice and rag dolls.

She knew the service was drawing to a close because the general energy level in the room began to buzz again. The congregation rose for the benediction, and as the bishop mentioned Jesus's name, they all fell again to their knees, leaving Ellie standing alone and aware. Sitting down beside Katie again, she felt the girl suddenly go stiff as a board. 'What is it?' she whispered, but Katie shook her head, tight-lipped.

The deacon was speaking. Katie strained forward, listening, and then closed her eyes in relief. Several rows ahead, where Sarah was sitting, Ellie noticed her chin sag to her chest. Ellie

put her hand on Katie's knee and traced a question mark.
'There will be no members' meeting,' Katie murmured, the
words laced with joy. 'No disciplining to be done.'

Ellie regarded her thoughtfully. She must have nine lives, to
have escaped the English legal system and the punitive channels of her own people too. After another hymn came the
dismissal, three and a half hours after the service had begun.
Katie ran off to the kitchen to set tables for the snack, Ellie
trying to follow and getting woefully tangled between the greet-
ings of others. Someone pushed her to a table where the ordained
men were eating, inviting her to sit down. 'No,' Ellie said, shaking
her head. It was clear, even to her, that there was a pecking
order, and that she shouldn't be eating first.

'You are a visitor,' Bishop Ephram said, gesturing to the
bench.

'I have to find Katie.'

She felt strong hands on her shoulders and looked up to find
Aaron Fisher steering her back to the table. 'It is an honor,' he
said, meeting her eye, and without a sound Ellie sank onto the
bench.

*Graduation day at Penn State was like nothing Katie had ever seen
– a pageant of color, punctuated by silver flashes of cameras that
instinctively made her start. When Jacob marched up to receive his
diploma in his stately black cap and gown, she clapped louder than
anyone else around her. She was proud of him – a curiously un-Amish
feeling, but valid all the same in this* Englischer *collegiate world.
Impressively, it had only taken him five years – including the one he
spent mastering the high school subjects he'd never learned. And
although Katie herself didn't see the purpose of going on past eighth
grade with your schooling when you were going to grow up and manage
a household anyway, she couldn't deny that Jacob needed this. She
had lain on the floor of his apartment and listened to him read aloud
from his books, and before she could catch herself she'd been swept
away by Hamlet's doubts; by Holden Caulfield's vision of his sister
on that merry-go-round; by Mr Gatsby's lonely green light.*

Suddenly the graduates tossed their hats in the air, like starlings scattering from the trees when the hammers rang out at a barn raising. Katie smiled as Jacob hurried toward her. 'You did wonderful gut,' she said, and hugged him.

'Thanks for coming.' Lifting his head, Jacob suddenly called out a greeting to someone across the green. 'There's someone I want you to meet.'

He drew her toward a man taller even than Jacob, wearing the same black robe, but with a blue sash over his shoulders. 'Adam!'

The man turned around and grinned. 'Hey, that's Dr Sinclair to you.'

He was a little older than Jacob, this she could see from the lines around his eyes, which made her think he laughed often, and well. He had hair the color of a honeycomb, and eyes that almost matched. But what made Katie unable to look away was the absolute peace that washed over her when she met his gaze, as if this one Englischer *had a soul that was Plain.*

'Adam just got his Ph.D.,' Jacob explained. 'He's the one whose house I'm renting.'

Katie nodded. She knew that Jacob had moved out of undergraduate housing and into a small home in town, since he was staying on as a teaching assistant at Penn State. She knew that the man who owned the home was going away to do research. She knew there would be two weeks' time when they were roommates, before the owner left on his trip. But she had not known his name. She had not known that you could stand this far away from a person and still feel as if you were pressed up tight against him, fighting to take a breath.

'Wie bist du heit,' she said, and then blushed, flustered that she had greeted him in Dietsch.

'You must be Katie,' he answered. 'Jacob's told me about you.' And then he held out his hand, an invitation.

Katie suddenly thought about Jacob's stories of Hamlet and Holden Caulfield and Mr Gatsby, and with perfect clarity understood how these studies of emotional conundrums might be just as useful in real life as learning how to plant a vegetable garden, or

hanging out the laundry. She wondered what this man had mastered,
to earn his Ph.D. With great deliberation, Katie took Adam Sinclair's
hand, and she smiled back.

After arriving home and having lunch, Aaron and Sarah went
off to do what most Amish did on Sunday afternoons: visit relatives and neighbors. Ellie, having unearthed an entire set of
Laura Ingalls's *Little House* books, sat down to read. She was
tired and irritable from the long morning, and the rhythmic
clop of horses pulling buggies along the main road was beginning to bring on a migraine.

Katie, who had been cleaning the dishes, came into the living
room and curled up in the chair beside Ellie. Eyes closed, she
began to hum softly.

Ellie glared at her. 'Do you mind?'

'Mind what?'

'Singing. While I'm reading.'

Katie scowled. 'I'm not singing. If it's bothering you, go somewhere else.'

'I was here first,' Ellie said, feeling like a seventh-grader. But
she got to her feet and headed toward the door, only to find
Katie following her. 'For God's sake, you have the entire living
room now!'

'Can I ask you a question? Mam said you used to come visit
Paradise in the summers, to stay on a farm like ours. Aunt Leda
told her. Is it true?'

'Yes,' Ellie said slowly, wondering where this was leading.
'Why?'

Katie shrugged. 'It's just that you don't seem to like it much.
The farm, I mean.'

'I like the farm just fine. I'm just not accustomed to having
to baby-sit my clients.' At the wounded look that crossed Katie's
face, Ellie sighed inwardly. 'I'm sorry. That was uncalled-for.'

Katie looked up. 'You don't like me.'

Ellie didn't know what to say to that. 'I don't know you.'

'I don't know you, either.' Katie scuffed the toe of her boot on the wooden floor. 'On Sunday, we do things different here.'

'I'd noticed. No chores.'

'Well, we still have chores. But we also have time to relax.' Katie looked up at her. 'I thought that maybe, it being Sunday, you and I could do things different, too.'

Ellie felt something tighten inside her. Was Katie going to suggest they skip town? Go find a pack of cigarettes? Give each other a few hours of no-holds-barred privacy?

'I was thinking that maybe we could be friends. Just for this afternoon. You could pretend that you met me coming to visit the farm you were at when you were a kid, instead of the way it really happened.'

Ellie put down her book. If she won Katie's friendship and got the girl to open enough to spill out the truth, she might not need Coop to come evaluate her at all. 'When I was a kid,' Ellie said slowly, 'I used to be able to skip stones farther than any of my cousins.'

A smile blossomed over Katie's face. 'Think you still can?'

They jostled through the door and struck out across the field. At the edge of the pond, Ellie reached for a smooth, flat rock and tossed it, counting as it bounced five times over the water. She wiggled her fingers. 'Haven't lost the touch.'

Katie picked up her own stone. Four, five, six, seven skips. With a broad smile, she turned to Ellie. 'Some touch,' she teased.

Ellie narrowed her eyes in concentration and tried again. A moment later, Katie did too. 'Ha!' Ellie crowed. 'I win!'

'You do not!'

'I beat you by a yard, fair and square!'

'That's not what I saw,' Katie protested.

'Oh, right. And your eyewitness accounts these days are *so* accurate.' When Katie stiffened beside her, Ellie sighed. 'I'm sorry. It's hard for me to separate from why I'm really here.'

'You're supposed to be here because you believe me.'

'Not necessarily. A defense attorney is paid to make a jury

believe whatever she says. Which may or may not be what her client has told her.' At Katie's baffled expression, Ellie smiled. 'It probably sounds very strange to you.'

'I don't understand why the judge doesn't just pick the person who's telling the truth.'

Reaching for a piece of timothy grass, Ellie set it between her teeth. 'It's not quite as simple as that. It's about defending people's rights. And sometimes, even to a judge, things aren't black and white.'

'It is black and white, if you're Plain,' Katie said. 'If you follow the *Ordnung*, you are right. If you break the rules, you get shunned.'

'Well, in the English world, that's communism.' Ellie hesitated. 'What if you didn't do it? What if you were accused of breaking a rule, but you were perfectly innocent?'

Katie blushed. 'When there's a members' meeting for discipline, the accused member has a chance to tell his story too.'

'Yeah, but does anyone believe him?' Ellie shrugged. 'That's where a defense attorney comes in – we convince the jury that the client may not have committed the crime.'

'And if he did?'

'Then he still gets acquitted. That happens sometimes, too.'

Katie's mouth dropped open. 'That would be lying.'

'No, that would be acting as a spin doctor. There are many, many different ways of looking at what's happened to bring someone to trial. It's only considered lying if the client doesn't tell the truth. Attorneys – well, we can say just about anything we want as an explanation.'

'So . . . you would lie for me?'

Ellie met her gaze. 'Would I have to?'

'Everything I've told you is the truth.'

Sitting up, Ellie crossed her legs. 'Well, then. What haven't you told me?'

A sparrow took off in flight, casting a shadow across Katie's face. 'It's not our way to lie,' she said stiffly. 'It's why a Plain person can stand up for himself in front of the congregation.

It's why defense attorneys don't have a place in our world.'

To her surprise, Ellie laughed. 'Tell me about it. I have never in my life stuck out like such a sore thumb.'

Katie's gaze traveled from Ellie's running shoes to her sundress to the small, dangling earrings she wore. Even the way Ellie sat – as if the grass was too scratchy to let the backs of her legs rest upon it – was slightly uncomfortable. Unlike the hordes of people who streamed into Lancaster County to get a glimpse of the Amish, Ellie had never asked for this. She had done Aunt Leda a favor, and it had mushroomed into an obligation.

Katie knew how she had felt, from her visits to Jacob. Putting on the costume of a wordly teenager had never made her one. Ellie might think she espoused individuality, but being yourself in a culture where other *Englischers* were busy being themselves was a far cry from being yourself in a culture where the people were all intent on being the same – but different from you.

A world that was crowded with people could still be a very lonely place.

'I can fix that,' Katie said aloud. With a big grin she reached into the lake, scooped up some water, and tossed it onto Ellie.

Sputtering, Ellie jumped up. 'What did you do that for?'

'*Wasser,*' Katie said, splashing her again.

Ellie shielded herself with her hands. 'What's a what?'

'No, *wasser*. It's Dietsch for water.'

After a moment, Ellie understood. She took this small gift and let it settle inside her. '*Wasser,*' she repeated. Then she pointed to the field. 'Tobacco?'

'*Duvach.*'

Katie beamed when Ellie tried the word. '*Gut! Die Koo,*' she said, gesturing at a grazing Holstein.

'*Die Koo.*'

Katie held out her hand. '*Wie bist du heit.* It's nice to meet you.'

Ellie slowly extended her own hand. She looked deeply into Katie's eyes for the first time since she'd arrived at the district court yesterday. The lightness of the afternoon, of the Dietsch lesson, fell away until all the two women knew was the pressure of their palms against each other, the heady hum of the crickets, and the understanding that they were starting over. '*Ich bin die Katie Fisher,*' Katie said quietly.

'*Ich bin die Ellie Hathaway,*' Ellie answered. '*Wie bist du heit.*'

'I'm going to get the popcorn before the movie starts,' Jacob said, standing. When Katie began to rummage through her pockets for the money her Mam always sent along, Jacob shook his head. 'My treat. Hey, Adam, keep an eye on her.'

Katie slouched in her seat, annoyed that her brother would think of her as a child. 'I'm seventeen. Does he think I'm going to wander away?'

Beside her, Adam smiled. 'He's probably more worried that someone's gonna steal his pretty little sister.'

Katie blushed to the roots of her hair. 'I doubt it,' she said. She was unused to compliments that referred to her beauty, rather than a job well done. And she was uncomfortable being alone with Adam, who had been invited by Jacob to join them.

Katie did not wear a watch, and she wondered how long it would be until the film began. This would be her fourth movie, ever. It was supposed to be a love story – such a funny concept, for a two-hour movie. Love wasn't supposed to be about a moment where you looked into a boy's eyes and felt the world spin from beneath your feet; when you saw in his soul all the things that were missing in yours. Love came slow and surefooted and was made of equal measures of comfort and respect. A Plain girl wouldn't fall in love, she'd sort of glance down and realize she was mired in it. A Plain girl knew she loved someone when she looked out ten years from now and saw that same boy standing beside her, his hand on the small of her back.

She was dragged from her thoughts by the sound of Adam's voice. 'So,' he said politely, 'do you live in Lancaster?'

'In Paradise. Well, on the edge of it.'

Adam's eyes lit up. 'On the edge of Paradise,' he said, smiling. 'Almost sounds like you're in for a nasty fall.'

*Katie bit her lower lip. She didn't understand Adam's jokes.
Trying to change the conversation, she asked him if his degree was
in English, like Jacob's diploma.*

*'Actually, no,' Adam said. Was he blushing? 'I work in para-
normal science.'*

'Para—'

'Ghosts. I study ghosts.'

*If he'd taken off all his clothes at that moment, it couldn't have
shocked Katie more. 'You study them?'*

*'I watch them. I write about them.' He shook his head. 'You
don't have to say it. I'm sure you don't believe in ghosts, like most
of the free world. When I tell people what my doctorate is in, they
think it's from some TV correspondence course, with a minor in air-
conditioning repair. But I came by it honestly. I started out as a
physics major, theorizing about energy. Just think about it – energy
can't be destroyed, only converted into something different. So when
a person dies, where does that energy go?'*

Katie blinked at him. 'I don't know.'

*'Exactly. It has to go somewhere. And that residue energy, every
now and then, shows up as a ghost.'*

*She had to look into her lap, or else she was liable to confess to
this man she hardly knew something she'd admitted to nobody.
'Ah,' Adam said softly. 'Now you think I'm crazy.'*

'I don't,' Katie said immediately. 'I really don't.'

*'It makes sense, if you think about it,' he said defensively. 'The
emotional energy that comes from a tragedy impresses itself onto a
scene – a rock, a house, a tree – just as if it's leaving a memory.
At the atomic level, all those things are moving, so they can store
energy. And when living people see ghosts, they're seeing the residue
of energy that's still trapped.' He shrugged. 'There's my thesis, in
a nutshell.'*

*Suddenly Jacob reappeared, carrying a bucket of popcorn. He set
it on Katie's lap. 'You telling her about your pseudo-academic
pursuits?'*

'Hey.' Adam grinned. 'Your sister is a believer.'

'My sister is naïve,' Jacob corrected.

'That's the other thing,' Adam said, ignoring him and turning to Katie. 'You don't bother trying to convince the disbelievers, because they'll never understand. On the other hand, if a person's ever had a paranormal experience – well, they practically go out of their way to find someone like me, who wants to listen.' He looked into her eyes. 'We all have things that come back to haunt us. Some of us just see them more clearly than others.'

In the middle of the night, Ellie awakened to a low moan. Pushing away the folds of sleep, she sat up and turned toward Katie, who was tossing softly beneath her covers. Ellie padded across the floor and touched the girl's forehead.

'Es dut weh,' Katie murmured. She suddenly threw back her covers, revealing two spreading, circular stains on the front of her white nightgown. 'It hurts,' she cried, running her hands over the damp spots on her gown and the bedding. 'There's something wrong with me!'

Ellie had friends – more and more of them, lately – who had gone through childbirth. They had joked about the day that their milk came in, turning them into torpedo-breasted comic book characters. 'There's nothing wrong. This is perfectly natural, after having a baby.'

'I didn't have a baby!' Katie shrieked. 'Neh!' She shoved Ellie away, sending her sprawling on the hard floor. 'Ich hab ken Kind kaht . . . mein hatz ist fol!'

'I can't understand you,' Ellie snapped.

'Mein hatz ist fol!'

It was clear to her that Katie wasn't even really awake yet, just terrified. Deciding not to deal with this on her own, she started out the bedroom door, only to run into Sarah.

It was a shock to see Katie's mother in her bedclothes, her cornsilk hair hanging past her hips. 'What is it?' she asked, kneeling at her daughter's bedside. Katie's hands were clamped over her breasts; Sarah gently drew them down and unbuttoned the nightgown.

Ellie winced. Katie was swollen, so rock-hard that a thin blue map of veins stood out, with tiny rivers of milk leaking from her nipples. At Sarah's urging, Katie passively followed her to the bathroom. Ellie watched as Sarah matter-of-factly massaged her daughter's painful breasts, coaxing a stream of milk into the sink.

'This is proof,' Ellie said flatly, finally. 'Katie, look at your body. You did have a baby. This is the milk, for that baby.'

'Neh, lus mich gay,' Katie cried, now sobbing on the toilet seat.

Ellie set her jaw and crouched down in front of her. 'You live on a dairy farm, for God's sake. You know what's happening to you right now. *You . . . had . . . a baby.'*

Katie shook her head. *'Mein hatz ist fol.'*

Ellie turned to Sarah. 'What is she saying?'

The older woman stroked her daughter's hair. 'That there's no milk; and that there was no baby. Katie says this is happening,' Sarah translated, 'because her heart's too full.'

6

Ellie

Let me just make this perfectly clear: I can't sew. Give me a needle and thread and a pair of trousers to be hemmed, and I am more likely than not to stitch the fabric to my own thumb. I throw out socks that get holes in the heels. I'd rather diet than let a seam out, and that's really saying something.

This is all a way of prefacing that when Sarah invited me to the quilting session she was holding in the living room, I wasn't suitably excited. Things had been strained between us since the previous night. This morning she had wordlessly handed Katie a long strip of white muslin to bind herself. An invitation to quilt was a concession of sorts, a welcome into her world that had previously not been extended. It was also a plea to just let last night pass for what it was.

'You don't have to sew,' Katie told me, pulling me by the wrist into the other room. 'You can just watch us.'

There were four women plus the Fishers: Levi's mother, Anna Esch; Samuel's mother, Martha Stoltzfus; and two cousins of Sarah's, Rachel and Louise Lapp. These women were younger, and brought along their smallest children – one an infant still swaddled, the other a toddler who sat on the floor at Rachel's feet and played with scraps of fabric.

The quilt was spread across the table with spools of white thread scattered over its top. The women looked up as I entered the room. 'This is Ellie Hathaway,' Katie announced.

'Sie schelt an shook mit uns wohne,' Sarah added.

Out of deference to me, Anna responded in English. 'How long will she be staying?'

'As long as it takes for Katie's case to come to trial,' I said.

As I sat down, Louise Lapp's little girl tottered to a standing position and lunged for the bright buttons on my blouse. To keep her from falling, I caught her up in my arms and swung her onto my lap, running my fingers up her belly to make her smile, reveling in the sweet, damp weight of a child. Her sticky hands grasped my wrists, and her head tipped back to reveal the whitest, softest crease in her neck. Too late, I realized that I was being overly friendly with the child of a woman who most likely did not trust me with her daughter's care. I looked up, prepared to apologize, and found all the women now regarding me with considerable esteem.

Well, I wasn't going to look a gift horse in the mouth. As the women bent to their stitches, I played with the little girl. 'Do you care to sew?' Sarah asked politely, and I laughed.

'Believe me, you'd rather I didn't.'

Anna's eyes sparkled. 'Tell her about the time you stitched Martha's quilt to your apron, Rachel.'

'Why bother?' Rachel huffed. 'You do a wonderful *gut* job telling the story yourself.'

Katie idly threaded a needle and bowed her head over a square of white batting, making small, even stitches without the benefit of a ruler or a machine. 'That's amazing,' I said, honestly impressed. 'They're so tiny, they almost seem to disappear.'

'No better than anyone else's,' Katie said, her cheeks reddening at the praise.

The sewing continued quietly for a few moments, women gracefully dipping toward and lifting from the quilt like gazelles coming to drink from a pool of water. 'So, Ellie,' Rachel asked. 'You are from Philadelphia?'

'Yes. Most recently.'

Martha snipped off the end of a piece of thread with her teeth. 'I was there, once. Went in by train. Whole lot of people hurrying around to go nowhere fast, if you ask me.'

I laughed. 'That's pretty much right.'

Suddenly a spool of thread tumbled from the table and

landed square on the head of the infant, sleeping in a small basket. He flailed and began to cry, loud, unstoppable sobs. Katie, who was closest, reached out to quiet him.

'Don't you touch him.'

Rachel's words fell like a stone into the room, stilling the hands of the women so that their palms floated over the quilt like those of healers. Rachel secured her needle by weaving it through the fabric and then lifted her son against her chest.

'Rachel Lapp!' Martha scolded. 'What is the matter with you?'

She would not look at Sarah or Katie. 'I just don't think I want Katie around little Joseph right now, is all. Much as I care for Katie, this here is my son.'

'And Katie's my daughter,' Sarah said slowly.

Martha rested her arm on Katie's chair. 'She's very nearly my daughter, too.'

Rachel's chin lifted a notch. 'If I'm not welcome here—'

'You're welcome, Rachel,' Sarah said quietly. 'But you are not allowed to make my Katie feel unwelcome in her own house.'

I sat breathless on the edge of my chair, the hot damp weight of Louise's sleeping girl on my chest, waiting to see who was going to come out the winner. 'You know what I think, Sarah Fisher,' Rachel began, her eyes flashing, and before she could finish the rest of the sentence, she was interrupted by a loud ringing.

The women, startled, began to look around them. With a sinking feeling I shifted the child to my left arm and pulled my cell phone out of my pocket with my free hand. The women watched, wide-eyed, as I punched a button and held the phone to my ear. 'Hello?'

'Good God, Ellie, I've been trying to reach you for days. Don't you keep this thing on?'

I was amazed the battery was even working after so long. And sort of hoping it would just quit, so that I wouldn't have to speak to Stephen. The Amish women stared, their feud temporarily forgotten. 'I have to take this call,' I said apologetically, and set the sleeping child into her mother's arms.

'A telephone?' Louise gasped, just as I left the room. 'In the *house*?'

I did not hear Sarah's explanation. But by the time I was speaking to Stephen in the kitchen, I heard the wheels of the Lapp sisters' buggy crunching out of the driveway.

'Stephen, this isn't the best time for me to talk.'

'Fine, we don't have to stay on long. I just need to know something, Ellie. There's a ridiculous rumor running around town that you're acting as a public defender for some Amish kid. And that the judge has you living on a farm.'

I hesitated. Stephen would never have let himself get into a position like this. 'I wouldn't call myself a public defender,' I said. 'We just haven't negotiated a fee yet.'

'But the rest? Christ, where are you, anyway?'

'Lancaster. Well, just outside Lancaster, in Paradise Township.'

I could picture the large blue vein in Stephen's forehead, swelling visibly right now. 'So this is what you call taking a breather?'

'It was completely unexpected, Stephen – a family obligation I needed to take care of.'

He laughed. 'A family obligation? Would the Amish be second cousins, twice removed, or would I be confusing them with the Hare Krishnas on your mother's side of the family? Come on, Ellie. You can tell me the truth.'

'I am,' I gritted out. 'This isn't a ploy to get attention; it couldn't be anything farther from that. In a long and convoluted way, I'm defending a relative of mine. I'm on the farm because it's part of the bail agreement. That's all.'

There was a beat of silence. 'I have to say, Ellie, it hurts that you felt like you had to keep this case a secret, instead of telling me what you were up to. I mean, if you were trying to build your reputation as a lawyer for sensational cases – and I do mean sensational in all definitions – I could have offered you advice, suggestions. Maybe even a leg up into my firm.'

'I don't want a leg up into your firm,' I said. 'I don't want sensational cases. And frankly, I can't believe that you've turned this whole thing into a personal affront against *you*.' Glancing down, I noticed that my hand had curled itself into a fist. Finger by finger, I relaxed.

'If this is the case I think it's going to be, you're going to need help. I could come out there as co-counsel; bring the firm on board.'

'Thanks, Stephen, but no. My client's parents barely approved one lawyer, much less a whole building full of them.'

'I could come out anyway, and let you bounce some ideas off. Or we could just sit on the porch swing and drink lemonade.'

For a moment, I was swayed. I could picture the freckles on the nape of Stephen's neck, and the angle at which he cocked his wrist when he was brushing his teeth. I could almost smell the scent of him, coming from the closets and the dressers and the bedclothes. There was something so easy about it, so familiar – and the world I had moved myself into was foreign at every turn. Stopping at the end of the day to see something I recognized, someone I had loved, would put my business with Katie back into the place it was supposed to be: my work, rather than my life.

I tightened my hand around the small phone and closed my eyes. 'Maybe,' I heard myself whisper, 'we ought to just wait and see what happens.'

I found Sarah sitting alone in the living room, her head bowed over the quilt. 'I'm sorry. For the phone.'

She waved away my apology. 'That was nothing. Martha Stoltzfus's husband has one in his own barn, for business. Rachel was just getting on her high horse.' With a sigh, she came to her feet and began to gather the spools of thread. 'Might as well tidy up here.'

I took two corners of the fabric to help her fold it. 'The quilting session seemed awfully short. I hope I wasn't the cause of it.'

'I think it would have been short today no matter what,' Sarah answered briskly. 'I sent Katie out to hang the wash, if you're looking for her.'

I knew a dismissal when I heard one. I started out, but hesitated at the doorway that led to the kitchen. 'Why would Rachel Lapp doubt Katie?'

'I'd think you ought to be able to figure out that one.'

'Well, I meant beyond the obvious. Especially since your bishop stood up for her . . ?'

Sarah set the quilt onto a shelf and turned to me. Although she was doing an admirable job of hiding her feelings, her eyes burned with shame that her friends had snubbed her own daughter. 'We look alike. We pray alike. We live alike,' she said. 'But none of these things mean we all think alike.'

Great white sails snapped in the wind as they were secured to the laundry line. The sheets wrapped their wide arms around Katie as she tried to hang them, her apron flying out behind her as she muttered with a mouthful of clothespins and beat them back. When she saw me, she stepped away from the clothesline, tossing the extra pins into a pail. 'Sure, you get here just when I'm done,' she complained, sitting down on the stone wall beside me.

'You did fine without me.' On one line hung a rainbow of shirts and dresses: dark green, wine, lavender, lime. Beside these danced the black legs of men's trousers. Sheets were stretched over the third clothesline, puffing out their swelled bellies. 'My mother used to hang our laundry,' I said, smiling. 'I remember poking sheets with a stick, pretending I was a knight.'

'Not a princess?'

'Hardly. They don't have any fun.' I snorted. 'I wasn't going to wait around for some prince, when I could very well save myself.'

'Hannah and me, we used to play hide-and-seek in the sheets. But we'd kick up the dirt, and they'd get streaked, and we'd have to wash them all over again.'

Tipping my head back, I let the wind play over my face. 'I used to believe that you could smell the sun on the sheets when you brought them in and made the beds.'

'Oh, but you can!' Katie said. 'The fabric soaks it up, in place of all the damp. Every action has an equal and opposite reaction.'

Newton's laws of physics seemed a bit advanced for an eighth-grade education, which was when Katie, like most Amish children, had stopped attending organized school. 'I didn't know physics was part of the curriculum here.'

'It's not. It's just something I heard.'

Heard? From who? The local Amish scientist? Before I could ask her, she said, 'I need to tend the garden.'

I followed, then settled down to watch her snap off the beans and gather them into her apron. She seemed thoroughly absorbed in her work, so much so that she jumped when I spoke. 'Katie, do you and Rachel usually get along?'

'*Ja.* I watch little Joseph all the time for her. At quilting, sometimes even during church.'

'Well, she sure didn't treat you like the favored family baby-sitter today,' I pointed out.

'No, but Rachel's always one to listen to what other folks say, instead of finding out for herself.' Katie paused, her fingers wrapped around the stem of a bean. 'I don't care what Rachel says, because truth always comes to light sooner or later. But it makes me feel bad to think that I might have something to do with making my mother cry.'

'What do you mean?'

'Well, Rachel's words hurt her more than me. I'm all my Mam's got, now. It's up to me to be perfect.'

Katie stood, the bounty in her apron sagging with its weight. She turned toward the house, only to see Samuel striding toward her.

He took off his hat, his blond hair matted down by sweat. 'Katie. How are you today?'

'Wonderful *gut*, Samuel,' she said. 'Just getting the beans for lunch.'

'It's a good crop you've got there.'

I listened, standing at a distance. Where was the talk of intimacy? Or even a light touch at the elbow or back? Surely Samuel had heard about the argument at the quilting; surely he was here to comfort Katie. I did not know if this was how courting was done in their world; if Samuel was holding back because I was present; or if these two young people truly had nothing to say to each other – something odd, if in fact they had created a baby together.

'Something came for you,' Samuel said. 'If you want to take a look.'

Ah, this was more like it – a private assignation. I lifted my eyes, waiting to hear what Katie had to say, and realized that Samuel had been speaking to me, not her.

'Something came for me? No one even knows I'm here.'

Samuel shrugged. 'It's in the front yard.'

'Well. All right.' I smiled at Katie. 'Let's go see what my secret admirer shipped this time.' Samuel turned, taking Katie's arm to lead her to the front of the house. Walking behind them, I watched as Katie very gently, very slowly, slipped from his grasp.

A squat corrugated cardboard box sat on the packed dirt in front of the barn. 'The police brought it,' Samuel said, staring at the covered carton as if he expected it to contain a rattlesnake.

I hefted it into my arms. The discovery from the prosecutor was not nearly the volume of other cases I'd had in the past – this one small box contained everything the police had gathered, up to this point. But then again, you didn't need a lot of proof for an open-and-shut case.

'What is it?' Katie asked.

She stood beside Samuel, that same sweet, bewildered look

on her face. 'It's from the prosecution,' I told her. 'It's all the evidence that says you killed your baby.'

Two hours later, I was surrounded by statements and documents and reports, none of which cast my client in a favorable light. There were holes in the case – for example, DNA testing had yet to prove that Katie was indeed the mother of the child, and the prematurity of the fetus cast doubt on its ability to survive outside the womb – but for the most part, the overwhelming evidence pointed to her. She'd been placed at the scene of the crime; she'd been tagged as someone who'd recently given birth; her blood was even found on the dead infant's body. The secrecy with which she'd tried to give birth made the prospect of someone else coming along and killing the baby seem ludicrous. On the other hand, it did offer up a motive for the prosecution: when you try so diligently to hide the act of birth, you're probably going to go to great lengths to hide the product of that act, as well. Which left the question of whether or not Katie was in her right mind when she'd committed the murder.

The first thing I needed to do was file a motion for services other than counsel. The court could pay for a psychiatric professional, someone far less likely than me to take Katie on pro bono; and the sooner I wrote up the motion, the sooner I'd have that check in my hand.

Getting off the bed, I knelt to reach beneath it for my laptop. The sleek black case slid along the polished wood floor, so wonderfully heavy with technology and synthetic fabric that it made me want to weep. I set it on the bed and unzipped it, lifting the hinged head of the computer and pressing the button to turn it on.

Nothing happened.

Muttering a curse, I rummaged in the pockets for the battery pack, and slipped it into the hardware. The computer booted up, beeped to alert me that the battery needed to be recharged, and then foundered to a bare, black screen.

Well, it wasn't the end of the world. I could work near an outlet until the battery recharged. An outlet . . . which didn't exist anywhere in Katie's house.

Suddenly I realized what it meant to me, a lawyer, to be working on an Amish farm. I was supposed to create a defense for my client without any of the normal, everyday conveniences accessible to attorneys. Furious – at myself, at Judge Gorman – I grabbed for my cell phone to call him. I managed to dial the first three numbers, and then the phone went dead.

'Jesus Christ!' I threw the phone so that it bounced off the bed. I didn't even have a battery for it; I'd have to recharge it through the cigarette lighter on a car. Of course, the nearest car was Leda's, a good twenty miles away.

Leda's. Well, that was one solution; I could do all my legal work over there. But it was a difficult solution, since Katie was not supposed to leave the farm. Maybe if I wrote the motion out by hand . . .

Suddenly, I stilled. If I wrote the motion out by hand, or if I managed to get my phone working again and called the judge, he'd tell me that the conditions for bail weren't working, and that Katie could cool her heels in jail until the trial. It was up to me to find a way out of this.

With determination, I stood up and headed downstairs, toward the barn.

From Katie I'd learned that the cows were not let out every day in the summer, it was too hot. So when I walked into the barn, the Holsteins chained to their stanchions lowed at me. One lurched to her feet, her udder huge and painfully pink, making me think of Katie the night before. Turning away, I walked between the two rows of cows, ignoring the occasional splash of urine into the grates behind them, hoping to find a way to make my computer work.

I had noticed that if any rules were relaxed on an Amish farm, it was due to economic necessity. For example, in the pristine milk room, a twelve-volt motor stirred the milk in the refrigerated bulk tank; and the vacuum milking machines were powered by a diesel engine that ran twice a day. These 'modern conveniences' were not worldly as much as practical; they kept the Amish in a competitive league with other suppliers of milk. I didn't understand much about diesel fuel or engines, but who knew? Maybe one could be adapted to run a Thinkpad.

'What are you doing?'

At the sound of Aaron's voice, I jumped, nearly striking my head on one of the steel arms of the bulk tank. 'Oh! You scared me.'

'You have lost something?' he asked, frowning at the corner where I'd been peering.

'No, actually, I'm trying to find something. I need to charge a battery.'

Aaron took off his hat and rubbed his forehead on the fabric of his shirt. 'A battery?'

'Yes, for my computer. If you want me to represent your daughter adequately in court, I'm going to have to prepare for her trial. That involves writing several motions beforehand.'

'I write without a computer,' Aaron answered, walking away.

I fell into step beside him. 'You may, but that's not what the judge will be expecting.' Hesitating, I added, 'I'm not asking for an outlet in the house; or even for Internet access or a fax machine – both of which I use excessively before trial. But you must understand that it's not fair to ask me to prepare in an Amish way, when the event I'm getting ready for is an English one.'

For a long time, Aaron stared at me, his eyes dark and fathomless. 'We will speak to the bishop about it. He is coming here today.'

My eyes widened. 'He is? For this?'

Aaron turned away. 'For other things,' he said.

*   *   *

Without a word, Aaron herded me into the buggy. Katie was already waiting in the back, her expression a signal that she didn't understand what was happening either. Aaron sat down on Sarah's right side and picked up the reins, clucking to the horse to set it trotting.

Another buggy pulled out behind us – the open carriage that Samuel and Levi drove to work. In a caravan we turned onto roads I had never traveled upon. They wound through fields and farms where the men were still working, and finally came to a stop at a small crossroads that was dotted with several other buggies.

The cemetery was neat and small, each marker the same approximate size, so that the very oldest ones were differentiated from the newest only by the chiseled dates. A small group of Amish stood in the far corner, their black dresses and trousers brushing the earth like the wings of crows. As Sarah and Aaron stepped from the buggy, they moved in unison, in greeting.

Too late, I realized that the Fishers were only their first stop. They circled me and Katie, touching her cheek and her arm and patting her shoulder. They murmured words of loss and sorrow, which sound the same in any language. In the distance, Samuel and Levi carried something from their wagon; the small, unmistakable shape of a coffin.

Stunned, I broke away from the little group of relatives to stand beside Samuel. Toes to the edge of the grave, he stood looking down at the tiny wooden box. I cleared my throat, and he met my gaze. Why is no one sympathizing with you? I wanted to ask, but the words stuck fast.

A car pulled slowly to a stop behind the carriages, and Leda and Frank got out, dressed in black. I looked down at my own jeans and T-shirt. If someone had mentioned to me that we'd be attending a funeral, I could have changed. But from the looks of things, no one had bothered to tell Katie this, either.

She accepted the sympathies of her relatives, flinching slightly every time someone spoke to her, as if suffering a physical blow. The bishop and the deacon, men I recognized from the church service, came to stand beside the open grave, and the small group gathered around.

I wondered what sense of responsibility had made Sarah and Aaron retrieve the body of an infant that they would not admit aloud was their grandchild. I wondered how Samuel felt to be standing on the fringe. I wondered what Katie made of all this, given her denial of the pregnancy altogether.

With her mother firmly holding her hand, Katie stepped forward. The bishop began to pray, and everyone bowed their heads – everyone except Katie. She looked straight ahead, then at me, then at the buggies – anywhere but in that grave. Finally, she turned her face to the sky like a flower, and smiled softly, inappropriately, as the sun washed over her skin.

But as the bishop invited everyone to silently recite the Lord's Prayer, Katie suddenly pulled away from her mother and sprinted to the buggy, climbing inside and out of sight.

I started after her. No matter what Katie had said up to this point, something about this funeral had apparently struck a chord. I had taken a step in her direction when Leda grasped my hand and stopped me with a brief shake of her head. To my surprise, I remained standing beside her. I found myself mouthing the words of the prayer; words I had not said in years; words I had forgotten I even knew. Then before Leda could stop me again, I hurried to the buggy and climbed in. Katie was huddled in a lump on the seat, head buried beneath her hands. Hesitantly, I stroked her back. 'I can imagine how hard this is for you.'

Slowly, Katie sat up, her spine poker-straight. Her eyes were dry; her lips curved the slightest bit. 'He's not mine, if that's what you're thinking.' She repeated, 'He's not mine.'

'All right,' I conceded. 'He's not yours.' I felt Aaron and Sarah climb into the buggy, turn the horse toward home. And with every rhythmic step I asked myself how Katie, who professed ignorance, had known that the infant was a boy.

Sarah had prepared a meal for the relatives who'd come to the funeral. She set platters of food and baskets of bread on a trestle table that had been moved onto the porch. Unfamiliar women hurried in and out of the kitchen, smiling shyly at me whenever they passed.

Katie was nowhere to be found, and even more strange, no one seemed to find this disturbing. I settled myself on a bench with a plate of food, eating without really tasting anything. I was thinking of Coop, and how long it would be before he got here. First the milk coming in, and now the burial of a tiny body – how much longer could Katie deny the birth of a baby before breaking down?

The bench creaked as a large, elderly woman sat down beside me. Her face was lined like the inner rings of a great sequoia, her hands heavy and swollen at the knuckles. She wore the same black horn-rimmed glasses I remembered my grandfather wearing in the 1950s. 'So,' she said. 'You're the nice lawyer girl.'

I could count on one hand the number of times in my career I'd heard the words *nice* and *lawyer* in the same sentence, much less the reference to my thirty-nine-year-old self as a girl. I smiled. 'That would be me.'

She reached across her plate and patted my hand. 'You know, you're very special to us. Standing up for our Katie this way.'

'Well, thank you. But it's my job.'

'No, no.' The woman shook her head. 'It's your heart.'

Well, I didn't know what to say to that. What mattered here was getting Katie acquitted, which had virtually nothing to do with my own opinion of her. 'If you'll excuse me,' I said, standing, planning on a quick escape. But no sooner had I turned than I ran into Aaron.

'If you would come with us,' he said, gesturing to the

bishop beside him. 'We can talk about that matter from earlier today.'

We walked to a quiet spot in the shade of the barn. 'Aaron tells me you have a problem with your legal case,' Ephram began.

'I wouldn't call it a problem with the case. It's more like a difficulty in logistics. You see, part of my job requires me to be plugged into technology. I need the tools of my trade to prepare the motions I'll be sending to the judge, as well as depositions that will come later on. If I hand the judge a handwritten legal text, he'll laugh me out of court – right after he puts Katie into jail, saying that the bail conditions aren't working out.'

'You are talking about using a computer?'

'Yes, specifically. Mine will run on batteries, but they're dead.'

'You can't get more of these batteries?'

'Not at the local Turkey Hill,' I said. 'They're expensive. I could recharge them, but that requires an outlet.'

'I will not have an outlet on my property,' Aaron interrupted.

'Well, I can't go into town and charge the battery for eight hours and leave Katie alone here, either.'

The bishop stroked his long, gray beard. 'Aaron, you remember when Polly and Joseph Zook's son had the asthma? You remember how much more important it was for the child to have oxygen than to adhere to the strict letter of the *Ordnung*? I think this is the same thing.'

'This is not the same at all,' Aaron countered. 'This isn't life or death.'

'Ask your daughter about that,' I shot back.

The bishop held up his hands. At that moment, he looked exactly like every judge I'd ever stood up to in a courtroom. 'The computer is not yours, Aaron, and I do not doubt your personal commitment to our ways. But like I told the Zooks, the ends justifies the means, in this case. For as long as the lawyer needs it, I will allow an inverter on this farm, to be used only by Miss Hathaway for the electric.'

'An inverter?'

He turned to me. 'Inverters convert twelve-volt current into one-hundred ten volt. Our businessmen use them to power cash registers. We can't use electric straight from a generator, but an inverter, it runs off a battery, which is okay by the *Ordnung*. Most families can't have inverters, because there's too much temptation. You see, the electric goes from diesel to generator to twelve-volt battery to inverter to any appliance – such as your computer.'

Aaron looked appalled. 'Computers are forbidden by the *Ordnung*. And inverters – they're on probation,' he said. 'You could plug a lightbulb into one!'

Ephram smiled. 'You could . . . but Aaron, you wouldn't. I will have someone bring Miss Hathaway an inverter today.'

Clearly miffed, Aaron looked away from the bishop. I was completely confounded by the bargain that had been struck, but grateful all the same. 'This will certainly make a difference.'

The bishop's warm hands enveloped mine, and for a moment, I felt my whole self settle. 'You have made adjustments for us, Miss Hathaway,' Ephram said. 'Did you think we would not make the same compromises for you?'

I don't know why the thought of bringing electricity onto the Fishers' land made me feel a little queasy, as if I were Eve holding out that apple with a come-hither grin. It wasn't as if I was going to find Katie off in the barn playing Nintendo, for God's sake. The inverter would probably collect dust between the times I booted up my Thinkpad to do work. Still, I found myself wandering aimlessly away from the barn and the house after the bishop's decision.

I heard Katie's voice before I even realized I'd walked to the pond. She sat among a high brace of cattails, almost hidden, her bare feet submerged in the water. 'I'm watching,' she said, her eyes fixed on a spot in the middle of the pond where there was absolutely nothing to see. She smiled and clapped, the single audience member for a show of her own making.

Okay, so maybe she *was* crazy.

'Katie,' I said quietly, startling her. She jumped to her feet, splashing me.

'Oh, I'm sorry!'

'It's hot. I could use a little spray.' I sat down on the bank. 'Who were you talking to?'

Her cheeks flamed. 'No one. Just myself.'

'Your sister again?'

Katie sighed, then nodded. 'She skates.'

'She skates,' I repeated, deadpan.

'*Ja,* about six inches above where the water is now.'

'I see. Isn't she having a little trouble without any ice?'

'No. She doesn't know it's summer; she's just doing what she was doing before she died.' Her voice dropped to a whisper. 'She doesn't seem to hear me, either.'

I looked at Katie for a long moment. Her *kapp* was slightly askew, a couple of loose tendrils curled about her ears. Her knees were drawn up, arms crossed loosely over them. She was not agitated or confused. She was just staring at the pond, at this alleged vision.

I picked a cattail and twisted the stem. 'What I don't understand is how you believe something you can't even see, but adamantly refuse to believe something that other people – doctors, and coroners, and my God, even your parents – all know for a fact happened.'

Katie lifted her face. 'But I do see Hannah, clear as day, wearing her shawl and her green dress and the skates that got passed down to her from me. And I never saw that baby, until it was already in the barn, wrapped up and dead.' Her brow furrowed. 'Which would you believe?'

Before I could answer, Ephram appeared with the deacon. 'Miss Hathaway,' the bishop said, 'Lucas and I must speak to our young sister here, for a moment.'

Even with the distance between us, I could feel Katie trembling, and the sharp scent of fear rising from her skin. She was shivering in a way that she hadn't even when a charge of murder was being hung around her neck. Her hand scrabbled over the matted reeds to find mine and slip beneath it. 'I would like my lawyer to be present, then,' she said, her voice no more than a whisper.

The bishop looked surprised. 'Well, Katie, what for?'

She could not even raise her eyes to the older man. 'Please,' she murmured, then swallowed hard.

The deacon and the bishop looked at each other, and Ephram nodded. The trembling, submissive creature beside me was nothing like the girl who'd looked me in the eye and told me there was no baby. She was nothing like the girl who'd spoken to me minutes before about what was visible to one person not being crystal clear to another. But she did bear a striking resemblance to the child I'd seen in court the moment I first arrived, the child who had been ready to let the legal system steamroll her rather than mount a defense.

'It's like this,' Ephram said uncomfortably. 'We know how hard things are, right now, and only bound to be getting more tangled. But there was a baby, Katie, and you being not married . . . well, you need to come to church, and make your things right.'

It was slight, but Katie inclined her head.

With a nod to me, the two men struck off across the field again. It took a full thirty seconds for Katie to get control of herself, and when she did, her face was as pale as a new moon. 'What was that about?' I asked.

'They want me to confess to my sin.'

'What sin?'

'Having a baby out of wedlock.' She started walking, and I hurried to keep up with her.

'What will you do?'

'Confess,' Katie said quietly. 'What else can I do?'

Surprised, I turned and blocked her path. 'You could start

by telling them what you told me. That you didn't have a baby.'

Her eyes filled with tears. 'I couldn't tell them that; I couldn't.'

'Why not?'

Katie shook her head, her cheeks bright. She ran into the waving sea of corn.

'Why not?' I yelled after her, my frustration rooting me to the ground.

The men who brought the inverter set it up for me in the barn. Attached to the generator beside the calving pen, it gave me a lovely view of the police tape still securing the crime scene, just in case I needed any inspiration to fight Katie's charges. Shortly after four o'clock I carried my files and my laptop out to the barn and began to act like a lawyer.

Levi, Samuel, and Aaron were milking the cows at their stanchions. Levi seemed resigned to the Amish equivalent of scut work – shoveling manure, scooping out grain – while the two older men wiped down the udders of the cows with what seemed to be the pages of a telephone book, and then hooked them up in pairs to a suction pump powered by the same generator that was indirectly running my computer. From time to time, Aaron would carry the container into the milk room and pour it into the bulk tank with an audible splash.

I watched them for a while, taken by their graceful routine and the kindness of their hands as they stroked the side of a cow's belly or scratched behind her ears. Smiling, I gingerly plugged in my laptop, made a quick and fervent prayer that this wouldn't surge and destroy my hard drive, and booted it up.

The screen rolled open in a wash of color, spotted with icons and toolbars. My screen saver came next, a computer graphic of sharks at the bottom of the ocean. I reached for one of the manila files I'd received from the prosecutor and spread it open on the hay. Leafing through its contents, I tried to formulate in my mind a motion for services other than counsel.

When I glanced up, Levi was gaping at the laptop from across the barn, his shovel propped forgotten at his side until Samuel walked over and cuffed him. But then Samuel looked himself, eyes widening at the burst of color and the realism of the sharks. His hand twitched, as if he was trying hard not to reach out and touch what he saw.

Aaron Fisher never even turned his head.

A cow bawled at the far end of the stanchions. The sweet hay and even sweeter feed tickled the inside of my nose. The tug-suck, tug-suck of the milking pump became a backbeat. Closing out this world, I focused and began to type.

7

The broad beam of light swept over her legs, then arched up the wall and the ceiling before repeating the circuit all over again. Katie came up on her elbows, heart pounding. Ellie was still asleep; that was a good thing. She crawled out of bed and knelt at the window. At first she could see nothing; then Samuel removed his hat and the moon caught the crown of his bright hair. Taking a deep breath, Katie slipped into her clothes and hurried out to meet him.

He was waiting with the flashlight, which he turned off the minute he saw her framed in the doorway. Once Katie walked outside, he caught her in his arms and pressed his lips against hers, hard. It made Katie freeze – he'd never moved this fast before – and she wedged her hands up between them to set her distance. 'Samuel!' she said, and immediately he stepped back.

'I'm sorry,' Samuel murmured. 'I am. It's just that I feel like you're slipping away.'

Katie lifted her eyes. She knew Samuel's face as well as her own; they'd grown up as family, as friends. He'd chased her into a tree once when she was eleven. He'd kissed her for the first time when she was sixteen, behind Joseph Yoder's calf shed. On the small of her back, she felt Samuel's hands move restlessly.

Sometimes when she pictured her life, it was like the telephone poles that marched along the length of Route 340 – year after year after year, stretching out all the way to the horizon. And when she saw herself like that, it was always with Samuel standing beside her. He was everything that was right for her; everything that was expected of her. He was her safety net. The thing was, most Plain folks never lifted their faces from the straight and narrow ground, to know that high above was the most wondrous tightrope you could ever have the chance to walk.

Samuel tipped his forehead against Katie's. She could feel his breath, his words, falling onto her, and she opened her lips to receive them. 'That baby wasn't yours,' he said urgently.

'No,' she whispered.

He tilted his face so that their mouths came together, wide and sweet as the sea. Their kiss tasted of salt, and Katie knew there were tears on both of their cheeks, but she did not recall which of them had passed the sorrow to the other. She opened herself to Samuel as she had never done before, understanding that this was a debt he had come to collect.

Then Samuel drew away from her and kissed her eyelids. He held her face between his hands and murmured, 'I've sinned.'

She raised her palms to cover his. 'You haven't,' she insisted.

'Yes. Let me finish.' Samuel swallowed. 'That baby. That baby, it wasn't ours.' He gathered Katie closer, burying his face in her hair. 'It wasn't ours, Katie. But I have been wishing it was.'

'Have you ever touched one?'

Adam looked up from the desk, smiling at the sight of Katie bent over one of his logbooks. 'Yeah,' he said. 'Well, sort of. You can't grab them, you just sort of feel them come over you.'

'Like a wind?'

Adam set down his pen. 'More like a shiver.'

Katie nodded, and very seriously turned back to her reading. This was the second time she'd visited Jacob this week — an unprecedented occurrence, apparently — and she'd scheduled the visit on a day when she knew that Jacob was working at the college until the afternoon. When Adam sat down beside her, Katie smiled. 'Tell me what it was like.'

'I was at an old hotel in Nantucket. I woke up in the middle of the night and found a woman looking out the window. She was wearing an old-fashioned dress, and the air was filled with this perfume – a scent I'd never smelled before, or since. I sat up and asked who she was, but she didn't answer. And then I realized that I could see the windowsill and the wooden mullions right through her body. She completely ignored me, then walked right past the window, through me. It felt . . . chilly. Made the hair rise on the back of my neck.'

'Were you frightened?'

'Not really. She didn't seem to know I was there. The next morning, I asked the proprietor, who told me that the hotel had been the home of a sea captain that drowned. It was supposedly haunted by his widow, who was still waiting for her husband to come home.'

'That's so sad,' Katie said.

'Most ghost stories are.'

For a moment, Adam thought she was going to cry. He reached out and touched Katie's head. 'Her hair, it was like yours. Thick and straight and longer than I'd ever seen.' As she blushed, he sat back and crossed his arms over his bent knees. 'Can I ask you a question now?'

'All right.'

'It's not that I'm not incredibly flattered you're so fascinated by my research . . . but you're the last person I would have expected to find it interesting.'

'Because I'm Plain, you mean?'

'Well, yeah.'

Katie touched her fingers to the words that Adam had typed out. 'I know these ghosts,' she said. 'I know what it's like to move around in the world, but not really be a part of it. And I know what it's like to have people stare right through you, and not believe what they are seeing.' Setting aside the book of research, Katie looked at Adam. 'If I exist, why can't they?'

Adam had once interviewed an entire bus of tourists who'd seen a battlefield at Gettysburg erupt with a battalion of soldiers who were not there. He'd recorded on infrared cameras the colder pockets of energy that surrounded a ghost. He had heard ghosts move crates in attics, slam doors, ring phones. Yet for all the years he had been doing his doctoral research, he'd had to fight for credibility.

Humbled, Adam reached for Katie's hand. He squeezed it gently, and then raised it to his lips to kiss the inside of her wrist. 'You are not a ghost,' he said.

George Callahan frowned at Lizzie's plate. 'Don't you ever eat anything? You're gonna blow over in a wind.'

The detective took a bite of the bagel in front of her. 'How come you're only happy when everyone around you is devouring something?'

'Must have something to do with being a lawyer.' He blotted his mouth with his napkin, then leaned back in his chair. 'You're going to need your energy today. You ever tried to get unsolicited information from the Amish?'

Lizzie let her mind spiral back. 'Once,' she said. 'That case with Crazy Charlie Lapp.'

'Oh, yeah – the schizophrenic kid who went off his meds and drove a stolen car down to Georgia. Well, take that case, and multiply the degree of difficulty by about a hundred.'

'George, why don't you let me do my job? I don't tell you how to try cases.'

'Sure you do. I just don't listen.' He leaned forward, propping his elbows on the table. 'Most neonaticides don't even make it to trial – they get plea-bargained. If the mother does get convicted, it's on a minimal charge. You know why that is?'

'Because no one on a jury wants to believe a mother's capable of killing her baby?'

'In part. But more often because the prosecution can't pin a motive on the crime, which makes it seem less like murder.'

Lizzie stirred her coffee. 'Ellie Hathaway might notice up an insanity defense.'

'She hasn't yet.' George shrugged. 'Look. I think this case is going to blow big, because of the Amish angle. It's a chance to make the county attorney's office shine.'

'It doesn't hurt, of course, that this is an upcoming election year for you,' Lizzie said.

George narrowed his eyes. 'It has nothing to do with me. This wasn't Mary coming into the barn to deliver the infant Jesus. Katie Fisher went there intending to have a baby, kill it, and hide it.' He smiled at the detective. 'Go prove me right.'

Ellie, Sarah, and Katie were in the kitchen pickling cucumbers when the car drove into the front yard. 'Oh,' Sarah said, moving the curtains aside for a better look. 'It's that detective coming around again.'

Ellie's hands froze in the middle of skinning a cucumber. 'She's here to question you all. Katie, go up to your room and don't come back until I tell you.'

'Why?'

'Because she's the enemy, okay?' As Katie hurried upstairs, Ellie turned to Sarah. 'You have to talk to her. Just tell her what you feel comfortable saying.'

'You won't be here?'

'I'll be keeping her away from Katie. That's more important.'

Sarah nodded just as there was a knock from outside. Waiting for Ellie to leave the room, she crossed the kitchen and opened the door.

'Hello, Mrs Fisher. I don't know if you remember me. I'm—'

'I remember you,' Sarah said. 'Would you like to come in?'

Lizzie nodded. 'I'd like that very much. I'd also like to ask you a few questions.' She surveyed the kitchen, with the bottles sealing on the stove and the piles of cucumbers heaped upon the table. 'Would that be all right?' When Sarah nodded stiffly, Lizzie took her notebook from her coat pocket. 'Can you tell me a little about your daughter?'

'Katie's a good girl. She is humble and giving and kind and she serves the Lord.'

Lizzie tapped her pencil against the paper, writing nothing at all. 'She sounds like an angel, Mrs Fisher.'

'No, just a good, Plain girl.'

'Does she have a boyfriend?'

Sarah twisted her hands beneath her apron. 'There have been a few, since Katie came into her running-around years. But the most serious has been Samuel. He works the farm with my husband.'

'Yes, we've met. How serious is serious?'

'It's not for me to say,' Sarah ventured, smiling shyly. 'That would be Katie's private business. And if they were thinking of marriage, it would be up to Samuel to go to the *Schtecklimann,* the go-between who'd come and ask Katie what her wishes are.'

Lizzie leaned forward. 'So Katie doesn't tell you everything about her personal life.'

'Of course not.'

'Did she tell you she was pregnant?'

Sarah looked down at the floor. 'I don't know.'

'At the risk of being rude, Mrs Fisher, either she told you, or she didn't.'

'She didn't tell me right out, but she wouldn't have volunteered that information, either. It's a very personal thing.'

Lizzie bit back her retort. 'You never noticed that her dresses were getting bigger? That she wasn't menstruating?'

'I have had babies, Detective. I know the signs of pregnancy.'

'But would you have recognized them if they were intentionally being hidden?'

'I guess the answer is no,' Sarah softly conceded. 'Still, it is possible that Katie didn't know what was happening herself.'

'She grew up on a farm. And she watched you through

your other pregnancy, right?' As Sarah bent her head, nodding, something sparked in Lizzie's mind. 'Has Katie ever exhibited a violent streak?'

'No. If anything, she was the opposite – always bringing in stray squirrels and birds, and feeding the calves whose mothers died birthing. Taking care of whoever needed caring.'

'Did she watch her little sister often?'

'Yes. Hannah was her shadow.'

'How did your youngest die, again?'

Sarah's eyes shuttered as she stepped back from herself. 'She drowned in a skating accident when she was seven.'

'I'm so sorry. Were you there at the time?'

'No, she and Katie were out at the pond by themselves.' When Lizzie did not ask another question, Sarah looked up at the detective, at the conclusion written across her face. 'You cannot be thinking that Katie had anything to do with her own sister's death!'

Lizzie raised her eyebrows. 'Mrs Fisher,' she murmured, 'I never said I did.'

In a perfect world, Lizzie thought, Samuel Stoltzfus would be gracing the pages of magazines dressed in nothing but Calvin Klein underwear. Tall, strong, and blond, he was so classically lovely that a woman of any faith would have had trouble turning him away – but Lizzie had been questioning the young man for twenty minutes, and knew that even if he looked like a Greek god, he sure as hell didn't have the smarts of Socrates. So far, although she'd verbally held up every single piece of medical evidence of his girlfriend's pregnancy, Samuel wouldn't budge from saying Katie hadn't had a baby.

Maybe denial was catching, like the flu.

Exhaling heavily, Lizzie backed off. 'Let's try another tack. Tell me about your boss.'

'Aaron?' Samuel seemed surprised, and with good reason; all the other questions had been about his relationship with Katie. 'He's a good man. A very simple man.'

'He seemed sort of stubborn to me.'

Samuel shrugged. 'He is used to doing things his way,' he said, then hastened to add, 'but of course he should, since this is his farm.'

'And after you're a member of the family? Won't it be your farm, then, too?'

Samuel ducked his head, clearly uncomfortable. 'That would be his decision.'

'Who else is going to take over the farm, especially once Katie marries? Unless he's got a son waiting in the wings that no one's mentioned.'

Without meeting her eye, Samuel said, 'He has no sons anymore.'

Lizzie turned. 'Was there another child that died? I was under the impression it was a little girl.'

'Yes, Hannah.' Samuel swallowed. 'No one else died. I meant that he has no sons. Sometimes, with the English, I forget how to say it.'

Lizzie eyed the blond man. Samuel stood to inherit the farm – as long as he managed to claim Katie Fisher. Having Aaron Fisher's grandchild would cement that deal. Had Katie killed the infant because she didn't want to be tied to Samuel? Because she didn't want him to inherit?

'Before the baby was found,' Lizzie asked, 'were you and Katie having any fights?'

He hesitated. 'I don't think I have to tell you this.'

'Actually, Samuel, you do. Because your girlfriend's on trial for murder here, and if you had any part in it you could be charged as an accessory. So – the fights?'

Samuel blushed. It made Lizzie stare; she'd never seen shame sprawled across the face of such a large man. 'Just small things.'

'Such as?'

'Sometimes she didn't want to kiss me good night.'

Lizzie grinned. 'That's a little like locking the barn door after the horse has run out.'

Samuel blinked at her. 'I don't understand.'

Now it was Lizzie's turn to blush. 'I just meant that a kiss seems fairly inconsequential once you've gotten her pregnant.'

His cheeks flamed brighter. 'Katie did not have a baby.'

Back to square one. 'Samuel, we've been over this. She had a baby. There's medical proof.'

'I don't know these English doctors, but I know my Katie,' he said. 'She says she didn't have that baby, and it's true; she couldn't have.'

'Why not?'

'Because.' Samuel turned away.

'Because isn't good enough, Samuel,' Lizzie said.

He turned around, his voice rising. 'Because we have never made love!'

Lizzie was silent for a moment. 'Just because she's never slept with you,' the detective gently pointed out, 'doesn't mean she hasn't slept with someone else.'

She waited for the words to sink in, the awful battering ram that knocked down the last of Samuel's defenses. The big man curled into himself, the brim of his hat touching his knees, his arms folded tight around his middle.

Lizzie remembered a case she'd worked on years ago, where the girlfriend of a jewelry store manager had cheated on her boyfriend and gotten pregnant. Rather than admitting to it, she saved face by claiming the guy had raped her and going to court. This newborn's murder might not hinge on an argument between Katie and Samuel, but the very opposite. Instead of admitting that she had slept with another man, going against her religious principles, hurting her family, and ruining her prospects with Samuel, Katie had simply gotten rid of the evidence of her transgression. Literally.

Lizzie watched Samuel's shoulders shake with emotion. Patting him once on the back, she left him to come to terms with the truth: It was not that he didn't believe Katie had had a baby; it was that he didn't want to.

★   ★   ★

'Would she do that?' Samuel whispered, holding onto Ellie's hands like a lifeline. 'Would she do that to me?'

She had never believed that you could see a heart break, yet here she was watching it. And it was much like the time she'd watched a skyscraper demolished in Philly, floor crumbling into floor until there was nothing but a memory hanging in the air. 'Samuel, I'm sorry. I barely know her well enough to make that judgment.'

'But did she say anything to you? Did she tell you his name?'

'We don't know there was another "he,"' Ellie said. 'The detective wants you to jump to conclusions, in the hope that you'll slip up and tell her something the prosecution can use.'

'I didn't say anything,' Samuel insisted.

'Of course not,' Ellie said dryly. 'I'm sure they have plenty to work with right now.' In fact, just the thought of it sent her head spinning: in a nutshell, here was the prosecution's motive – Katie committed murder to cover up an indiscretion.

Samuel looked at Ellie seriously. 'I would do anything for Katie.'

'I know.' And Ellie did. The question was, just how far did Samuel's promise extend? Could he simply be a very good actor, and have known all along about his girlfriend's pregnancy? Even if Sarah hadn't noticed, Samuel would have easily discovered physical differences in Katie during a simple embrace – and would naturally have known if he wasn't the father. Without any Fisher sons, Samuel stood to inherit the farm – as long as he managed to claim Katie. A Lancaster County farm was a tremendous boon, the real estate value of some of these properties reaching into the millions. If Katie had given birth and then married the father of the child, Samuel would be left out in the cold. It was a clear motive for murder – but pointed at a very different suspect.

'I think you need to speak to Katie,' Ellie said gently. 'I'm not the one who's going to be able to give you the answers.'

'We were going to be together. She told me so.' Samuel's voice was shaking; although no tears had fallen, they were shining in his eyes. Another thing about heartbreaks – you could not watch one without feeling your own heart suffer a hairline fracture as well. Samuel turned away from Ellie, his shoulders rounded. 'I know that it's the Lord's way to forgive her, but I can't do that right now. Right now, all I want to know is who she was with.'

Ellie nodded, and silently thought, You're not the only one.

Vines twined around the footing of the railroad bridge, stretching toward the high water mark and the rivets that anchored steel to concrete. Katie rolled up the legs of her jeans and took off her shoes and socks, following Adam into the shallow water. Pebbles bit at the arches of her feet; on the slick, smoother stones, her heels slipped. As she reached for the pillar to steady herself, she felt Adam's hands grasp her shoulders. 'It's December, 1878,' he whispered. 'An ice storm. The Pennsylvania Line's carrying two hundred and three passengers headed toward New York City for Christmas. The train derails there, just at the edge of the bridge, and the cars tumble over into the icy water. One hundred and eighty-six people die.'

His breath fanned against the side of her neck, and then just as suddenly, he stepped away from her. 'Why aren't there a hundred and eighty-six ghosts, then?' Katie asked.

'For all we know, there are. But the only one that's been seen by a number of different people has been Edye Fitzgerald.' Adam walked back to the bank of the river and sat down to fiddle with a long, flat mahogany box. 'Edye and John Fitzgerald were newlyweds, on their way to New York City for their honeymoon. John survived the crash, and supposedly kept going into the wreckage with the relief workers, calling out for his wife. After identifying her body, he went to New York City alone, took the honeymoon suite in some fancy hotel, and killed himself.'

'That's a sin,' Katie said flatly.

'*Is it? Maybe he was just trying to get back to Edye again.*'
*Adam smiled faintly. 'I'd like to check out that suite, though, and
see if he's haunting it.' He opened the cover of the wooden case.
'Anyway, there are over twenty accounts of people who've seen
Edye walking around in the water here, people who've heard her
calling John's name.'*

*He withdrew two long L-shaped rods from the box and twirled
them in his hands like a sharpshooter. Katie watched, wide-eyed.
'What can you do with those?'*

'*Catch a ghost.' At her shocked expression, he grinned. 'You
ever use dowsing rods? I guess not. People play around with these
to find water, or even gold. But they'll pick up on energy, too.
Instead of pointing down, you'll see them start to quiver.'*

*He began to walk around the cement pylon so soundlessly that
the water barely whispered over his legs. His hands curved around
the rods, his head bowed to his task.*

*She could not imagine her parents doing what John and Edye
had done in the extremes of love. No, if a spouse died, that was
the natural course of things, and the widow or widower went on
with his business. Come to think of it, she'd never seen her Dat
even give her Mam a quick kiss. But she could remember the way
he kept his arm around her the whole day of Hannah's funeral;
the way he'd sometimes finish his meal and beam at Mam like
she'd just hung the moon. Katie had always been taught that it
was similar values and a simple life that kept a husband and wife
together – and after that, passion came privately. But who was
to say it didn't come before? That sigh pressing up from the inside
of your chest; the ball of fire in the pit of your stomach when he
brushed your arm; the sound of his voice curling around your
heart – couldn't those things bind a man and a woman forever,
too?*

*Suddenly Adam stilled. His hands were shaking slightly as the
rods jumped up and down. 'There's something . . . right here.'*

Katie smiled. 'A cement pillar.'

*A dark shadow of disappointment passed over Adam's face so
quickly she wondered if she had imagined it. The rods began to*

jerk more forcefully. Adam wrenched away from the spot. 'You think I'm making this up.'

'I don't—'

'You don't have to lie to me. I can see it on your face.'

'You don't understand,' Katie began.

Adam thrust the rods at her. 'Take these,' he challenged. 'Feel it.'

Katie curled her hands over the warm spots his own hands had left. She stepped gingerly toward the place where Adam had been standing.

At first it was a shiver that ran up her spine. Then came an unspeakable sorrow, falling over her like a fisherman's net. Katie felt the rods tugging, as if someone was standing at the other end and grabbing onto them like a lifeline. She bit her lower lip, fighting to hold on, understanding that this restlessness, this unseen energy, this pain – this was a ghost.

Adam touched her shoulder, and Katie burst into tears. It was too much – the knowledge that the dead might still be here on earth; that all those years, all those times she'd seen Hannah, Katie hadn't been losing her mind. She felt Adam's arms close around her, and she tried to hold herself at a distance, embarrassed to find herself sobbing into his shirt. 'Ssh,' he said, the way one would approach a wild, wary animal. 'It's all right.'

But it wasn't all right. Was Hannah carrying around the same despair that Katie had sensed in Edye Fitzgerald? Was she still calling out for Katie to save her?

Adam's lips were warm against Katie's ear. 'You felt her,' he whispered with awe, and Katie nodded against his palm.

Katie felt the quivering again, but this time it was coming from inside her. Adam's eyes were bright, the blue you see when you twirl in a cornfield and fall dizzy onto your back to gaze up at the sky. With her heart pounding and her head spinning, she thought of Edye and John Fitzgerald. She thought of someone who would love her so, he'd spend eternity calling her name. 'Katie,' Adam whispered, and bent his head.

She had been kissed before; dry, hard busses that felt like a bruise. Adam rubbed his mouth gently over hers, so that her lips tingled and her throat ached. She found herself leaning into him. He tasted of coffee and peppermint gum; he held her as if she was going to break.

Adam drew back suddenly. 'My God,' he said, taking a step back. 'Oh, my God.'

Katie tucked her hair behind her ear and blushed, staring at the ground. What had gotten into her? This was not the way for a Plain girl to carry on. But then, she wasn't Plain now, was she? Wearing these clothes Jacob had gotten her; with her hair English-styled loose and free, she felt like someone entirely different. Someone who might believe in ghosts. Someone who might believe in love at first sight, in love that lasts forever.

Finally, gathering her courage, Katie looked up. 'I'm sorry.'

Slowly, Adam shook his head. His mouth, his beautiful mouth, quirked at the corner. He lifted her palm and kissed the center of it, a token to hold tight and slip into her pocket as a keepsake. 'Don't be,' he said, and took her into his arms again.

Ellie stormed into the bedroom she shared with Katie, slamming the door behind her.

'Did she leave?'

The question stopped Ellie in her tracks. 'Who?'

'The detective. The woman who drove up before.'

God, she had completely forgotten about Lizzie Munro roaming the farm. 'As far as I know she's out interviewing the goddamned herd,' Ellie snapped. 'Sit up. You and I, Katie Fisher, are going to have a talk.'

Startled, Katie curled from her bed into a sitting position. 'What – what's the matter?'

'This is what's the matter: The investigator for the prosecution is downstairs getting a precious commodity – facts – from your friends and relatives. And me, I've been cooling my heels here for a week, and can't even get a straight answer out of you.' Katie opened her mouth, but Ellie silenced her by raising her hand. 'Don't. Don't even think about saying that you've already told me the truth. You know that baby you didn't have? Your boyfriend Samuel just told me that you didn't sleep with him to conceive it.'

Katie's eyes went wide, so that a ring of white shone around the blue irises. 'Well, no. I wouldn't do that before taking marriage vows.'

'Of course not,' Ellie said sarcastically. 'So now we have a virgin birth.'

'I didn't—'

'You didn't have a baby! You didn't have sex!' Ellie's voice rose, shaking. 'God, Katie, how do you expect me to defend you?' She stood above Katie, her anger flowing over the girl like heat. 'You have a guy walking around out there devastated to find out that he's not your one and only. You duck your head and *yes, yes* the bishop when he suggests that you might have had intercourse. But you sit here like some damn block of cement, unwilling to budge the tiniest bit to give me something to work with!'

Katie bent back under the force of Ellie's wrath. She crossed her arms over her stomach and turned away from Ellie. 'I love Samuel, I do.'

'And who else, Katie? *Who else?*'

'I don't know.' By now she was sobbing. Her hands crept up to cover her face; her *kapp* became unpinned and fell to the floor. 'I don't know. I don't know who it was!'

'We're talking about a sexual partner, for God's sake – not what cereal you had for breakfast a week ago. It's not something that you typically forget!'

Katie wound herself into a fetal position on the bed, crying and rocking her body back and forth. 'What aren't you telling me?' Ellie asked. 'Were you drunk?'

'No.'

'High?'

'No!' Katie buried her face in the pillow. 'I don't remember who touched me!'

Katie's cries wound around Ellie's chest, squeezing so

tightly she could barely find the strength to breathe. With a groan of surrender, she sat down on the mattress and gathered the girl close, stroking her hair and whispering words of comfort.

Katie felt like a child in her arms. An overgrown toddler who'd knocked over a vase with a ball, never knowing that she'd done something that would make the rest of the world rear up and roar. A big child, but one just as lost, just as needy, just as desperate for forgiveness.

A terrible suspicion began to rise in Ellie, filling her heart and lungs and mind with a powerful and sudden rage. She clamped it down, calming herself before she lifted Katie's chin. 'Did someone rape you?'

Katie stared at her, her swollen eyes drifting closed. 'I don't remember,' she whispered.

For the first time since meeting Katie, Ellie believed what she was saying.

'Oh, Christ.' Lizzie lifted her loafer and stared at the muck and manure stuck to the sole. They just weren't paying her enough for this interrogation, and Aaron Fisher could go hang for all she cared. She raised her head and sighed, then started off across the field again. Fisher, seeing her approach, pulled his team of mules to a stop.

'If you are looking for the way home,' Fisher said in accented English, 'it's that way.' He pointed toward the main road.

Lizzie bared her teeth at him. Just her luck to find an Amishman who fancied himself a stand-up comic. 'Thanks, but I've already found what I've been searching for.'

That brought him up short. Lizzie let him stew a minute, imagining all the grisly pieces of evidence that might turn up in a murder investigation. 'What would that be, Detective?'

'You.' Lizzie shaded her eyes. 'I wonder if you've got a minute.'

'I have many minutes, all of them used toward a common

purpose.' He clucked to the horses, and Lizzie jogged beside them until the farmer stopped again.

'Care to share it with me?'

'To run my farm,' Aaron said. 'If you will excuse—'

'I'd think you might be able to spare a few precious seconds to save your daughter from going to jail, Mr Fisher.'

'My daughter is not going to jail,' he said stubbornly.

'It's not for you to decide.'

The farmer took off his hat. He looked tired, suddenly, and much older than Lizzie had originally thought. 'It's not for you to decide either, but for the Lord. I trust in His judgment, as does my daughter. Good day, now.' He tapped the reins, and the mules jumped forward in unison, the plowing equipment groaning through the earth.

Lizzie watched him go. 'Too bad God won't be sitting on that jury,' she murmured, and then began the long walk back to the farmhouse.

Ellie finished wiping up the last of the pickling spices that dusted the kitchen table. It was beastly hot in the kitchen – God, what she'd do for air conditioning, or an electric fan – but she had promised Sarah she'd take care of the cleanup detail, since she'd missed a good portion of the actual canning work while she was consoling Katie.

And what was she to make of that last confrontation? Mysteries were beginning to fall into place in her mind, as neatly as tumblers in a lock – Katie's selective amnesia, her denial of the pregnancy and the birth, Samuel's stunned expression when they'd last spoken. For the first time since she'd arrived at the farm, Ellie did not feel revulsion at the thought of the neonaticide Katie had committed, but pity.

As a defense attorney she'd supported her share of clients who'd committed heinous crimes, but she instinctively worked harder when she could make herself understand what had brought them to that point. The woman who'd murdered her husband in his sleep was less of a monster when you factored in that the man had beaten her for thirty years. The rapist with a swastika tattoo across the bridge of his nose was far less intimidating when you thought of him as a boy being abused by his stepfather. And the Amish girl who killed her newborn couldn't be forgiven, but certainly understood, if the father of the child had sexually assaulted her.

On the other hand, it was the final nail in Katie's coffin. In terms of motive, it made very good sense for a young woman to want to kill the baby conceived in an act of rape. Which meant that – no matter how much Ellie might sympathize with Katie, no matter how much she hoped to get her counseling – no mention of rape would ever be made during her defense.

Ellie wrung out the sponge in the sink. She wondered if Katie would start to confide in her now. She wondered if she ought to go upstairs again, so that Katie would not awaken alone.

At the sound of the door opening behind her, Ellie shut off the faucet and wiped her hands on the voluminous apron she'd borrowed from Sarah. 'I'm glad you're back,' she said, facing away from the door.

'I must say, that's a surprise.'

Ellie whirled around to find Lizzie Munro standing there instead of Sarah. The investigator's gaze traveled from Ellie's sweat-soaked hair to the hem of her apron.

Folding her arms across her waist, Ellie straightened, trying to look as commanding as possible given her attire. 'You ought to get that crime scene tape down. There are people here trying to get on with their lives.'

'It's not my tape. Call the state police.'

'Give me a break, Detective.'

Lizzie shrugged. 'Far as I'm concerned, they should have taken it down days ago. We have everything we need.'

'You think you do.'

'This case will be won on forensic evidence, Ms Hathaway. Clear away the smoke and mirrors, and there's a dead baby left behind.'

Ellie smirked. 'You sound like a prosecutor.'

'Professional hazard.'

'Interesting, then, that for such an open-and-shut case you'd feel the need to interview the Fishers.'

'Even here in the shadow of Philadelphia, we know how to cover our asses during an investigation.'

Ellie took a step forward. 'Look, if you think this is about pitting a big-city legal operation against a small-town county attorney, you can tell George right now—'

'Tell George yourself. I'm not a courier.' Lizzie glanced up the stairs. 'I'd like to speak to Katie.'

Ellie laughed out loud. 'I bet you would. Personally, I'd like a margarita and central air.' She shrugged. 'You knew when you came here I wasn't going to let you near my client. And I'm sure George will understand when you tell him you couldn't get a statement from the defendant *or* her father.'

Lizzie's eyes widened. 'How did you—?'

'Inside advantage,' Ellie said smugly.

The detective started toward the door. 'I can see how this place would start to wear on you,' she said, gesturing toward Ellie's apron. 'Sorry to interrupt your . . . uh, big-city legal operation.'

Ellie stared at the door as it closed after Lizzie. Then she took off the apron, folded it neatly over a chair, and went to check on her client.

Levi craned his neck one more time to make sure that Aaron and Samuel were still busy in the fields, then ran the flat of his hand along the curved hood of Lizzie Munro's car. It was as red as the apples that grew beside his Aunt Frieda's house, and as smooth as the tiny waterfall that ran over the dam in the Fishers' creek. The metal was warm to the touch. Levi closed his eyes and imagined sitting behind the wheel, revving the gas, flying down the road.

'Ever seen one of these before?'

The voice nearly made him jump out of his skin. Levi

turned, an apology trembling on his lips, and found himself staring at the lady detective who'd come the day they'd found the dead baby. 'A sixty-six Mustang convertible, one of the last of a dying breed.' She set her hand just where his had been, patting it like it had feelings, like it was one of their own horses. 'Want to look at the engine?'

She reached inside the car and turned the ignition, then suddenly the hood popped up. The detective released the latch and opened it to reveal its spinning, working insides. 'A small-block V8, with a three-speed manual transmission. This sweetheart can fly.' She smiled at Levi. 'You ever travel over a hundred miles an hour?'

Eyes wide, Levi shook his head.

'Well, if you see any state troopers – neither have I.' She winked at him, then reached inside again. The car immediately stilled, leaving behind the faintest trace of exhaust.

The detective grinned at Levi. 'I know you're not the chauffeur – so what do you do around here?'

Levi nodded toward the fields. 'I work with Samuel.'

'Oh, yeah?'

'He's my cousin.'

The detective raised her brows. 'I guess you know Katie pretty well then, too.'

'Well, *ja*. Everyone knew they were gonna be getting married soon enough. They've been courting for a year, now.'

'What's taking him so long to ask?'

Levi shrugged. 'It's not the wedding season yet, for one thing. That's November, after the harvest. But even that's only going to happen if Samuel can keep her from picking fights.'

'Katie?'

'She makes Samuel wonderful mad sometimes.' Levi gently reached out with his thumb, hoping the detective couldn't see, and touched the side of the car again.

'Maybe they should just find other people to court,' the detective suggested.

'That would be even worse for Samuel. He's been after Katie forever.'

The detective nodded solemnly. 'I suppose that her parents are expecting to get Samuel as a son-in-law, too.'

'Sure.'

'Would they be disappointed if Samuel and Katie broke up?'

Levi squinted at her. 'Broke up?'

'Split. Started seeing other people.' The detective sighed. 'Found others to court.'

'Well, Sarah's counting on a wedding come fall. And Aaron, he'd be sorry, for sure.'

'Seems like he might be angry, more than sorry. He comes off as a pretty strict dad.'

'You don't know him,' Levi said. 'Even if Katie wouldn't marry Samuel, he wouldn't cut her off like he did Jacob.'

'Jacob,' the detective repeated.

'*Ja*, you know. Katie's brother.'

'*Jacob*. Of course.' She smiled at Levi and opened the driver's door to the car, then revved the engine. To his surprise, she held out her hand to him. 'Young man, you've been an unexpected delight.' They shook, and then Levi watched her drive off in the V8 Mustang, gradually picking up speed.

In the middle of the night, Katie felt a hand cover her nose and mouth. Thrashing at the pillows, forgetting where she was for a moment, she grabbed at the arm and bit at the fingers. She heard a muffled oath, and then the hand disappeared – only to be replaced by the soft, insistent pressure of a mouth against hers.

In that instant the sleep surrounding her melted away and she was in Jacob's apartment, on his couch, Adam's body spread over hers like a quilt. He drew back, touching his forehead to Katie's. 'I can't believe you bit me like that.'

In the darkness, she smiled. 'I can't believe you scared me like that.' Katie rubbed her hand over his cheek, rough with a night's beard. 'I'm glad you decided to stay.'

She could see his teeth flash. 'Me too,' Adam said.

He'd put off going to New Orleans for another week. And Katie had constructed an elaborate story about staying over at Mary Esch's house, all the while planning to come to State College instead. Even her mother did not know this time that she was at Jacob's.

Adam's finger traced a path from her throat to her collarbone. 'I've wanted to do this all day. Do you realize your brother didn't even go to the bathroom between four and nine tonight?'

Katie giggled. 'I'm sure he did.'

'No. I know, because the last time I touched you, it was just after lunch.' He lay on his side, sharing her pillow, so close that his breath fell into her own mouth.

She stretched forward, just enough to kiss him. It was new to her, being the leader. She still felt shy every time she kissed Adam, instead of letting him kiss her. But once, when she had done it, he'd raised her hand to his chest, and she felt the rapid tattoo of his heart. A strange thing, to think she had that power over him.

He pinned her on her back and leaned over her, his hair falling to tangle with her own. She let her mind run like a river, let her arms reach and grab hold. She felt Adam's hands moving over her shoulders, sloping down her sides.

And then they were underneath her T-shirt. His palm burned like a brand on the skin of her breast. Her eyes flew open, and she began to shake her head. 'Adam,' she whispered, tugging at his hair. 'Adam! You can't!'

Now her heart was hammering, and her stomach flipped with fear. Plain boys didn't do this, at least not the ones she'd known. She thought of Samuel Stoltzfus, with his serious eyes and his slow smile – Samuel, who had driven her home from the singing last Sunday and had blushed when he held her hand to help her out of the courting buggy.

Adam spoke, a quiver against her own throat. 'Please, Katie. If you just let me look at you, I'll do whatever you want.'

Too frightened to move, she hesitated, then yielded. Adam inched her T-shirt up, exposing her navel, her ribs, the pink beads of her nipples. 'You see,' he whispered, 'there's nothing plain about you.'

He tugged the fabric back down and gathered her into his arms. 'You're shaking.'

Katie buried her face against his neck. 'I . . . I've never done that before.'

Adam kissed her callused hand. It made her feel cherished, as if she were a princess instead of a farm girl. Then he sat up, untangling himself from her arms.

Katie frowned, thinking that she'd done something wrong; thinking that she hadn't done enough. 'Where are you going?'

'I made you a promise. I said I'd do whatever you wanted, if you let me see you. I'm guessing that right now, you want me to go away.'

She sat up, cross-legged, and reached for him. 'That's not what I want,' she said.

It had been a long, strenuous day for Samuel, working beside Aaron in the fields. The whole way home he'd watched Silver plodding along, and he'd been unaware of Levi's chatter. He could not stop thinking about Katie, about what she might have done. What he wanted was a hot meal, a hotter shower, and the sweet oblivion that came with sleep.

At his parents' home, he unhitched his buggy and led the horse into the barn. There was another buggy in the yard; someone visiting with his mother, maybe. Gritting his teeth at the thought of being polite, Samuel lumbered heavily onto the front porch, where he stood for a moment gathering his thoughts before heading inside.

He was staring at the main road, watching the cars cross with their bright headlights and throaty engines, when the front door opened behind him. His mother stood there, surrounded by the soft yellow light that spilled from inside the house. 'Samuel! What are you doing out here?' She reached for his arm and dragged him into the kitchen, where Bishop Ephram and Lucas the deacon were sitting with steaming cups of coffee. 'We've been waiting for you,' Samuel's mother scolded. 'Sometimes I think you come home via Philadelphia.'

Samuel smiled, a slow unraveling. '*Ja*, you can't keep Silver from the entrance ramps to those fancy highways.'

He sat down, nodding at the two men, who couldn't seem to look him in the eye. His mother excused herself, and a moment later Samuel heard her heavy footsteps treading up the stairs. Steepling his fingers in front of him, he tried to act calm, but inside his stomach was rolling like the tiller in the fields. He had heard of what it was like to be called to account for your sins, but never experienced it firsthand. From the looks of things, the bishop and the deacon didn't like the prospect any more than Samuel himself.

The bishop cleared his throat. 'We know what it's like to be a young man,' Ephram began. 'There are certain temptations . . .' The voice trailed off, unraveling at the edges like one of Samuel's mother's balls of yarn.

Samuel looked from Lucas to Ephram. He wondered what Katie had told them. He wondered if Katie had told them anything at all.

Katie, for whom he would have laid down his life; for whom he would have gladly been shunned for six weeks' time; with whom he'd wanted to spend the rest of his days, filling a house with children and serving God. Katie, who had had a baby.

Samuel bowed his head. Any minute now, they'd ask him to come to church to make his things right, and if they asked him, he'd go, as was expected. You didn't argue once the bishop laid a sin against you; it just wasn't done. But suddenly Samuel realized that this awkward hesitation of Ephram's was a gift. If Samuel spoke first, if Samuel spoke now – that sin might never be laid against him at all.

'Lucas, Ephram,' he said, in a voice so steady that it could not be his own, 'I want to marry Katie Fisher. I will tell you and the preachers and all our brothers and sisters this if you wish next *Gemeesunndaag*.'

A broad smile split the white mass of Ephram's beard. He turned to the deacon and nodded, satisfied.

Samuel tightened his fingers on his knees, almost to the point of pain. 'I want to marry Katie Fisher,' he repeated. 'And I will. But you should know something else right now – I was not the father of her baby.'

8

Ellie

My favorite place on the farm was the milk room. Thanks to the bulk refrigeration tank, it stayed cool, even at the hottest times of the day. It smelled like ice cream and winter, and the white walls and spotless floor made it a fine place to sit down and think. Once the inverter had charged the batteries of my laptop, I'd take my computer there to do my work.

It was where Leda found me when she decided to grace me with a visit ten days after I'd become an official resident of the Fisher farm. As I sat typing with my head bowed, the first things that came into my range of vision were her Clark sandals – something I hadn't seen in a while. The Amish women who didn't wear boots wore the ugliest sneakers I'd ever seen in my life, no doubt some bulk lot even Kmart couldn't stand on its shelves. 'It's about time,' I said, not bothering to lift my head.

'Now, I couldn't come any quicker, and you know that,' Leda said.

'Aaron would have gotten over it.'

'It wasn't Aaron. It was you. If I hadn't given you a chance to get your feet wet, you would have crawled into the trunk of my car and stowed away like a fugitive.'

I snorted. 'Well, you'll be thrilled to know that not only have my feet gotten wet, they've also gotten stuck in the mud, nearly run over by a buggy, and come *this* close to being urinated on by a heifer.'

Laughing, Leda leaned against the stainless steel sink. 'Bet Marcia Clark didn't have details like that in her book.'

'Fabulous. The best-seller I eventually write will be shrink-wrapped with the *Farmer's Almanac*.'

Leda smiled. 'I hear Katie got a clean bill of health?'

I nodded. We had gone to the doctor for a checkup yesterday, and the OB had pronounced Katie healing well. Physically, she would be fine. Mentally – well, that was still up in the air.

I closed the file I'd been working on and popped the disc from its drive. 'You couldn't have timed this better. Guess who's about to become my paralegal?'

She held up her hands to ward me off. 'Don't even think it, honey. The most I know about the law is that possession is nine-tenths of it.'

'But you know how to use a computer. You used to send me e-mail.' I sighed, thinking of how long it would be before I could access my account. 'I need you to print a file and deliver it to the superior court. Needless to say, my laser printer's not running.'

'I'm surprised you even have your computer here. How upset did Aaron get?'

'The bishop took the decision out of his hands. He's very supportive of Katie.'

'Ephram's a good man,' Leda said faintly, her mind far away. 'He was very kind to me when I was excommunicated. It meant a lot to Aaron and Sarah to have him come to the baby's funeral.'

I shut off the computer, unplugged it from the inverter, and stood. 'Why'd they do that? Have a funeral, I mean.'

Leda shrugged. 'Because the baby was their responsibility.'

'It was Katie's.'

'A lot of Amish folks will have a service for a stillborn baby.' She hesitated, then looked at me. 'That's what it says on the stone – Stillborn. I suppose that was the only way Aaron and Sarah could live with what's happened.'

I thought about a girl who might have been sexually assaulted, and then might completely block the incident and the after-effects – including a pregnancy – out of her mind. 'According to the ME, that baby wasn't stillborn, Leda.'

'According to the prosecutor, Katie killed the baby. I don't believe that either.'

I scuffed my sneaker along the cement floor of the milk room, contemplating how much I should confide in her. 'She might have,' I said carefully. 'I'm going to have a psychiatrist come out and talk to her.'

Leda blinked. 'A psychiatrist?'

'Katie's not only denying the pregnancy and the birth – but also the conception. I'm beginning to wonder if she might have been raped.'

'Samuel is such a fine boy, he—'

'The baby wasn't Samuel's. He's never had sex with Katie.' I took a step forward. 'Look, this has nothing to do with the defense. In fact, if Katie was raped, it gives her an emotional motive to want to get rid of the newborn. I just think that Katie might need someone to talk to – someone more qualified than me. For all I know, Katie comes in contact with the guy every single day, and God only knows how that's affecting her.'

Leda was quiet for a moment. 'Maybe the man wasn't Amish,' she said finally.

I rolled my eyes. 'Why not? Samuel may be one thing, but that doesn't mean there isn't some Amish boy out there who got carried away in the heat of the moment and forced Katie to do something she didn't want to. And besides, I can count on one hand the number of English people Katie's talked to since I've been here.'

'Since you've been here,' she repeated.

Leda was shifting in her seat, a miserable mottled flush rising over her cheeks. Clearly, being on the farm had clouded my mind, or I would have realized that with an excommunicated aunt, Katie probably had more access to worldly people and places than most Amish girls. 'What haven't you told me?' I said quietly.

'Once a month she goes to State College on the train. To the university. Sarah knows about it, but they tell Aaron that Katie's come to visit me. I'm her cover, and since Aaron isn't about to come to my house to check up on his daughter, I'm a good one.'

'What's at the university?'

Leda exhaled softly. 'Her brother.'

'How on earth do you expect me to defend Katie when no one's willing to cooperate?' I exploded. 'My God, Leda, I've been here nearly two weeks, and nobody bothered to mention that Katie has a brother she visits once a month?'

'I'm sure it wasn't intentional,' Leda hurried to explain. 'Jacob was excommunicated, like me, because he wanted to continue his schooling. Aaron took the high road, and said if Jacob left the church, he wouldn't be his son any longer. His name isn't mentioned in the house.'

'What about Sarah?'

'Sarah's an Amish wife. She yields to her husband's wishes. She hasn't seen Jacob since he left six years ago – but she secretly sends Katie as her emissary, once a month.' Leda jumped as the automatic stirring machine came to life, mixing the milk in the bulk tank. She raised her voice over the hum of the battery that powered it. 'After Hannah, she couldn't have any more children. She'd had a batch of miscarriages between Jacob and Katie, anyway. And she couldn't stand the thought of losing Jacob like she'd lost Hannah. So, indirectly, she didn't.'

I thought of Katie taking the train all the way to State College by herself, wearing her *kapp* and her pinned dress and her apron, attracting stares. I imagined her fresh-faced innocence lighting the room at a frat party. I pictured her fighting off the groping hands of a college boy, who at nineteen knew more about the ways of the world than Katie would learn in a lifetime. I wondered if Jacob knew that Katie had been pregnant; if he could tell me the father of the baby. 'I need to talk to him,' I said, wondering whether it would be faster to drive or take the train.

Then I groaned. I couldn't go; I had Coop coming sometime this afternoon to interview Katie.

If I had learned anything in ten days, it was that the Amish way was *slow*. Work was painstaking, travel took forever, even church hymns were deliberate and lugubrious. Plain people didn't check their watches twenty times a day. Plain people didn't hurry; they just took as much time as it needed for something to be done.

Jacob Fisher would simply have to wait.

'Why didn't you tell me you have a brother?'

Katie's hands froze on the hose that she was hooking up to the outside faucet. She looked away, and if I hadn't known better I would have believed she was deciding whether or not to lie to me. 'I *had* a brother,' she said.

'Rumor has it he's alive and well and living in State College.' I tied the ends of the apron I'd borrowed from Sarah, shucked off my sneakers, and stepped into the rubber barn boots she'd loaned me. I wasn't going to win any fashion awards, but then again, I was on my way to hose down heifers. 'Rumor has it you visit him from time to time, too.'

Katie wrenched the faucet open, then tested the nozzle of the hose. 'We don't talk about Jacob here anymore. My father doesn't like it.'

'I'm not your father.' Katie began walking into the field with the hose, and I fell into step behind her, swatting away a patch of mosquitoes that circled my face. 'Isn't it hard, visiting Jacob on the sly?'

'He takes me to movies. And he bought me a pair of jeans to wear. It's not hard, because when I'm with him, I'm not Katie Fisher.'

I stopped walking. 'Who are you?'

She shrugged. 'Just anyone. Just any other girl in the world.'

'It must have been very upsetting when your father kicked him out of the house.'

Katie yanked again on the hose. 'It was upsetting even before that, when Jacob was lying about his schooling. He should have just confessed at church.'

'Ah,' I said. 'The way you're going to. Even though you're innocent.'

The mosquitoes hovered in an arc above Katie, a halo. 'You don't understand us,' she accused. 'Just because you've lived here for ten days doesn't mean you know what it's like to be Plain.'

'Then make me understand,' I said, turning so that she had to stop, or walk around me.

'For you, it's all about how you stand out. Who is the smartest, the richest, the best. For us, it's all about blending in. Like the patches that make up a quilt. One by one, we're not much to look at. But put us together, and you've got something wonderful.'

'And Jacob?'

She smiled wistfully. 'Jacob was like a black thread on a white background. He made the decision to leave.'

'Do you miss him?'

Katie nodded. 'A lot. I haven't seen him in a while.'

At that, I turned. 'How come?'

'The summer here, it's busy. I was needed at home.'

More likely, I thought, she wouldn't have been able to hide a pregnant belly in a pair of Levi's. 'Did Jacob know about the baby?'

Katie continued walking, tugging on the hose.

'Was it someone you met there, Katie? Some college boy, some friend of Jacob's?'

She mulishly set her jaw, and finally we came to the pen where the one-year-old cows were kept. On days this hot, they were sprayed with water to be made more comfortable. Katie twisted the nozzle, letting the water trickle onto her bare feet. 'Can I ask you something, Ellie?'

'Sure.'

'Why don't you talk about your family? How could you move out here and not have to make a phone call to them saying where you'd be?'

I watched the cows milling in the field, lowering their heads to the fresh grass. 'My mother's dead, and I haven't spoken to my father in a few years.' Not since I became a defense attorney, and he accused me of selling out my morals for money. 'I never got married, and my boyfriend and I just ended our relationship.'

'How come?'

'We sort of outgrew each other,' I said, testing the answer on my lips. 'Not surprising, after eight years.'

'How can you be boyfriend and girlfriend for eight years and not get married?'

How to describe the intricacies of 1990s dating to an Amish girl? 'Well, we started out thinking we were right for each other. It took us that long to find out we weren't.'

'Eight years,' she scoffed. 'You could have had a whole bunch of kids by now.'

At the thought of all that time wasted, I felt my throat close with tears. Katie dipped her toe in the small puddle of mud forming beneath the nozzle of the hose, clearly embarrassed at having upset me. 'You must miss him.'

'Not Stephen, so much,' I said softly. 'Just that bunch of kids.'

I waited for Katie to make the connection, to say something about her own circumstances in relation to mine – but once again she surprised me. 'You know what I noticed when I was with Jacob? In your world, people can reach each other in an instant. There's the telephone, and the fax – and on the computer you can talk to someone all the way around the world. You've got people telling their secrets on TV talk shows, and magazines that publish pictures of movie stars trying to hide in their homes. All those connections, but everyone there seems so lonely.'

Just as I started to protest, Katie handed me the hose and hopped over the fence. Reaching for the nozzle again, she turned the water on and waved it over the cows, who bellowed and tried to dodge the spray. Then, with a grin, she turned the hose on me.

'Why, you little—!' Soaked from my hair to my ankles, I climbed the fence and started to run after her. The cows got

between us, milling in circles. Katie shrieked as I finally grabbed
the hose and saturated her. 'Take that,' I laughed, then slipped
on the wet grass and landed on my bottom in a slick of mud.

'Excuse me? I'm looking for Ellie Hathaway.'

At the sound of the deep voice, both Katie and I turned,
the nozzle in my hand spraying the shoes of the speaker
before he managed to jump out of the way. I stood up, wiping
mud off my hands, and grinned sheepishly at the man on the
other side of the heifer pen, a man staring at my boots and
apron and the muck all over me. 'Coop,' I said. 'It's been a
while.'

Ten minutes later when I came downstairs fresh from a shower,
I found Coop sitting on the porch with Katie and Sarah. A
platter of cookies was on the wicker table, and Coop held a
sweating glass of ice water in his hand. He stood up as soon
as he saw me.

'Still a gentleman,' I said, smiling.

He leaned forward and kissed me on the cheek, and to my
surprise a hundred memories rushed at me – the way his hair
had always smelled of wood smoke and apples, the curve of
his jaw, the imprint of his fingers splayed over my back. Dizzy,
I stepped back and did my best not to look uncomfortable.

'These ladies have been kind enough to keep me company,'
he said, and Katie and Sarah bent their heads together, whispering like schoolgirls.

Sarah came to her feet. 'We'll leave you to your caller,' she
said, nodding at Coop as she walked back into the house. Katie
headed toward the garden, and I sat down. After twenty years,
Coop had grown into his looks. His features – just a little too
sharp in college – had roughened with time, chiseling his skin
with a scar here and a laugh line there. His black hair, which
once hung to his shoulders, was neatly trimmed and feathered
with gray. His eyes were still that clear pale green that I had
only seen twice in my life: on Coop, and once from the window
of a plane when I was traveling to the Caribbean with Stephen.

'You've aged well,' I said.

He laughed. 'You make it sound like I'm a bottle of wine.' Leaning back in his chair, he grinned at me. 'You look pretty good, yourself. Especially compared to about fifteen minutes ago. I'd heard defense litigation was a dirty business, but I never took it literally.'

'Well, it's sort of like method acting. The Amish aren't a particularly trusting lot, when it comes to outsiders. When I look like them, work with them, they open up.'

'Must be hard, being stuck here away from home.'

'Is that John Joseph Cooper the psychiatrist asking?'

He started to say something, then shook his head. 'Nah. Just Coop, the friend.'

I shrugged, deliberately looking away from his careful gaze. 'There are things I miss – my coffee maker, for one. Downshifting in my car. *The X-Files*, and *ER*.'

'Not Stephen?'

I had forgotten that the last time I saw Coop, we'd been with our significant others. We met in the lobby during the intermission of a performance by the Philadelphia Symphony. Although we'd been in touch occasionally for business reasons, I had never before met his wife, who was fine-boned and blond, and fit against his side as neatly as a matched jigsaw puzzle piece. Even after all those years, just the sight of her was a sucker punch.

'Stephen isn't in the picture,' I admitted.

Coop regarded me for a moment before saying, 'I'm sorry to hear that.'

I was a grown-up; I could get through this. Taking a deep breath, I summoned a smile and clapped my hands on my knees. 'Well. You didn't come all the way out here to talk to me—'

'But I would have, Ellie,' Coop said, his voice soft. 'I forgave you a long time ago.'

It would have been easy to pretend that I had not heard him; to simply launch into a discussion about Katie. But you can't speak to someone partly responsible for making you who you are without unearthing a little bit of that history. Maybe Coop had forgiven me, but I hadn't.

Coop cleared his throat. 'Let me tell you what I found out about Katie.' He dug in a briefcase and pulled out a pad of yellow legal paper covered with his chicken-scratch hand-writing. 'There are two camps of psychiatric explanations for neonaticide. The minority attitude is that women who kill their newborns have gone into a dissociative state that lasts throughout the pregnancy.'

'Dissociative state?'

'A very concentrated focus state, where a person blocks out all but the one thing they're doing. In this case, these women fracture off a bit of their consciousness, so that they're living in a fantasy world where they're not pregnant. When the birth finally occurs, the women are totally unprepared. They've dissociated from the reality of the event, experiencing memory lapses. Some women even become temporarily psychotic, once the shock of the birth slams through that shell of denial. In either case, the excuse is that they're not mentally present at the moment of the crime, so they can't be held legally accountable for their actions.'

'Sounds very *Sybil* to me.'

Coop grinned and handed me a list of names. 'These are some psychiatrists who've testified the past few years with the soft approach. They're clinical psychiatrists, you'll see – not forensic ones. That's because the majority of forensic psychiatrists who deal with neonaticides say the women are not in a dissociative state – just detached from the pregnancy. They feel dissociation might occur at the moment of birth. Plus, even I'd tell you that some dissociation is entirely normal, given the pain of childbirth. It's like when you cut yourself chopping vegetables, and you kind of stand there for a second and say, "Wow, that's a deep one." But you don't go chopping off your hand after that to eliminate the problem.'

I nodded. 'Then why do they kill the babies?'

'Because they have no emotional connection to them – it's

like passing a gallstone. At the moment of murder, they aren't out of touch with reality – just frightened, embarrassed, and unable to face an illegitimate birth.'

'In other words,' I said flatly, 'patently guilty.'

Coop shrugged. 'I don't have to tell you how insanity defenses go over with a jury.' He handed me another list, this one three times as long as the first. 'These psychiatrists have supported the mainstream view. But every case is different. If Katie's still refusing to admit to what's happened in the face of a murder charge and medical evidence of pregnancy, there may be something more at work creating that defense mechanism.'

'I wanted to talk to you about that. Is there any way to find out if she was raped?'

Coop whistled. 'That would be a hell of a reason to get rid of a newborn.'

'Yeah. I'd just like to be the one to find out, instead of the prosecutor.'

'It's going to be tough, so many months after the fact, but I'll keep it in mind when I'm talking to her.' He frowned. 'There's another option, too – that she's been lying all along.'

'Coop, I'm a defense attorney. My bullshit meter is calibrated daily. I'd know if she was lying.'

'You might not, El. You have to admit you're a little close to the situation, living here.'

'Lying isn't one of the hallmarks of the Amish.'

'Neither is neonaticide.'

I thought of the way Katie would blush and stammer when she was confronted with something she didn't want to talk about. And then I thought of how she'd looked every time she denied having a baby: her chin jutting straight, her eyes bright, her focus right on me. 'In her mind, that baby never happened,' I said quietly.

Coop considered this. 'Maybe not in her mind,' he answered. 'But that baby was here.'

*   *   *

Katie fisted her hands in her lap, looking as if she'd been sentenced to an execution. 'Dr Cooper just wants to ask you some questions,' I explained. 'You can relax.'

Coop smiled at her. We were all sitting by the creek, far enough away from the house for privacy. He slipped a tape recorder out of his pocket, and I quickly caught his eye and shook my head. Unfazed, Coop reached for his pad instead. 'Katie, I just want to start off by telling you that whatever you say isn't going to go beyond us. I'm not here to tattle on you; I'm just here to help you work through some of the feelings you must be having.'

She looked at Ellie, then back at Coop.

He grinned. 'So – how are you feeling?'

'All right,' she said, wary. 'Good enough that I don't need to talk to you.'

'I can understand why you feel that way,' Coop responded pleasantly. 'A lot of people do, who've never spoken to a psychiatrist. And then they figure out that sometimes it's easier to talk to a stranger about personal things than it is to talk to a family member.'

I knew Coop was watching the same things I was – how Katie's spine had become just a little less stiff, how her hands had uncurled in her lap. As his voice continued to wash over her, as his eyes held hers, I wondered how anyone stood a chance of keeping secrets from him. There was an affability to Coop, an effortless charm, that immediately made you feel like you had an intimate connection to him.

Then again, I had.

Shaking my attention back to my client, I listened to Coop's question. 'Can you tell me about your relationship with your parents?'

Katie looked at me as if she didn't understand. What was a perfectly normal question for a clinical interview seemed silly, given the Amish. 'They are my parents,' she said haltingly.

'Do you spend a lot of time with them?'

'*Ja*, out in the fields or in the kitchen, at meals, at prayer.' She blinked at Coop. 'I'm with them all the time.'

'Are you close to your mother?'

Katie nodded. 'I'm all she's got.'

'Have you ever had seizures, Katie, or head trauma?'

'No.'

'How about very bad bellyaches?'

'Once.' Katie smiled. 'After my brother dared me to eat ten apples that weren't ripe.'

'But not . . . recently?' She shook her head. 'How about losing big chunks of time . . . you suddenly realize that hours have passed, and you can't remember where you've been or what you've done?'

At that, inexplicably, Katie blushed again and said no.

'Have you ever had hallucinations – seen things that aren't really there?'

'Sometimes I see my sister—'

'Who died,' I interrupted.

'She drowned at the pond,' Katie explained. 'When I'm there, she comes too.'

Coop didn't even blink, as if seeing ghosts were the normal course of one's day. 'Does she speak to you? Tell you to do anything?'

'No. She just skates.'

'Does it bother you to see her?'

'Oh, no.'

'Have you ever been very sick? Had to go to the hospital?'

'No. Not until this last time.'

'Let's talk about that,' Coop said. 'Do you know why you were hospitalized?'

Katie's cheeks flamed and she stared into her lap. 'It was for a woman's problem.'

'The doctors said you had a baby.'

'They were wrong,' Katie said. 'I didn't.'

Coop let the denial roll right off his back. 'How old were you when you started menstruating, Katie?'

'Twelve.'

'Did your mother explain what was happening?'

'Well, a little. But I knew. I'd seen the animals and such.'

'Do you and your parents talk about sex?'

Katie's eyes widened, absolutely scandalized. 'Of course not. It's not right, not until a girl's gotten herself married.'

'Who says it's not right?'

'The Lord,' she said promptly. 'The church. My parents.'

'Would your parents be upset if they found out you were sexually active?'

'But I'm not.'

'I understand. But if you were, what do you think would happen?'

'They'd be very disappointed,' Katie answered quietly. 'And I'd be put in the *bann*.'

'What's that?'

'It's when you break a rule, and the bishop finds out. You have to confess, and then, for a little while anyway, you're shunned.' Her voice lowered to a whisper. 'You're cut off, is all.'

For the first time I saw it through Katie's eyes – the stigma of being an outcast in a community where sameness was so highly valued.

'If you were in trouble, Katie, would you turn to your mother or father for help?'

'I would pray,' she said. 'And whatever happened would be the Lord's will.'

'Have you ever drunk alcohol, or taken drugs?'

To my great shock, Katie nodded. 'I had two beers, once, and peppermint schnapps, when I was with my gang.'

'Your *gang*?'

'Other young people who are my friends. We're called the Sparkies. Most Plain kids my age join up with a gang when they come into their *Rumspringa*.'

'*Rumspringa?*'

'Running-around years. When we're fourteen or fifteen.'

Coop looked at me, but I raised my brows. This was the first I was hearing of it. 'So – what made you join the Sparkies?'

'They were right for me. Not too crazy, but still fun. We have a few fellows who'll buy beer at the Turkey Hill and race their buggies after midnight down Route 340, but most of the wild kids would rather join the Shotguns or the Happy Jacks – they hold hops, and drive around in plain sight, and really become *Sod* – worldly. We get together on Sunday nights and sing hymns, mostly. But sometimes,' she admitted shyly, 'we do other things.'

'Like?'

'Drink. Dance to music. Well, I used to do that, but now I leave after the singing when things are getting a little crazy.'

'How come?'

Katie fisted her hands in the grass. 'Now I'm baptized.'

Coop's brows raised. 'Haven't you been since you were a baby?'

'No, we get baptized when we're older. For me, it was last year. We make the choice to stand before God and agree to live by the *Ordnung* – those rules I was talking about.'

'When you went to these singings, and drank and danced, did your parents know?'

Katie looked toward the house. 'All the parents know that the kids are up to something; they just look the other way and hope it isn't too dangerous.'

'Why would they accept behavior like this, but be disappointed by sexual activity?'

'Because it's a sin. The singings – well, it's kind of like a fling with being English. Folks believe if their kids have a chance to try it once or twice, they'll still give up worldly things and take on the responsibility of living Plain.'

'Do most kids?'

'*Ja.*'

'Why?'

'All their friends are Plain. And their family. If they don't join the church, they won't be like everyone else. Plus, they have to be baptized, if they want to get married.'

'Do you? Want to get married?'

'Who doesn't?' Katie said.

Coop grinned. 'Well, Ellie for one,' he joked under his breath, just loud enough for me to hear. I was so busy turning over his words in my mind, and what they meant, that I nearly missed his next question.

'Have you ever kissed a boy, Katie?'

'Ja,' she said, blushing again. 'Samuel. And before him, John Beiler.'

'Samuel is your boyfriend?'

Was, I thought.

'Have you and your boyfriend ever had sexual intercourse?'

'No!'

Coop hesitated. 'Does he kiss you anywhere but on the lips?'

'On the neck,' she murmured. 'My forehead.'

'What about on your breasts, Katie? Your belly?'

Katie inched her bare feet out from beneath her skirt and set them one by one into the running creek. 'Samuel wouldn't do that.'

'Have you ever let anyone else kiss or touch you?' Coop gently pressed. When she didn't answer, he softened his voice even more. 'Do you want to have babies one day, Katie?'

She lifted her face, the sun lighting her cheeks and her eyes. 'Oh, yes,' she whispered. 'More than anything.'

The moment Katie was out of earshot I verbally pounced on Coop. 'What do you think?'

He lay back on the grassy bank. 'That I'm not in Kansas anymore. I need a crash course in Amish life before I evaluate her further.'

'When you find the university offering the night session, will you sign me up?' I sighed. 'She said she wants children.'

'Most women who commit neonaticide do. Just not at this time.' He hesitated. 'Then again, it's also possible that to her, this baby never existed.'

'So you don't think she's lying. You think she really blocked out having that baby.'

Coop was silent for a moment. 'I wish I could tell you for sure. The general public seems to believe that shrinks can tell better than the average Joe whether someone's lying through her teeth, but you know what, El? It's a myth. It's too early, really, to make a judgment. If she is lying, she's awfully good at it, and I can't imagine it was part of her upbringing.'

'Well, did you come up with anything conclusive?'

He shrugged. 'I think it's safe to say that she's not psychotic right now.'

'Ghosts notwithstanding?'

'There's a big difference between a figment of one's imagination and a psychotic delusion. If her sister was appearing and telling her to kill her baby, or saying the Devil was living under the silo, that would be another story.'

'I don't care if she's psychotic now. What about when she delivered the baby?'

Coop pinched the bridge of his nose between his thumb and forefinger. 'It's clear she's blocking out the pregnancy, and the act that led to it, but you didn't need me to tell you that.'

'What about rape?' Ellie asked.

'That's tough to call, too. She's so skittish about sex I can't figure out if it's due to religious background or to assault. Even having consensual sex with someone not Amish might be enough to put up a wall in Katie's mind. You heard how fearful she is of being shunned. If she developed a relationship with an outsider, she might as well kiss her Amish life good-bye.'

I had been there long enough to know that wasn't quite right. You were always welcomed back – you just had to admit to your sins. 'Actually, she could confess, and go back to the church.'

'Unfortunately, just because others would forgive her doesn't mean that she would forget. She'd be carrying that around for the rest of her life.' Coop turned to me. 'Given her upbringing, it's not surprising that her mind is working overtime to block out what's happened.'

I flopped onto my back beside him. 'She tells me she didn't kill the baby. She tells me she didn't have the baby. But there's proof that she did have the baby—'

'And if she lied about the one thing,' Coop finished for me, 'then she's probably lied about the other. However, lying presumes conscious knowledge. If she's dissociating, she can't be blamed for not knowing the truth.'

Coming up on my elbow, I smiled sadly. 'But can she be blamed for committing murder?'

'That,' Coop said, 'depends on a jury.' He tugged me upright. 'I'd like to keep talking to her. Walk her through the night before the birth.'

'Oh, you don't have to do that. I mean, it's incredibly nice of you and far beyond the call of duty, but you must have more important things to do.'

'I said I'd help you, El, and I haven't exactly done a crackerjack job yet. I'll drive out in the evenings and talk to her after leaving the office.'

'And meanwhile, your wife's sitting home eating dinner alone. Weren't you the one who told me psychiatrists are the ones who can't keep their own personal relationships together?'

Coop nodded. 'Yeah. Which is probably why I got divorced about a year ago.'

I turned toward him, my mouth dry. 'You did?' He looked down at his shoes, at the rush of the creek; and I wondered why it was so easy to speak of Katie, and so difficult to speak of ourselves. 'Coop, I'm sorry.'

He reached out to the bark of a tree and plucked off a neon inchworm, which curled tight as a drum in the hollow of his palm. 'We all make mistakes,' Coop said softly. He reached for my hand and held it up beside his, just as the worm began to move; traveling, stretching, a small bright bridge between us.

It took me a half hour to convince Sarah that if I left Katie in her custody for the morning, I wouldn't be breaking any laws, and chances were incredibly slim that any representative of the court would come ambling by to realize I wasn't around. 'Look,' I said finally, 'if you want me to gather up a defense strategy for Katie, I need flexibility.'

'Dr Cooper drove out here,' Sarah fretted.

'Dr Cooper doesn't have to bring half a million dollars' worth of laboratory equipment with him,' I explained. In fact, I had worked so hard just to guarantee myself the two hours I needed to meet with Dr Owen Zeigler that I was faintly disappointed to realize I had no desire to be in the neonatal pathology lab at the University of Pennsylvania Medical Center. I kept thinking of sick infants, dead infants, infants born at risk to women over forty, and all I wanted to do was hightail it back to the Fishers' farm.

Owen, a man with whom I'd worked once in the past, had a Moon Pie face, a bright bald head, and a round middle that balanced on his knees whenever he hiked himself up onto one of the high stools in front of the microscopes. 'The placental culture showed mixed flora, including diphtheroids,' he said. 'Which basically means there was crap floating around.'

'Are you saying it might have affected the results?'

'No. It's perfectly normal, considering the placenta had been lying around in a barn.'

I narrowed my eyes. 'Then tell me something that's abnormal.'

'Well, the death of the neonate. Looks like a live birth to me,' he said, and my hopes plummeted. 'Based on the hydrostatic test, air made it to the alveoli.'

'Speak English, Owen.'

The pathologist sighed. 'The baby breathed.'

'That's a definite, then?'

'You can tell if a newborn, even a preemie, has breathed air or just inhaled fluid, when you look at the alveoli in the lungs. They get rounded. It's more conclusive than the hydrostatic test itself, because lungs may float if artificial respiration was attempted.'

'Yeah, right,' I muttered. 'She gave it mouth to mouth, and then killed it.'

'You never know,' Owen said.

'So what made it stop breathing?'

'The medical examiner is crying suffocation. But that's not conclusive.'

I climbed onto a stool beside the pathologist. 'Tell me more.'

'There are petechiae in the lungs, which suggests asphyxia, but they could have formed before or after death. As for the bruising on the neonate's lips, all that means is that it was pressed up tightly against something. That something could have been the mother's collarbone, for all we know. In fact, if the newborn was suffocated with something soft, like the shirt it was wrapped in or the mother's hand, the findings are virtually indistinguishable from SIDS.'

He reached forward and took from my hand the glass slide I'd been absently playing with. 'Bottom line: the baby could very well have died without anyone laying a hand on him. At thirty-two weeks, it's a viable neonate, but just barely.'

I frowned. 'Would the mother have known if the baby was dying right before her eyes?'

'Depends. If it was choking on mucus, she could have heard it. If it was suffocating, she'd see it gasping, turning blue.' He turned off his microscope and slipped the slide – marked clearly BABY FISHER – into a small box containing others.

I tried to imagine Katie paralyzed by fear, by the awareness of this tiny premature infant struggling to breathe. I pictured her watching it, wide-eyed, too stunned to intervene; and then realizing too late what had happened. I saw her wrapping it in a shirt and trying to hide it, before anyone could discover what had gone wrong.

I envisioned her standing in a court of law, still, on trial for failing to seek proper medical attention after delivering the baby. Negligent homicide – not first-degree murder. But a felony, nonetheless; one that carried with it a jail sentence.

Extending my hand to Owen, I smiled. 'Thanks anyway,' I said.

*　　　*　　　*

On Saturday night, I headed upstairs at about ten o'clock and drew the green shades on the eastern side of the room. I took a shower and thought of Coop, wondered what he might be doing – seeing a movie? Eating out at a five-star restaurant? I was wondering if he still wore a T-shirt and boxers to bed when Katie came into the room. 'What's the matter with you?' she asked, peering at my face.

'Nothing.'

Katie shrugged, then yawned. 'Boy, I'm tired,' she said, but her bright eyes and the bounce in her step completely contradicted her words. As she walked into the bathroom, I turned off the bedroom light and crawled into bed, letting my eyes adjust to the darkness. Katie returned, sat down on the edge of her bed, and took off her boots. Then she slid between the sheets, fully dressed.

I came up on an elbow, amused. 'Aren't you forgetting something?'

'I'm cold, is all.'

'There's another quilt in the closet, up on top.' I thought of her rolling over in the middle of the night and having one of the pins that secured her dress jab her chest.

'This is fine.'

'Suit yourself.' I rolled over, staring at the wall, and suddenly remembered being sixteen years old and going to sleep in all my clothes, so that I could sneak out of the house when I saw the headlights of my best friend's car and go to the party a football jock was throwing while his parents were out of town. Sitting up, I glared at Katie's huddled body. 'Where are you planning on going?'

Her jaw dropped – guilty as charged.

'Correction,' I said. 'Where are *we* planning on going?'

She drew herself to a sitting position. 'On Saturday nights, Samuel comes,' Katie confessed. 'We visit on the porch, or in the living room. Sometimes we stay up until morning.'

Well, whatever 'visiting' encompassed, I already knew that it didn't include having sex. Katie's embarrassment stemmed from a basic Amish principle about dating – it was strictly your own business, and for some reason I didn't understand, Plain teens went out of their way to pretend that they were doing anything *but* meeting their boyfriend or girlfriend.

Katie's eyes gleamed in the dark, her gaze focused on the window. For a moment, she looked so much like any other lovesick teenager that I wanted to touch her; just cup my hand over the curve of her cheek and tell her to make this moment last, because before she knew it she'd be like me, a witness to someone else's moment. I didn't know how to say that, given the circumstances, Samuel might not come. That the baby she could not admit to bearing had changed the rules.

'Does he throw pebbles? Or use a ladder?' I asked softly.

Realizing I was not going to give her secret away, Katie smiled slowly. 'A flashlight.'

'Well.' I felt duty-bound to dispense some advice for the upcoming tryst, but what could I say to a girl who'd already had a baby and was accused of killing it? 'Be careful,' I said finally, settling under the covers again.

I slept fitfully, waiting to see that flashlight beam. At midnight, Katie was still lying awake in bed. At two-fifteen, she got up and sat in the rocking chair beside the window. At three-thirty, I knelt down beside her. 'He's not coming for you, sweetheart,' I whispered. 'In less than an hour, he'll have to start the milking.'

'But he always—'

I turned her face so that she was looking at me, and shook my head.

Stiffly, Katie got up and walked to bed. She sat down and traced the pattern of the quilt, lost in her own thoughts.

I had seen the looks on clients' faces at the moment they were sentenced to five years, ten, life in prison. In most cases, even when they knew it was likely to be coming, the truth hit them like a wrecking ball. Sentencing would be a piece of cake for Katie, compared to this: the understanding that her life would no longer be as it once was.

She was quiet for a long time, running her finger over the seams of her handiwork. Then she spoke, her voice rising thin as a trail of smoke. 'When you're quilting, one missed stitch ruins the whole bunch.' With a rustle of covers, she turned to me. 'You pull on it,' she whispered, 'and they all unravel.'

Aaron and Sarah spent the Sunday off from church visiting friends and relatives, but Katie and I declined their invitation to come along. Instead, after we finished the chores, we went to the creek to fish. I found the rods just where she said they'd be in the shed and met her in the field, where she was overturning a clod of earth to pluck out worms for bait. 'I don't know,' I said, watching them wriggle pink over her palm. 'I'm having second thoughts.'

Katie dropped several into a small jelly jar. 'You said you used to fish when you were a kid, here on the farm.'

'Yeah,' I said. 'But that was a thousand years ago.'

She smiled up at me. 'You always do that. Make yourself out to be some old woman.'

'Get back to me when you're thirty-nine, and tell me how you feel.' I walked at her side, the rods canted over my shoulder.

The creek was running strong, thanks to a few days of rain. The water tumbled over rocks, forked around sticks. Katie sat down at the water's edge and took a worm out of the jar, then reached for one of the poles. 'When Jacob and I used to have fishing contests, I always caught the biggest— Ouch!' Drawing back her hand, she popped her thumb into her mouth to suck away the blood. 'That was stupid of me,' she said a moment later.

'You're tired.' She lowered her eyes. 'We all do crazy things when we care about someone,' I said carefully. 'So you waited up all night. So what?' I reached for a worm, swallowed, and baited my own hook. 'When I was your age, I got stood up before my senior prom. I bought a hundred-and-fifty-dollar strapless dress that wasn't beige or cream, mind you, but ecru, and I sat in my room waiting for Eddie Bernstein to pick me up. Turns out he'd asked two girls to the dance and decided that Mary Sue LeClare was more likely to put out.'

'Put out?'

I cleared my throat. 'Um, it's an expression. For having sex.'

Katie's brows rose. 'Oh, I see.'

Uncomfortable, I dunked my line into the water. 'Maybe we should talk about something else.'

'Did you love him? Eddie Bernstein?'

'No. The two of us were always vying for highest grade-point average, so we got to know each other pretty well. I didn't fall in love until I got to college.'

'Why didn't you get married then?'

'Twenty-one is awfully young to get married. Most women like to have a few years to get to know themselves, before getting to know marriage and children.'

'But once you have a family, there's so much more you learn about yourself,' Katie pointed out.

'Unfortunately, by the time I came around to that way of thinking, my prospects had dimmed.'

'What about Dr Cooper?'

I dropped my fishing rod, then grabbed it up again. 'What about him?'

'He likes you, and you like him.'

'Of course we do. We're colleagues.'

Katie snorted. 'My father has colleagues, but he doesn't sit a little too close to them on the porch swing, or smile extra long at something they've said.'

I scowled at her. 'I would think that you, of all people, would respect my right to privacy regarding my own personal affairs.' *Affairs,* I thought. Wrong word.

'Is he coming here today?'

I started. 'How would you know that?'

'Because you keep looking up the driveway, like I did last night.'

Sighing, I decided to come clean. If nothing else, maybe it would spur her to honesty. 'Coop was the boy in college.

The one I didn't marry when I was twenty-one.'

She suddenly leaned back to pull a thrashing sunfish out of the brook. Its scales caught the sunlight; its tail thumped between Katie and me. She lifted it with her thumb in its mouth, and set it into the water for a second chance.

'Which one of you quit?' she asked.

I didn't pretend to misunderstand. 'That,' I said softly, 'would have been me.'

'I wasn't feeling well at dinner,' Katie told us, her eyes fixed on a point somewhere beyond Coop's shoulder. 'Mam told me to go on up and lie down, and she'd clean the dishes.'

Coop nodded, encouraging. He'd been here for two hours now, interviewing Katie about the night of the alleged murder. To my great surprise, Katie was being cooperative, if not forthcoming.

'You felt sick,' Coop prompted. 'Was it a headache? Stomachache?'

'It was chills all over, with a headache. Like the flu.'

I hadn't had children myself, but those symptoms seemed to suggest a virus rather than impending labor. 'Did you fall asleep?' Coop asked.

'*Ja,* after a little bit. And then I woke up in the morning.'

'You don't remember anything between the time you went to bed sick, and the time you woke up in the morning?'

'No,' Katie said. 'But what's so strange about that? I don't usually remember anything between when I fall asleep and I wake up, except a dream every now and then.'

'Did you feel sick when you woke up?'

Katie blushed furiously. 'A little.'

'The same headache and chills?'

She ducked her head. 'No. It was my time of the month.'

'Katie, was the flow heavier than usual?' I asked, and she nodded. 'Did you have cramps?'

'Some,' she admitted. 'Not bad enough to keep me from doing my chores.'

'Were you sore?'

'You mean like my muscles?'

'No. Between your legs.'

After a sidelong look at Coop, she murmured to me, 'It burned a little bit. But I thought it was maybe part of the flu.'

'So,' Coop said, clearing his throat, 'you got up and did your chores?'

'I started to cook breakfast,' Katie answered. 'There was something big going on down at the barn, and then the *Englischer* police came, and Mam stuck her head in long enough to tell me to make extra food for them.' She stood up, pacing the length of the porch. 'I didn't go into the barn until Samuel came to tell me what was happening.'

'What did you see?'

Her eyes were bright with tears. 'The tiniest baby,' she whispered. 'Oh, the very tiniest one I'd ever seen.'

'Katie,' Coop said softly, 'had you seen that baby before?'

She gave her head a quick shake, as if she was trying to clear it.

'Did you touch the baby?'

'No.'

'Was it wrapped up?'

'In a shirt,' she whispered. 'So that just his face was showing, and it looked like he was sleeping, like Hannah used to look when she was in her crib.'

'If the baby was wrapped up, if you never touched it. . . how do you know it was a boy?'

Katie blinked at Coop. 'I don't know.'

'Try hard, Katie. Try to remember the moment you knew it was a boy.'

She shook her head, crying harder now. 'You can't do this to me,' she sobbed, and then she turned on her heel and ran.

'She'll come back,' I said, staring off in the direction Katie had fled. 'But it's nice that you're worried.'

Coop sighed and leaned back on the porch swing. 'I pushed

her to the edge,' he said. 'Came right up against that world she's been living in in her mind. She had to shut down, or else concede that her logic doesn't work.' He turned to me. 'You believe she's guilty, don't you?'

It was the first time since I'd been here that anyone had actually put the question to me. The Fisher family, their Amish friends and relatives – everyone in the community seemed to treat Katie's murder charge as some bizarre finger-pointing that they had to simply accept, but not believe. However, I wasn't looking at a girl I'd known all my life – just a mountain of evidence that seemed damning. From the police reports to my recent discussion with the neonatal pathologist, everything I had seen so far suggested that Katie had either actively or passively caused the death of her child. The concealment of the pregnancy – that was premeditation. The threat of losing Samuel, as well as her parents' respect; the fear of being excommunicated – that was motive. The ongoing denial of hard facts – well, my gut feeling was that with an upbringing like Katie's, it was the only way to deal with something she'd known damn well was wrong.

'I have three choices for my defense, Coop,' I said. 'Number one: she did it and she's sorry, and I throw her on the mercy of the court. But that would mean putting her on the stand, and if I do, they'll know she's not sorry at all – hell, she doesn't even believe she committed the crime. Number two: she didn't do it, someone else did. A nice defense, but highly unlikely, given that it was a premature birth that occurred in secret at two in the morning. And number three: she did it, but she was dissociating at the time, and she can't really be convicted of a crime if she wasn't mentally there.'

'You believe she's guilty,' Coop repeated.

I couldn't look him in the eye. 'I believe this is my only chance to get her off.'

Aaron and I walked into the barn in the later afternoon – me heading for my computer, Aaron intent on delivering feed to the cows. Suddenly, he stopped beside me. The barn was charged with the scent of something about to happen. One of the ballooned cows in the calving pen was bellowing, a tiny hoof sticking out from between her hind legs. Swiftly, Aaron reached for a pair of long rubber kitchen gloves and went into the pen, pulling at the hoof until a miniature white face emerged beside a second hoof. Aaron tugged and tugged, and I watched with wonder as the calf emerged bloody, with the sound of a seal being broken.

It landed, sprawled, on the hay. Aaron knelt before it and brushed a blade of straw over its face. The little nose wrinkled, sneezed, and then the calf was breathing, standing, nuzzling its mother's side. Peering under its leg, Aaron grinned. 'It's a heifer,' he announced.

Well, of course it was. What was he expecting – a whale?

As if he could read my mind, he laughed. 'A *heifer*,' he repeated. 'Not a bull.'

Peeling off his gloves, he got to his feet. 'How's that for a miracle?'

The mother rasped her tongue along the wet whorls of her baby's hide. Mesmerized, I stared. 'That'll do just fine,' I murmured.

When she heard that Mary Esch was hosting a singing, Katie got down on her knees and begged to be allowed to go. 'You can come along,' she said, just in case that was liable to sway me. 'Please, Ellie.'

I knew, from what she'd told Coop and me, that this was a social event. It would give me an opportunity to see Katie react around other Amish boys, boys who might have been the father of her baby. So, five hours later, I was sitting beside Katie on the front bench of the buggy, en route to a hymn sing. I'd ridden in the Fisher buggy before, but it hadn't seemed quite so precarious from the backseat. Gripping the edge, I asked, 'How long have you been driving?'

'Since I was thirteen.' She caught my gaze and grinned.

'Why? Wanna take the reins?'

There was something about Katie tonight – a sparkle, a hope – that made my eyes keep coming back to her. After we arrived, she tied up the horse beside a batch of other buggies, and we went inside the barn. Mary kissed Katie on the cheek and whispered something that made Katie cover her mouth and laugh. I tried to blend into the background and stared at the girls with their creamy complexions and their rainbow-colored dresses, the boys with their fringed bangs and furtive glances. I felt like a chaperone at a high school dance – overbearing, critical, and uncomfortably old. And then I saw a familiar face.

Samuel stood with a group of slightly older boys; the ones, I assumed, that had been baptized like him yet still remained single. His back was to Katie, and he was listening to another boy's conversation – from the looks of it, a rude story about either a fat woman or a horse. When the group broke into laughter, Samuel smiled faintly, then walked off.

The teenagers began to drift toward two long picnic tables. The first had a bench of girls sitting opposite a bench of boys. The second was reserved for couples: girls and boys sat side by side, their entwined hands hidden in the folds of the girl's skirt. A young woman I had never met approached me. 'Ms Hathaway, can I show you to a seat?'

I had been expecting a barrage of questions about my identity, but I should have known better. The power of word of mouth was mighty in the Amish community; these kids had heard about me for nearly two weeks. 'Matter of fact,' I said, 'I just might stand back here and watch.'

The girl smiled and took a seat at the singles table, whispering to her friend, who then glanced at me from beneath her lashes. Katie sat at the end of the couples table, leaving a spot beside her. As if nothing at all had happened the night before, she smiled at Samuel as he came toward the table.

He kept walking.

With Katie watching every step, Samuel slid into a spot at

the singles' table. Nearly every pair of eyes followed his progress, then darted back to Katie, but no one said a word. Katie bowed her head, her neck drooping low as a cygnet's, her cheeks bright.

As the high notes of a hymn rose toward the ceiling, as the mouths of the girls rounded with sound and the voices of boys grew magically deeper, I took a slow step toward the couples table. I climbed over the bench seat and sank down beside Katie, who did not look at me. I placed my hand, palm facing up, on her knee and counted: a quarter note, a half, a full measure before she took what I was offering.

With my back turned, I never would have been able to identify them as Amish teens. The buzz and chatter, the giggling, the clink of glasses and plates as the snacks were served, all seemed familiar and English. Even the dark and shifting shapes in the corners – couples looking for a spot to get closer – and the odd pair who wandered outside, their faces burning with an internal fever, seemed far more suited to my world than Katie's.

Katie sat like a queen bee on a stool, surrounded by loyal girlfriends speculating on the cause of Samuel's defection. If she was being comforted by them, it wasn't working. She looked shell-shocked, as if two consecutive nights of rebuff were too much for her to accept.

Then again, she was having trouble accepting more than one fact of life these days.

Suddenly the group of girls cleaved and fell back in two halves. Hat in his hands, Samuel stepped forward toward Katie. 'Hello,' he said.

'Hello.'

'Could I take you home?'

Some of the girls patted Katie's back, as if to say that they knew it would come out all right the whole time. Katie kept her face averted. 'I have my own buggy. And Ellie's with me.'

'Maybe Ellie could drive home herself.'

That was my cue to speak up. I stepped forward from where I had been shamelessly eavesdropping and smiled. 'Sorry, guys. Katie, you're welcome to a private moment, but only if it doesn't involve me, a swaybacked mare, and a set of reins.'

Samuel glanced at me. 'My cousin Susie said she'd drive you back to the Fishers', if you're willing. And then I can take her back home after.'

Katie waited, yielding to my wishes. 'All right,' I sighed. I wondered if Susie was even old enough to have a learner's permit in my world.

I watched Katie climb into the open buggy Samuel had brought. I hauled myself into the family carriage we'd arrived in, beside a slip of a girl with thick Coke bottle glasses who was my designated driver. Just before they drove off, Katie waved to me and smiled nervously.

The ride home was a long, silent fifteen minutes. Susie was far from the budding conversationalist; she seemed to have been struck dumb by her close proximity to someone who wasn't Amish. When she asked to use the bathroom just as we arrived at the Fishers', I jumped at the sound of her voice. 'Sure,' I said. 'Go on inside.'

It wasn't good hostessing, but I wasn't about to leave before Katie arrived. Just in case.

I sat in the buggy, because I had no idea how to unhook the horse from its traces. A moment later, the light clop of hooves on packed dirt announced the arrival of Samuel's horse.

I should have let them know I was there. Instead I sank into the dark recesses of the buggy, waiting to hear what Katie and Samuel had to say.

'Just tell me.' Samuel's voice was so soft I would not have heard it if not for the wind that carried it close. 'Tell me who it was.' At Katie's silence, he began to grow frustrated. 'Was it John Lapp? I've seen him staring at you. Or Karl Mueller?'

'It was no one,' Katie insisted. 'Stop it.'

'It was *someone*! Someone touched you. Someone held you. Someone made that baby!'

'There was no baby. There was no baby!' Katie's voice rose in pitch, in volume, and then I heard a thump as she jumped down from the buggy and ran into the house.

I stepped out of my hiding spot and sheepishly looked at Samuel, and Susie, who'd collided with Katie at the door of the Fishers' home.

'There was a baby,' Samuel whispered to me.

I nodded. 'I'm sorry.'

E. Trumbull Tewksbury arrived shortly after lunchtime, wearing his G-man aviator sunglasses and his buzz cut and his black suit. He looked around the farm as if he was scoping it for assassins or terrorists, and then asked where he could set up. 'The kitchen,' I said, leading him inside, to where Katie was already waiting.

A former FBI man, Bull now administered lie detector tests in the private sector. Basically, he was a suitcase for hire. He'd come out before on my behalf to clients' homes with his portable equipment, and exuded enough of his past training to invite both an air of solemnity for the occasion, and a vague threat suggesting that – criminal or not – the client had better be telling the truth.

Of course, this was probably the first time he'd had to get the thumbs-up from an Amish bishop to administer a test, what with the requisite tape recorder and microphone and battery pack that was part and parcel of a lie detector. But, since church permission had been granted, even Aaron was grudgingly leaving us alone. It was just me, Katie, and for moral support, Sarah, holding tight to her daughter's hand.

'Breathe deeply,' I said, leaning closer to Katie. She was absolutely terrified, like several of my former clients. Of course, I didn't know if that was due to guilt, or because she had never seen so many bells and whistles in one place. However, since the machine reacted to nerves, Katie's fear had to be nipped in the bud, no matter what was causing it.

'I'm just going to be asking you some questions,' Bull said.

'You see here? This is just a little bitty tape recorder. And this part is a microphone.' He tapped it with his fingernail. 'And this thing, it's no different from those earthquake seismographs.'

Katie's fingers were white where they held Sarah's hand. Beneath her breath she was whispering in the dialect, words that were becoming familiar to me after many evenings with the Fishers: '*Unser Vater, in dem Himmel. Dein Name werde geheiliget. Dein Reich komme. Dein Wille geschehe auf Erden wie im Himmel.*'

In all my years of practice, I'd never had a client reciting the Lord's Prayer before a lie detector test.

'Just relax,' I said, patting her arm. 'All you have to do is say yes or no.'

In the end, it wasn't me who managed to calm Katie down. It was Bull himself, who – bless his Pentagonal heart – struck up a distracting conversation about Jersey cows and the cream content of their milk. Watching her mother chat with the strange man about a familiar topic, Katie's shoulders softened, then her spine, then finally her resolve.

The tape began to turn incrementally. 'What's your name?' Bull asked.

'Katie Fisher.'

'Are you eighteen?'

'Yes.'

'Do you live in Lancaster?'

'Yes.'

'Have you been baptized Amish?'

'Yes.'

I listened to the preliminary questions I'd drafted from my seat beside Bull, a seat where I could see the needle on the lie detector and the printout of responses. So far, nothing was out of the ordinary. But nothing he'd asked so far could be considered a provocative question, either. This went on for a few minutes, loosening Katie's tongue up, and then we began to get down to the real reason we were all here.

'Do you know Samuel Stoltzfus?'

'Yes,' Katie said, her voice a little more thready.

'Did you have sexual relations with Samuel Stoltzfus?'

'No.'

'Have you ever been pregnant?'

Katie looked at her mother. 'No,' she said.

The needle remained steady.

'Have you ever had a baby?'

'No.'

'Did you kill your baby?'

'No,' Katie said.

Trumbull turned off the machine and ripped off the long printout. He marked a couple of places where the needle had wavered slightly, but he and I both knew that none of the responses indicated an out-and-out lie. 'You passed,' he said.

Katie's eyes widened with delight, then she gave a small cry and hugged Sarah hard. When she pulled back, she turned to me, smiling. 'This is good? You can tell the jury this?'

I nodded. 'It's definitely a step in the right direction. Usually, though, we do two tests. It's that much more proof.' I nodded to Bull, asking him to set up again. 'Besides, you've already gotten over the hard part.'

Much more relaxed, Katie sat down in her seat and patiently waited for Bull to adjust the microphone to her mouth. I listened to her give the same answers to the same batch of questions.

Katie finished, her cheeks pink, and smiled at her mother. Bull pulled the printout free and circled several spots where the needle had gone sky-high – in one case, running off the top edge of the paper. This time around, Katie had lied in response to three questions: about being pregnant, about having the baby, about killing it.

'Surprising,' Bull murmured to me, 'since she was so much more at ease this time around.' He shrugged, and began to disconnect wires. 'Then again, maybe that's why.'

It meant that I couldn't use the previous test as evidence – not without submitting to the prosecution this final test too, which Katie had failed miserably. It meant that the outcome of the lie detector examination was inconclusive.

Bright-eyed and blissfully unaware, Katie looked up at me. 'Are we finished?'

'Yes,' I said softly. 'We certainly are.'

It was Katie's job to feed the calves. After a couple of days they were taken from their mothers and housed in little plastic igloos that were queued up outside the barn like a row of doghouses. We each carried a bottle – they were fed formula, so that they didn't take milk from their moms that might otherwise provide income. 'You can have Sadie,' she said, referring to the little calf that had been born in front of me days before. 'I'll take Gideon.'

Sadie had turned into quite a pretty little calf. No longer bloody with afterbirth, she reminded me of a black-and-white map, with huge continents spread across her bony hips and knobby back. Her rough nose twitched at the smell of the formula. 'Hey, little girl,' I said, patting the sweet block of her head. 'Are you hungry?'

But Sadie had already found the nipple of the bottle and was now intent on yanking it out of my hands. I tipped it up, frowning at the chain that haltered her to her little prison of a Quonset hut. I knew that the milk cows didn't much mind being hooked to their stanchions, but this was just a baby. What trouble could she possibly get into?

While Katie's back was to me, I slipped the hook on the calf's collar from the tethering chain. Just like I figured, Sadie didn't even notice. Her throat chugged up and down as she managed to drain every last drop of the bottle, and then butt her head underneath my arm.

'Sorry,' I said. 'We've run dry.'

Katie smiled at me over her shoulder, where Gideon – a little older, a little less greedy – was still summarily slurping his bottle. And that was the moment when Sadie vaulted over me, kicking me hard in the stomach as she sprang for freedom.

'Ellie!' Katie cried. 'What did you do!'

I could not answer, much less breathe. I rolled around in the dirt in front of the little igloo, clutching my side.

Katie ran after the calf, which seemed to have developed springs on the bottoms of her hooves. Sadie ran in a half circle and then began to curve back toward me. 'Grab her front legs,' Katie yelled, and I dove for Sadie's knees, crumbling the rest of her body in a neat tackle.

Panting, Katie dragged the chain to where I was bodily restraining the calf and clipped her collar secure again. Then she sat down beside me to catch her breath. 'Sorry,' I gasped. 'I didn't know.' I watched Sadie slink back to the shade of her igloo. 'Hell of a good tackle, though. Maybe I ought to try out for the Eagles.'

'Eagles?'

'Football.'

Katie stared blankly at me. 'What's that?'

'You know, the game. On TV.' I could see I was getting nowhere. 'It's like baseball,' I finally said, remembering the school-age children I'd seen with their gloves and balls. 'But different. The Eagles are a professional team, which means that the players get a lot of money to be in the game.'

'They make money for playing games?'

Put that way, it sounded positively stupid. 'Well, yeah.'

'Then what do they do for work?'

'That is their work,' I explained. But it seemed strange even to me, now – compared to the day-to-day existence of someone like Aaron Fisher, whose job directly involved putting food into his family's mouth, what was the value of tossing a ball through an end zone? For that matter, what was the value of my own career, making a living with words instead of with my hands?

'I don't understand,' Katie said honestly.

And sitting on the Fisher farm, at that moment, neither did I.

* * *

I turned to Coop, amused. 'You got a divorce because of a *bank dispute*?'

'Well, maybe not exactly.' His teeth flashed in the moonlight. 'Maybe that was just the straw that broke the camel's back.'

We were sitting on the back of a contraption I'd seen Elam and Samuel and Aaron dragging behind a team of mules, and trying hard not to cut our feet. Wicked prongs stuck like fangs from three deadly pinwheels attached to the base, and it seemed to me an instrument of torture, although Katie had told me it was a tetter, used to fluff up the cut hay so that it could dry better before baling. 'Let me guess. Credit card debt. She had a weakness for Neiman Marcus.'

Coop shook his head. 'It was her ATM password.'

I laughed. 'Why? Was it some embarrassing nickname she had for you?'

'I don't know what it was. That was the dispute.' He sighed. 'I'd left my wallet at home, and we'd gone out to dinner. We needed to get cash from one of the bank machines, so I took her card from her purse and said I'd go. But when I asked for her password, she clammed up.'

'In all fairness,' I pointed out, 'you're not supposed to tell your password to anyone.'

'You probably had a client whose husband cleaned her out and ran off to Mexico, right? Thing is, Ellie, I'm not one of those guys. I never was. And she just wouldn't back down. Wouldn't trust me with this one thing. It made me wonder how much more she was holding back from me.'

I worried a button on my cardigan, unsure of what to say. 'Once, when Stephen and I had been together, oh, I don't know – six years? – I got the flu. He brought me breakfast in bed – eggs, toast, coffee. It was sweet of him, but he'd brought the coffee with cream and sugar. And for six years, every day, I'd been sitting down across from him and drinking it black.'

'What did you do?'

I smiled faintly. 'Thanked him up one side and down another,

and dated him for two more years,' I joked. 'What other choice
did I have?'

'There are always choices, Ellie. You just don't like to see
them.'

I pretended not to hear Coop. Staring out over the tobacco
field, I watched fireflies decorating the greenery like Christmas
lights in July. 'That's *duvach*,' I said, remembering the Dietsch
word Katie had taught me.

'Changing the topic,' Coop said. 'Good old Ellie.'

'What do you mean by that?'

'You heard me.' He shrugged. 'You've been doing it for
years.'

Eyes narrowing, I turned toward him. 'You have no idea
what I've been doing—'

'That,' he interrupted, 'was not my choice.'

I crossed my arms, annoyed. 'I understand this is a professional hazard for you, but some people prefer not to drag up
the past.'

'Still touchy about what happened?'

'Me?' I laughed, incredulous. 'For someone who says he's
forgiven me, you sure as hell harp on our history together.'

'Forgiving and forgetting are two completely different things.'

'Well, you've had twenty years to put it out of your mind.
Maybe you could manage to do that for the length of time
you're involved with my client.'

'Do you really think I'm driving way the hell out here twice
a week to meet pro bono with some Amish girl?' Coop reached
out and cupped my cheek with his palm, my anger dissolving
in the time it took to draw a startled breath. 'I wanted to see
you, Ellie. I wanted to know if you'd gotten what you wanted
all those years ago.'

He was so close now that I could see the sparks of gold in
his green eyes. I could feel his words on my skin. 'You take
your coffee black,' he whispered. 'You brush your hair a
hundred strokes before you go to bed. You break out in hives
if you eat raspberries. You like to shower after you make love.

You know all the words to "Paradise by the Dashboard Light"
and you keep quarters in your pockets at Christmastime, to
give to the Salvation Army Santas.' Coop's hand slid to the
back of my neck. 'What did I leave out?'

'A-T-T-Y,' I whispered. 'My ATM password.'

I leaned toward him, tasting him already. Coop's fingers
tightened, massaging, and as I closed my eyes I thought how
many stars there were here, how deep the night sky was, how
this was a place where you could lose yourself.

Our lips had just touched when we broke apart again, startled by the sound of footsteps running down the driveway.

We had followed Katie on foot for nearly a mile now, stumbling along in silence so that she wouldn't see us. She was the
one who was carrying the flashlight, however, so we were
clearly at a disadvantage. Coop held my hand, squeezing it in
warning when he saw a branch in our path, a rock, a small rut
in the road.

Neither of us had spoken a word, but I was certain that
Coop was thinking the same thing I was: Katie was off to meet
someone she didn't want to meet with me around. Which left
Samuel out of the running, and cast into perfect light the
absent, unknown father of her baby.

I could see a farmhouse rising in a gray mountain just
beyond us, and wondered if that was where Katie's lover lived.
But before I could speculate any further, Coop yanked me to
the left, into a small fenced yard that Katie had entered. It took
a moment to realize that the small, white stones were actually
grave markers – we were in the cemetery where Sarah and
Aaron had buried the body of the dead infant.

'Oh, my God,' I breathed, and Coop's hand came up to
cover my mouth.

'Just watch her.' His words fell softly into my ear. 'This
could be the wall tumbling down.'

We crouched at a distance, but Katie seemed oblivious,
anyway. Her eyes were wide and slightly glazed. She propped

the flashlight against another marker, so that it formed a spotlight as she knelt down on the freshly packed grave and touched the headstone.

STILLBORN, just as Leda said it read. I watched Katie's finger trace each letter. She hunched over – was she crying? I started toward her, but Coop held me back.

Katie lifted what looked like a small hammer and a chisel, and touched it to the stone. She pounded once, twice.

Coop couldn't stop me this time. 'Katie!' I called, running toward her, but she did not turn around. I squatted beside her and gripped her shoulders, then pulled the chisel and hammer out of her hands. Tears were running down her face, but her expression was perfectly blank. 'What are you doing?'

She looked at me with those vacant eyes, and then suddenly reason rose up behind them. 'Oh,' she squeaked, covering her face with her hands. Her body began to shake uncontrollably.

Coop swung her into his arms. 'Let's get her home,' he said. He started toward the cemetery gate, Katie sobbing against his chest.

I knelt at the grave, gathering the chisel and the hammer. Katie had managed to chip off some of the carving on the stone. A pity for Aaron and Sarah, who had paid dearly for that marker. I traced the remaining letters: STILL.

'Maybe she was sleepwalking,' Coop said. 'I've had patients whose sleep disorders wreaked havoc on their lives.'

'I've been sleeping in the same room with her for two weeks, and I haven't seen her get up once to even go to the bathroom.' I shivered, and he slid his arm around me. On the small wooden bench at the edge of the Fishers' pond, I moved infinitesimally closer.

'Then again,' he hypothesized, 'maybe she's starting to realize what happened.'

'I'm missing the logic here. Why would admitting that you'd been pregnant lead to defacing a gravestone?'

'I didn't say she admitted it to herself. I said she's starting to take in some of the proof we've been throwing at her, and in some way, she's trying to reconcile it. Unconsciously.'

'Ah. If the headstone for the baby isn't there, the baby never existed.'

'You got it.' He exhaled slowly, then said thoughtfully. 'There's enough here, Ellie. You'll be able to find a forensic shrink who'll back you up on an insanity defense.'

I nodded, wondering why Coop's support didn't make me feel any better. 'You're going to keep talking to her, right?'

'Yeah. I'll do whatever I can to break the fall, when it comes. And it's coming.' He smiled gently, adding. 'As *your* psychiatrist, I have to tell you that you're getting too personally involved in this case.'

That made me smile. '*My* psychiatrist?'

'With pleasure, ma'am. Can't think of anyone else I'd rather treat.'

'Sorry. I'm not crazy.'

He kissed a spot behind my ear, nuzzling. 'Yet,' he murmured. He turned me in his arms, letting his mouth travel over my jaw and my cheek before resting lightly against my lips. With a little shock I realized that after all these years, after all this time, I still knew him – the Morse-code pattern of our kisses, the places his hands would fall on my back and my waist, the feel of his hair as my fingers combed through it.

His touch brought back memories and left a litter of new ones. My heart pumped hard against Coop's chest; my legs twined over his. In his arms, I was twenty again, the whole world spread in front of me like a banquet.

I blinked and suddenly the pond and Coop came back into focus. 'Your eyes are open,' I whispered into his mouth.

He stroked my spine. 'The last time I closed them, you disappeared.' So I kept my eyes wide, too, and was stunned by the sight of two things I'd never thought to see: myself, coming full circle; and the ghost of a girl who walked on water.

I pulled back in Coop's arms. Hannah's ghost? No, it couldn't be.

'What is it?' Coop murmured.

I leaned into him again. 'You,' I said. 'Just you.'

9

Sometimes, when Jacob Fisher was sitting in the tiny closet-sized office he shared with another graduate student in the English department, he pinched himself. It was not so long ago, really, since he had hidden Shakespearean plays under bags of feed in the barn; since he had stayed up all night reading by the beam of a flashlight, only to stumble through his chores the next morning, drunk with what he'd learned. And now here he was, surrounded by books, paid to analyze and teach to young men and women with the same stars in their eyes that Jacob had had.

He settled in with a smile, happy to be back at work after two weeks out of town, assisting a professor emeritus on a summer lecture circuit. At a knock on his door, he glanced up from the anthology he was highlighting. 'Come in.'

The unfamiliar face of a woman peeked around the edge of the door. 'I'm looking for Jacob Fisher.'

'You found him.'

Too old to be one of his students; plus, students didn't tend to dress in business suits. The woman brandished a small wallet, flashing ID. 'I'm Detective-Sergeant Lizzie Munro. East Paradise Township police.'

Jacob gripped the arms of his chair, thinking of all the buggy accidents he'd seen growing up in Lancaster County, all the farm machinery that had accidentally caused death. 'My family,' he managed, his mouth gone dry as the desert. 'Did something happen?'

The detective eyed him. 'Your family is healthy,' she said after a moment. 'Mind if I ask you a few questions?'

Jacob nodded and gestured to the other grad student's desk chair. He hadn't had news of his family in nearly three months, what with summer being so busy and Katie unable to come. He'd been meaning to call his Aunt Leda, just to keep in touch, but then he got wrapped up in his work and dragged off on the lecture tour. 'I understand you grew up Amish, in East Paradise?' the detective asked.

Jacob felt the first prick of unease on his spine. Being English for so long had made him wary. 'Do you mind if I ask what this is in reference to?'

'A felony was allegedly committed in your former home-town.'

Jacob closed the anthology he'd been reading. 'Look, you guys came to talk to me after the cocaine incident too. I may not be Amish anymore, but that doesn't mean I'm supplying drugs to my old friends.'

'Actually, this has nothing to do with the narcotics cases. Your sister has been charged with murder in the first degree.'

'*What?*' Gathering his composure, he added, 'Clearly, there's been a mistake.'

Munro shrugged. 'Don't shoot the messenger. Were you aware of your sister's pregnancy?'

Jacob could not keep the shock from his face. 'She . . . had a baby?'

'Apparently. And then she allegedly killed it.'

He shook his head. 'That's the craziest thing I've ever heard.'

'Yeah? You ought to try my line of work. How long since you last saw your sister?'

Calculating quickly, he said, 'Three, four months.'

'Before that did she visit you on a regular basis?'

'I wouldn't say regular,' Jacob hedged.

'I see. Mr Fisher, did she develop any friendships or romantic interests when she was visiting you?'

'She didn't meet people here,' Jacob said.

'Come on.' The detective grinned. 'You didn't introduce her to your girlfriend? To the guy whose chair I'm sitting on?'

'She was very shy, and she spent all her time with me.'

'You were never apart from her? Never let her go to the library, or shopping, or to the video store by herself?'

Jacob's mind raced. He was thinking of all the times, last fall, that he'd left Katie in the house while he went off to class. Left her in the house that he was subletting from a guy who delayed his research expedition not once, but three times. He looked impassively at the detective. 'You have to understand, my sister and I are two different animals. She's Amish, through and through – she lives, sleeps, and breathes it. Visiting here for her – it was a trial. Even when she did come in contact with outsiders here, they had about as much effect on her as oil on water.'

The detective flipped to a blank page in her notebook. 'Why aren't you Amish anymore?'

This, at least, was safe ground. 'I wanted to continue my studies. That goes against the Plain way. I was working as a carpentry apprentice when I met a high school English teacher who sent me off with a stack of books that might as well have been gold, for all I thought they were worth. And when I made the decision to go to college, I knew that I would be excommunicated from the church.'

'I understand this caused some strain in the relationship between you and your parents.'

'You could say that,' Jacob conceded.

'I was told that to your father, you're as good as dead.'

Tightly, he answered, 'We don't see eye to eye.'

'If your father banished you from the household for wanting a diploma, what do you think he would have done if your sister had a baby out of wedlock?'

He had been part of this world long enough to understand the legal system. Leaning forward, he asked softly, 'Which one of my family members are you accusing?'

'Katie,' Munro said flatly. 'If she's as Amish as you say she is, then it's possible she was willing to do anything – including commit murder – to *stay* Amish and to keep your father from finding out about that baby. Which includes hiding the pregnancy, and then getting rid of the baby when it was born.'

'If she's as Amish as I say she is, then that would never happen.' Jacob stood abruptly and opened the door. 'If you'll excuse me, Detective, I have work to do.'

He closed the door and stood behind it, listening to the detective's retreating footsteps. Then he sat down at his desk and picked up the telephone. 'Aunt Leda,' he said a moment later. 'What in the world is going on?'

By the time the church service drew to a close that Sunday, Katie was light-headed, and not just from the pressing summer heat, intensified by so many bodies packed into one small home. The bishop called a members' meeting, and as those who hadn't been baptized yet filed out to play in the barn, Ellie leaned close to her. 'What are they doing?'

'They have to leave. So do you.' She saw Ellie staring at her trembling hands, and she hid them under her thighs.

'I'm not budging.'

'You must,' Katie urged. 'It will be easier that way.'

Ellie stared at her in that wide-eyed owl way that sometimes made Katie smile, and shook her head. 'Tough beans. Tell them to take it up with me.'

In the end, though, Bishop Ephram seemed to accept that Ellie was going to sit in on the members' meeting. 'Katie Fisher,' one of the ministers said, calling her forward.

She didn't think she was going to be able to stand, her knees were knocking so hard. She could feel eyes on her: Ellie's, Mary Esch's, her mother's, even Samuel's. These people, who would bear witness to her shame.

It didn't matter whether or not she'd had a baby, when you got right down to it. She had no intention of discussing her private matters in front of the congregation, in spite of what Ellie had tried to explain to her about a Bill of Rights and kangaroo courts. Katie had been brought up to believe that rather than defend yourself, you'd best step up and take the medicine.

With a deep breath, she walked to the spot where the ministers were sitting.

When she knelt on the floor, she could feel the ridge of the oak boards pressing into her skin and she gloried in this pain, because it kept her mind off what was about to happen. As she bowed her head, Bishop Ephram began to speak. 'It has come to our attention that the young sister has found herself in a sin of the flesh.'

Every part of Katie was on fire, from her face to her chest to the very palms of her hands. The bishop's gaze was on her. 'Is this offense true?'

'Yes,' she whispered, and she might have imagined it, but she could have sworn that in the silence she heard Ellie's defeated sigh.

The bishop turned to the congregation. 'Do you agree to place Katie under the *bann* for a time as she considers her sin and comes to repentance?'

Each person in the room got a vote, a hand in meting out her punishment. It was rare, in cases like this, that someone wouldn't agree – after all, it was a relief to see a sinner confessing and beginning the process of healing. '*Ich bin einig,*' she heard: I am agreed; each member repeating the words in succession.

Tonight, she would be shunned. She would have to eat at a separate table from her family. She would spend six weeks in the *bann*; still spoken to and loved, but for all that, also apart and alone. With her head bowed, Katie could pick out the soft voices of her baptized girlfriends, the reluctant sigh of her own mother, the stiff resolve of her father. Then she heard the voice that she knew best of all, the deep, rough rumble of Samuel. '*Ich bin . . .*' he said, stumbling. '*Ich bin . . .*' Would he disagree? Would he stand up for her, after all that had passed?

'*Ich bin einig,*' Samuel said, as Katie let her eyes drift shut.

The church service had been held at a nearby farm, so Ellie and Katie opted to walk home. Ellie slung her arm around the girl's shoulders, trying to cheer her up. 'It's not like you've got a scarlet A on your chest,' she joked.

'A what?'

'Nothing.' Pressing her lips together, Ellie said softly, 'I'll eat with you.'

Katie flashed her a brief, grateful look. 'I know.'

They walked in silence for a few moments, Ellie scuffing at rocks in the path. Finally she turned to Katie. 'I've got to ask you something, and it's going to make you angry. How come you're willing to admit in front of a whole congregation that you had a baby, but you can't do the same for just me?'

'Because it was expected of me,' Katie said simply.

'I expect it of you, too.'

She shook her head. 'If the deacon came to me and said he wanted me to make my things right because I'd been skinny-dipping in the pond, even if I hadn't done it, I'd say yes.'

'How?' Ellie exploded. 'How can you let them railroad you like that?'

'They don't. I could stand up and say it wasn't me skinny-dipping, I have a birthmark on my hip you didn't see – but I never would. You saw what it was like in there – it's much more embarrassing to talk about the sin than to just get the confession over with.'

'But that's letting the system walk all over you.'

'No,' Katie explained. 'That's just letting the system work. I don't want to be right, or strong, or first. I just want to be part of them again, as soon as I can.' She smiled gently. 'I know it's hard to understand.'

Ellie willed herself to remember that the Amish system of justice was not the American system of justice, but that both had functioned rather well for hundreds of years. 'I understand, all right,' she said. 'It's just that it's not the real world.'

'Maybe not.' Katie sidled out of the way of a car, one with a tourist hanging half out the window trying to photograph her from behind. 'But it is where I live.'

*　　　*　　　*

Katie stood anxiously at the end of the lane, holding a flashlight. She had taken risks before, especially where Adam was involved, but this would be the gamble of a lifetime. If anyone found her with this Englischer, she'd be in trouble for sure – yet Adam was leaving, and she could not let him go without taking this opportunity.

In the end, Adam hadn't gone to New Orleans to find his ghosts. He transferred the grant money to a whole different locale – Scotland – and reorganized his plans so that he'd leave in November. If Jacob noticed anything odd about the arrangement, it was Adam's generous offer to let Jacob stay on as a housemate in spite of the change of circumstances. Jacob was so grateful not to have to move that he did not bother to see anything else – such as the ease with which his sister and his roommate conversed, or the way Adam sometimes steadied her with a hand on her back when they walked across the campus, or the fact that in all these months, Adam had not dated a single girl.

A car approached, slowing at the end of every driveway. Katie wanted to wave, shout, make Adam see her, but instead she waited in the shadow of the bushes, stepping out into his headlights only when he came close. Adam turned off the car and got out, silently studying Katie's clothes. Walking up to her, he touched the stiff organdy of her kapp, then gently pricked the ball of his thumb on the straight pin that held her dress together at the neck. She felt foolish, suddenly, dressed Plain – he was accustomed to her in jeans and sweaters. 'You must be cold,' he whispered.

She shook her head. 'Not so much.'

He started to slip off his coat, to give it to her, but she ducked away. For a moment, neither of them spoke. Adam looked over Katie's head to the faint silver edge of the silo, jutting against a seamless sky. 'I could go,' he said softly. 'I could leave and we could pretend that I never came here after all.'

In response, Katie reached for his hand. She lifted it, staring at the fine long fingers, stroking the softness of his palm. This was not a hand that had pulled reins and hauled feed. She brought it to her lips and kissed the knuckles. 'No. I've been waiting for you for years.'

She didn't mean it the way Englischer *girls would have, as an exaggeration, accompanied by a pout and a stamp of the foot. Katie's words were literal, measured, true. Adam squeezed her hand, and let her lead him into the world where she'd grown up.*

Sarah watched her daughter chopping vegetables for dinner, and then turned her attention to setting the table. Tonight, and for many nights from now, Katie couldn't eat at it – that was part of carrying out the letter of shunning. For the next six weeks, Sarah would have to live apart from her in the same house: pretend that Katie was no longer a large part of her life, give up praying with her, limit their conversation. Why, it was like losing a child. Again.

Sarah frowned at her dining area: it was really one long table, with two bench seats on either side – as she was unable to have more children, there wasn't much call for a bigger one. She looked over at Katie's back, painfully stiff, as if she was trying to keep Sarah from noticing how very much this hurt.

Sarah went into the living room and moved a gas lamp from a card table, one she sometimes pulled out when her cousins came over to play gin rummy. She dragged it by its front legs into the kitchen, and arranged the tables so that there was no more than an inch of space between them. She took a long, white cloth from the drawers of her china cabinet and billowed it over the two tables, so that when it came to rest, if you were not looking closely, you could not tell that it wasn't one big rectangle. 'There,' she said, smoothing it, moving the silverware that was set at Katie's usual place over to a spot on the card table. She hesitated, then moved her own silverware closer to the edge of the regular table, closer to where Katie would sit to eat. 'There,' she repeated, and went again to work at her daughter's side.

One of the chores that Ellie had been assigned was getting Nugget grain and water. The big quarter horse had scared her at first, but they seemed to have come to an understanding.

'Hey, horse,' she said, sidling into the stall with the scoop of sweet grain. Nugget whinnied and stamped his foot, waiting for Ellie to get out the way so that he could settle down to business. 'Don't blame you,' she murmured, watching his heavy head bend to the fragrant, honeyed oats. 'The food's about the best thing this place has going.'

She knew by now how well the Amish treated their buggy horses – after all, if a horse broke down you couldn't take it into the local Ford dealer for a tune-up. Even Aaron, whose quiet stoicism still managed to catch her off guard, was gentle and patient with Nugget. Apparently quite a judge of horseflesh, he was occasionally asked to accompany a neighbor to the horse auctions held on Monday afternoons, just to offer his opinion.

Ellie stretched out her hand tentatively – she was still a little afraid that those big square yellow teeth would clamp onto her wrist and never let go – and stroked the horse's side. He smelled of dust and grass, a clean, mealy scent. Nugget pricked up his ears and snorted, then tried to wedge his nose beneath her armpit. Surprised, Ellie laughed, and patted his head as if he were a pet dog. 'Cut it out,' she said, but she was smiling as she unlatched the hook of the nearly empty rubber water bucket from the eye on the wall and carried it outside to the hose.

She had just turned the corner of the barn when someone snaked out and grabbed her, one hand clamped over her mouth. The bucket fell and bounced. Fighting down the quick surge of panic, Ellie bit down on the fingers that covered her mouth and an instant later drove her elbow into her abductor's gut, all the while thanking God that Stephen had gotten her self-defense lessons for Christmas two years ago.

She whirled around, her hands in a ready stance, and glared at the man, who was doubled over in pain. There was something vaguely familiar about him – the bright cap of his hair and the lithe, rangy spread of his body – and it annoyed Ellie that she could not put a name to the face. 'Who the fuck are you?'

One arm rubbing his middle, the man lifted his gaze. 'Jacob Fisher.'

'Well, you shouldn't have grabbed at me,' Ellie said a few minutes later, standing across from Katie's brother in the hayloft of the barn. 'It's a good way to get yourself killed.'

'I've been away for a while, but you rarely find black belts wandering around Amish farms.' Jacob's smile dimmed. 'You rarely find murdered babies, either.'

She sat down on a bale of hay, trying to read his face. 'I've been trying to call you.'

'I've been out of town.'

'So I realized. I assume that by now you know there have been charges brought against your sister?' Jacob nodded. 'Has the prosecution's detective found you yet?'

'Yesterday.'

'What did you tell her?'

Jacob shrugged. At his reluctant silence, Ellie braced her elbows on her knees. 'Let's get something straight right now,' she said. 'I didn't ask for this case; it sort of adopted me. I don't know what your opinion is of lawyers in general, but I'm guessing that since you've lived English for some time, you assume we're all sharks, like the rest of the free world. Frankly, Jacob, I don't care if you think I'm Attila the Hun – I'm still the best chance your sister has of getting off. You should understand better than your Amish relatives how serious a charge this is against her. Whatever I can find out from you that helps your sister's case will be held in the strictest confidence, and will help me decide what to do to defend her, but – no matter what you tell me – I'm still going to defend her. Even if you open up your mouth right now and tell me she killed that baby in cold blood, I'll still try to get her off any way I can, and then get her the psychiatric help she needs. However, I'd like to think that you're going to give me information that paints a slightly different scenario.'

Jacob walked to the high window in the hayloft. 'It's beautiful here. Do you know that it's been six years since I've been back?'

'I know how hard this must be,' Ellie said. 'But Katie never would have been charged if there wasn't sufficient evidence for the police to believe she'd killed the baby.'

'She didn't tell me she was pregnant,' Jacob confessed.

'I don't think she admitted it to herself. Is there anyone you know of that she might have been intimate with?'

'Well, Samuel Stoltzfus—'

'Not here,' Ellie interrupted. 'In State College.'

Jacob shook his head.

'Did she ever show any inclination to leave the Amish church like you did?'

'No. She wouldn't have been able to stand it, being cut off from our Mam and Dat. From everyone. Katie's not . . . how can I say this? She used to come visit me, you know, and go to parties and eat Chinese food and wear jeans. But you can take a fish out of the pond and dress it up in sheep fur, and that's never going to make it a lamb. And sooner or later, without that water, it's going to die.'

'*You* didn't,' Ellie said.

'I'm not Katie. I made a decision to leave the church, and once I made that decision, it led to other choices. I grew up Plain, Ms Hathaway, but I've thrown a punch. I've taken theology courses that question the Bible. I've owned a car. All things that I never would have believed I could do.'

'Wouldn't the same hold true for Katie? Maybe she made a decision to stay Amish – and therefore found herself forced to do things you'd never believe she could do.'

'No, because of one fundamental fact. When you're English, you make decisions. When you're Plain, you yield to a decision that's already been made. It's called *gelassenheit* – submitting to a higher authority. You give yourself up for God's will. You give yourself up for your parents, for your community, for the way it's always been done.'

'That's interesting, but it doesn't stand up against the autopsy report of a dead infant.'

'It does,' Jacob said firmly. 'Committing a murder is the most arrogant act there is! To decide you have the power of God, to take someone else's life.' He stared at Ellie, his eyes bright as beacons. 'People think Plain folks are stupid, that they let the world walk all over them. But Plain folks – they're smart; they just don't know how to be selfish. They're not selfish enough to be greedy, or pushy, or proud. And they're certainly not selfish enough to kill another human being with intent.'

'The Amish faith isn't what's on trial, here.'

'But it should be,' Jacob countered. 'My sister could not commit murder, Ms Hathaway, simply because she's Amish through and through.'

Lizzie Munro narrowed her eyes behind her safety goggles, raised her arms, and blew ten rounds from her 9-millimeter Glock into the heart of the life-size target at the far end of the shooting range. As she reeled it forward to judge her marksmanship, George Callahan whistled and popped out his earplugs. 'Glad to know you're on our side, Lizzie. You've got a real gift.'

She ran a finger appreciatively over the hole that had been blown into the target's paper chest. 'Yeah. And to think, my grandmother only wanted me to take up embroidery.' She holstered her gun and then rolled the kinks out of her shoulders.

'Must say, I'm kind of surprised to see you here.'

Lizzie raised a brow. 'How come?'

'Well, how many Amish do you plan to find armed and dangerous?'

'Hopefully none,' Lizzie answered, sliding into her suit jacket. 'I do this for relaxation, George. Beats decoupage.'

He laughed. 'We've got the pretrial hearing coming up next week.'

'Five weeks flies when you're having fun, huh?'

'I wouldn't call it fun,' George said. They walked out of the shooting range and began to stroll across the police academy's lush grounds. 'Actually, that's why I'm here. I just wanted to be sure we'd covered the state's collective ass before I go in.'

Lizzie shrugged. 'I didn't get squat from the brother, but I can go back and see if he'll talk again. The evidence is fairly cut-and-dried. The only thing that's missing is the donor of the sperm, but even that really doesn't matter, since the motive's there either way. If it was an Amish boy, then she killed the baby to keep from ruining her chances with the big blond boyfriend. If it was a regular kid from outside the community, then she killed the baby to keep from fessing up to a relationship with an outsider.'

'We seized on Katie Fisher as a suspect quickly,' George mused. 'I wonder if we overlooked someone.'

'She was bleeding like a stuck pig; that's why we seized on her,' Lizzie said. 'She had that baby, and it was two months premature – so who else could have known it was her time? We already know she hid it from her parents, so they're out of the picture. She wasn't going to tell Samuel, since it wasn't his baby. Even if she wanted to tell her brother or her aunt that the contractions had started, she couldn't very well whip out her cell phone at two in the morning.'

'We can tie her conclusively to birth, but not to murder.'

'We've got motive and logic on our side. You know that ninety percent of murders are committed by someone with a personal relationship to the victim. Do you realize that number goes up to nearly a hundred percent when it's a newborn involved?'

George stopped, and laughed down at her. 'You angling to be second chair, Lizzie?'

'Conflict of interest. I'm already testifying for the state.'

'Well, that's a shame, because I think you could single-handedly convince a jury of Katie Fisher's guilt.'

Lizzie grinned up at him. 'You're right,' she said. 'But everything I know I've learned from you.'

In the wee hours of the morning, one of the cows had given birth. Aaron had been up most of the night, because the calf hadn't been turned right. His arms hurt from being inside the cow, from the contractions that squeezed and bruised him. But look at what he had to show for it: this little wonder, black tumbled with white, wavering on its clothespin legs beside the supportive wall of its mother.

He began to spread fresh hay in the pen as the calf suckled at its mother. In a day, the baby would be taken away and put on a bottle.

You see, a small voice needled. Babies get taken from their mothers all the time.

He managed to push the thought away just as Katie came in through the barn door. Fragrant steam rose from the mug of coffee she held out to him. 'Oh, another calf,' she said, her eyes lighting. 'Isn't he a sweet one?'

Aaron could recall his daughter with nearly every calf that had been born on the farm, and that was a goodly number. She'd bottle-fed the babies since she was nearly as tiny as the calves she was caring for. Aaron could remember the first time he showed her how you could stick your finger in a calf's mouth, where there were no upper teeth to bite. He could remember explaining how a calf's tongue would curl around you and draw you in, sandpaper rough and powerfully strong. And he could remember the way her eyes widened when, that very first time, it was just as he'd said.

As the head of this family, it had been his responsibility to teach his offspring the Plain way of life – how to give themselves up to God, how to navigate a path between what was right and what was wrong. He watched Katie kneel in the fresh hay, rubbing the crazy whorls of hair that still stuck in damp spirals on the calf's back. It reminded him too much of what had happened weeks ago. Closing his eyes, he turned away from her.

Katie stood slowly and spoke, her voice as wobbly as the newborn animal. 'It's been five days since the kneeling confession. Are you never gonna talk to me again, Dat?'

Aaron loved his daughter; he wanted nothing more than to take her onto his lap like he had when she was just a little thing, and the world had been no bigger for her than the span of his own arms. But he was to blame for Katie's sin and Katie's shame, simply because he had not been able to prevent it. And it was his job, too, to see through the consequences – however painful they might be.

'Dat?' Katie whispered.

Aaron held up a hand, as if to ward her off. Then he picked up the coffee mug and turned away, heading out of the barn with the stooped shoulders and heavy gait of a much older, much wiser man.

'Have you had enough?'

Coop spoke over the litter of dishes on the table between them, and Ellie could not answer at first. She couldn't eat another bite, but she had not had enough. She didn't think she could ever get enough of the buzz and the chatter, the heady mix of society perfumes, the sound of cars jockeying about on the street below the rooftop restaurant.

Ellie watched the light from the chandelier spring rainbows from her glass of chardonnay, and she grinned.

'What's so funny?' Coop asked.

'Me,' Ellie said, a laugh bubbling up from inside her. 'I feel like I ought to keep checking my shoes for manure.'

'Five weeks on a farm doesn't quite make you Daisy Mae. Besides, your dress is considerably more flattering than bib overalls.'

Ellie fluttered her hands over her waist and her hips, reveling in the feel of the silk shantung against her skin. She never would have believed Leda capable of picking something so simple and sexy off the rack at Macy's, but then again, lots of things had been surprising her lately. Including the side-long glances that Sarah and Katie had given each other at lunch, clearly in on a secret they did not care to share with Ellie. And including the unexpected arrival of Coop, taking her breath away with his dark suit and silk tie and small bouquet; thoughtful enough to have carted along Leda as a conspirator who came bearing formal wear and high heels and who was resolved to play warden for Katie while Coop took Ellie to dinner in Philadelphia.

The wine – it made her limbs loose and liquid, made her feel that a hummingbird had taken the place of her heart. 'I can't believe we drove two hours to a restaurant,' Ellie murmured. It was a gorgeous one, to be sure, with a Saturday-night orchestra and the lights of the city rising in its floor-to-ceiling windows – but the thought of Coop traveling all the way to the Fishers', and then all the way back to Philly, made Ellie feel things she was not ready to feel.

'One and a half hours, actually,' Coop corrected. 'And hey, it took some time to find a place that served decent chow-chow.'

Ellie groaned. 'Oh, please, don't mention that dish.'

'Maybe some pickled tripe would hit the spot?'

'No,' she laughed. 'And if you even think the word "dumpling" I won't be held accountable for my actions.'

Coop glanced at her empty plate, which had once had a perfectly grilled piece of swordfish upon it. 'I take it the fruits of the sea aren't big in the Fisher household?'

'If Sarah can't put it in a thick, rich sauce, it doesn't get to the table. I'm going to gain so much weight there I won't fit into my suits when it comes time to go to trial.'

'Ah, but that's the point. You have to get fat enough for the judge to believe that you never slipped away from that farm, not even for a low-cal lunch.'

Ellie stretched in her seat like a cat. 'I like slipping away from the farm,' she said. 'I needed to slip away. Thank you.'

'Thank *you*,' he said. 'My dinner companions are never this entertaining. You're certainly the first one who's mentioned manure.'

'You see? Already I've lost my edge. Maybe I ought to do what Katie suggested.'

'What did Katie suggest?'

'She said – let me make sure I get this right – that if I knew

I wanted a good-night kiss, I should make sure to bump up against you on the turns, and comment on your horse.'

Coop burst out laughing. 'This is what you two talk about?'

'We're just a couple of girls having a slumber party.' Ellie smiled widely. 'Have I told you what a fine horse you have?'

'You know, I don't believe you have.'

Ellie leaned forward. 'Quite the stud.'

'I've got to get you drinking more often.' Coop stood, tugging on her hand. 'I want to dance with you.'

Ellie let herself be dragged upright. 'But that'll mean the ball's going to come to an end,' she moaned. 'I'll turn back into a pumpkin.'

'Only if you keep eating Sarah's dumplings.' Coop pulled her close, and began to turn her slowly around the dance floor.

Ellie rested her head beneath his chin. Their hands were twined like ivy, growing up between their hearts; and his thumb grazed the bare skin of her shoulder. She closed her eyes as his lips grazed her temple, and let herself be led in gentle circles. For a moment she stopped thinking of Katie, of the trial, of her defense, of anything but the incredible heat of Coop's hand on her back. The melody stopped, and as the musicians put down their instruments for a break and couples left the parquet floor, Ellie and Coop remained in each other's arms, simply staring.

'I think I might like to see where you stable that horse,' Ellie murmured.

Coop regarded her carefully. 'It's not much of a barn, as barns go.'

'I don't mind.'

And he smiled so brilliantly that she basked in it, that she did not notice how the temperature had dropped even after they were outside and driving to his apartment with the windows rolled down. She sat as close to him as the console would allow, their hands tangled on the stick shift. When they reached his home, Coop turned the key in the lock and pushed open the door, apologizing from the very first moment. 'It's sort of a mess. I didn't know—'

'It's all right.' Ellie stepped into the room carefully, as if too heavy a footfall might shatter the magic. She took in the glass of cola, flat, sweating a ring on the glass coffee table; the psychiatric journals littering the floor like lily pads; the running shoes knotted together at the laces and hung over the rungs of a ladderback chair. None of the furniture matched.

'Kelly got most of it,' he said quietly, reading her mind. 'These were the things she didn't want.'

'I think I remember the coffee table from college.'

Ellie walked to the bookshelf, to the state-of-the-art stereo system. 'They say you can tell a lot about a person from their CD collection,' Coop said. 'You trying to figure me out?'

'Actually, I'm looking at the wires. It's been a while since I've seen so many of them.' She touched her finger to a small photograph, one that showed Ellie hanging upside down from the limb of an apple tree, a limb above the one Coop himself had been sitting on to take the photo. 'I remember this from college, too,' she said softly. 'You still have it?'

'I dug it out, recently.'

'You kept telling me to stop laughing,' Ellie murmured. 'And I kept telling you to take the damn picture before my shirt crept up again and I flashed the world.'

Coop grinned. 'And I said—'

'"What's the matter with that?"' Ellie interrupted. 'What *was* the matter, Coop?'

'I've thought about it,' he said, loosely linking his arms behind her. 'And for the life of me, El, I can't remember.' He slid his hands up her sides. His kiss, open-mouthed, breathed fire into her. Ellie tugged his shirt from the back of his pants and skimmed her palms over the muscles of his back, pushing closer and closer until she felt his heart balanced just above hers.

They fell together onto the couch, scattering a stack of papers. His hands tangled in her hair, pulling her down, as she worked at his belt and zipper. Coop tightened his embrace. 'Can you feel that?' he whispered. 'My body remembers you.'

And just like that, she was eighteen again, pinned like a

butterfly beneath Coop's confidence. Back then, she'd loved him so much and so well that it took months to realize that what Coop made her feel was not necessarily what she wanted. Back then, she had told him a lie to let him down easy, one that hurt all the more because it was so far from the truth: that she did not love him enough. 'I can't do this,' she said out loud, the words that she didn't have the strength to utter when she was in college. She pushed at Coop's chest, at his legs, so that she was sitting up on the end of the couch, clutching the bodice of her dress together.

Reason came back to him by degrees. 'What's the matter?'

'I can't.' Ellie couldn't even look at him. 'I'm so sorry. I ought to just . . . go.'

His jaw tightened. 'What's the excuse this time?'

'I have to get back to Katie.'

'It's not me you need to keep your distance from, it's your little Amish client. You're her *lawyer*, Ellie. Not her *mother*.' Coop snorted. 'You're not scared of some judge or bail contingency. You're terrified that for once in your life you'll start something, and you won't get it right.'

'You don't know anything about—'

'For Christ's sake, Ellie, I know more about you than you do. Straight A's, dean's list, Phi Beta Kappa. You've turned cartwheels to get the toughest cases, and you've won nearly every one – even the ones that make you sick to think about. You never got married, just stayed in a relationship you should have gotten out of years ago, because you didn't really care enough about it to give a shit if it got screwed up. You're perfectly willing to leave me with blue balls as long as it means you don't risk getting in over your head, because then you'd have a vested interest in the outcome, and frankly, we don't have a successful track record. You're a classic type-A perfectionist, and you're unwilling to go out on a limb because it just might break underneath you.'

By the time Coop finished, he was yelling. Ellie stood and hobbled around, trying to find her heels. Her head hurt, nearly as much as her heart. 'Don't you psychoanalyze me.'

'You know what your problem is? If you never go out on that limb, you're missing a hell of a view.'

Ellie managed to jam her feet into her shoes and find her purse. 'You flatter yourself,' she said evenly.

'Is it just me, Ellie, or do you lead all guys on and then do a complete turnaround? What kind of power did Stephen have over you, to keep you from running away all those years?'

'He didn't love me!' As the words exploded in the still room, Ellie turned her back on Coop. She had been many things to Stephen – a roommate, a legal sounding board, a sexual partner – but never the one to share his life. And because of that, she'd never felt suffocated. She'd never felt the way she'd felt twenty years earlier, with Coop. 'There,' she said, her voice shaking. 'Is that what you wanted to hear?' Stricken, Ellie made her way to the door. 'Don't bother getting up. I'll find my own ride back.'

Coop stared at her, at the pain that seemed to flow from an untapped source, pain that filled the confines of his small apartment long after she'd gone.

Once, before Samuel had been baptized in the church, he'd driven an automobile. One of his friends, Lefty King, had bought one secondhand and kept it hidden behind his father's tobacco shed, where the old man pretended it didn't exist every time he came across it. Samuel had marveled at the fluid ride, at the amazing fact that you could idle in neutral without the car running toward the edge of the road to graze.

He was thinking of that car tonight, as he took Mary Esch home in his courting buggy. There was but a slice of moon, the kind Mam used to say looked like a cookie almost all eaten up, which gave him the perfect cover for what he had in mind.

Thing about Mary was, she didn't stop talking. She was his third cousin, so it hadn't seemed too strange when he'd come and asked her to go for an ice cream. And Samuel guessed she was pretty enough, with hair as dark and rich as a newly plowed field and a tiny ribboned bow of a mouth. But the reason

Samuel had picked her, out of all the others, was that she was Katie's best friend, and this was the closest he could come to her.

Himmel, she was chattering on now about her little brother Seth, who'd fallen into the pig trough that afternoon when he was trying to tightrope-walk on the fence that edged the pen. Samuel clucked to his horse and pulled gently on the reins, so that the buggy stopped at a small turnaround at the top of the hill.

Mary was talking so fast and furious it took her a minute to see that they weren't moving. 'Why did you stop?' she asked.

Samuel shrugged. 'Thought it was a nice night.'

She looked at him a little strangely, and for good reason. The sky was a thick, cloudy soup, the only visible light coming from that tiny bite of moon. 'Samuel,' she said, her gaze going all milky the way girls' eyes sometimes could, 'is it that you need someone to talk to?'

He felt his heart swelling like the blacksmith's bellows, fit to burst from his chest. Do it now, he told himself, or you never will. 'Mary,' he said, and then he hauled her into his arms, grinding his mouth hard against hers.

She wasn't Katie, that was his only thought. She didn't taste like Katie, like vanilla, and the size of her was all wrong in his arms, and when he pushed harder the enamel of their teeth scraped. He groped for her breast, aware that she was trying to shove him back and getting frightened, but also aware that at least once, someone had done this and more to his Katie.

'Samuel!' Mary broke away from him with a mighty effort and scrambled to the far end of the courting buggy. 'What on earth has gotten into you?'

Her face was blotched, her eyes wide and terrified. Good God, had he done that to her? Was this what he'd been brought to?

'I'm . . . I'm sorry . . .' Samuel hunched around his shame, hugging his arms to his chest. 'I didn't mean . . .' He buried his face in his shirt and tried to keep the tears from coming.

He was not a good Christian, not at all. Not only had he just attacked poor Mary Esch; he could not accept Katie's confession. Forgive her? He couldn't even get past the bare facts of it.

Mary's soft hand lit on his shoulder. 'Samuel, let's just go home.' He felt the buggy jostle as she jumped down and switched places with him, so that she could drive.

Samuel wiped hastily at his eyes. 'I'm not feeling so wonderful *gut*,' he admitted.

'No kidding,' Mary said with a little smile. She reached over and patted his hand. 'You'll see,' she said with sympathy. 'Everything is going to be all right.'

Superior Court Judge Phil Ledbetter turned out to be female.

It took Ellie nearly a full thirty seconds to absorb that fact, as she sat in the judge's chambers with George Callahan for the pretrial hearing. Phil – or Philomena, as her brass nameplate said – was a small woman with a tight red perm, a no-nonsense pinch to her mouth, and a voice with a chirp to it. Her broad desk was littered with photos of her children, all four of whom had the same trademark red hair. This was not, on the whole, good for Katie. Ellie had been banking on a male judge, a judge who would know nothing about childbirth, a judge who would feel vaguely uncomfortable skewering a young girl being tried for neonaticide. A female judge, on the other hand, who knew what it was like to carry a child and hold it in your arms the minute it came into the world, would be more likely to hate Katie at first sight.

'Ms Hathaway, Mr Callahan, why don't we get started?' The judge opened the file on the desk in front of her. 'Is discovery complete?'

'Yes, Your Honor,' said George.

'Do either of you have any motions to file? Ah, here's one from you, Ms Hathaway, about barring the press from the courtroom. Why don't we deal with this one right now?'

Ellie cleared her throat. 'It's contrary to my client's religion

to be in court at all, Your Honor. But even out of the sphere
of the courtroom, the Amish are averse to photography. It's
their way of taking the Bible to the letter,' she explained. '"You
shall not make for yourself a graven image or a likeness of
anything." Exodus 20:4.'

George interrupted. 'Your Honor, didn't we separate church
and state about two centuries ago?'

'It's more than that,' Ellie continued. 'The Amish think that
if a photograph is taken of you, you might take yourself too
seriously or try to make a name for yourself, which goes against
their spirit of humility.' She looked hard at the judge. 'My client
is already compromising her religious principles to come to
trial, Your Honor. If we have to go through this farce at all, we
can at least make it comfortable for her.'

The judge turned. 'Mr Callahan?'

George shrugged. 'Heck, yes. Let's make it comfortable for
the defendant. And while we're at it, why not give the prisoners
in the State Pen featherbeds and a gourmet chef? With all due
respect to Ms Hathaway, and to her client's religion, this is a
public trial, a *public* murder. The press has first-amendment
rights to report it. And Katie Fisher gave up certain constitutional rights when she violated some of the major ones.' He
turned to Ellie. 'Forget graven images – what about "Thou
shalt not kill"? If she didn't want notoriety, she shouldn't have
committed murder.'

'No one's proved that she has,' Ellie shot back. 'Frankly,
Your Honor, this is a religious matter, and Mr Callahan is
walking a fine line between derision and defamation. I think—'

'I know what you think, counsel; you've made yourself
painfully clear. The press will be allowed into the courtroom,
but cameras and video equipment will be barred.' The judge
turned a page in the file. 'Something else leaps out at me, Ms
Hathaway. There's obvious speculation, due to the nature of
the alleged crime, that you might be considering a plea of
insanity. As I'm sure you know, the deadline's passed for noticing
up a defense.'

'Your Honor, those deadlines can be extended for good cause, and I need a forensic psychiatrist to look at my client before I consider any theories of defense at all. However, you haven't yet ruled on my motion for services other than counsel.'

'Oh, yes.' The judge lifted a piece of paper edged with rose-buds down the margins – bubble-jet printer stationery that Leda apparently used to print the file from Ellie's disk. 'I must say, this is the prettiest motion I've ever had filed.'

Ellie groaned silently. 'I apologize for that, Your Honor. My current working conditions are . . . less than ideal.' At George's snicker, she turned resolutely toward the judge. 'I need the State to pay for an evaluation before I notice up anything.'

'Hey,' George said, 'if you get a forensic shrink, then I get a forensic shrink. I want the girl evaluated for the State.'

'Why? I'm just asking for the money to pay a psychiatrist, so that I can come to a conclusion about how to defend my client. I'm not saying I'm running an insanity defense yet. All I'm admitting to is that I'm an attorney, not a psychiatrist. If I decide to go with insanity, I'll turn over the reports and you can have your own shrink look at my client, but as it stands, I won't let her be seen by any state psychiatrist until I notice up that defense.'

'You can have your psychiatrist,' the judge said. 'How much do you need?'

Ellie scrambled to recall a typical fee. 'Twelve hundred to two thousand.'

'All right. Consider yourself funded with a two-thousand-dollar cap, unless I hear cause for more than that. If there are any other motions due, I want them within thirty days. We'll have our final pretrial in six weeks. Does that give you two enough time?'

Ellie and George murmured their assent, and the judge rose. 'If you'll excuse me, I'm due in court.' She breezed past, leaving them alone in chambers.

Ellie shuffled her papers together while George clicked his

pen and hooked it back inside his suit jacket pocket. 'So,' he said, smirking. 'How's the milking going?'

'You oughtta know, farm boy.'

'I may be a country lawyer, Ellie, but I got my degree in Philly, just like you.'

Ellie stood. 'George, do me a favor and find someplace to go. I've seen enough horse's asses in the past few weeks.'

George laughed and picked up his portfolio, then held the door open for Ellie. 'If I had as shitty a case as you do, I guess I'd be in a foul mood, too.'

Ellie walked past him. 'Don't guess,' she said. 'You're bound to be wrong.'

Coop had asked Katie to walk him through the days leading up to the birth, hoping to jar a memory, although in an hour's time there had been no major breakthroughs. He leaned forward. 'So you were doing the wash. Tell me what it felt like when you bent down to reach into that basket of wet clothes.'

Katie closed her eyes. 'Good. Cool. I took one of my Dat's shirts and rubbed it on my face, because I was so hot.'

'Was it hard to bend down?'

She frowned. 'It hurt my back. I felt a crick in it, like I sometimes do before it's my time of the month.'

'How long had it been since your time of the month?'

'A long time,' Katie admitted. 'I thought about that when I hung my drawers up to dry.'

'You knew that skipping menses was a sign of pregnancy,' Coop said gently.

'*Ja*, but I'd been late before.' Katie picked at the hem of her apron. 'I kept telling myself that.'

Coop's eyes narrowed. 'Why?'

'Because . . . because I . . .' Katie's face contorted, reddened.

'Tell me,' he urged.

'When I first missed my time,' Katie said, tears streaming down her cheeks, 'I told myself not to worry about it. And then I stopped worrying, for a little while. But I was so tired, I could barely stay awake after dinner. And when I put on my apron, I had to work hard to make the straight pins go through the same holes as always.' She took a shuddering breath. 'I thought – I thought I might be – but I wasn't big like my Mam with Hannah.' Her hands moved to her belly. 'This was nothing.'

'Did you ever feel something moving inside you? Kicking?'

Katie was silent for so long Coop was about to ask another question. Then, suddenly, her voice came, quiet and sad. 'Sometimes,' she confessed, 'it would wake me up at night.'

Coop lifted her chin, forcing her to meet his gaze. 'Katie, on that day you hung the laundry, on that day your back hurt so much, what did you know?'

She looked into her lap. 'That I was pregnant,' she breathed.

Coop stilled at the admission. 'Did you tell your mother?'

'I couldn't.'

'Did you tell anyone?'

She shook her head. 'The Lord. I asked Him to help me.'

'What time that night did you wake up with cramps?'

'I didn't.'

'All right,' Coop said. 'Then when did you go out to the barn?'

'I didn't.'

He rubbed the bridge of his nose. 'Katie, you knew you were pregnant when you went to sleep that night.'

'Yes.'

'Did you think you were pregnant the next morning?'

'No,' Katie answered. 'It was gone. I just knew all of a sudden.'

'Then something must have happened between that night and the next morning. *What happened*?'

Katie blinked back fresh tears. 'God answered my prayers.'

By silent agreement, neither Ellie nor Coop spoke of the fiasco in his apartment a few nights earlier. They were colleagues, polite and professional, and as Ellie listened to Coop talk about his session with Katie, she tried not to feel as if something was missing.

In the privacy of the barn, Coop watched the wheels turn in Ellie's mind as she analyzed Katie's admission of pregnancy. 'She cried?'

'Yeah,' Coop answered.

'That would be evidence of remorse.'

'She cried, but not about the baby – about the mess she'd gotten into. Plus, she's still amnesiac about how she became pregnant. And instead of a birth, we have divine intervention.'

Ellie smiled a little. 'Well, that would be a novel defense.'

'What I'm saying, Ellie, is that you shouldn't be throwing a victory party just yet. She hid a pregnancy, and today she admitted to it. First off, that's shady. Often amnesia victims present false memories – the story they've heard from the press and from the family, and worse, once they tell it they believe this new story fiercely, when it may not be accurate at all. But, just for the hell of it, let's say that Katie's on the square here, and truly did just remember being pregnant. Maybe there will be more admissions, as her defense mechanisms break down. But maybe there won't be. What just happened is therapeutic for Katie, but not for you and your defense – no one ever doubted that she had the baby, except for Katie herself. And hiding a pregnancy isn't normal, but it's not outside the range of the law, either.'

'I know what she's on trial for,' Ellie snapped.

'I know you do,' Coop said. 'But does she?'

Adam stood behind her, his hands fisted over her own on the dowsing rods. 'You ready?' he whispered, as a barn owl cried. They stepped forward, walking the perimeter of the pond, their shoes crunching on the dry field grass. Katie could feel Adam's heart pounding, and she wondered why he too seemed on edge; wondered what on earth he had to lose.

The rods began to shake and jump, and Katie instinctively drew back against Adam. He murmured something she did not hear, and together they fought to hold onto the sticks. 'Take me back there,' he said, and Katie closed her eyes.

She imagined the cold of that day, how you could pinch together your nostrils and feel them stick, how when you removed your mittens to lace up your skates, your fingers grew thick and red as sausages. She imagined the whoop of delight Hannah had let out when she skated off to the center of the pond, shawl flying out behind her. She imagined her sister's bright blond hair glinting through her kapp. *Most of all, she remembered the feel of Hannah's hand in hers when they walked down the slippery hill to the pond, small and warm and utterly trusting in Katie's ability to keep her from falling.*

The pressure on the dowsing rods stopped, and Katie opened her eyes when Adam sucked in his breath. 'She looks just like you,' he whispered.

Hannah skated away from them, making figure eights about six inches above the surface of the water. 'The pond was higher then,' Adam said. 'That's why she seems to be floating.'

'You see her,' Katie murmured, her heart lifting. She dropped the dowsing rods and threw her arms around Adam. 'You can see my sister!' Belatedly suspicious, she drew back to quiz him. 'What color are her skates?'

'Black. And they look like hand-me-downs.'

'And her dress?'

'Kind of green. Light, like sherbet.'

Adam led her to the bench at the edge of the pond. 'Tell me what happened that night.'

Katie painted with words: Jacob's escape to the barn, the spangles on the figure-skating champion she'd been dreaming about, the scrape of Hannah's blades on the thin patches of ice. 'I was supposed to be looking out for her, and instead all I could think of was me,' she said finally, miserably. 'It was my fault.'

'You can't think that. It was just something horrible that happened.' He touched Katie's cheek. 'Look at her. She's happy. You can feel it.'

Katie lifted her face to his. 'You've already told me that the ones who come back, the ones who become ghosts, have pain left behind. If she's so happy, Adam, why is she still here?'

'What I told you,' Adam gently corrected, 'is that the ones who come back have an emotional connection to the world. Sometimes it's pain, sometimes it's anger . . . but Katie, sometimes it's just love.' His words rose softly between them. 'Sometimes they stay because they don't want to leave someone behind.'

She remained perfectly still as Adam bent toward her. She waited for him to kiss her, but he didn't. He stopped just a breath away, fighting for the willpower to keep from touching her.

Katie knew he would be leaving the next day, knew that he moved in a world that would never be her own. She placed her palms on his cheeks. 'Will you haunt me?' she whispered, and met his lips halfway.

Katie was cleaning the tack used by the mules and by Nugget when a voice startled her.

'They made you pick up my chores,' Jacob said sadly. 'I never even thought to ask you about it.'

Her hand at her throat, she whirled around. 'Jacob!'

He opened his arms, and she flew into them. 'Does Mam know—'

'No,' he said, cutting her off. 'And let's keep it that way.' He hugged her tightly and then held her at arm's length. 'Katie, what's happened?'

She buried her face against his chest again. He smelled of pine and ink, and was so solid, so strong for her. 'I don't know,' she murmured. 'I thought I did, but now I can't be sure.'

She felt Jacob distance himself again, and then his eyes dipped down to her apron. 'You had . . . a baby,' he said uneasily, then swallowed. 'You were pregnant when you last saw me.'

She nodded and bit her lower lip. 'Are you awful mad about it?'

He slid his hand down her arm and squeezed her hand. 'I'm not mad,' he said, sitting down on the edge of a wagon. 'I'm sorry.'

Katie sat beside him and leaned her head on his shoulder. 'I am too,' she whispered.

    ★   ★   ★

Mary Esch came visiting on Sunday, wearing Rollerblades and bearing a Frisbee. Ellie could have run up and hugged the girl. It was just what Katie needed in light of these newfound recollections about the baby – a moment to just be a teenager again, without any responsibilities. While Ellie washed the dishes from lunch, Mary and Katie ran around the front yard, their skirts belling as they leaped into the air to snatch the neon disc.

Hot and winded, the girls collapsed on the grass outside the kitchen window, which Ellie had opened to catch the faint breeze. She could hear snatches of conversation drifting up over the rush of the faucet: '. . . seen the fly that landed on Bishop Ephram's nose,' '. . . asked about you,' '. . . not so lonely, not really.'

Mary closed her eyes and rubbed the cold glass of a root beer bottle against her forehead. 'I think it's hotter than any summer I ever remember,' she said.

'No.' Katie smiled. 'You just put things out of your mind when they're not right in front of you, is all.'

'Still, it's awful hot.' She put down the bottle and fluted her skirt over her bare toes, unsure of what else to say.

'Mary, has it got so bad that all we can talk about is the weather?' Katie said quietly. 'Why don't you ask me what you really want to ask?'

Mary looked into her lap. 'Is it awful, being shunned?'

Katie shrugged. 'It's not so bad. The mealtimes are tough, but I have Ellie with me, and my Mam tries to make it all work out okay.'

'And your Dat?'

'My Dat isn't so good at trying to make it all work out,' she admitted. 'But that's how he is.' She took her friend's hand. 'In six weeks, it'll all go back to being the way it was.'

If anything, this made Mary look even more upset. 'I don't know about that, Katie.'

'Well, sure you do. I've made my things right. Even if Bishop Ephram asks me to step down at communion time, I won't have to be under the *bann*.'

'That's not what I mean,' Mary murmured. 'It's the way others might act.'

Katie slowly turned. 'If they can't forgive my sin, they shouldn't be my friends.'

'For some people, it's going to be harder to pretend nothing happened.'

'It's the good Christian thing to do,' Katie said.

'*Ja,* but it's hard to be Christian when it was your girl,' Mary answered quietly. She fiddled with the strings of her *kapp*. 'Katie, I think Samuel might want to see someone else.'

Katie felt the air go out of her, like a pillow punched in the middle. 'Who told you that?'

Mary did not answer. But the red burn in her friend's cheeks, the obvious discomfort at bringing up the very private notion of a beau, made Katie realize exactly what had happened. 'Mary Esch,' she whispered. 'You *wouldn't.*'

'I didn't want to! I pushed him away after he tried to kiss me!'

Katie got to her feet, so angry she was shaking. 'Some friend you are!'

'I am, Katie. I came here so you wouldn't have to hear it from someone else.'

'I wish you hadn't.'

Mary nodded slowly, sadly. She pulled her socks from the bellies of her Rollerblades and buckled the skates onto her feet. Gliding smoothly out of the driveway, she did not look back.

Katie held her elbows tight at her sides. Any movement, she thought, and she might fly apart in a thousand different pieces. She heard the screen door open and slam, but she remained staring over the fields, where Samuel was working with her father.

'I heard,' Ellie said, touching her shoulder from behind. 'I'm sorry.'

Katie tried to keep her eyes wide, so wide that the tears in them couldn't quite trickle over the edges. But then she turned and threw herself into Ellie's arms. 'It's not supposed to be like this,' she cried. 'It wasn't supposed to happen this way.'

'Ssh. I know.'

'You don't know,' Katie sobbed.

Ellie's hand fell, cool, on the back of her neck. 'You'd be surprised.'

Katie desperately wanted Dr Polacci to like her. Ellie had said that the psychiatrist was being paid a great deal of money to come to the farm and meet with her. She knew that Ellie believed whatever Dr Polacci had to say would be extremely useful when it came time for trial. She also knew that ever since she had told Dr Cooper about the pregnancy, he and Ellie had been too stiff with each other, and Katie thought it was all somehow tied together.

The psychiatrist had puffy black hair and a face like the moon and a wide ocean of body. Everything about her urged Katie to jump, knowing that no matter how she landed, she'd be safe.

She smiled nervously at Dr Polacci. They were sitting in the living room, alone. Ellie had fought to be there, but Dr Polacci suggested that her presence might keep Katie silent. 'I'm someone she confides in,' Ellie had argued.

'You're one more person to confess in front of,' the psychiatrist answered.

They talked in front of her like she was stupid, or a pet dog – like she had no opinion whatsoever about what was happening to her. In the end, Ellie had left. Dr Polacci had made it clear that she was here to help Katie get acquitted. She'd said that Katie should tell her the truth, because she surely didn't want to go to jail. Well, Dr Polacci was right on that count. So pretty much, Katie had spent the past hour telling her everything that she had told Dr Cooper. She was careful about her choice of words – she wanted the most precise recollection. She wanted Dr Polacci to go back to Ellie and say, 'Katie's not crazy; it's all right for the judge to let her go.'

'Katie,' Dr Polacci asked now, drawing her attention, 'what was going through your mind when you went to bed?'

'Just that I felt bad. And I wanted to go to sleep so that I could wake up and be better.'

The psychiatrist marked something down on her notepad. 'Then what happened?'

She had been waiting for this, for the moment when the small flashes of light that had been bursting in her mind these past few days would fly from her mouth like a flock of scattering starlings. Katie could almost feel the cut of the pain again, slicing like a scythe from her back to her belly with such a sharp, reaching pull from inside that she found herself knotted in a ball by the time she could breathe again. 'I hurt,' she whispered. 'I woke up and the cramps were bad.'

Dr Polacci frowned. 'Dr Cooper told me that you haven't been able to remember labor pains, or the birth of the baby.'

'I haven't,' Katie admitted. 'The first thing that came to me was that I was pregnant – I told Dr Cooper how I remembered trying to bend down and feeling something stuck in the middle there that I had to work my way around. And since then, I keep remembering things.'

'Like what?'

'Like that the light in the barn was already on, when it was way too early for the milking.' She shuddered. 'And how I was trying and trying to hold it in, but I couldn't.'

'Did you realize that you were giving birth?'

'I don't know. I was awfully scared, because it hurt so much. I just knew that I had to be quiet, that if I yelled out or cried someone might hear.'

'Did your water break?'

'Not all at once, like my cousin Frieda's did when she had little Joshua, right in the middle of the barn-raising lunch. The ladies sitting on both sides of her on the bench got soaked. This was more like a trickle, every time I sat up.'

'Was there blood?'

'A little, on the insides of my legs. That's why I went outside – I didn't want it to get on the sheets.'

'Why not?'

'Because I wash 'em, but my Mam takes them off the beds. And I didn't want her to know what was happening.'

'Did you know you were going to go to the barn?'

'I didn't plan it, exactly. I never really got to thinking about what would happen . . . when it was time. I just knew that I had to get out of the house.'

'Did anyone in the household wake up as you left?'

'No. And there was no one outside, or in the barn. I went into the calving pen, because I knew it had the cleanest hay put out for the expecting cows. And then . . . well, it was like I wasn't there for a little while. Like I was somewhere else, just watching what was happening. And then I looked down, and it was out.'

'By "it" you mean the baby.'

Katie looked up, a little dazed to think of the result of that night in those terms. 'Yes,' she whispered.

'Approximately two hundred to two hundred and fifty neonaticides occur each year, Ms Hathaway. And those are only the ones that are reported.' Teresa Polacci walked beside Ellie along the stream that bordered the farm. 'In our culture, that's reprehensible. But in certain cultures, such as the Far East, neonaticide is still acceptable.'

Ellie sighed. 'What kind of woman would kill her own newborn?' she asked rhetorically.

'One who's single, unmarried, pregnant for the first time with an unwanted baby conceived out of wedlock. They're usually young, between the ages of sixteen and nineteen. They don't abuse drugs or alcohol, or have run-ins with the law. No, they're the girls who walk the neighbor's dog as a favor when they're on vacation; the ones who study hard to get good grades. Often they're overachievers, oriented toward pleasing their parents. They are passive and naïve, afraid of shame and rejection, and occasionally come from religious backgrounds where sex is not discussed.'

'I take it from your comments that you think Katie fits the mold.'

'In terms of the profile, and her religious upbringing, I've rarely seen a closer case,' Dr Polacci said. 'She certainly had more reason than most girls in this day and age to face shame and persecution both within her family and without if she admitted to premarital sex and pregnancy. Hiding it became the path of least resistance.'

Ellie glanced at her. 'Hiding it suggests a conscious decision to cover up.'

'Yes. At some point she knew she was pregnant – and she intentionally denied it. Curiously enough, she wasn't the only one. There's a conspiracy of silence – the people around the girl usually don't want her to be pregnant, either, so they ignore the physical changes, or pretend to ignore them, which just plays into the system of denial.'

'So you don't believe that Katie went into a dissociative state.'

'I never said that. I do believe it's psychologically impossible to be in a dissociative state for the entire term of a pregnancy. Katie – like many other women I've interviewed who have committed neonaticide – consciously denied her pregnancy, yet then unconsciously dissociated at the time of the birth.'

'What do you mean?' Ellie asked.

'That's when the moment of truth occurs. These women are extremely stressed. The defense mechanism they've had in place – denial – is shattered by the arrival of the infant. They have to distance themselves from what's occurring, and most of these women – Katie included – will tell you it didn't feel like it was happening to them, or that they saw themselves but couldn't stop it – a true out-of-body experience. Sometimes the appearance of the baby even triggers a temporary psychosis. And the more out of touch with reality the women are at that moment, the more likely they are to harm their newborns.

'Let's look at Katie, specifically. Thanks to her brother's experience, she's been living with a very primitive survival script in her head, believing that if Mom and Dad find out her secret, she'll be excommunicated and forced out of the household. So there's this covert idea in her mind that it's somehow okay to get rid of your children. Then she goes into labor. She can't deny the baby's existence anymore – so she does to the baby what she's afraid will happen to her – she throws it out. The dissociative state lasts long enough for the birth and the murder, and then she reverts to using denial as a defense mechanism, so that when she's confronted by the police, she immediately says she didn't have a baby.'

'How can you tell that she dissociated at all?'

'When she speaks about giving birth, she shuts down a little. She doesn't rely on other defense mechanisms – for example, denial, or something more primitive.'

'Wait a second,' Ellie said, stopping. 'Katie admitted to giving birth?'

'Yes, I have it on tape.'

Ellie shook her head, feeling oddly betrayed. 'She didn't fold when Coop pressed her.'

'It's not unusual for a client to admit something crucial to a forensic psychiatrist that she hasn't admitted to a clinical psychiatrist. After all, I'm not talking to her to make her feel comfortable, but to keep her from going to jail. If she lies to me, she's hurting herself. It's my job to uncover the can of worms; it's the clinical psychiatrist's job to help stuff them back in.'

Ellie glanced up. 'She told you about killing the infant too?'

The psychiatrist hesitated. 'Actually, no. She says she still can't remember two specific points: the conception of the baby, and the murder.'

'Could she have been in a dissociative state both times?'

'It's entirely possible that she dissociated during the birth of the baby and during the killing. In fact, since her recollections don't match entirely with the forensic records you've given me, the discrepancy flags just that. But as for the sex . . . well, that's not something these women usually forget.'

'What if it was traumatic for her?' Ellie asked.

'You mean a rape? It's possible, but usually women admit to being raped, unless they're protecting someone. My gut feeling is that there's more to Katie's story on that particular point.'

Ellie nodded. 'And the killing?'

'Katie recounted in great detail the night before the delivery, the actual birth, and falling asleep with the infant in her arms. She says the baby was gone when she woke up, along with the scissors she used to cut the umbilicus.'

'Did she look for the baby?'

'No. She went back to her room to sleep, entirely consistent with women who commit neonaticide – the problem's out of sight, out of mind.'

Ellie's head was spinning. 'How long was she unconscious in the barn?'

'She said she doesn't know.'

'It couldn't have been long, based on the police reports,' Ellie mused aloud. 'What if—'

'Ms Hathaway, I realize what you're thinking. But remember – up until now, Katie didn't recall the birth of the baby. Tomorrow, who knows? She may recall in excruciating detail how she smothered it. As much as we might want to think she didn't kill that infant, we have to take her recollections with a grain of salt. By the mere definition of dissociation, there are gaps of time and logic missing for Katie. Chances are awfully good that she did indeed kill the baby, even if she's never able to verbally admit to it.'

'So you believe that she's guilty,' Ellie said.

'I believe that she fits the profile of many other women I've interviewed who killed their newborns while in a dissociative state,' the psychiatrist corrected. 'I believe that her pattern of behavior is consistent with what we know of the phenomenon of neonaticide.'

Ellie stopped walking along the stream's edge. 'Is my client sane, Dr Polacci?'

The psychiatrist exhaled heavily. 'That's a loaded question. Are you talking medically sane, or legally sane? Medical insanity suggests that a person is not in touch with reality – but a person in a dissociative state *is* in touch with reality. She looks and appears normal while in a totally abnormal state. However, legal insanity has nothing to do with reality – it hinges on cognitive tests. And if a woman commits murder while in a dissociative state, she most likely will not understand the nature and quality of the act, or know that what she's doing is wrong.'

'So I can use an insanity defense.'

'You can use whatever you want,' Polacci said flatly. 'You're really asking if an insanity defense can get your client off. Frankly, Ms Hathaway, I don't know. I will tell you that juries usually want to know practical issues: that the woman is safe, and that this won't happen again – both of which are affirmative for most women who commit neonaticide. Best-case scenario? My testimony can give the jury something to hang their hats on – if they want to acquit, they will, as long as there's something they can point to to rationalize their actions.'

'Worst-case scenario?'

Dr Polacci shrugged. 'The jury learns more about neonaticide than they ever wanted to know.'

'And Katie?'

The psychiatrist fixed her gaze on Ellie. 'And Katie goes to jail.'

Katie felt like the green twig that she was mangling in her own hands – bent double backward, nearly ready to break. She fought the urge to stand up and start pacing, to look out the hayloft window, to do anything but speak to her attorney right now.

She understood the point of the drill – Ellie was trying to get her ready for what would certainly be an unpleasant grilling by the forensic psychiatrist who'd been hired by the State. Ellie had said Dr Polacci believed Katie was holding back about how the baby was conceived. 'And,' she'd finished, 'I'll be damned if you spill the beans to the prosecution's expert.'

So now they were in the hayloft – she and Ellie, who'd somehow become so ruthless and unforgiving that every now and then Katie had to turn and make sure her face was familiar.

'You don't remember having sex,' Ellie said.

'No.'

'I don't believe you. You said you didn't remember the pregnancy or the birth, and lo and behold, three days later, you're a veritable font of information.'

'But it's true!' Katie felt her hands sweating; she wiped them on her apron.

'You had a baby. Explain that.'

'I already did, to Dr—'

'Explain how it was conceived.' At Katie's prolonged silence, Ellie wearily propped her head in her heads. 'Look,' she said. 'You're bluffing. The psychiatrist knows it and I know it, and Katie, you know it too. We're all on the same goddamned side, here, but you're making it twice as hard for us to defend you. I know of one Immaculate Conception, and yours wasn't it.'

With resignation Katie's gaze fluttered to her lap. What would it mean, to come clean? To confess, as she had for the bishop and the congregation? 'Okay,' Katie said finally, softly. She swallowed hard. 'I was visiting my brother, and we went to a graduation party at one of the fraternity houses. I didn't want to go, but Jacob did, and I didn't want him to feel badly for having me there like . . . what is it you say? Like a fifth wheel. We went to the party, and it was very crowded, very hot. Jacob went to get us something to eat and didn't come back for a while. In the meantime, a boy came up to me. He gave me a glass of punch and said I looked like I needed it. I told him I was waiting for someone, and he laughed, and said, "Finders, keepers." Then he started to talk to me.'

Katie walked to the rear of the hayloft, fingering the spikes on a rake propped against the far wall. 'I must have drunk some of the punch while he was talking, without really thinking about it. And it made me feel just awful – all sick to my stomach, and my head spinning like a top. I stood up to try to see Jacob in the crowd, and the whole room tilted.' She bit her lip. 'The next thing, I was lying on a bed I didn't recognize, with my clothes all . . . and he was . . .' Katie closed her eyes. 'I . . . I didn't even know his name.'

She bent her head to the wooden wall, feeling the rough plane of the board against her forehead. Her entire body was shaking, and she was afraid to turn and see Ellie's expression.

She didn't have to. Ellie embraced her from behind. 'Oh, Katie,' she soothed. 'I'm so sorry.'

Katie turned in her arms, this safe place, and burst into tears.

This time, when Katie finished telling the story, she was grasping Ellie's hand for support. If she was aware of the tears streaming over her cheeks, she made no mention of it. Ellie itched to wipe them away, to catch Katie's eye and smile and tell her she'd done a great job.

Dr Polacci, who'd been called back for the confession, looked from Katie to Ellie, and back again. Then she lifted her hands and began clapping, her expression impassive. 'Nice story,' she said. 'Try again.'

'She's lying,' Dr Polacci said. 'She knows exactly where and when she conceived that baby, and that charming little date rape story wasn't it.'

Ellie bristled at the thought that Katie was lying; at the thought that Katie had been lying deliberately to her. 'We're not talking about an average teenager who fabricates excuses for her parents and spends the night horizontal in the back of her boyfriend's four-by-four.'

'Exactly. This story was just *too* good. Too calculated, too rehearsed. She was telling you what you wanted to hear. If she'd been raped, she would have admitted to it by now in her sessions with the clinical psychiatrist, unless she was protecting the rapist, which her tale didn't support. And then there's the small matter of the graduation party held three months after a June graduation – I'm assuming she conceived in October, based on the medical examiner's report.'

It was that glaring inconsistency that finally broke through Ellie's defenses. 'Shit,' she muttered. At a sudden thought, Ellie glanced up. 'If she's lying about not remembering having sex, is she lying about not remembering the murder?'

The psychiatrist sighed. 'My gut feeling still tells me no. When I pushed her on conception, she got fuzzy on me – said things are just sort of out of reach in her mind. When I pushed her about the murder, I got a flat denial of the crime, and that hard break – she fell asleep holding the infant; she woke up and it was gone. The two amnesic episodes differ – which leads me to believe she's consciously denying one, and subconsciously dissociating about the other.'

Dr Polacci patted Ellie's shoulder. 'I wouldn't take this too hard. Actually, it's sort of a compliment. Katie feels so close to you that she wants to live up to your expectations, even if it means coming up with a false recollection. In some ways, you've become a parent figure.'

'Living up to parental expectations,' Ellie huffed. 'Isn't that what got her here in the first place?'

Dr Polacci chuckled. 'In part. That, along with some guy. Some guy who's got a hold on her like I've never seen.'

The night was so warm that Ellie had climbed outside the quilt and was now lying on top of it with her nightgown hiked to her thighs. She stayed perfectly still, trying to listen for Katie's breathing, wondering how long it would take for the two of them to fall asleep.

It made no sense to Ellie, this new obsession she had with the truth. As a defense attorney she usually had to stick her fingers in her ears to keep from hearing an admission she did not legally want to hear. But she would have traded her twelve-volt inverter for ten minutes inside Katie Fisher's head.

Then she heard it, the faintest of sighs. 'I'm sorry,' Katie said quietly.

Ellie did not bother to look at her. 'What is the apology for, exactly? The baby's murder? Or the more mundane crime of making me look like an idiot in front of my own witness?'

'You know what I'm sorry for.'

There was a long silence. 'Why did you do it?' Ellie finally asked.

She could hear Katie rolling onto her side. 'Because you needed to hear it so badly.'

'What I need is for you to stop lying to me, Katie. About this, and about what happened after that baby was born.' She passed a hand down her face. 'What I need is to turn the clock back, so this time I can refuse your case.'

'I only lied because you and Dr Polacci were so sure I knew something,' Katie said, her voice thick with tears. 'I don't, Ellie. I promise I don't. I'm not crazy, like you think . . . I just can't remember. About how the baby got made, or how it got killed.'

Ellie didn't say a word. She heard the quiet creak of the bed as Katie curled on her side and cried. She clenched her fists to keep from going to the girl, then crawled beneath her own blanket and counted the minutes it took for Katie to fall asleep.

Samuel wiped the sweat off his brow and yanked another bull calf off its feet. After all these years helping Aaron, he had castration down to a science. He waited until the animal had gotten the urge to kick out of him, then slipped the rubber ring of the elestrator around the scrotum and let it constrict. Within seconds the two-month-old calf was up on its feet, casting an aggrieved, sidelong look at Samuel before heading out to pasture again.

'He's a sturdy one,' a voice said, startling Samuel.

He turned to find Bishop Ephram standing on the other side of the fence. '*Ja*, he'll bring Aaron enough beef.' Smiling at the older man, Samuel let himself out through the gate. 'If you're looking for Aaron, I think he's in the barn.'

'Actually, I was looking for you.'

Samuel hesitated, wondering what charge the bishop might want to lay against him this time, then berating himself for even thinking such a thing. He'd had plenty of visits from the bishop in his life, and he'd never associated a single one with shame or wrongdoing. Until everything had gone wrong with Katie.

'*Komm,*' Ephram said. 'Walk a ways.' Samuel fell into step beside him. 'I remember when your father got you your first calf.'

It wasn't an extraordinary gift for an Amishman to his son: the proceeds from the sale of the meat were put into a bank account for the boy's later use, when he wanted to purchase his own home or farm. Samuel smiled, recalling the bull calf that had gained a thousand pounds in a year.

He still had the money the beef had brought in, as well as other calves that had followed. He'd been saving it, or so he thought, for his life with Katie.

'Your technique's a little better these days,' Ephram said. 'As I recall, that first bull kicked you but good, in a place that don't take to kicking.' He grinned through the snow of his beard. 'It was touch and go there, for a while, who exactly was gonna be castrated.'

Samuel's face burned with the memory, but he laughed. 'I was nine years old,' he reasoned. 'The bull weighed more than me.'

Ephram stopped walking. 'Whose fault was it?'

'Fault?'

'The kick. The fact that you got hurt at all.'

Frowning, Samuel shrugged. 'The bull's, I suppose. I sure didn't do it to myself.'

'No. But if you'd been holding it tighter, what do you think might have happened?'

'It wouldn't have been able to get in a wild blow, you know that. Certainly, I learned my lesson. I've never been kicked again.' Samuel exhaled. He had work to do for Aaron. He didn't have the patience for Ephram's ramblings today. 'Bishop,' he said, 'you didn't come here to talk to me about that bull.'

'Didn't I?'

He jammed his hat on his head. 'Aaron will be needing me by now.'

Bishop Ephram put his hand on Samuel's arm. 'You're right, Brother. Why should we talk about ancient history, after all?

Once that bull kicked you, you got rid of it right away.'

'No, I didn't. You remember how big he got. He was a fine steer.' Samuel scowled. 'By the time I put the money into the bank, I barely remembered that he'd kicked me at all.'

The old man peered at him. 'No. But when you were lying on your back in the pasture that day, howling and grabbing your privates, I bet you never would have guessed things could turn out so good in the end.'

Samuel slowly swung his head toward the bishop. 'You didn't come here to talk about that bull,' he repeated softly.

Bishop Ephram raised his brows. 'Didn't I?'

Dr Brian Riordan traveled by private jet, accompanied by two men who looked like football linebackers past their prime and a tiny mouse of a girl who jumped whenever he beckoned her to carry through some task on his behalf. He was well known in forensic psychiatry circles as being one of the foremost critics of the insanity defense, particularly when used to acquit murderers. He'd made his very strong beliefs known in trials all over the United States, and in fact kept a map in his office covered with brightly colored pins, signifying the court systems in which he'd had a hand in putting away a criminal who might otherwise have gotten off on pure sympathy.

He also looked patently out of place on a farm.

Compared to Dr Polacci, Dr Riordan was a formidable species. Even from the doorway of the kitchen, where Ellie could observe the interview, she could see Katie trembling.

'Ms Fisher,' Riordan said, after introducing himself, 'I've been retained by the prosecution. What that means is that whatever you say to me will go to court. You cannot say something off the record; there's no confidentiality. Do you understand?'

Ellie listened as Riordan walked Katie through the birth, asking her to recount the events in the present tense. 'It's lying there,' Katie said softly, 'right between my legs.'

'Is it a boy or a girl?'

'A boy. A tiny, tiny boy.' She hesitated. 'It's moving around.'

Ellie felt her face grow warm. She turned away, fanning herself with one hand.

'Is it crying?' Riordan asked.

'No. Not till I cut the cord.'

'How do you cut it?'

'My Dat keeps a pair of scissors hanging on a peg outside the calving pen. That's what I use. And then there's blood, all over the place, and I'm thinking that I won't be able to clean this up, ever. I push down on the end of the cord, and tie it off . . . with twine, I think. Then it starts crying.'

'The baby?'

'*Ja*. It starts crying loud, real loud, and I try to hold him up against me to keep him quiet, but that doesn't help. I rock it tight and give it my knuckle to suck on.'

Ellie leaned against the wall. She pictured this fragile infant, rooting around the bodice of Katie's nightgown. She imagined the little face, the translucent eyelids, and suddenly there was a weight in her arms, heavy as a lost opportunity. How could anyone's actions, in this case, be defended? 'Excuse me,' she announced, bustling into the kitchen. 'I need a glass of water. Anyone else?'

For her interruption, Riordan gave her a dirty look. Ellie concentrated on filling a glass without her hand shaking, on drinking just a little before she had to hear her client recount this baby's death.

'What happens next, Katie?' Riordan asked.

Katie squinted, shook her head, then sighed. 'I don't know. I wish I did, I wish like you can't imagine. But one minute I'm praying for the Lord to help me, and the next minute I'm waking up. The baby is gone.' Ellie bowed her head over the sink. 'A miracle,' Katie added.

Riordan stared at her. 'You're kidding, right?'

'No.'

'How long were you passed out in the barn?'

'I don't know. I guess about ten, fifteen minutes.'

The psychiatrist folded his hands in his lap. 'Did you kill the baby during that time?'

'No!'

'You're sure?' She nodded emphatically. 'Then what did happen to him?'

No one had ever asked Katie before; as Ellie watched the girl struggle for an answer, she realized how shortsighted this had been. 'I . . . don't know.'

'You must have an idea. Since someone killed that baby, and it wasn't you.'

'M-m-maybe it just died,' Katie stammered. 'And someone hid it.'

Ellie silently groaned. And maybe that was Katie's subconscious doing a voluntary confession. 'Do you think that's what happened?' Riordan asked.

'Someone could have come in and killed it.'

'Does that seem likely to you?'

'I – I'm not sure. It was sort of early . . .'

'Middle of the night, I'd figure,' Riordan interjected. 'Who would have known you were there giving birth?' He watched her wrestle with the question. 'Katie,' he said firmly, *'what happened to the baby?'*

Ellie watched the girl's disintegration: the trembling lower lip, the welling eyes, the shaking spine, as Katie shook her head and repeatedly denied criminal responsibility. She waited for Riordan to do something to comfort Katie, but then realized that he'd already aligned his sympathies elsewhere. He'd been retained by the prosecution; it would be unethical for him to offer comfort when he'd been called in for the express purpose of helping to lock Katie away.

Ellie approached her client and knelt. 'Do you think we could take a minute?'

She didn't wait for Riordan's response. Instead she slipped an arm around Katie's shoulders, trying to ignore the way the girl had balled up her apron and now sat huddled over it, cradling it in her arms as if it were an infant.

Riordan batted his eyes and adopted an impassioned falsetto. 'Katie Fisher wasn't there at the time of the baby's death. Her body, maybe, but not her mind. At the time that infant died, she was in a mental fortress made of her own guilt.' He lowered his voice to his own natural tones and grinned at the county attorney. 'Or something along those lines.'

George laughed. 'Does that psychoanalytic bullshit actually work at trials?'

Riordan took a mint from a jar on the desk. 'Not if I have anything to say about it.'

'You're sure that when Hathaway noticed up insanity, she was thinking of dissociation?'

'Trust me, it's the designer defense tailored to neonaticide. Psychologically, the discrepancies between Katie's story and the forensic evidence can be explained either by dissociation, or flat-out lying – and you can figure out which of those two options the defense is going to seize upon. But brief episodes of dissociation do not constitute insanity.'

Riordan shrugged, popping a mint into his mouth. 'The other thing about dissociative states is that if you give Ms Hathaway enough rope, she'll hang herself. There's no way for her expert to prove that the dissociation was caused by the mental stress of giving birth, rather than the mental stress of committing murder. It's a chicken-and-egg thing.'

'I can go somewhere with this.' George grinned and leaned back in his chair.

'Straight to the state prison.'

George nodded. 'Do we need to cover any of the psychological ramifications of being Amish?'

Riordan stood, buttoned his jacket. 'Why?' he said. 'Murder's murder.'

As he kissed her, leaves rained down over them, spotting his back with the rich reds of the maples and the guinea gold of the oaks. Her shawl was spread over the crabgrass like the wingspan of a great black hawk, providing a makeshift blanket. Katie moved her hands from Adam's hair to his shoulders as he began to unfasten her dress. He gently speared each straight pin into the bark of the tree behind them, and she loved him for that – for being thoughtful enough to consider what this would be like for her, after.

The apron came off, and her dress fell open. Katie closed her eyes, embarrassed, but then felt Adam bend to her breast, drawing on her through the fine cotton of her underwear. She held his head there; she imagined that he was drinking from the bowl of her heart.

He had not said he loved her, but that did not matter. It was how he acted, how he treated her, that was a truer measure than any words he could say – deeds were the proof of affection for her people, not three little syllables that signified nothing. Adam would tell her when it was over; when it would not cheapen what was happening between them.

Then he shed his own clothes. Just by looking now, you could not say that one was Plain and one was not. That was the last conscious thought Katie had, and then Adam pressed his body full against hers, the heat of his skin taking away her speech, her fears.

He was heavy and full between her legs. With one hand, he lifted her knee, so that her body made a cradle for him. Then Adam looked down at her, his expression grave. 'We can stop,' he whispered. 'Right now, if you want.'

Katie swallowed. 'Do you want to stop?'

'About as much as I'd like to be drawn and quartered.'

She lifted her hips, an invitation, and felt him losing himself in her, stretching her so that it made her eyes smart. She thought of all the tourists who stood beneath the crossroads sign about five miles east, the one that said INTERCOURSE, PA, and how they'd giggle and point up at it while someone snapped their picture. She thought of her flesh giving way to Adam's, the sweetest yielding of all. And then Adam reached between them and touched her. 'Come with me,' he whispered.

She thought he meant tomorrow, when he left for Scotland. She thought he meant forever. But then she felt her body spinning tighter *and tighter, and scattering like the bright white seeds of a milkweed. As she caught her breath, more leaves fell on them, a benediction. Adam lay by her side, smiling and stroking her hip. 'You okay?'*

Katie nodded. If she spoke, she would tell him the truth: she was not okay at all, but horribly empty, now that she knew what it was like to be filled.

He wrapped her in her shawl, and it made her feel physically ill. 'No.' She pushed at his hands, shimmying away from the light wool. 'I don't want it.'

Sensing the change in her, Adam drew her closer. 'Listen, now,' he said firmly. 'We didn't do anything wrong.'

But Katie knew it was a sin, had known from the moment she made the decision to lie with Adam. However, the transgression wasn't making love without the sanction of marriage. It was that for the first time in her life, Katie had put herself first. Put her own wants and needs above everything and everyone else.

'Katie,' Adam said, his voice rough, 'talk to me.'

But she wanted him to speak. She wanted him to carry her far away from here, and hold her close all over again, and tell her that two worlds could be bridged with a look, with a touch. She wanted him to say that she belonged to him, and that he belonged to her, and that in the grand scheme of things that was really all that mattered.

She wanted him to tell her that when you loved someone so hard and so fierce, it was all right to do things that you knew were wrong.

Adam remained silent, searching her face. Katie felt the heat of him, of them, seeping between her thighs. They would not be going to Scotland together. They would not be going anywhere. She reached for her shawl and pulled it around her shoulders, knotting it just below the spot where her heart was breaking. 'I think,' she said softly, 'you'd better leave.'

Katie was finding it harder and harder to fall asleep. In those floating moments just before she drifted off, she would feel the scratch of hay under her thighs, or smell fear, or see the moon glinting off the stretched skin of her belly. She would think of the things she had told Dr Polacci and Dr Riordan and feel ill. And then she'd roll onto her side, to watch Ellie sleep, and feel even worse.

She hadn't expected to like Ellie. At first, Katie had been furious to find herself stuck with a jailer who didn't trust her, to boot. But as uncomfortable as Katie might have found the situation, Ellie must have found it even more uncomfortable. This was not her home; these were not her people – and as she had pointed out several times, now, usually in fits of anger, this was not a situation of her own making.

Well, it isn't my fault, either, Katie thought. And yet she had seen that baby wrapped in the horse blankets. She had watched its coffin lowered into the ground. It was *someone's* fault.

Katie had not killed the baby, she knew this as well as she knew the sun would come up in the morning. But then, who had?

There was once a homeless man who'd taken up shelter inside Isaiah King's tobacco shed. But even if a vagrant had been in the barn that morning, he'd have no cause to take a newborn out of Katie's arms, kill it, and hide it. Unless he was crazy, like Ellie was making her out to be.

Katie knew that she would have sensed if someone else was in the barn that morning. And even if she hadn't, the animals would have. Nugget would have been whinnying for a treat, like he always did when a person came to call; the cows would have been lowing in anticipation of milking. From the little bits and pieces Katie could recall, there had only been calm.

Which meant someone had slipped in after her.

She had racked her brain over and over, wishing for something she could give to Ellie on a silver platter, some piece of evidence so strong that it would make everything clear. But who would have cause to be up at that hour?

Her father. The very thought shamed Katie. Her Dat sometimes came down to check on the cows due to deliver – but he was there to help give life, not take it away. Had he found Katie lying with a newborn – well, he would have been shocked, even angry. But justice for him would come from the church, not from his own hands.

Samuel. If he'd come early for the milking, he might have found her asleep in the barn with the newborn. For sure, he'd have every right to be upset. Could he have hurt the baby before he realized what he'd done? Impossible, Katie thought, not Samuel. Samuel didn't jump to conclusions; he thought slowly. And he was too honest to lie to the police. Suddenly Katie brightened, remembering another alibi for Samuel: he always brought along Levi. He wouldn't have been alone in the barn long enough to commit a crime.

But that left no one else – no one but Katie herself. And here, in the very deepest part of the night, she pulled the quilt tighter around herself and let herself wonder if Dr Polacci and Ellie might be right after all. If you didn't remember something happening, was it because it never had happened? Or because you wished it hadn't?

Katie rubbed her temples. She drifted off to sleep, borne along on the memory of the high, thin cry of a baby.

The flashlight shining in her eyes woke Ellie. 'For God's sake,' she muttered, flinging a look at Katie, fast asleep, and then crossing to the window. If Samuel had come to tender an apology, it would have been nice for him to pick a time other than one in the morning. Ellie peered out the window, ready to give him a piece of her mind, and then realized that the man standing out in front of the house was Coop.

After dressing quickly in the shirt and shorts she'd had on the previous day, Ellie hurried down to meet him. She put her finger to her lips when she stepped onto the porch, and walked a distance from the house. Folding her arms across her chest, she nodded at the flashlight. 'Samuel tip you off to that trick?'

'Levi,' Coop said. 'The kid's a real corker.'

'Did you come to show me that you understand Amish courting rituals?' As soon as she said it, she wanted to take it back. As if, after the way things had gone the other night, Coop might want to include her in anything even marginally resembling a courting ritual.

He sighed. 'I came to say I'm sorry.'

'In the middle of the night?'

'I would have called, but damn if I couldn't find a listing for the Fishers. I had to find my handy-dandy flashlight and attend to the matter in person.'

Ellie felt a smile twitch at her lips. 'I see.'

'No, you don't.' He reached for her hand, pulling her down the path toward the pond. 'I am truly sorry that things didn't work out for you with Stephen. I never meant to humiliate you.'

'Could have fooled me.'

'You hurt me once, El. Badly. I guess on some level I wanted to make you feel as rotten as I did back then.' He grimaced. 'Not very enlightened of me.'

Ellie faced him. 'I wouldn't have asked you to help with Katie's case if I'd known you were still carrying a grudge, Coop. I thought after twenty years you would have moved past that.'

'But if I'd moved past that,' Coop reasoned, 'it would mean I'd moved past you.'

Ellie could feel the night closing in around her. Crazy, she thought, a pulse hammering at her throat. This is crazy. 'I noticed up insanity,' she blurted out.

Coop nodded, accepting the quick change of subject, and Ellie's need for it. 'Ah.'

'What does that mean?'

He stuffed the flashlight under his arm and tucked his hands in his pockets, striking off again as Ellie followed. 'You know what it means, because you've probably thought it through yourself. Katie's not insane. Then again, I suppose as her attorney you can tell the jury she's Queen Elizabeth, if that's bound to get her acquitted, and we all know she hasn't got a drop of royal blood in her, either.'

'What's harder to swallow, Coop: that a young, frightened girl snapped and smothered her baby without realizing what she was doing – or that a stranger came into the barn at two

in the morning, after a girl had given birth two months shy of
her due date, and murdered the baby while she was asleep?'

'Insanity defenses rarely win, El.'

'Neither does reasonable doubt, when it looks absolutely
unreasonable.' They had reached the pond, and Ellie sank down
onto the iron bench and drew up her knees. 'Even if she didn't
kill that baby, the best way to get her to walk is to convince the
jury that she did, without cognitively knowing what she was
doing. It's the most sympathetic defense I've got.'

'Hell, lawyers lie all the time,' Coop said.

She snorted. 'You don't have to tell me. I've done it. . . God,
I can't even count by now.'

'You're damn good at it, too.'

'Yeah,' Ellie said. 'That I am.'

Coop reached for her hand. 'Then how come it's eating you
up inside?'

She let the façade drop, the one she'd been holding in place
since explaining to Katie that they were going to use the insanity
defense to get her off, even though she wasn't insane.

'You want me to tell you why it's killing you?' Coop said
easily. 'Because pleading insanity means Katie did it, even if
she was cognitively off on Mars. And deep down, you just like
Katie too much to want to admit that.'

Ellie sniffed. 'You're way off base. You know what a client
relationship is like – personal feelings don't enter into it. I've
managed to keep a straight face while I told a jury that a child
molester was a pillar of the community. I've made a serial
rapist look like a choirboy. It's what I *do*. What I personally
feel about my clients has nothing to do with what I say to
defend them.'

'You're absolutely right.'

That stopped Ellie flat. 'I am?'

'Yeah. The issue here is that a long time ago, Katie stopped
being a client. Maybe from the very start, even. She's related
to you, however distantly. She's likable, young, confused – and
you've fallen into the role of surrogate mother. But your feel-

ings for her are a mystery, because for all intents and purposes she discarded something you'd kill to have – a child.'

Ellie squared her shoulders, ready to laugh this observation off, but found that no smart comment sprang to her lips. 'Am I so easy to read?'

'No need,' Coop murmured. 'I already know you by heart.'

'So how do I fix it? If I don't separate my personal relationship with her from my professional one, I'm never going to win her case.'

Coop smiled. 'When are you going to learn that there are all kinds of ways to win?'

'What do you mean?' she asked, wary.

'Sometimes when you think you've lost, you actually wind up coming out far ahead.' He grasped her chin in his hand, and kissed her lightly. 'Just look at me.'

Ellie did. She saw the remarkable Caribbean green of his eyes, but more importantly, the history in them. She saw the little scar beneath his jaw that he'd gotten in a bicycle fall at age six. And the crease in his cheek that would cave into a dimple at the slightest hint of a smile.

'I'm sorry for what I said to you the other night,' Coop said. 'And I think I'll even cover my ass by apologizing for what I just told you now, too.'

'I probably needed to hear it. And every now and then, to be slapped up the side of the head, most likely.'

'I should warn you now, I'm not that kind of man.'

She leaned toward him. 'I know.'

Their kisses were frantic and close, as if they were intent on getting inside each other's skin. Coop's hands roamed over her back and her breasts. 'God, I've missed you,' he breathed.

'It's only been five days.'

Coop stopped abruptly, then touched her face. 'It's been forever,' he said.

With her eyes closed, she believed him. She could imagine the music of the Grateful Dead crackling across the courtyard, wafting through the open window of her dorm room, where she and Coop lay tangled on the narrow bed. She could still see the curtain of beads that hung in the doorway of the closet, a crystalline rainbow, and the beady eyes of the squirrel who perched on the windowsill, watching them.

She felt him peel off her shirt and unsnap her shorts. 'Coop,' she said, suddenly nervous. 'I'm not twenty anymore.'

'Damn.' He continued to push her shorts down. 'I guess that means I'm not, either.'

'No, really.' She took his hand from the waistband of her shorts and brought it to her mouth. 'I don't look like I used to look.'

He nodded sympathetically. 'It's that scar, isn't it – the one from your pacemaker surgery?'

'I didn't have pacemaker surgery.'

'Then what are you worried about?' He kissed her lightly. 'El, if you weighed two hundred pounds and had grown hair on your chest, I wouldn't care. When I look at you, no matter what I should be seeing, I'm picturing a girl who's still in college – because the minute I fell in love with you, time stopped.'

'I don't weigh two hundred pounds.'

'Not an ounce over one-eighty,' Coop agreed, and she hit him on the arm. 'Are you gonna keep distracting me, or are you going to let me make love to you?'

Ellie smiled. 'I don't know. Let me think on it.'

Grinning, he kissed her. Her arms twined around his neck, and she pulled him closer. 'You know,' he said, the words hot against her skin, 'you weren't twenty when I undressed you the other night, either.'

'No, but I was drunk.'

Coop laughed. 'Maybe I ought to try that. Because this damn bench is hard enough to make me feel every single one of my thirty-nine decrepit years.' In a quick move, he pulled her off the seat, rolling so that he'd bear the brunt of the fall as they went down on the grass.

Ellie landed on top of him, her legs sprawled, her face an inch from Coop's. 'Are you gonna keep distracting me,' she murmured, 'or are you going to let me make love to you?'

Coop's arms tightened on the small of her back. 'I thought you'd never ask,' he said, and touched his lips to hers.

Katie was sitting at the table, nursing a glass of fresh milk from the ubiquitous pitcher in the refrigerator, when Ellie crept into the house like a teenager. Seeing the light, she poked her head into the kitchen. 'Oh,' she said, surprised to find Katie there. 'Why are you up?'

'Couldn't sleep,' Katie said. 'How about you?' But she knew, from the moment she'd seen Ellie, where she had been and what she'd been doing. The grass in her hair; the color in her cheeks. She smelled of sex.

For a moment Katie was so jealous she felt it rise inside her like a tide, and she couldn't take her eyes off Ellie because all she wanted was to feel what Ellie was feeling now. It was marked on her, as sure as if his touch still glowed fluorescent on her skin.

'I went for a walk,' Ellie said slowly.

'And you fell.'

'No . . . why?'

Katie shrugged. 'How else would you have gotten leaves in your hair?'

Self-conscious, Ellie reached up. 'What are you,' she said with a smile, 'my mother?'

Katie thought of Ellie, being touched and held and kissed. She thought of Adam, and instead of the soft swelling she usually felt in her lower stomach there was just a bitter ball. 'No. And you're not my mother, either.'

Ellie stiffened. 'That's true.'

'You think you are. You want me to crawl up on your lap and cry my heart out so you can make it all better. But you know what, Ellie? Mothers don't have the power to make it all better, no matter what you think.'

Stung, Ellie narrowed her eyes. 'This coming from a true expert on motherhood.'

'I know more than you,' Katie shot back.

'The difference between you and me,' Ellie said evenly, 'is that I would give anything to have a baby, and you couldn't wait to get rid of one.'

Katie's eyes widened, as if Ellie had slapped her. Then, in a lightning change, they filled with tears that she wiped away with the backs of her hands. 'Oh, God,' she said, keening, her arms crossed over her middle. 'Oh, God, you're right.'

Ellie stared at her. 'Did you kill the baby, Katie?'

She shook her head. 'I fell asleep. I fell asleep, I swear to you and to God, holding it.' Her face contorted with pain. 'But I might as well have killed it, Ellie. I *wished* it away. I wished for months and months that it would just disappear.'

She was doubled over now, sobbing so hard that she could not catch her breath. Ellie swore softly and embraced Katie tightly. 'That's just wishing,' she soothed, stroking the bright fall of the girl's hair. 'Wishing doesn't make it happen.'

Katie pressed her burning cheek against Ellie's chest. 'You're not my mother . . . but sometimes I wish you were.' She felt what she expected to: Ellie's arms closing around her with even greater force. Katie shut her eyes and imagined being held not by Ellie, but by Adam – her smile in his eyes, her name on his lips, her heart tight with the knowledge of being loved, no matter what.

10

Ellie

OCTOBER

After three months with the Fishers, I sometimes found it hard to believe that not so long ago, I thought a crimper had something to do with curling one's hair, and that being shocked referred to a person, rather than a bundle of wheat. Preparations for Katie's trial fell, unfortunately, in the middle of harvesting season, and any hopes I harbored about getting support from her family in the creation of our insanity defense were quickly put to rest. In Aaron Fisher's mind, getting the tobacco in on time and the silos filled were the household priorities.

And like it or not, I was part of that household.

I walked along behind Katie in the rich tobacco field, three acres so lush that they might have been a rice paddy. 'This one,' she said, instructing me on which leaves were ready to pick.

'They all look the same to me,' I complained. 'They're all green. Aren't you supposed to wait until things start to go brown before you pick them?'

'Not tobacco. Look at the size, here.' She snapped a leaf off and set it gently in a basket.

'Think of all the lung cancer, right here in this field,' I murmured.

But it didn't bother Katie. 'It's a cash crop,' she said simply. 'With dairy farming, it's hard to turn a profit.'

I bent down, ready to snap off my first leaf. 'No!' Katie cried. 'That's too small.' She held up another, larger leaf.

'Maybe I should just jump ahead to the next step. Stuffing

it into pipes, or sticking the surgeon general's warning on the box.'

Katie rolled her eyes. 'The next step is to hang it, and if you can't figure out the picking, I'm not going to let you get close to a five-foot-long sharpened stick.'

I laughed and bent to the plants again. As much as I hated to admit it, I was in better shape than I'd ever been in my life. My work as an attorney had always exercised my mind, but not my body; by default, living with the Fishers, I was stretching the limits of both. The Amish believed that hard physical labor was a basic tenet of living, and almost never employed outsiders as farmhands because they couldn't live up to the standard workday. Although Aaron had never said as much to me, I knew he was expecting me to break down in a citified, sobbing puddle, or sneak from the fields for a glass of lemonade before harvest was finished – things that would point to the obvious fact I wasn't one of them. All of which made me even more determined to do my share, if only to prove him wrong. To that end, I'd spent a week in early August standing bundles of wheat on end as the cutter spit them out, until my back was knotted and my skin was covered with chaff. I'd matched the rest of the family in that field, minute for minute. In my mind was the thought that if I earned Aaron's respect on familiar, fertile ground, I might earn his respect on my own turf.

'Ellie, are you coming or not?'

Katie stood with her hands on her hips, her full basket planted between her feet. I'd been picking leaves as my mind wandered too, because my own basket was nearly filled. God only knew if the tobacco I'd chosen was ready for harvest – I took some of the bigger leaves and stuck them on top, so Katie wouldn't notice. Then I followed her to the long shed that had been empty the few months I'd been living on the farm.

There were large gaps in the slatted walls of the shed, so that the air traveled through in a light breeze. I sat down on a hay bale beside Katie and watched her pick up a skewer as tall as she was. 'You poke the leaves through the stem,' she instructed. 'Like cranberries on string, for your Christmas trees.'

Now, *this* I could do. Balancing my own stick against the hay bale, I began to line the leaves up a few inches apart, so that they'd be able to dry. I knew that by the time we were finished, the small field of tobacco would be bare, all the leaves hanging on poles stacked to the rafters of this shed. In the winter, when I was long gone, the family would strip the tobacco and sell it down South.

Would Katie be here to help?

'Maybe when we're done with this, we could talk about the trial.'

'Why?' Katie said, her attention focused on piercing the stems of her leaves. 'You're going to say what you want to, anyway.'

I let the comment roll off my back. In the months since Katie had been interviewed by the forensic psychiatrists, I had marched along with my insanity defense, although I knew it upset her. In her mind, she hadn't killed that baby, so an inability to recall the murder had nothing to do with insanity. Every time I asked her for her assistance – with lines of questioning, with the sequence of events of that horrible night – she turned away. Her skittishness about the defense had turned her into a wild card, which made me even more grateful I hadn't decided to go with reasonable doubt. For an insanity defense, Katie would never have to take the stand.

'Katie,' I said patiently. 'I've been in a lot more courts than you have. You're going to have to believe me.'

She stabbed a leaf onto the end of the stick. 'You don't believe me.'

But how could I? Her story, since the beginning of this farce, had changed several times. Either I could make the jury think that was due to dissociation, or they would simply assume she'd been lying. Intentionally, I speared a leaf through the midpoint, instead of the stem. 'No,' Katie said, reaching for it. 'You're doing it wrong. Watch.'

With relief, I settled down into letting her be the expert.

With any luck, even without help from Katie I would have
enough testimony from Dr Polacci to get her acquitted. We
worked side by side in silence, the dust motes rising in the glow
that filtered through the shed's walls. When our baskets were
almost empty, I looked up. 'You want to pick some more?'

'Only if you want to,' Katie answered, deferring – as the
Amish always did – to someone else's opinion.

The door to the shed flew open, the sun backlighting a tall
man in a suit. It had to be Coop; although he usually dressed
casually when he visited Katie, occasionally he drove straight
from the office – and at any rate, he was the only male I could
think of who'd be wearing anything other than suspendered
trousers. I stood, a smile on my face as he walked inside.

'You,' Stephen said, grinning, 'are one tough woman to
find.'

For a moment I could not move. Then I set down the stick
and managed to find my voice. 'What are you doing here?'

He laughed. 'Well, that's not quite the hello I was thinking
of during the drive, but I can see you're meeting with a client.'
Stephen offered his hand to Katie. 'Hi there,' he said. 'Stephen
Chatham.' Glancing around the shed, he stuffed his hands in
his pockets. 'Is this some kind of occupational therapy?'

I could barely grasp the fact that Stephen was here. 'It's a
cash crop,' I said finally.

All the while, Katie was darting glances at me, wisely
remaining silent. I could not look at Stephen without imagining Coop standing beside him. Stephen didn't have Coop's
pale green eyes. Stephen looked too polished. Stephen's smile
seemed practiced, instead of a flag unfurled.

'You know, I'm actually quite busy,' I hedged.

'The only case I see you actively working on involves ten-
packs of Marlboro Lights. Which is why you ought to thank
me. I'm guessing that access to law libraries in Amish country
is limited at best, so I took the liberty of pulling some verdicts
for you to look over.' He reached into a portfolio and extracted
a thick sheaf of papers. 'Three neonaticides that walked under

Pennsylvania law. One of which, believe it or not, was an insanity defense.'

'How did you know I noticed up insanity?'

Stephen shrugged. 'This case is generating a lot of buzz, Ellie. Word gets around.'

I was about to respond when Katie suddenly pushed between us, running from the shed without a backward glance.

Sarah invited Stephen to dinner, but he didn't want to accept the invitation. 'Let me take you out,' he suggested. 'We can go to one of those homey Amish places in town, if you want.'

As if, leaving this household, the first thing I'd want to do is eat the same thing all over again. 'They're not Amish,' I said, just to be fractious. 'Anyone who's truly Plain wouldn't advertise their religion on the sign.'

'Well, then, there's always McDonald's.'

I glanced into the kitchen, where Sarah and Katie were hard at work preparing dinner – a chore that I'd be helping with, had Stephen not arrived. Sarah peered over her shoulder at us, caught my eye, and turned away quickly in embarrassment.

Folding my arms across my chest, I said, 'How come you can't eat here?'

'I just thought that you'd—'

'Well, you thought wrong, Stephen. I'd actually prefer to have dinner with the Fishers.' I could not say why, but it was important to me that Sarah and Katie know I'd rather be with them than Stephen. That they understand I wasn't pining to get away as quickly as possible.

Somehow, over the past few months, these people had become my friends.

Stephen held up his hands, crying peace. 'Whatever you want, Ellie. Dinner with Ma and Pa Kettle will be just fine.'

'Oh, for God's sake, Stephen. Maybe they dress differently and pray more often than you do, but that doesn't mean that they can't hear you being an idiot.'

Stephen sobered quickly. 'I didn't mean to offend anyone.

I only figured after – what, four months here? You might be anxious for a little intellectual banter.' He took my hand, tugging me out of the range of the doorway, so that Sarah and Katie couldn't see us. 'I've missed you,' he said. 'Truth is, I wanted you all to myself.'

I saw him coming closer to kiss me and froze – a deer in the headlights, unable to stop what was about to happen. Stephen's mouth was warm on mine, his hands crossing the map of my back, but my mind was running. After eight years, how could being in Stephen's arms feel less comfortable than being in Coop's?

With a small, tight smile, I flattened my hands against Stephen's chest. 'Not now,' I whispered. 'Why don't you walk around the farm while I help with supper?'

An hour later, when the family gathered at the table, all my doubts about Stephen were laid to rest. He bowed his head solemnly at the silent prayer; he used his charm on Sarah until she couldn't pass him a serving dish without blushing the color of a plum; he talked about silage as if the subject interested him even more than the law. I should have known that this would be fine: the Fishers were generous and friendly; Stephen was a consummate actor. By the time Sarah served the main course – a pot roast, chicken pie, and turkey stroganoff – I had relaxed enough to take my first bite of food.

Katie was telling a hilarious story about the time the cows got out of the barn in the middle of a snowstorm when there was a knock at the door. Elam went to open it, but before the older man could get there, the visitor let himself in. 'Hey,' Coop said, shrugging out of his coat. 'Am I too late for dessert?'

Like me, he'd become an adopted member of the Fisher family. After the first month, even Aaron stopped objecting with mutinous silence when Sarah graciously offered him dinner on the days he met with Katie or visited me. His eyes lit on mine and warmed – that was all the contact we allowed each other, in front of others. Then he saw Stephen sitting next to me.

Stephen was already getting to his feet, one hand on my shoulder and the other extended. 'Stephen Chatham,' he said, smiling quizzically. 'Have we met?'

'John Cooper. And yes, I think we have,' Coop said, so smoothly I could have kissed him right then and there. 'At the opera.'

'Symphony,' I murmured.

Both men looked at me.

'Coop's taken Katie on as a patient,' I explained.

'Coop,' Stephen repeated slowly, and I saw him making the synaptic connections: the abbreviated nickname, the snapshots jammed into the back of my college yearbook, the conversations we'd had under a blanket of darkness about our past lovers, when we were still safe and secure in each other's arms. 'That's right. You knew Ellie from Penn.'

Coop looked at me reluctantly, as if he didn't trust himself to control whatever emotions might play across his face. 'Yeah. It's been a while.'

I had never been more thankful for the Amish belief that intimate relationships were matters only for the interest of the two people involved. Katie was meticulously cutting the meat on her plate; Sarah found something to attend to in the kitchen; the other men began to discuss when they were planning to fill the silos. Drawing a deep breath, I sat down. 'Well,' I said, my voice high and bright. 'Who's hungry?'

Outside, a light wind whistled through the trees, playing them like pipes. Stephen and I walked beneath the overturned bowl of the sky, close enough to feel each other's body heat without actually touching. 'The whole case is riding on the forensic psychiatrist,' I told him. 'If the jury doesn't buy her, Katie's screwed.'

'Then let's hope the jury buys her,' Stephen said gallantly, when I knew he was thinking that we didn't have a prayer.

'Maybe it won't come to that. Maybe I'll get a mistrial.'

Stephen pulled the lapels of his coat up. 'How's that?'

'I motioned for one on the grounds that Katie won't be tried by a jury of her peers.'

He smiled slyly. 'Meaning there won't be a single Amish body among the twelve?'

'Yup.'

'I thought participation in the legal system was against their religion?'

'It might as well be. Like I said: she won't be tried by a jury of her peers.'

Stephen burst out laughing. 'God, El. You're never gonna win it, but it's one hell of an appealable issue. This backwater judge isn't going to know what hit her.' He stepped in front of me in one smooth maneuver, so that I walked into his open arms. 'You are something else,' he murmured against my ear.

Maybe it was the way I lighted in his embrace, or the millisecond it took my body to relax against his – something made Stephen draw back. He spread his hand against my cheek, curving his thumb along my jaw. 'So,' he said softly. 'It's like that?'

For a moment, I hesitated, spinning a web in my mind that I could use to catch him as he fell, the same way I'd lied to Coop when I broke up with him years ago. I had always believed that some lies could do more good than harm, and therein lay the justification: *I'm not good enough for you; I'm too busy to concentrate on a relationship right now; I just need some time to myself.*

Then I thought of Katie, kneeling in front of her congregation and telling them what they wanted to hear.

I covered his hand with my own. 'Yeah. It's like that.'

He pulled our linked fingers down between us, swinging like a pendulum. Stephen, who had always looked so sure of himself, suddenly seemed hollow and fragile, like the husks of maple seeds that helicoptered down from the trees.

He lifted my hand so that my fingers opened like a rose. 'Does he love you?'

'He does,' I said, swallowing, slipping my hand into my pocket.

'Do you love him?'

I didn't respond right away. I turned my head, so that I could see the yellow rectangle of light that was the kitchen window, and the silhouettes of Sarah and Coop bent over the double sink. Coop had volunteered to clear the table with her, so that Stephen and I could take a walk on our own. I wondered if he was thinking of me; if he had any doubt about what I was saying.

Stephen was smiling faintly when I looked at him again. He held a finger to my lips. 'Asked and answered,' he said; then gently kissed my cheek and walked off toward his car.

I wandered for a while by myself, down the stream and toward the pond, where I sat on the small bench. This break from Stephen was what I had wanted when I left Philadelphia, yet that didn't stop me from feeling like I had been sucker-punched. I drew up my knees and watched the moon scrawl calligraphy on the surface of the water, listened to the creaks and trills of the earth going still for the night.

When he came, all he did was hold out his hand. Without a word I stood, went into Coop's arms, and held on tight.

Sarah leaned against her shovel and raised her face to the sky. 'Every time we fill the silos,' she mused, 'that's how I know the weather's going to turn.'

I wiped the sweat off my brow for what must have been the hundredth time that day. 'Maybe if we concentrate it will turn in the next five minutes.'

Katie laughed. 'Last year when we filled the silos it was eighty degrees. Indian summer.'

Sarah shaded her eyes, squinting into the fields. 'Oh, they're coming!'

The sight took my breath away. Aaron and Samuel were driving the team of mules, which pulled a gasoline-powered corn binder. The contraption was over six feet tall, with knives in the front for cutting down the field corn, and a mechanism that bundled it into sheaves. Beside it, Levi drove another team that pulled a wagon. Coop stood in the back, tossing the tall bundles of corn that came off the binder into the flatbed.

Coop grinned and waved when he saw me. He was wearing jeans, a polo shirt, and one of Aaron's broad-brimmed hats to keep the sun off his face. He was so proud you'd think he'd cut every stalk himself.

'Look at you,' Katie said, nudging against me. 'You've gone all *ferhoodled*.'

I hadn't a clue what it meant, but it certainly sounded the way I felt. I smiled back at Coop and waited for him to jump down from the wagon. Levi, with all the self-importance of a preteen, swaggered toward the conveyor belt beneath the silo and hooked it up so that the gas engine could run the belt and the chopping machine and the big fan that blew the corn up a chute to the silo.

Sarah climbed into the wagon bed to toss down the first sheaf of corn; then I followed. Bits of husk and stalk stuck to my cheeks and the back of my neck. The chopped corn was damp and sweet, with a tang to it that reminded me of alcohol. Then again, the silage fed to the herd all winter was just a step away from fermented corn mash. Maybe that's why cows always looked so placid – they spent the winter drunk.

As Aaron tended to the horses and Coop and Levi hauled corn over the lip of the wagon, Samuel jumped down. With great curiosity I watched him approach Katie. It had to be uncomfortable for her, seeing him day in and day out on the farm when their relationship had taken such a turn for the worse – but recently, Katie had grown even more upset. Every time Samuel came within ten feet of her, she did her best to escape. I'd chalked it up to her nervousness about the impending trial, until Sarah casually mentioned that November was the month for weddings; soon enough, the couples who intended to get married would be published in church.

If things had gone slightly different, Katie and Samuel would have been one of them.

'Here,' Samuel said. 'Let me.' He rested his hand on Katie's shoulder and took the tall bundle of corn from her hands. With sure, strong motions, he set the heavy stack on the conveyor belt while Katie stood back and watched.

'Samuel!' At Aaron's shout, Samuel gave an apologetic grin and relinquished his position to Katie again.

She immediately reached up for another sheaf of corn. The bristling stalks groaned to the top of the belt. The mules, unhitched now, stamped and shuffled. And although she did not say a word, as Sarah worked with her daughter, she was smiling.

Teresa Polacci was coming to go over the testimony for her direct examination on a day when heavy gray clouds had been rolling across the sky for hours, threatening a downpour. In the milk room, where I sat in front of my computer, the wind pressed up against the windows and screamed beneath the cracks of the doors.

'So after we discuss dissociation,' I mused aloud, 'we'll—' I broke off as a kitten began to use my leg as a clawing post. 'Hey, Katie, do you mind?'

On her belly on the linoleum floor, with the rest of the litter of barn kittens crawling over her back and legs, Katie sighed. She got to her hands and knees, knocking off all but one cat, which rode on her shoulder, and pulled the kitten off my jeans.

'All right. So we go through the basic profile of a woman who commits neonaticide, talk about dissociation, and then walk through your interview with Dr Polacci.'

Katie turned. 'Will I have to sit there and listen to you say all these things?'

'You mean in the courtroom? Yeah. You're the defendant.'

'Then why don't you just let me do it?'

'Get on the stand, you mean? Because the prosecutor would rip you to pieces. If Dr Polacci tells your story, the jury is more likely to find you sympathetic.'

Katie blinked. 'What's so unsympathetic about falling asleep?'

'First off, if you stand up there and say that you fell asleep and didn't kill the baby, it goes against our defense. Second, your story is harder for the jury to believe.'

'But it's the truth.'

The psychiatrist had warned me about this – that Katie might be mulishly set on her amnesic explanation of events for some time yet. 'Well, Dr Polacci's testified in dozens of cases like this one. If you got on the stand, it would be the first time. Don't you feel a little safer going with an expert?'

Katie rolled one of the kittens into a ball in the palm of her hand. 'How many cases have you done, Ellie?'

'Hundreds.'

'Do you always win?'

I frowned. 'Not always,' I admitted. 'Most of the time.'

'You want to win this one, don't you?'

'Of course. That's why I'm using this defense. And you should go along with it because you want to win, too.'

. Katie held her hand high so that one of the kittens leaped over it. Then she looked right at me. 'But if you win,' she said, 'I still lose.'

The smell of sawdust carried on the air and the high whine of hydraulic-powered saws sliced through the sky as nearly sixty Amishmen puzzled together the wooden skeleton of a huge barn wall. All shapes and sizes and ages, the men wore carpenter's pouches around their waists, stuffed with nails and a hammer. Young boys, let out early from school for the event, scrambled around in an effort to be useful.

I stood on the hill with the other women, my arms crossed as I watched the magic of a barn raising. The four walls lay flat on the ground, assembled two-dimensionally at first. A handful of men stationed themselves along what would be the western wall, taking positions a few feet apart from each other. The man whose barn this would be, Martin Zook, took a spot a distance apart. On a count given by him in the Dialect, the others picked up the frame of the wall and began to walk it upright. Martin came up behind them, holding the wall in place with a long stick, while Aaron took up a stick to secure the far side. Ten more men swarmed to the base of the wall, hammering it into place in a volley of staccato pounding. One man began to walk along the cement foundation, setting nails with a single swipe of his hammer at intervals along the wood base that joined it, while a pair of eager schoolboys trailed him, using three or four sharp blows to drive the nails home.

Mixed with the sweet, raw scent of new construction was the heavier tang of the men's sweat as they hoisted the other walls into place, secured them, and climbed the wooden rigging like monkeys to fasten the boards of the roof. I thought of the workers who'd put a new roof on our house when I was sixteen and in awe of men's chests: parading on the black tar paper, their feet canted at an angle, their heads wrapped in bandannas and their torsos bare, their boomboxes beating. These men seemed to be working twice as hard as that long-ago crew; yet not a single one had given into the heat past rolling up the sleeves of their pale shirts.

'Fine day for this,' Sarah said behind my back to another woman, as they set out dishes on the long picnic tables.

'Not too hot, not too cold,' the woman agreed. She was Martin Zook's wife, and I had been introduced to her, but I couldn't remember her name. She bustled past Sarah and laid a platter of fried chicken on the table. Then she cupped her hands around her mouth and yelled, *'Komm esse!'*

Almost in unison, everyone laid down his hammer and nails and untied his canvas waist pouch. The boys, who still had energy, ran ahead to an old washtub set outside the kitchen, filled with water. A bar of Ivory soap bobbed on its surface. Huddled shoulder to shoulder, the boys slipped the soap from one fist to another with squelching fart noises and lots of grinning. They patted their forearms dry with light blue towels, giving up their spots at the washtub to the red-faced, sweating men.

Martin Zook sat down, his sons on his right and his left. Men fell into empty spots at the table. Martin lowered his head, and for a moment the only sound was the creak of the benches beneath the men and the measured beat of their breathing. Then Martin looked up and reached for the chicken.

I would have expected boisterous conversation – at the very least, discussion of how much longer it would take to finish the barn. But hardly anyone spoke. Men shoveled food into their mouths, too hungry for niceties.

'Save room, now,' Martin's wife said, leaning over the table with a refilled platter of chicken. 'Sarah made her squash pie.'

When Samuel spoke, it was all the more arresting because of the lack of chatter at the table. 'Katie,' he said, surprising her so that she jumped, 'is this your potato salad?'

'Why, you know it is,' Sarah answered. 'Katie's the only one who puts in tomatoes.'

Samuel took another helping. 'Good thing, since that's how I've grown to like it.'

The others at the table continued to devour their lunch, as if they had not been witness to the furious blush that rose on Katie's face, or Samuel's slow smile, or this uncharacteristically public championing. And a few minutes later when the men rose, leaving us behind to clean up, Katie was still staring off in the direction of the barn.

The Tupperware had been cleaned and returned to the women who'd brought the food. Nails had been gathered up in brown paper bags, and hammers tucked beneath the bench seats of buggies. The barn stood proud and raw and yellow, a new silhouette carved into a sky as purple as a bruise.

'Ellie?'

I turned, surprised by the voice. 'Samuel.'

He was holding his hat in his hands, running it around and

around by the brim like an exercise wheel. 'I thought you maybe would like to see the inside.'

'Of the barn?' In all the hours we'd been at the barn raising, I hadn't seen a single woman stray toward the construction site. 'I'd love to.'

I walked beside him, unsure of what to say. The last true private conversation we'd had had ended with Samuel sobbing over Katie's pregnancy. In the end, I took the Amish way out – I did not say anything, but instead moved companionably alongside him.

The barn seemed even larger from the inside than from the outside. Thick beams crossed over my head, fragrant pine that would be here for decades. The high gambrel roof arched like a pale, artificial sky; and when I touched the posts that supported the animal stalls, a confetti of sawdust rained down on me.

'This is really something,' I said. 'To build a whole barn in a single day.'

'It only looks like such a big thing when it's one man by himself.'

Not much different from my own philosophy to my clients – although having an ardent attorney by your side to help you out of a bind paled in comparison to having fifty friends and relatives ready in an instant.

'I need to talk to you,' Samuel said, clearly uncomfortable.

I smiled at him. 'Talk away.'

He frowned, puzzling out my English, and then shook his head. 'Katie . . . she's doing all right?'

'Yes. And that was a nice thing you did for her, today at lunch.'

Samuel shrugged. 'It was nothing.' He turned, gnawing at his thumbnail. 'I've been thinking about this court.'

'You mean the trial?'

'*Ja*. The trial. And the more I think about it, it's not so different from anything else. Martin Zook didn't have to look up at that pile of lumber all by himself.'

If this was some roundabout Amish reasoning, I was missing the mark. 'Samuel, I'm not quite sure—'

'I want to help,' he interrupted. 'I want to work with Katie in the court so she don't have to be all alone.'

Samuel's face was dark and set; he had given this much thought. 'Building a barn isn't forbidden by the *Ordnung*,' I said gently. 'But I don't know how the bishop will feel if you willingly take the role of character witness in a murder trial.'

'I will speak to Bishop Ephram,' Samuel said.

'And if he says no?'

Samuel tightened his mouth. 'An English judge won't care about the *Meidung*.'

No, a superior court judge wouldn't give a damn if a witness was being shunned by his religious community. But Samuel might. And Katie.

I looked over his shoulder at the sturdy walls, the right angles, the roof that would keep out the rain. 'We'll see,' I answered.

'Now what?'

Katie snipped off a thread between her teeth and looked up at me. 'Now you're done.'

My jaw dropped. 'You're kidding.'

'Nope.' Katie spread her hands over the small quilt, a log cabin pattern with hints of yellow, purples, deep blues, and a streak of rose. When I had first arrived at the Fishers, shamelessly unable to sew on a button, Sarah and Katie decided I was a worthy cause. With their help, I'd learned how to baste and pin and sew. Each night when the family gathered after dinner – to read the newspaper, or play backgammon or Yahtzee, or – like Elam – just doze off and snore, Katie and I would bend over the small frame of my quilt, and piece it together. And now it was finished.

Sarah lifted her face from her mending. 'Ellie's done?'

Beaming, I nodded. 'Want to see?'

Even Aaron put down the paper. 'Of course,' he joked.

'This is the biggest event since Omar Lapp sold his twenty acres to that real estate developer from Harrisburg.' He lowered his voice. 'And just about as unlikely.' But he was grinning, too, as Katie helped me unfasten the quilt from the frame and hold it up to my chest with pride.

I knew that if Katie had completed a quilt, she wouldn't show it off so, and it would have been far more worthy of praise. I knew that the stitches on her side of the quilt were neat and even as baby teeth, while mine scurried drunk across the marked pencil lines. 'Well, that's just fine, Ellie,' Sarah said.

Elam, in the La-Z-Boy, opened one eye. 'Won't even keep her feet warm in the winter.'

'It's supposed to be small,' I argued, then turned to Katie. 'Isn't it?'

'*Ja.* It's like a baby quilt. For all those children still to come,' she said with a smile.

I rolled my eyes. 'Don't go holding your breath.'

'Most Plain women your age are only half done with having their children.'

'Most Plain women my age have been married for twenty years,' I pointed out.

'Katie,' Sarah warned, 'leave Ellie be.'

I folded my quilt as carefully as a fallen soldier's flag and hugged it. 'See? Even your mother agrees with me.'

A terrible silence fell over the room, and almost immediately I realized my mistake. Sarah Fisher didn't agree with me – at forty-three, she'd have given her right arm to be still bearing children, but the decision had been taken out of her hands.

I turned to her. 'I'm sorry. That was very tactless of me.'

Sarah was still for a moment, then she shrugged and took the quilt. 'You'd like me to iron this for you?' she asked, hurrying from the room before I could tell her that I'd rather she sit down and relax.

I looked around, but Katie and Aaron and Elam were back

in their seats, quietly occupied, as if I had never spoken thought-
lessly at all.

In the next instant there was a knock at the door, and I rose
to answer it. I could tell from the look that crossed between
Aaron and Elam that in their minds, a caller arriving this late
on a weeknight was a sure messenger of trouble. My hand had
just reached the knob when the door swung open, pushed from
the outside. Jacob Fisher stood there. He met my stunned gaze
first, a wry and nervous smile playing over his lips. 'Hey-Mom-
I'm-home,' he said breezily, a parody of TV sitcoms that only
the two of us would even understand. 'What's for supper?'

Sarah came running first, drawn by the sound of a son she
had not seen in years. Her hand clapped over her mouth, her
eyes smiling through tears, she was a yard away from Jacob
when Aaron stopped her by simply slashing his arm through
the air and saying, 'No.'

He advanced on his son, and in deference Sarah melted
against the wall. 'You are no longer welcome here.'

'Why, Dat?' Jacob asked. 'It's not because the bishop said
so. And who are you to make a rule stronger than the *Ordnung*?'
He stepped further inside. 'I miss my family.'

Sarah gasped. 'You will come back to the church?'

'No, Mam, I can't. But I want badly to come back to my
home.'

Aaron stood toe to toe with his son, his throat working.
Then, without saying a word, he turned and walked out of the
room. A few seconds later a door slammed in the rear of the
house.

Elam patted Jacob on the shoulder, then moved slowly in
the direction his own son had gone. Sarah, tears running down
her face, held her hands out to her oldest child. 'Oh, I can't
believe this. I can't believe it's you.'

As I watched her, I understood why a mother would starve
herself to feed a baby; how there was always time and room
for a child to curl close to her side; how she could be soft

enough to serve as a pillow and strong enough to move heaven and earth. Sarah's fingers traced the slopes and planes of Jacob's face: beardless, older, different. 'My boy,' she whispered. 'My beautiful boy.'

In that moment, I could see the girl she had been at eighteen – slender and strong, shyly offering up this brand-new infant to her young husband. She squeezed Jacob's hands, wanting him all to herself, even when Katie leaped up like a puppy to get her own embrace. Jacob met my gaze over the women's heads. 'Ellie, it's good to see you again.'

Jacob had quickly agreed to serve as a character witness for Katie – the best I could do, since there was no way her mother or father was going to set foot on the witness stand. I had been working on his direct examination questions just that day. However, I'd planned to rehearse with him in State College, simply because I believed it was too difficult to sneak him close to the farm without raising Aaron's suspicions. But now it looked as if Jacob was playing by his own rules.

He let Sarah lead him into the kitchen for some hot chocolate – was that still his favorite? – and one of the muffins she'd made that morning. I noticed, and I'm sure Jacob did too, that when he settled down to eat, the baptized members of the family stood, overjoyed at the reconciliation but still unable to sit at a table with an excommunicated Amishman.

'Why did you come back?' Katie asked.

'It was time,' Jacob answered. 'Well, it was time for you and Mam to see me, anyway.'

Sarah looked away. 'Your father was wonderful mad when he found out Katie had been coming to visit you. We disobeyed him, and he's smarting.' She added, 'It's not that he doesn't want to see you, or that he doesn't love you. He's a fine man, hard on others – but hardest on himself. When you made the decision to leave the church, he didn't blame you.'

Jacob snorted. 'That's not how I remember it.'

'It's true. He blamed himself, for being your father and not bringing you up in a way that made you want to stay.'

'My book learning had nothing to do with him.'

'Maybe to you,' Sarah said. 'But not to your Dat.' She patted Jacob's shoulder and kept her hand there, as if she was loath to let him go. 'All these years, he has been punishing himself.'

'By banishing me?'

'By giving up the one thing he wanted more than anything else,' Sarah answered quietly. 'His son.'

Jacob stood abruptly and looked at Katie. 'You want to take a walk?'

She nodded, radiant to be singled out. They had nearly reached the back door when Sarah called to Jacob, 'You'll stay the night?'

He shook his head. 'I won't do that to you,' he said softly. 'But whether he likes it or not, Mam, I'll keep coming back.'

Sometimes when I was lying in my bed at the Fishers', I wondered if I would ever be able to adapt back to city living. What would it be like to fall asleep to the sound of buses chugging, instead of owls? To close my eyes in a room that never got completely dark, thanks to the neon signs and floodlamps on the streets? To work in a building so high off the ground that I could not smell the clover and the dandelions under my feet?

That night the moon rose yellow as a wolf's eye, blinking back at me in my bed, where I waited for Katie to return from her walk with Jacob. I had hoped to talk to him about his testimony a little bit, but he and Katie had disappeared and had not come back, not by the time Elam made his way back to the *grossdawdi haus*, nor when Aaron returned from a last check on the livestock and headed upstairs in silence, nor even when Sarah went from room to room, turning off gas lanterns for the night.

In fact, it was well after two in the morning when Katie finally slipped into the bedroom. 'I'm awake,' I announced. 'So don't worry about keeping quiet.'

Katie paused in the act of removing her apron, then nodded and continued. Keeping her back modestly turned, she slipped off her dress and hung it on one of the wooden pegs lining the walls, then pulled her nightgown over her head.

'It must have been nice, having Jacob all to yourself.'

'Ja,' Katie murmured, with none of the enthusiasm I would have expected.

Concerned, I came up on one elbow. 'You all right?'

She managed a smile. 'Tired, is all. We talked some about the trial, and it wore me out.' After a moment she added, 'I said you would be telling everyone I was crazy.'

Not quite the terminology I'd have used, but there you had it. 'What does Jacob think?'

'He said you were a good lawyer, and you knew what you were doing.'

'Bright boy. What else did he say?'

Katie shrugged. 'Stuff,' she said quietly. 'Stuff about himself.'

Leaning back again, I folded my arms beneath my head. 'I bet he threw your father for a loop tonight.'

When there was no response, I assumed Katie had fallen asleep. I jumped when she swung out of bed in a quick motion and yanked on the blinds. 'That moon,' she muttered. 'It's too light to get any rest.'

The blackout shades in the bedroom were hunter green, like every other blackout shade in the house. It was one of the ways you could tell an Amish place from an English one – the color of the shades, and the lack of electrical wires winnowing toward the house.

'How come the shades are green?' I asked, certain that there was an explanation for this, as for every other oddity of Amish life.

Katie's face was turned away from me, her voice coated thick. If not for the mundane question I'd asked, I would have thought she was crying. 'Because,' she said, 'that's the way it's always been.'

*   *   *

I had gotten into the habit of taking only coffee in the morning, certain that my exit from the Fishers' would coincide with an angioplasty if I didn't watch myself more closely. But the day of the final pretrial hearing, when I came down to the kitchen wearing my red knock-'em-dead power suit, Sarah handed me a platter of eggs and bacon, flapjacks, toast, and honey. She even pushed me to have seconds. She was feeding me like she fed Aaron and Samuel, men who worked long, hard hours in order to preserve her way of life.

After only a moment's thought to my triglycerides, I ate everything she stacked on my plate.

Katie was stationed at the sink while I ate, washing the bowls and pans used to cook. She was wearing her lavender dress and her best apron – her Sunday clothes – for the trip to the superior court. Although she would not be sitting in on the hearing, I wanted the judge to know that she was still firmly in my custody.

She turned to set a freshly washed mixing bowl on the counter, but it slipped out of her hand. 'Oh!' she cried, grasping for it, fumbling in a comedy of errors to keep it from shattering on the floor. With pure luck, she managed to catch it, and hugged it close to her middle – only to move too quickly and knock a pitcher off the counter with her elbow, sending pottery shards and orange juice across the kitchen floor.

One look at the mess, and Katie burst into tears. Sarah scolded her gently in Dietsch, while Katie knelt to pick up the biggest slivers of the broken pitcher. I set my napkin on the table and got down on the floor to help her. 'You're jittery.'

Katie rocked back on her heels. 'It's just . . . all of a sudden, Ellie, this is very real.'

Sarah reached between us, mopping up the orange juice with a dish towel. Over her strong back I met Katie's gaze and smiled. 'Trust me. I know what I'm doing.'

I knew it had rattled George Callahan to pass Katie, sitting serene and sweet on a bench just outside the judge's chambers. He kept peering beyond the court reporter who'd come for the private hearing into the open doorway, where Katie was visible. 'What's your client doing here?' he finally hissed at me.

I made a big show out of craning my neck and studying Katie. 'Praying, I think.'

'You know what I mean.'

'Oh, why did I bring her to court? Well, gosh, George. You should understand better than anyone. It's part of the bail contingency.'

Judge Ledbetter bustled in. 'Sorry I'm late,' she said, taking a seat behind her desk. She opened a file and scanned it. 'Might I just say, Ms Hathaway, how glad I am that you finally got around to noticing up your insanity defense?' She turned a page. 'Any motions either of you plan to submit?'

'I've filed a motion to dismiss, Your Honor,' I said.

'Yes, I know. Why?'

'Because my client is being denied a constitutional right – a fair trial among her peers. However, not a single Amishman or woman will be sitting on that jury. In our society – in our system – her peers do not exist.' I took a deep breath as the judge's eyes narrowed slightly. 'I would consider asking for a trial in front of a judge, or even asking for a change of venue, but neither applies here – either of those options would still compromise her right to fair trial. A typical jury that's a cross-section of America is not a cross-section of an Amish community, Your Honor. And if my client is not judged by people who understand her faith and her upbringing and, well, her world – then she's at a marked disadvantage.'

The judge turned to the district attorney. 'Mr Callahan?'

'Your Honor, the fact remains that Ms Fisher broke a law of the United States government. She is going to be tried in a United States court of law. It doesn't matter if she's Amish, Buddhist, or Zulu – she played with fire, and she is now required to deal with the consequences of her actions.'

'Oh, please. She's not an international terrorist who set off a bomb in the World Trade Center. She's an American citizen, which entitles her to objective treatment under the law.'

George turned, and said under his breath, 'American citizens pay taxes.'

'Excuse me, I don't think the court reporter quite got that,' the judge commented.

I smiled at her. 'The county attorney was just erroneously making assumptions about my client's fiscal responsibility. The Amish pay taxes, George. If they're self-employed, they don't pay Social Security, because they don't use Medicare or Medicaid or any of the other services it funds, since they believe in caring for their own elderly. If they're employed by someone else, they get Social Security taken out of their paychecks and never use a penny of it. The Amish don't pay gasoline taxes, but they pay real estate taxes, which support public schools they don't even use. They also don't take advantage of federal agriculture subsidies, welfare, and student loans.' Turning to the judge, I said, 'This is my point exactly, Judge Ledbetter. If the prosecutor in this case is already coming into court with preconceived misconceptions about the Amish, that prejudice will be multiplied by twelve on a traditional jury.'

The judge pinched the bridge of her nose. 'You know, Ms Hathaway, I've actually given this motion of yours a great deal of thought. It's extremely distressing for me to think that a United States citizen might, simply by religious affiliation, not be able to get a fair trial. What you said in your brief is absolutely valid.'

'Thank you, Your Honor.'

'Unfortunately for you and your client, what Mr Callahan just said in response is absolutely valid as well. We have a defendant on trial for murder here, not for stealing a pack of gum. It's irresponsible to dismiss a trial of such magnitude. And although I think we can all pretty much guarantee that not a single Amish person will sit on that jury, the truth is, Ms Hathaway, your client wouldn't get a jury of her peers no matter what court in America this case winds up in. At least in Lancaster she'll have the next best thing: twelve people who live and work in this community with the Amish on a daily basis. Twelve people who, one hopes, are slightly more knowledgeable about their Amish neighbors than the average cross-section of America.' She looked directly at me. 'I'm going to deny your motion to dismiss, Ms Hathaway, but I thank you for bringing up a provocative subject.' The judge flattened her hands on top of her desk. 'Now, if there's nothing else, I'd like to set the date for jury selection.'

'Three and a half weeks,' I said, letting the sheet float down over the bed in Elam's *grossdawdi haus*. 'That's when the trial starts.'

Sarah tucked in the linens across from me and exhaled with relief. 'I can't wait until it's over,' she said. Turning troubled eyes to Katie, she asked, 'Was it upsetting to be there?'

'Katie spent the hearing sitting on a bench outside the judge's office. At the trial, she'll be sitting beside me at the defense table. The prosecutor's never going to be able to get the chance to upset her, because she won't be on the witness stand. That was part of the reason we decided to use an insanity defense.'

Katie finished stuffing the final pillow into a fresh case. At that last sentence, she cried out, so softly that I was surprised both Sarah and I had heard it. 'Will you stop? Will you please just stop?' With an anguished groan, she turned on her heel and left.

Sarah picked up her skirts and began to hurry after Katie, but I stayed her with a hand on her arm. 'Please,' I said gently. 'Let me.'

At first I didn't see her, curled into a small knot in the rocking chair. I closed the door and sat down on my bed, then used a strategy I'd learned from Coop – I just shut up and waited. 'I can't do this,' she said, her face still buried against her knees. 'I can't live this way.'

Every nerve in my body snapped alert. As a defense attorney, I'd heard those words dozens of times – usually prefacing a gut-wrenching confession. At this point, even if Katie told me she'd murdered that infant in cold blood, I would still use the insanity defense to get her off – but I also knew I'd fight a lot harder for her if I could believe, for whatever reason, that she truly didn't know what she had been doing at the time. 'Katie,' I said. 'Don't tell me anything.'

That got her attention. 'After months of pushing me, you say that?'

'Tell Coop, if you have to. But I'm going to mount a much more compelling defense if we don't have the conversation you want to have.'

She shook her head. 'I can't let you get up there and lie about me.'

'It's not a lie, Katie. Even you don't know what happened, exactly. You told Coop and Dr Polacci there are things you can't remember.'

Katie leaned forward. 'I do remember.'

My pulse began to pound behind my temples. 'Your memory keeps changing, Katie. It's changed at least three times since I met you.'

'The father of the baby is a man named Adam Sinclair. He owned the apartment that Jacob rents in State College. He left before he ever found out. . . that I was having a baby.' Her words were soft, her face even softer. 'I blocked it all out, at first. And by the time I could admit what had happened, it was too late. So I kept pretending things were the way they had always been.

'I fell asleep after I had the baby in the barn. I was going to go inside and take him to my mother, Ellie, but my legs were too shaky to stand. I just wanted to rest a minute. And then the next thing I knew, I woke up.' She blinked at me. 'The baby was gone.'

'Why didn't you go to look for it?'

'I was so scared. More scared than I was about my parents finding out, because the whole time I was telling myself that this was the Lord's will, I think I knew what I was going to discover. And I didn't want to.'

I stared hard at her. 'You still could have killed that baby, Katie. You could have sleepwalked. You could have smothered him without knowing what you were doing.'

'No.' By now, she was crying again, her face red and blotchy. 'I couldn't have, Ellie. Once I saw that baby, I wanted him. I wanted him so much.' Her voice fell to a whisper. 'In my life, that baby was the best thing – and the worst thing – I'd ever done.'

'Was the baby alive when you fell asleep?'

She nodded.

'Then who killed it?' I stood up, angry. Eleventh-hour confessions were not the stuff of great defenses. 'It was two in the morning, it was two months before your due date, and no one knew you were pregnant. Who the hell else came in there and killed that baby?'

'I don't know,' Katie sobbed. 'I don't know, but it wasn't me, and you can't go into that trial and tell them I did.' She looked up at me. 'Don't you see what's happened since I started lying? My whole world has come apart, Ellie. A baby's died. Everything's gone wrong.' She fisted her hands and buried them in her apron. 'I want to make my things right.'

The very thought sent me reeling. 'We're not talking about a confession in front of a bunch of ministers, Katie. That may get you redemption in the Amish church, but in a court of law, it'll get you fifteen years to life.'

'I don't understand—'

'No, you don't. That's why you hired me, an attorney – to lead you through the court system. The only way you're going to be acquitted is if I get up there and use a good defense. And the best one we've got is insanity. No jury in the world is going to buy you on the witness stand, saying that you fell asleep and woke up and whaddaya know, the baby was missing. And so very conveniently dead, too.'

Katie set her jaw. 'But it's the truth.'

'The only place the truth is going to save you from a charge of first-degree murder is in a perfect world. A court is far from a perfect world. From the moment we walk in there, it's not about what really happened. It's about who has the best story to sell to the jury.'

'I don't care if it's a perfect world or not,' Katie said. 'It's not my world.'

'You tell the truth on the stand, and the only world you're going to know is the State Penitentiary.'

'If that's the Lord's will, then I'll accept it.'

Furious, I glared at her. 'You want to play martyr? Go ahead. But I'm not going to be sitting next to you while you commit legal suicide.'

For a while Katie was silent. Then she turned to me, eyes wide and clear. 'You have to, Ellie. Because I need you.' She sat beside me on the bed, so close that I could feel the heat from her body. 'I'm not going to fit into that English court-room. I'm going to stand out, with how I dress, and how I think, because I'm not English. I don't know about murder and witnesses and juries, but I do know how to fix things in my life when they're messed up. If you make a mistake and you repent, you're forgiven. You're welcomed back. If you lie, and keep lying, there won't be a place for you.'

'Your community looked the other way when it came to hiring me,' I said. 'They'll understand why you need to do this, too.'

'But *I* won't.' She folded her hands together, as if she were in prayer. 'Maybe these lies will get me free, like you say, and I won't have to go to the English jail. But Ellie, then where do I go? Because if I lie to save myself there, I won't be able to come back here.'

I closed my eyes and thought about the church service where Katie had gotten down to confess. I thought about the faces of the others sitting in that hot, cramped room as they passed judgment – not vindictive, not spiteful . . . but relieved, as if Katie's humility made them all a little bit stronger. I thought of the afternoon when we'd all worked to bring in the corn; how it had felt to be a part of something bigger than myself.

I thought of Sarah's face, when she laid eyes on Jacob for the first time in years.

What good was a personal victory to someone who'd spent her life losing herself for the greater good of everyone else?

Katie's hand, callused and small, slipped into my own. 'All right,' I sighed. 'Let's see what we can do.'

II

Do not let your left hand know
what your right hand is doing.
> – Matthew 6:3

11

Judge Philomena Ledbetter watched the attorney fumble her pen for the third time since she'd entered chambers. For a big-city legal eagle, Ellie Hathaway seemed as skittish as a lawyer knee-deep in her first litigation – all the more bizarre, given the fact that just yesterday, she'd been confident and competent. 'Counselor,' the judge said, 'you called us back for a discussion?'

'Yes, Your Honor. I felt there was a need for more argument before the trial. Certain . . . circumstances have come to light.'

Sitting on her right, George Callahan snorted. 'In the ten hours since we last met?'

Judge Ledbetter ignored his comment. She wasn't too thrilled herself to be called in on short notice and forced to juggle her schedule to make accommodations. 'Would you care to elaborate, Ms Hathaway?'

Ellie swallowed. 'I would not normally do this, I want to say that up front. And this is not my choice. Due to confidentiality I can't say everything, but my client believes – that is, I believe . . .' She cleared her throat. 'I need to withdraw my defense of guilty but mentally ill.'

'Excuse me?' George said.

Ellie straightened her spine. 'In its place, we're entering a plea of not guilty.'

Judge Ledbetter frowned. 'I'm sure you know that at this point—'

'Believe me, I know everything. I don't have a choice, Your Honor. In order to keep my ethical obligations to the court and to my client, I have to do this. I'm just trying to give you as much notice as I've had.'

Predictably, George exploded. 'You can't do this three and half weeks before the trial!'

'Why should it make any difference to you?' Ellie snapped. 'You were supposed to be trying to prove all along she wasn't insane – and now I'm telling you you're right. This isn't about me screwing up your prosecution, George; it's about me screwing up my own defense.' Taking a deep breath, she turned toward the judge. 'I'd like more time to prepare, Your Honor.'

The judge raised her brows. 'Wouldn't we all, Ms Hathaway,' she said dryly. 'Well, I'm sorry, but you're on the docket for three and half weeks from now, and this is your decision.'

With a terse nod, Ellie gathered her things and stormed out of chambers, leaving both the county attorney and the judge wondering what had just transpired.

Ellie hurried out of the judge's chambers and through the hallways of the superior court, then burst through the front doors of the building and stopped dead, staring at the bleak, bare arms of the trees and the overcast sky. She had absolutely no idea what to do next. Her mind was running a million places at once – damn good thing, since she had less than a month to mount a defense that was a 180-degree reversal of what she'd been planning.

She set down her briefcase so that it lolled against her ankle, and slowly sank to the courthouse steps. Then, squandering time she could ill afford, she wondered how she was going to manage to win when she was coming from so far behind.

It took Ellie a half hour to track down Jacob, who had spent the night in Lancaster – but not at his parents' home. Leda opened the door at Ellie's knock, a smile on her face, but Ellie shoved right past her, her gaze locked on the young man swilling milk from the carton in front of the open refrigerator. 'You little shit,' she growled.

Jacob started, spilling milk on the front of his flannel shirt. 'What?'

'You're supposed to be helping me, dammit. You're supposed to tell me anything you can that might help your sister's case.'

'I did!'

'Does the name Adam Sinclair fall into that category?'

Leda stepped forward to keep Ellie from jumping at Jacob again, but not before Ellie saw the flat dimming of the eyes that comes with being found out. He stayed his aunt, telling her it was all right, and then turned to Ellie. 'What about Adam?'

'He was your roommate?'

'And my landlord.'

Ellie crossed her arms. 'And the father of Katie's child.'

Jacob ignored Leda's gasp. 'I didn't know for sure, Ellie. I just suspected.'

'A suspicion would have been nice to know – oh, about three months ago. God, is anyone going to be straight with me before we get to trial?'

'I thought you were using an insanity defense,' Leda said.

'Talk to your niece about that.' Ellie turned to Jacob. 'All I know is, she goes out with you for two hours last night, comes home, and refuses to let me defend her the way I want to. What the hell did you say?'

Jacob closed his eyes. 'I wasn't talking about her,' he groaned. 'I was talking about me.'

Ellie could feel a headache coming on. 'Keep going.'

'I told Katie the reason I came back was the same reason I left in the first place – I couldn't live a lie. I couldn't let people pretend I was something I really wasn't. Six years ago, all I wanted was book learning, but I let people think I was happy being Plain. And now, I'm an associate professor, but what I miss more than anything is my family.' He looked up at Ellie, stricken. 'When Hannah drowned, I thought it was my fault. I should have been out there watching the two of them, but I was hiding in the barn, trying to read. I said to Katie that for the second time in my life, I was watching my sister go under – but this time the sister was her, and this time I was hiding what happened when she came to visit me.'

'Then you knew she got pregnant when—'

'I didn't know. I suspected as much, after talking to you and the prosecution's investigator.' He shook his head. 'I didn't mean for Katie to take me literally. I just wanted her to see it my way.'

'Well, you succeeded,' Ellie answered flatly. 'She's modeling herself after her honest brother now. She wants to confess on the witness stand, and pretend the jury's her congregation.'

'But I told her the insanity defense was a good one!'

'Apparently, that part of the conversation didn't leave quite as strong an impression.' Ellie steepled her hands in front of her. 'I need to know where to find Adam Sinclair.'

'I haven't been in touch with him – even my rent checks go to a property management agency. Sinclair's been out of the country since last October,' Jacob said. 'And he hasn't been in contact with Katie to even know about the pregnancy.'

'If you haven't been in touch with him, then how do you know he's still gone? Or that Katie hasn't been writing to him all this time?'

Without a word, Jacob got off the chair and walked upstairs. He returned a minute later holding a stack of letters, bound with a rubber band. 'They come to my place every two weeks, like clockwork,' he said. 'To Katie, care of me. The return address hasn't changed. The postmark's from Scotland. And I know Katie hasn't been writing to him because I never gave her a single one of these.'

Torn between professional curiosity and personal affront for Katie, Ellie bristled. 'This is a federal offense, you know.'

'Great. You can defend me after you're through with Katie.' Jacob pushed his hands through his hair and sat down again. 'I didn't do it to be a jerk. I was trying, actually, to be a hero. I just didn't want Katie to have to face what I did when I decided to go English – turning her back on our folks and finding her way in a place that's so big and unfamiliar it can keep you awake all night. I didn't know Katie was pregnant, but even I could see that she was attracted to Adam – she hung around him like a puppy – and I knew that if the feeling was fueled, eventually Katie was going to have to make a choice between two worlds. I thought that if there was a clean break when he left, she'd forget about him, and everything would work out for the best.'

'Does your sister know you have these letters?'

Jacob shook his head. 'I was going to tell her last night. But she was so upset already, about the trial coming up so fast, that it seemed like one extra heartache.' He grimaced, flexed his hands on the edge of the table. 'I suppose I should give them to her today.'

Ellie stared at the neat, block type that formed the letters of Katie's name. At the thin-skinned blue airmail stationery, folded and stamped and sealed. 'Not necessarily,' she said.

Technically, Ellie should have dragged Katie into Philadelphia with her, but at this point she'd managed to screw up the legal process so much that bending the requirements for Katie's bail couldn't possibly get her into any greater trouble. She didn't even know why she was driving toward Philly, actually, until she pulled into the parking lot of the medical complex where Coop's office was located.

The address was familiar, but Ellie had never been there before. She found herself standing in front of the directory, touching her finger to the brass plate stamped with Coop's name. In his office, when a pretty young secretary asked to help her, a stab of jealousy took Ellie's breath away. 'He's with a patient,' the woman said. 'Would you care to wait?'

'Please.' Ellie took a seat and began to leaf through a magazine that was six months old, without seeing a single page.

After a few minutes there was a buzz on the secretary's intercom, a muted conversation, and then Coop opened the door to the inner sanctum. 'Hi,' he said, his eyes dancing. 'I hear this is an emergency.'

'It is,' Ellie replied, feeling better than she had since Katie had turned the world upside down. She followed Coop in and let him close the door. 'I need urgent medical attention.'

He took her into his arms. 'Well, you know, I'm a psychiatrist. I treat the mind.'

'You treat all of me,' Ellie said. 'Don't sell yourself short.'

When Coop kissed her, Ellie clung to him, rubbing her cheek against the crisp flat of his shirt. He eased her onto his lap in one of the overstuffed armchairs.

'Now, what would Dr Freud have to say about this?' she murmured.

Coop shifted, his erection strong beneath her legs. 'That a cigar isn't always a cigar.' He groaned, then tumbled her into the chair as he stood up to pace. 'I've only got a ten-minute window before the next patient arrives, and I'd rather not tempt fate.' He stuffed his hands in his pockets. 'To what do I owe this visit?'

'I was hoping for a freebie,' Ellie confessed.

'Well, I'd be happy to take you up on that later—'

'I meant a clinical consult, Coop. My head's a mess.' She buried her face in her hands. 'I'm no longer using an insanity defense for Katie.'

'How come?'

'Because it goes against her code of morality,' Ellie said sarcastically. 'I'm just so glad I get to defend the first alleged murderer in history with an unshakable sense of ethics.' She got up and walked to the window. 'Katie told me who the baby's father was – a professor friend of Jacob's who never knew about the pregnancy. And now that she's turned over this new leaf of honesty, she won't let me get up there and say she dissociated and killed the baby, since she swears it's not the truth.'

Coop whistled. 'You couldn't convince her—'

'I couldn't say anything. I'm not dealing with a client who understands the way courts operate. Katie believes with all her heart that she can say her piece and she'll be pardoned. Why shouldn't she? That's the way it works in her church.'

'Let's assume that it's the truth, that she didn't kill the baby,' Coop said.

'Well, there are some other unalienable truths, too. Like the fact that the baby was born alive, and that it somehow was found dead and hidden.'

'Okay. So what does that leave you with?'

Ellie sighed. 'Someone else killed it – which, as we've already discussed, is virtually impossible to use as a defense.'

'Or else the baby died on its own.'

'And walked, postpartum, to the tack room to bury itself under a stack of blankets?'

Coop smiled faintly. 'If Katie wanted that baby, and woke up to find it dead, maybe that was the point when she lost touch with reality. Maybe she got rid of the corpse in a dissociative state, and can't remember now.'

'Concealment of death is still a crime, Coop.'

'But not of nearly the same proportion,' he pointed out. 'There's a pathos to trying to keep from consciously admitting a loved one's death that doesn't come into play if you also caused that death.' He shrugged. 'I'm no lawyer, El, but it looks to me like you've got one thing to go with – that the baby died on its own, and that was what Katie's mind tried to cover up. And you've got to have some expert you can pull out of your hat who'll twist the autopsy report, right? I mean, she gave birth early. What premature infant is going to make it without an incubator and lights and the services of a neonatal ICU?'

Ellie tried to turn that strategy over in her mind, but her thoughts kept snagging on something that stuck out as sharp and as stubborn as a splinter. It had been accepted, from the autopsy report forward, that Katie had delivered at thirty-two weeks. And no one – Ellie included – had bothered to question that. 'How come?' she asked now.

'How come what?'

'How come Katie, a healthy eighteen-year-old girl in better physical shape than most women her age, went into premature labor?'

*   *   *

Dr Owen Zeigler looked up as Ellie distracted him for the tenth time with a tremendously loud crunch of pork rinds. 'If you knew what those did to your body, you wouldn't eat them,' he said.

'If you knew when the last time I ate was, you wouldn't bother me.' Ellie watched him hunch over the autopsy report again. 'So?'

'So. In and of itself prematurity isn't an issue. Preterm labor is a fairly frequent occurrence, there's no good treatment for it, and OBs don't know what causes it most of the time. In your client's case, however, the preterm labor was most likely caused by the chorioamnionitis.' Ellie stared at him blankly. 'That's a pathological diagnosis, not a bacteriological one. It basically means that there was marked acute inflammation of the amniotic membranes and villi.'

'Then what caused the chorioamnionitis? What does the ME say?'

'He doesn't. He implies that the fetal tissues and the placenta were contaminated, so the cause wasn't isolated and identified.'

'What usually causes chorioamnionitis?'

'Sexual intercourse,' Owen said. 'Most of the infectious agents that cause it are bacteria living in the vagina on a regular basis. Put two and two together—' He shrugged.

'What if intercourse wasn't a viable option?'

'Then an infectious agent entering by another route – like the mother's bloodstream or a urinary tract infection – would have caused it. But is there evidence to support that?' Owen tapped a page of the autopsy. 'This keeps catching my eye,' he admitted. 'The liver findings were overlooked. There's necrosis – cell death – but no evidence of inflammatory response.'

'Translation for those of us who don't speak pathologese?'

'The ME thought that the liver necrosis was based on asphyxia – a lack of oxygen – his assumed cause of death. But it's not – those lesions just don't make sense; they point to something other than asphyxia. Sometimes you see hemorrhagic necrosis due to anoxia, but pure necrosis is unusual.'

'So where *do* you see that?'

'With congenital heart abnormalities, which this baby didn't have – or with an infection. Necrosis might occur several hours before the body can mount an inflammatory response to an infection that a pathologist is able to see – and it's possible the baby died before that happened. I'll get the tissue blocks from the ME and do a Gram's stain to see what I come up with.'

Ellie's hand stopped midway to her mouth, the pork rind forgotten. 'Are you saying it's possible that the baby died of this mystery infection, and not asphyxia?'

'Yeah,' the pathologist said. 'I'll let you know.'

That night, there was going to be a frost. Sarah had heard from Rachel Yoder, who'd heard from Alma Beiler, whose rheumatoid arthritis swelled her knees to the size of melons every year before the first drop of temperature. Katie and Ellie were sent out to the garden to pick the remaining vegetables – tomatoes and squash and carrots as thick as a fist. Katie gathered the food in her apron; Ellie had taken a basket from inside the house. Ellie peered under the broad-backed leaves of the zucchini plant, looking for strays that had made it this far into the harvest season. 'When I was little,' she mused, 'I used to think that babies came from vegetable patches like this.'

Katie smiled. 'I used to think babies came from getting poked with needles.'

'Vaccines?'

'Mmm-hmm. That's how the cows got pregnant; I'd seen it done.' Ellie had, too; artificial insemination was the safest way to breed the milking herd. Katie laughed out loud. 'Boy, did I kick up a fuss when my Mam took me to get a measles shot.'

Ellie chuckled, then sawed a squash off a vine with a knife. 'When I found out for real about babies, I didn't believe it. Logistically, it didn't seem like it would work.'

'I don't think so much about where babies come from now,' Katie murmured. 'I wonder about where they go.'

Rocking back on her heels, Ellie gingerly set down the knife.

'You're not going to make another confession right now, are you?'

Smiling sadly, Katie shook her head. 'No. Your defense strategy is safe.'

'What defense strategy?' Ellie muttered, and at Katie's panicked glance she scrambled to cover her own words. 'I'm sorry. I just don't quite know what I'm going to do with you now.' Ellie sank down between the rows of bean plants, picked bare weeks ago. 'If I had never walked into that courtroom – if I had let you try to defend yourself the way you wanted – you would have been declared incompetent to stand trial. You would have been acquitted, most likely, with the promise of psychiatric care.'

'I'm not incompetent, and you know it,' Katie said stubbornly.

'Yes, and you're not insane. We've already had this conversation.'

'I'm also honest.'

'Amish?' Ellie said, hearing incorrectly. 'I think the jury will get that, given your clothes.'

'I said *honest*. But I'm Amish, too.'

Ellie yanked at the curly head of a carrot. 'They might as well be synonyms.' She tugged again, and as the root came flying out of the ground, she suddenly realized what she'd said. 'My God, Katie, you're Amish.'

Katie blinked at her. 'If it's taken you this many months to notice, I don't—'

'That's the defense.' A grin spread over Ellie's face. 'Do Amish boys go to war?'

'No. They're conscientious objectors.'

'How come?'

'Because it isn't our way to be violent,' Katie replied.

'Exactly. The Amish live according to the literal teachings of Christ. That means turning the other cheek just like Jesus – not just on Sundays, but every single minute of the day.'

Puzzled, Katie said, 'I don't understand.'

'Neither will the jury, but they will by the time I'm finished,'

Ellie said. 'You know why you're the first Amish murder suspect in East Paradise, Katie? Because – quite simply – if you're Amish, you don't commit murder.'

Dr Owen Zeigler liked Ellie Hathaway. He had worked with her once before, on a case involving an abusive husband who'd beaten his pregnant wife and caused her to lose her twenty-four-week fetus. He liked her no-nonsense style, her boy's haircut, and the way her legs seemed to reach all the way to her neck – something anatomically impossible, but stimulating all the same. He had no idea who or what her client was this time around, but the way things were shaping up, Ellie Hathaway was going to get her reasonable doubt – however slim it might be.

In the owl-eye of his microscope, Owen scrutinized the results of the Gram's stain. There were clusters of dark blue Gram-positive short rods, cocco-bacillary in shape. According to the culture results of the autopsy, these had been identified as diphtheroids – basic contaminants. But there were a hell of a lot of them, making Owen wonder if they were truly diphtheroids after all.

Ellie, actually, had planted the seed of doubt. What if those Gram-positive rods were signs of an infectious agent? A cocco-bacillary organism could easily be misinterpreted as a rod-shaped diphtheroid, especially since the microbiologist who'd performed the test hadn't done the Gram stain.

He slipped the slide from the scope, cradled it in his palm, and walked down the hospital hall to the lab where Bono Gerhardt worked. Owen found the microbiologist huddled over a catalog of reagents. 'You picking out your spring bulbs?'

The microbiologist laughed. 'Yeah. I can't decide between Holland tulips, herpes simplex virus, or cytokeratin.' He nodded at the slide Owen had brought. 'What's that?'

'I'm thinking either Group B beta-hemolytic strep or listeria,' Owen said. 'But I was hoping you might be able to tell me for sure.'

*　　　*　　　*

Shortly before ten o'clock, the members of the Fisher family would put down whatever they were doing and gravitate, as if pulled by a magnet, to the center of the living room. Elam would say a short German prayer, and then the others would all bow their heads in silence for a moment, offering up their own tribute to God. Ellie had watched it for months now, always recalling that first suspicious conversation she'd had with Sarah about her own faith. The discomfort she'd initially felt had given way to curiosity, and then to indifference – she'd finish reading whatever article she'd been skimming in the *Reader's Digest* or one of her own law books, and then go up to bed when the others rose.

Tonight, she and Sarah and Katie had been playing Scrabble. It had gotten almost giddy, with Katie insisting that phoneti-cally spelled words of Dietsch be allowed to count. When the cuckoo clock chimed ten times, Katie dumped her tray of letters into the box, followed by her mother. Aaron, who'd been in the barn, came inside on the wings of a frigid swirl of air. He hung up his coat and went to kneel beside his wife.

But that night, when Elam said the Lord's Prayer, he recited it in English. Surprised by the overture – the Amish prayed in German, or at the very least, Dietsch – Ellie found her lips moving along. Sarah, whispering too, lifted her head. She looked at Ellie, then shifted the slightest bit to her right, to make a space.

How long had it been since Ellie had prayed, really prayed, not a last-minute send-up as the jury was filing in or when the highway patrolman had caught her doing eighty-five miles per hour? What did she have to lose? Without responding to her own questions, Ellie slipped from her chair and knelt beside Sarah as if she belonged, as if her thoughts and hopes might be answered.

'Bono Gerhardt,' the man said, sticking out his hand. 'Charmed.'

Ellie smiled at the microbiologist Owen Zeigler had intro-duced her to. The man was only about five foot four and wore a surgical scrub cap on his head, printed with zebras and monkeys. A Guatemalan worry doll was pinned to his lapel. Around his neck were headphones, which snaked into a Sony Discman in his right pocket. 'You missed the incubation,' he said, 'but I'll forgive you for coming in after the first act.'

Bono led her to a table, where several slides were waiting. 'Basically, we're trying to identify the organism Owen found by using an immunoperoxidase stain. I cut more sections of the paraffin block of tissue, and incubated them with an antibody that will react with listeria – that's the bacteria we're trying to ID. Over here are our positive and negative controls: bona fide samples of listeria, courtesy of the veterinary school; and diphtheroids. And now, lady and gentleman, the moment of truth.'

Ellie drew in her breath as Bono set a few drops of solution onto the first specimen.

'This is horseradish peroxidase, an enzyme bound to an antibody,' Bono explained. 'Theoretically, this enzyme's only gonna go where the listeria are.'

Ellie watched him attend to all the slides on the table. Finally, he brandished a small vial. 'Iodine?' she guessed.

'Close. It's just a dye.' He added drops to each sample and then anchored the first slide beneath a microscope. 'If that's not listeria,' Bono murmured, 'bite me.'

Ellie looked from one man to the other. 'What's going on?'

Owen squinted into the microscope. 'You remember I told you that the necrosis in the liver was probably due to an infection? This is the bacteria that caused it.'

Ellie peered into the scope herself, but all she could see were things that looked like tiny bits of fat rice, edged in brown.

'The infant had listeriosis,' Owen said.

'So he didn't die of asphyxia?'

'Actually, he did. But it was a chain of events. The asphyxia was due to premature delivery, which was caused by chorioamnionitis – which was caused by listeriosis. The baby contracted the infection from the mother. It's fatal nearly thirty percent of the time in unborn fetuses, but can go undetected in the mothers.'

'Death by natural causes, then.'

'Correct.'

Ellie grinned. 'Owen, that's fabulous. That's just the sort of information I was hoping for. And where did the mother pick up the infection?'

Owen looked at Bono. 'This is the part that you're not going to like, Ellie. Listeriosis isn't like strep throat – you don't go around contracting it on a daily basis. The odds of infection are roughly one in twenty thousand pregnant women. Maternal infection usually occurs after consumption of contaminated food, and with today's technology, the specific contaminants are pretty well negated by the time the food's available for consumption.'

Ellie crossed her arms, impatient. 'Food like what?'

The pathologist hunched his shoulders. 'What's the chance that your client drank unpasteurized milk while she was pregnant?'

12

Ellie

The little library at the superior court was directly above Judge Ledbetter's chambers. Although I was supposed to be researching recent case law concerning judgments on murders of children under the age of five, I had spent considerably more time these past two hours staring at the warped wooden floor, as if I might will through the slats a softness of heart.

'I can hear you thinking out loud,' said a deep voice, and I turned in my seat to find George Callahan standing behind me. He pulled up a chair and straddled it. 'You're sending vibes to Phil, right?'

I searched his face for signs of rivalry, but he only looked sympathetic. 'Just some light voodoo.'

'Yeah, I do it too. Fifty percent of the time, it even works.' George smiled, and, relaxing, I smiled back. 'I've been looking for you. I've got to tell you – I don't feel like a million bucks sending some little Amish girl to jail for life, Ellie. But murder's murder, and I've been trying to come up with a solution that might work for all of us.'

'What's your offer?'

'You know she's looking at life, here. I can give you ten years if she pleads guilty to manslaughter. Look, with good behavior, she'll be out in five or six years.'

'She won't survive in prison for five or six years, George,' I said quietly.

He looked down at his clasped hands. 'She's got a better chance of making it through five years than fifty.'

I stared, hard, at the floor above Judge Ledbetter's chambers. 'I'll let you know.'

*   *   *

Ethically, I had to bring a plea offered by the prosecution to my client. I'd been in this position before, where I had to relate an offer that I didn't think was in our best interests, but this time I was nervous about my client's response. Usually, I could convince someone that taking our chances at trial would be in his or her best interests, but Katie was a whole different story. She'd been brought up to believe that you gave an apology and then accepted whatever punishment was meted out. George's plea would allow Katie to bring this fiasco to an end, in a way that made perfect sense to her.

I found her doing the ironing in the kitchen. 'I need to talk to you.'

'Okay.'

She smoothed the arm of one of her father's shirts – lavender – and pressed it flat with an iron that had been heated on the stove. Not for the first time, I realized that Katie would make the perfect wife – in fact, she'd been groomed for just that. If she was sentenced to life in prison, she'd never get that opportunity. 'The county attorney offered you a plea bargain.'

'What's that?'

'It's a deal, basically. He reduces the charge and sentence, and in return you have to say you were wrong.'

Katie flipped the shirt over and frowned. 'And then we still go to trial?'

'No. Then it's over.'

Katie's face lit up. 'That would be wonderful!'

'You haven't heard his terms,' I said dryly. 'If you plead guilty to manslaughter, instead of Murder One, you'll get a sentence of ten years in prison, instead of life. But with parole you'll probably only have to be in jail half that time.'

Katie set the iron on its edge on the stove. 'I would still go to jail, then.'

I nodded. 'The risk in accepting the offer is that if you go to trial and get acquitted, you don't go to jail at all. It's like settling for something, when you haven't seen what's out there.'

But even as I said it, I knew it was the wrong explanation. An Amishman took what he was given – he didn't hold out for the best, because that would only come at someone else's expense, someone who didn't get the best.

'Will you get me acquitted, then?'

It always came down to this, with clients who were offered a plea. Before they ceded to my advice, they wanted the assurance that things were going to come out in our favor. In most cases of my career, I'd been able to say yes with fervor, with conviction – and I then went on to prove myself right.

But this was not 'most cases.' And Katie was no ordinary client.

'I don't know. I believe I could have gotten you off with temporary insanity. But with the abbreviated length of time I've had to prepare this new defense, I just can't say. I *think* I can get you acquitted. I *hope* I can get you acquitted. But Katie . . . I can't give you my word.'

'All I have to do is say I was wrong?' Katie asked. 'And then it's over?'

'Then you go to jail,' I clarified.

Katie lifted the iron and pressed it so hard against the shoulder of her father's shirt that the fabric hissed. 'I think I will take this offer,' she said.

I watched her run the iron over and between the button-holes, this girl who had just decided to go to prison for a decade. 'Katie, can I tell you something as your friend, instead of your lawyer?' She glanced up. 'You don't know what prison is like. It's not only full of English people – it's full of bad people. I don't think this is the way to go.'

'You don't think like me,' Katie said quietly.

I swallowed my reply and counted to ten before I let myself speak again. 'You want me to accept the plea? I will. But first I'd like you to do something for me.'

I'd been to the State Correctional Institution at Muncy before, courtesy of several female clients of mine who were still serving out their sentences. It was a forbidding place, even to a lawyer accustomed to the reality of prison life. All women sentenced in Pennsylvania went to the diagnostic classification center at Muncy, and then either stayed on to serve out their sentence or got moved to the minimum security institution at Cambridge Springs in Erie. But at the very least, Katie would spend four to six weeks here, and I wanted her to see what she was getting herself into.

The warden, a man with the unfortunate name of Duvall Shrimp and the more unfortunate habit of staring at my breasts, gladly ushered us into his office. I gave no explanations for Katie, no matter how odd it seemed to have a young Amish girl sitting next to me while I asked for a generic tour of the facility, and to Duvall's credit, he didn't ask. He led us through the control booth, where the barred door slammed shut behind Katie and made her draw in her breath.

The first place he took us was the dining hall, where long tables with benches framed a center aisle. A straggly line of women moved like a single snake at the serving counter, picking up trays filled with unappetizing lumps in different shades of gray. 'You eat in the hall,' he said, 'unless you're in the restricted housing unit for disciplinary behavior, or one of the capital case inmates. They eat in their cells.' We watched factions of prisoners separate to different tables, eyeing us with undisguised curiosity. Then Duvall led us up a staircase, into the block of cells. A television mounted at the end of the hallway cast a puddle of colored light over the face of one of the women, who dangled her arms through the bars of the cell and whistled at Katie. 'Whoo-ee,' she catcalled. 'Ain't you a little early for Halloween?'

Other prisoners laughed and snickered, brazenly standing in their tiny cages like exhibits in a circus sideshow. They stared at Katie as if she was the one on display. As she walked past the last cell in the row, whispering a prayer beneath her breath, a prisoner spat, the small splat landing just beside Katie's sneaker.

In the exercise yard, Duvall grew chatty. 'Haven't seen you around. You been defending men instead of women?'

'About even. You haven't seen me around because my clients get acquitted.'

He jerked his chin in Katie's direction. 'Who's she?'

I watched her walk the perimeter of the empty yard, stop at the corner, and view the sky, framed as it was by curls of razor wire. In the tower above Katie's head were two guards, holding rifles. 'Someone who believes in seeing the property before signing the lease,' I said.

Katie approached us, pulling her shawl more tightly around her shoulders. 'That's all,' Duvall said. 'Hope it was everything you thought it was cracked up to be.'

I thanked him and ushered Katie back to the parking lot, where she got into the car and sat in absolute silence for most of the two-hour trip. At one point she fell asleep, dreamed, and whimpered quietly. Keeping one hand on the wheel, I used the other to smooth her hair, soothe her.

Katie woke up as we got off the highway in Lancaster. She pressed her forehead to the window and said, 'Please tell George Callahan that I do not want his deal.'

I finished the last words of my opening argument with a flourish and turned at the sound of clapping. 'Excellent. Direct and persuasive,' Coop said, coming forward from the shadows in the barn. He gestured at the lazy cows. 'Tough jury, though.'

I could feel heat rising to my cheeks. 'You're not supposed to be here.'

He linked his hands at the small of my back. 'Believe me. This is exactly where I'm supposed to be.'

With a shove on his chest, I pushed away. 'Really, Coop. I have a trial tomorrow. I'll be lousy company.'

'I'll be your audience.'

'You'll be a distraction.'

Coop grinned. 'That's the nicest thing you've ever said to me.'

Sighing, I started to walk back to the milk room, where my computer was glowing green. 'Why don't you go inside and let Sarah cut you a piece of pie?'

'And miss all this excitement?' Coop leaned against the bulk milk tank. 'I think not. You go on ahead. Do whatever you were going to do before I showed up.'

With a measured glance, I sat down on the milk crate that served as my chair and began to review the witness list for tomorrow's trial. After a moment, I rubbed my eyes and turned off the computer.

'I didn't say a word,' Coop protested.

'You didn't have to.' Standing, I offered him my hand. 'Walk with me?'

We wandered, lazy, through the orchard on the north side of the farm, where the apple trees stood like a coven of arthritic old women. The perfume of their fruit twisted around us, bright and sweet as ribbon candy. 'The night before a trial, Stephen would cook steak,' I said absently. 'Said there was something primitive about devouring fresh meat.'

'And lawyers wonder why they're called sharks,' Coop laughed. 'Did you eat steak, too?'

'Nope. I'd get into my pajamas and lip-synch to Aretha Franklin.'

'No kidding?'

I tilted back my head and let the notes fill my throat. 'R-E-S-P-E-C-T!'

'An exercise in self-esteem?'

'Nah,' I said. 'I just really like Aretha.'

Coop squeezed my shoulder. 'If you'd like, I can sing backup.'

'God, I've been waiting my whole life for a guy like you.'

He turned me in his arms and touched his lips to mine. 'I certainly hope so,' he said. 'Where are you going to go, El, when this is all over?'

'Well, I . . .' I didn't know, actually. It was something I'd avoided thinking about: the fact that when I stumbled into Katie Fisher's legal quandary, I'd been on the run myself. 'I could go back to Philadelphia, maybe. Or stay at Leda's.'

'How about me?'

I smiled. 'You could stay at Leda's too, I suppose.'

But Coop was absolutely serious. 'You know what I'm saying, Ellie. Why don't you move in with me?'

Immediately, the world began to close in on me. 'I don't know,' I said, looking him squarely in the eye.

Coop stuffed his hands into his pockets; I could see how hard he was fighting to keep from making a disparaging comment about my treatment of him in the past. I wanted to touch him, to ask him to touch me, but I couldn't do that. We had been standing on the edge of this point once before, a hundred years ago, and for all that the cliff looked the same and the drop just as steep; I still couldn't catch my breath.

But we were older, this time. I wasn't going to lie to him. He wasn't going to walk away. I reached out for an apple and handed it to him.

'Is this supposed to be an olive branch, or are you feeling biblical?'

'That depends,' I said. 'Are we talking psalms or sacrificial offerings?'

Coop smiled, a sweet conciliation. 'Actually, I was thinking of Numbers. All that begetting.' He tangled his fingers with mine, leaned back into the soft grass, and pulled me down on top of him. With his hands angling my head, he kissed me, until I could barely hold a thought, much less a thread of my defense strategy. This was safe. This, I knew.

'Ellie,' Coop whispered, or maybe I imagined it, 'take your time.'

'Okay,' I said, in my best impression of a prosecutor, 'here's my offer: You let me unhook that water bucket, and you're looking at two to five. Carrots, I mean.'

Nugget shook his heavy head and stomped at me, as belligerent as any defense attorney turning down a lousy plea bargain. 'Guess we're going to have to go to trial,' I sighed, and ducked into the stall. The horse shoved me with his nose, and I scowled at him. 'Stubbornness sure runs in this family,' I muttered.

In response, the rotten beast took a nip at my shoulder. Yelping, I dropped the water bucket and backed out of the stall. 'Fine,' I said. 'Go get your own damn drink.' I turned on my heel, but was stopped by a faint sound overhead, like the mew of a kitten.

'Hello?' I called. 'Anyone here?'

When there was no response, I began to climb the narrow ladder to the hayloft, where the bales of hay and the grain for livestock were kept. Sarah was sitting in one corner, crying, her face buried in her apron to muffle the noise.

'Hey,' I said gently, touching her shoulder.

She started, hurriedly wiping her face. '*Ach,* Ellie. I just came up here for . . . for . . .'

'For a good cry. It's all right, Sarah. I understand.'

'No.' She sniffed. 'I have to get back to the house. Aaron will be coming in for lunch soon'

I forced her to meet my gaze. 'I'm going to do my best to save her, you know.'

Sarah turned away, staring out at the neat, symmetrical fields. 'I should never have put her on that train to see Jacob . . . Aaron was right all along.'

'There was no way you could have known that Katie would meet an English boy and get pregnant.'

'Couldn't I?' Sarah said softly. 'This is all my fault.'

My heart went out to the woman. 'She might have chosen to go on her own. It might have happened anyway.'

Sarah shook her head. 'I love my children. I love them, and look what's happened.'

Without hesitation, I embraced her. I could hear her words, hot against my collarbone. 'I'm her mother, Ellie. I'm supposed to fix it. But I can't.'

I took a deep breath. 'Then I'll have to.'

Getting to the trial was an exercise in politics. Leda and Coop and Jacob all arrived at the farm at about 6:30 A.M., each in a separate car. Katie and Samuel and Sarah were immediately shuttled to Coop's car, because he was the only driver who had not been excommunicated. Neither Jacob nor Leda felt comfortable leaving their car on Aaron Fisher's property, so Leda had to follow Jacob back to her house to drop off his Honda before they returned to pick me up. We had almost reached the point where I was certain we were going to be late when Aaron strode out of the barn, his eyes fixed on the passengers in Coop's car.

He'd made it clear that he would not attend the trial. Although the bishop would surely have understood Aaron's involvement in this particular lawsuit, Aaron could not condone it himself. But maybe there was more to him than I'd thought. Even if his principles kept him from accompanying his daughter to her trial, he would not let her go without a proper good-bye. Coop unrolled the back window so that Aaron could stick his head inside and speak to Katie.

But when he leaned close, all he said, softly, was, 'Sarah, *komm*.'

With downcast eyes, Katie's mother squeezed her hand and then slipped from the car. She fell into place beside her husband, her eyes bright with tears that she did not let fall even as her husband turned her by the shoulders and led her back to the house.

Leda was the first one to notice the vans. Sprawled across the parking lot of the superior court, they were crowned with satellite dishes and emblazoned with an alphabet soup of station call letters. Closer to the courthouse was one row of reporters holding microphones and another row of cameramen rolling tape, facing each other as if they were getting ready to do the Virginia reel instead of comment on the fate of a young girl.

'What on earth?' Leda breathed.

'That's debatable,' I muttered. 'Reporters aren't a human life form.'

Suddenly Coop's face appeared at my window. 'What are they doing here? I thought you won that motion.'

'I got the cameras removed from the courtroom itself,' I said.

'Outside is anybody's turf.' Since the day the judge had ruled, I hadn't given much thought to the media issue – I'd been too busy trying to create a new defense. But it was naïve to think that just because the cameras would not be present meant that the interest in the story would likewise absent itself. I grabbed my briefcase and got out of the car, knowing that I had about two minutes before everyone realized who I was. Tapping on the rear window of Coop's car, I pulled Katie's attention from the knot of press.

'Come on,' I said. 'It's now or never.'

'But—'

'There's no other way, Katie. Somehow we're going to have to break right through them to walk up the steps to the court-house. I know it's not what you want, and it's certainly not what I want, but we don't have a choice.'

Katie closed her eyes briefly before getting out of the car. Praying, I realized, and I wished in vain that she were asking God to make them all come down with a plague. Then, with a grace that belied her age, Katie stepped out and put her hand into mine.

Awareness rolled like a tidal wave as one reporter after another caught sight of Katie's *kapp* and apron. Cameras swiveled; questions fell around our feet like javelins. I could feel her wince at each flash; and I thought of Dorian Gray's portrait, the life draining out. Bewildered, she kept her face tucked down and trusted me to lead her up the stairs. 'No comment,' I shouted, parting the reporters like the prow of a great ship, pulling Katie in my wake.

I knew the building well enough after several visits, so I immediately took Katie to the nearest ladies' room. Checking beneath the stalls to make sure they were empty, I leaned against the door to prevent anyone else coming in. 'You're all right?'

She was shaking, and her eyes were wide with confusion, but she nodded. '*Ja*. It just wasn't what I expected.'

It wasn't what I had expected either, and I had an obliga-tion to tell her that it was going to get significantly worse before it got better, but instead I took a deep breath and managed to taste, deep in my lungs, the scent of Katie's fear. Shoving her out of the way, I ran for the nearest stall and threw up until there was nothing left in my stomach.

On my knees, with my face fired and hot, I pressed my forehead against the cool fiberglass wall of the stall. It was only by taking shallow breaths that I managed to turn and rip off a piece of toilet paper to wipe my mouth.

Katie's hand fell like a question on my shoulder. 'Ellie, are *you* all right?'

Nerves, I thought, but I wasn't about to admit that to my own client. 'Must have been something I ate,' I said, tossing Katie my brightest smile and getting to my feet. 'Now. Shall we go?'

Katie kept running her hands over the smooth, polished wood of the defense table. There were places the finish had been rubbed raw, worn by the hands of endless defendants who'd sat in the very same place. How many of them, I wondered, had truly been innocent?

Courtrooms, before the fact of a trial, were not the bastions of serenity depicted on TV shows about the law. Instead, they were a bustle: the clerk shuffling for the right file, the bailiff blowing his nose in a spotted handkerchief, the people in the gallery talking headlines over Styrofoam cups of coffee. Today it was even louder than usual, and I could make out distinct sentences through the general buzz. Most involved Katie, who was on display just as surely as a zoo animal, removed from her natural habitat for the curiosity of others.

'Katie,' I said softly, and she jumped a foot.

'How come they haven't started yet?'

'It's still early.' Now her hands were tucked beneath her apron, her eyes darting over the activity in the front of the courtroom. Her gaze lit upon George Callahan, six feet away at the prosecutor's table.

'He looks kind,' she mused.

'He won't be. His job is to get the jury to believe all the bad things he's going to say about you.' I hesitated, then decided in Katie's case, it would be best to know what's coming. 'It's going to be hard for you to hear, Katie.'

'Why?'

I blinked at her. 'Why will it be hard?'

'No. Why will he lie about me? Why would the jury believe him and not me?'

I thought about the rules of forensic evidence, the distinctions between casting a motive and spinning a false tale, the psychometric profiles that had been written on juries – all idiosyncrasies that Katie would not understand. How did one explain to an Amish girl that in a trial, it often came down to who had the best story? 'It's the way the legal system works in the English world,' I said. 'It's part of the game.'

'Game,' Katie said slowly, turning the word in her mouth until it softened. 'Like football!' She smiled up at me, remembering our earlier conversation. 'A game with winning and losing, but you get paid for it.'

I felt sick to my stomach again. 'Yeah,' I said. 'Exactly.'

'All rise; the Honorable Philomena Ledbetter presiding!'

I got to my feet and made sure Katie was doing the same as the judge bustled in from the side door of the courtroom. She climbed the steps, her robes billowing out behind her. 'Be seated.' Her eyes roamed the gallery, narrowing on the concentrated band of media representatives in the rear. 'Before we begin might I remind the press that the use of cameras or video photography is forbidden in this courtroom, and if I see a single violation, I'll toss the lot of you into the lobby for the remainder of the trial.'

She turned her attention to Katie, measuring her in silence before she spoke to the county attorney. 'If the prosecution's ready, you may begin.'

George Callahan strolled toward the jury box, as if he'd long been friends with every member. 'I know what you're thinking,' he said. 'This is a trial for murder – so where's the accused? Surely that little Amish girl sitting over there, wearing her apron and her little white cap, couldn't have killed a fly, much less another human being.' He shook his head. 'You all live in this county. You all see the Amish in their buggies and at their farm stands. If you know nothing else about them, you at least have picked up on the fact that they're a highly religious group that keep to themselves and don't make waves. I mean, really – when was the last time you heard of an Amish person being brought up on felony charges?

'Last year, that's when. When the idyllic bubble of Amish life was burst by two of its youth, peddling cocaine. And today, when you hear how this young woman cold-bloodedly killed her own newborn infant.'

He ran his hand along the rail of the jury box. 'Shocking, isn't it? It's hard to believe any mother would kill her own child, much less a girl who looks as innocent as the one sitting over there. Well, let me put your mind to rest. During the course of this trial you'll learn that the defendant is *not* innocent – in fact, she's a proven liar. For six years, she's been sneaking off her parents' farm to spend nights and weekends on a college campus, where she lets down her hair and dresses in jeans and tight sweaters and parties like any other teenager. She lied about that – just like she lied about the fact that she'd gotten pregnant during one of these wild weekends; just like she lied about committing murder.'

He turned toward Katie, pinned her with his gaze. 'So what's the truth? The truth is that shortly after two A.M. on July tenth, the defendant awakened with labor pains. The truth is that she got up, tiptoed to the barn, and in silence gave birth to a live baby boy. The truth is that she knew if the baby was discovered, life as she knew it would be over. She'd be thrown out of her home, out of her church, and out of her community. So the truth is, she did what she had to do to keep the lie intact – she willfully, deliberately, and premeditatedly killed her own baby.'

George flicked his eyes away from Katie and turned back to the jury. 'When you look at the defendant, look past the quaint costume. That's what she wants you to see. See instead a woman smothering a crying baby. When you listen to the defendant, pay attention to what she has to say. But remember that what comes out of her mouth can't be trusted. This so-called sweet little Amish girl hid a forbidden pregnancy, murdered a newborn with her bare hands, and fooled everyone around her while it was happening. Don't let her fool you.'

The jury was made up of eight women and four men, and I vacillated between thinking that worked for or against us. Women would be likely to feel more sympathy for an unwed teen – but more contempt for someone who killed her newborn. What it all boiled down to, of course, was how willing this particular mix of people was to look for a loophole.

I squeezed Katie's trembling hand beneath the defense table and stood. 'Mr Callahan would like you to believe that a certain party in this courtroom is an expert when it comes to not telling the truth. And you know what? He's right. The thing is, Katie Fisher isn't that person. Actually, it's me.' I raised my hand and waved it cheerfully. 'Yep, guilty as charged. I'm a liar and I'm rather good at it, if I say so myself. So good that it's made me a pretty accomplished attorney. And although I'm not about to put words in the county attorney's mouth, I bet he's bent the facts a time or two himself.' I raised my brows at the jury. 'You guys hear all the jokes – I don't have to tell you about lawyers. Not only do we lie well, but we get paid a lot to do it.'

I leaned against the railing of the jury box. 'Katie Fisher, on the other hand, doesn't lie. How do I know this, for a fact? Well, because I wanted to use a defense of temporary insanity today. I had experts who were going to stand up here and tell you that Katie didn't know what she was doing the morning she gave birth. But Katie wouldn't let me. She said she wasn't insane, and she hadn't murdered her baby. And even if it meant risking her conviction, she wanted you, the jury, to know that.'

I shrugged. 'So here I am, a lawyer armed with a novel

weapon – the truth. That's all I've got to contradict the prosecution's allegations: the truth, and perhaps a clearer eye. Nothing that Mr Callahan will show you is conclusive proof, and for good reason – Katie Fisher did not murder her newborn. Having lived with her and her family now for several months, I know something that Mr Callahan does not – that Katie Fisher is Amish, through and through. You don't "act" Amish, like Mr Callahan is suggesting. You live it. You are it. Through the course of this trial, you'll come to understand this complex, peaceful group, as I have. Maybe a suburban teenager would give birth and stuff the baby in the toilet, but not an Amish woman. Not Katie Fisher.

'Now, let's look at some of Mr Callahan's points. Did Katie sneak away repeatedly to a college town? Yes, she did – see, I'm telling you the truth. But what the prosecutor left out is why she was going there. Katie's brother, her only remaining living sibling, decided to leave the Amish church and study at college. Her father, hurt by this decision, restricted contact with this son. But family means everything to Katie, as to most Amish, and she missed her brother so much she was willing to risk anything to see him. So you see, Katie wasn't living a lie. She was maintaining a love.

'Mr Callahan also suggested that Katie needed to hide the illegitimate pregnancy, or else suffer being kicked out of her faith. However, you will learn that the Amish are forgiving. Even an illegitimate pregnancy would have been accepted by the church, and the infant would have grown up with more love and support than is found in many homes in our own communities.'

I turned toward Katie, who was regarding me with wide, bright eyes. 'Which brings me to Mr Callahan's final point: why, then, would Katie Fisher kill her own baby? The answer is simple, ladies and gentlemen. *She didn't.*

'The judge will explain to you that to convict Katie, you have to believe the prosecution beyond a reasonable doubt. By the time this trial's over, you'll have more than a reasonable doubt, you'll have a whole wagon full of them. You will see that there's no way for the prosecution to prove that Katie killed her baby. They have no physical witnesses to the fact. They have nothing but speculation and dubious evidence.

'On the other hand, I'm going to show you that there were a number of ways that baby might have died.' I walked toward Katie, so that the jury would be staring at her as well as me. 'I'm going to show you why the Amish don't commit murder. And most importantly,' I finished, 'I'm going to let Katie Fisher tell you the truth.'

13

Lizzie Munro would never have laid odds on the fact that one day, she'd be testifying against an Amish murder suspect. The girl was sitting at the defense table next to that high-powered attorney of hers, head bowed and hands clasped like one of those godawful Precious Moments figurines Lizzie's mother liked to litter her windowsills with. Lizzie herself hated them – each angel too calculatedly cute, each shepherd boy too doe-eyed to be taken seriously. Similarly, looking at Katie Fisher gave Lizzie the overwhelming urge to turn away.

She focused instead on George Callahan, dapper in his dark suit. 'Can you state your name and address?' he asked.

'Elizabeth Grace Munro. 1313 Grand Street, Ephrata.'

'Where are you employed?'

'At the East Paradise Township Police Department. I'm a detective-sergeant.'

George didn't even have to ask her the questions; they'd been through this opening act so often she knew what was coming. 'How long have you been a detective?'

'For the past six years. Prior to that, I was a patrol officer for five years.'

'Can you tell us a little bit about your work, Detective Munro?'

Lizzie leaned back in the witness chair – for her, a comfortable place. 'For the most part, I investigate felony cases in East Paradise Township.'

'Roughly how many are there?'

'Well, we took about fifteen thousand calls last year, total. Of those, there were only a handful of felonies – mostly we see misdemeanors.'

'How many murders occurred last year?'

'None,' Lizzie answered.

'Of those fifteen thousand calls, do many take you into Amish homes?'

'No,' she said. 'The Amish will call the police in if there's theft or damage to their properties, and occasionally we'll have to book an Amish youth for DUI or disorderly conduct, but for the most part they have a fairly minimal relationship to local law enforcement authorities.'

'Detective, could you tell us what happened on the morning of July tenth?'

Lizzie straightened in her chair. 'I was at the station when someone called to report finding a dead infant in a barn. An ambulance had been dispatched to the scene, and then I went out there as well.'

'What did you find when you arrived?'

'It was about five-twenty A.M., near sunrise. The barn belonged to an Amish dairy farmer. He and his two employees were still in the barn, milking their cows. I taped the front and back door of the barn to secure the scene. I went into the tack room, where the body had been found, and spoke to the EMTs. They said the baby was newborn and premature, and couldn't be resuscitated. I took down the names of the four men: Aaron and Elam Fisher, Samuel Stoltzfus, and Levi Esch. I asked if they'd seen anything suspicious or if they'd disturbed anything in the barn. The youngest boy, Levi, had been the one to find the baby. He hadn't touched anything but a couple of horse blankets on top of the dead infant, which was wrapped in a boy's shirt. Aaron Fisher, the owner of the farm, said that a pair of scissors used to cut baling twine was missing from a peg near the calving pen. All four men told me that no one had been found in the barn, and that no women in the household had been pregnant.

'After that, I went through the stalls, looking for a lead. The MCU of the state police was called in, as well. It was fairly impossible to take prints off the rough wooden beams and the hay, and any partial prints we found matched those of family members who would have had reason to be in the barn.'

'At this point, were you suspecting foul play?'

'No. I wasn't suspecting much of anything, other than abandonment.'

George nodded. 'Please continue.'

'Finally, we found the site of the birth – in a corner of the calving pen fresh hay had been scattered to cover up matted blood. At the spot where the baby's body had been discovered, we found a footprint in the dirt floor.'

'Did you determine anything about the footprint?'

'It would have belonged to a barefoot woman who wore a size seven shoe.'

'What did you do next?'

'I tried to find the woman who'd given birth. First I interviewed Aaron Fisher's wife, Sarah. I found out that she'd had a hysterectomy nearly a decade ago, and was unable to have children. I questioned the neighbors and their two teenage girls, all of whom had alibis. By the time I got back to the farm, the Fishers' daughter, Katie, had come downstairs. In fact, she came into the tack room where the medical examiner was with the newborn's body.'

'What was her reaction?'

'She was very disturbed,' Lizzie said. 'She ran out of the barn.'

'Did you follow her?'

'Yes. I caught up with her on the porch. I asked Ms Fisher if she'd been pregnant, and she denied it.'

'Did that seem suspicious to you?'

'Not at all. It was what her parents had told me, too. But then I noticed blood running down her legs and pooling on the floor. Although she was reluctant, I had her forcibly removed by the EMTs and taken to the hospital for her own personal safety.'

'At this point what was running through your mind?'

'That this girl needed medical attention. But then I wondered if perhaps the defendant's parents had never known she was pregnant – if she'd hidden the truth from them, like she'd tried to hide it from me.'

'How did you discover that she'd hidden the truth?' George asked.

'I went to the hospital and spoke to the defendant's doctor, who confirmed that she had delivered a baby, was in critical condition, and needed emergency treatment to stop the vaginal bleeding. Once I knew that she had lied to me about the pregnancy, I got warrants to search the farm and the house, and to get a blood test and DNA from the baby and from the defendant. The next step was to match the blood in the hay of the calving pen to that of the defendant, the blood on the baby's body to that of the defendant, and the blood type in the baby's body to that of the defendant.'

'What came of the information you got from these warrants?'

'Underneath the defendant's bed was a bloody nightgown. In her closet were boots and shoes in a size seven. All the lab tests positively linked the blood in the barn to the defendant, and the blood on and in the baby to the defendant.'

'What did this lead you to believe?'

Lizzie let her gaze rest lightly on Katie Fisher. 'That in spite of her denial, the defendant was the mother of that baby.'

'At this point, did you believe that the defendant had killed the baby?'

'No. Murder's rare in East Paradise, and virtually unheard of in the Amish community. I believed, at this point, that the baby was stillborn. But then the medical examiner sent me the autopsy report, and I had to refine my conclusions.'

'Why?'

'Well, for one thing, the baby had been born alive. For another, the umbilical cord had been cut by scissors – which made me think of the scissors Aaron Fisher said were missing; scissors from which we might have lifted a print. The newborn had died of asphyxia, but the medical examiner found fibers deep in the baby's mouth that matched the shirt it had been wrapped in, suggesting that he had been smothered. That was when I realized that the defendant was a potential suspect.'

Lizzie took a sip of water from a glass perched beside the witness stand. 'After that, I interviewed everyone close to the defendant, and the defendant herself. The defendant's mother confirmed that a younger child had died many years ago, and that she had no idea her daughter was pregnant – nor any reason to think so. The father wouldn't speak to me at all. I also interviewed Samuel Stoltzfus, one of the hired hands and coincidentally the defendant's boyfriend. From him I learned that he'd planned to marry the defendant this fall. He also told me that the defendant had never had sexual intercourse with him.'

'What did that lead you to believe?'

Lizzie raised her brows. 'At first I wondered if he'd found out that Katie Fisher had two-timed him – and if he'd smothered the baby out of revenge. But Samuel Stoltzfus lives ten miles from the Fisher farm with his parents, who confirmed that he was sleeping there during the window of time the medical examiner said death occurred. Then I began to think that maybe I had it backward – that the information pointed to the defendant, instead. I mean, here was a motive: Amish girl, Amish parents, Amish boyfriend – and she gets pregnant by someone else? That's an excuse to hide the birth, maybe even get rid of it.'

'Did you interview anyone else?'

'Yes, Levi Esch, the second hired hand on the farm. He said that the defendant had been sneaking to Penn State for the past six years to meet with her brother. Jacob Fisher did not live like the Amish anymore, but like any other college student.'

'Why was that relevant?'

Lizzie smiled. 'It's a lot easier to meet a guy other than your Amish boyfriend when a whole new world is at your fingertips – one with booze and frat parties and Maybelline.'

'Did you speak to Jacob Fisher, too?'

'Yes, I did. He confirmed the defendant's secret visits and

said he had not known of his sister's pregnancy. He also told me that the reason the defendant had to visit him behind her father's back was because he was no longer welcome at home.'

George feigned confusion. 'How come?'

'The Amish don't attend school past eighth grade, but Jacob had wanted to continue his education. Breaking that rule got him excommunicated from the Amish church. Aaron Fisher took the punishment one step further, and disowned Jacob. Sarah Fisher followed her husband's wishes, but sent her daughter to visit Jacob covertly.'

'How did this affect your thinking about the case?'

'All of a sudden,' Lizzie said, 'things became more clear. If I were the defendant, and I knew that my own brother had been exiled for something as simple as studying, I'd be very careful not to break any rules. Call me crazy, but having a baby out of wedlock is a more severe infraction than reading Shakespeare on the side. That means if she didn't find a way to hide what had happened, she was going to be tossed out of her home and her family, not to mention her church. So she concealed the pregnancy for seven months. Then she had the baby – and concealed that, too.'

'Did you determine the identity of the father?'

'We did not.'

'Did you consider any other suspects, beside the defendant?'

Lizzie sighed. 'You know, I tried to. But too much didn't add up. The birth occurred two and a half months early, in a place with no phone and no electricity – which means no one could have been called, or have known about it, unless they were living at the farm and heard the defendant's labor. As for a stranger coming by, what's the chance of someone dropping in unannounced at two A.M. on an Amish farm? And if a stranger did show up, why kill the baby? And why wouldn't the defendant have mentioned this?

'So that left me with family members. But only one of them had lied about the pregnancy and birth to my face. For only one of them were the stakes frighteningly high should news of this baby get out. And for only one of them did we have evidence placing her at the scene of the crime.' Lizzie glanced at the defendant's table. 'In my opinion, the facts clearly show that Katie Fisher smothered her newborn.'

When Ellie Hathaway stood up to do her cross-examination, Lizzie squared her shoulders. She tried to remember what George had said about the attorney's ruthlessness, her ability to worm answers out of the most stubborn witnesses. From the looks of her, Lizzie didn't doubt it a bit. Lizzie could hold her own with the boys in the department, but Ellie Hathaway's cropped hair and angular suit made it seem as if any of the softer edges of her personality had long been hacked away.

Which is why Lizzie nearly fell over in her seat when the attorney approached her with a genuine, friendly smile. 'Did you know I used to spend summers here?'

Lizzie blinked at her. 'At the courthouse?'

'No,' Ellie laughed, 'contrary to popular belief. I meant in East Paradise.'

'I did not know that,' Lizzie said stiffly.

'Well, my aunt lives here. Used to own a little farm.' She grinned. 'But that was before real estate taxes went as high as the new cellular towers.'

At that, Lizzie chuckled under her breath. 'That's why I rent.'

'Your Honor,' George interrupted, giving his witness a warning look, 'I'm certain the jury doesn't need to hear Ms Hathaway's stroll down memory lane.'

The judge nodded. 'Is there a point to this, counselor?'

'Yes, Your Honor. It's that growing up around here, you get to watch the Amish quite a bit.' She turned to Lizzie. 'Wouldn't you agree?'

'Yes.'

'You said you hadn't booked many Amish. When was the last one?'

Lizzie backpedaled mentally. 'About five months ago. A

seventeen-year-old who drove his buggy into a ditch under the influence.'

'And before that? How long had it been?'

She tried, but she couldn't remember. 'I don't know.'

'But a good length of time?'

'I'd say so,' Lizzie admitted.

'In your dealings . . . both professional and personal . . . have you found the Amish to be fairly gentle people?'

'Yes.'

'Do you know what happens when an unwed Amish girl has a baby?'

'I've heard that they take care of their own,' Lizzie said.

'That's right, and Katie wouldn't have been excommunicated – only shunned for a while. Then she'd be forgiven and welcomed back with open arms. So where's the motive for murder?'

'In her father's actions,' Lizzie explained. 'There are ways around excommunication if you want to keep in touch with family members who've left the church, but Aaron Fisher didn't allow them when he banished the defendant's brother. That severe fact was in the back of her mind, all the time.'

'I thought you didn't interview Mr Fisher.'

'I didn't.'

'Ah,' Ellie said. 'So now you're psychic?'

'I interviewed his son,' Lizzie countered.

'Talking to a son won't tell you what's in the father's mind. Just like looking at a dead baby doesn't tell you that its mother killed it, right?'

'Objection!'

'Withdrawn,' Ellie said smoothly. 'Do you find it odd that an Amish woman is being accused of murder?'

Lizzie looked at George. 'It's an aberration. But the fact is, it happened.'

'Did it? Your scientific proof confirms that Katie had that baby. That's indisputable. But does having that baby necessarily lead to killing that baby?'

'No.'

'You also mentioned that you found a footprint in the dirt near where the infant's body was found. In your mind, this links Katie to murder?'

'Yes,' Lizzie said. 'Since we know that she wears a size seven. It's not convicting evidence in and of itself, but it certainly adds support to our theory.'

'Is there any way to prove that this specific footprint was made by Katie's foot?'

Lizzie folded her hands together. 'Not conclusively.'

'I wear a size seven shoe, Detective Munro. So theoretically, it could have been my foot that made that print, correct?'

'You weren't in the barn that morning.'

'Did you know that a size seven adult woman's shoe is also approximately equivalent in length to a size five child's shoe?'

'I didn't.'

'Did you know that Levi Stoltzfus wears a size five shoe?'

Lizzie smiled tightly. 'I do now.'

'Was Levi barefoot when you arrived at the farm?'

'Yes.'

'Had Levi, by his own admission, been standing on the floor near that pile of horse blankets to reach for one when he happened to find the body of the infant?'

'Yes.'

'So is it possible that the footprint you're chalking up to evidentiary proof of Katie committing murder actually belonged to someone else who was in the same spot for a completely innocent reason?'

'It's possible.'

'All right,' Ellie said. 'You said the umbilical cord was cut with scissors.'

'Missing scissors,' Lizzie interjected.

'If a girl was going to kill her baby, Detective, would she bother to cut the cord?'

'I have no idea.'

'What if I told you that clamping and cutting the cord prompts the reflex that makes the newborn breathe on its own? Would it make sense to do that, if you're going to smother it a few minutes later?'

'I suppose not,' Lizzie answered evenly, 'but then again, I doubt most people know that cutting the cord leads to breathing. More likely, it's a step in the birthing process they've seen on TV. Or in this case, from watching farm animals.'

Taken down a peg, Ellie stepped back to regroup. 'If a girl was going to kill her baby, wouldn't it be easier to cover it up with hay and leave it to die of exposure?'

'Maybe.'

'Yet this baby was found wiped clean, lovingly wrapped. Detective, what murderous young mother is going to swab and swaddle her baby?'

'I don't know. But it happened,' Lizzie said firmly.

'That brings me to another point,' Ellie continued. 'According to your theory, Katie hid the pregnancy for seven months and sneaked into the barn to deliver the baby in absolute silence – going to great lengths to keep anyone from finding out that a baby ever existed either in utero or out. So why on earth would she leave it in a place that she knew very well would be crawling with people doing the milking a few hours later? Why not dump the baby in the pond behind the barn?'

'I don't know.'

'Or in the manure pile, where it wouldn't have been found for some time?'

'I don't know.'

'There are a lot of places on an Amish farm where the body of a baby could be disposed of that are far more clever than under a pile of blankets.'

Shrugging, Lizzie replied, 'No one said the defendant was clever. Just that she committed murder.'

'Murder? We're talking basic common sense here. Why cut the cord, get the baby breathing, swaddle it, kill it – and then leave it where it's sure to be discovered?'

Lizzie sighed. 'Maybe she wasn't thinking clearly.'

Ellie rounded on her. 'And yet by the very terms of a charge of murder, you allege that she was cognizant of this act, that she premeditated this act, that she committed it with intent? Can you be deliberate and confused all at the same time?'

'I'm not a psychiatrist, Ms Hathaway. I don't know.'

'No,' Ellie said meaningfully. 'You don't.'

When Katie and Jacob had been small, they'd played together in the fields, zigzagging through the summer cornfields as if they were a maze. Incredible, how thick and green those walls could grow, so that she could be a foot away from her brother just on the other side, and never know it.

Once, when she was about eight, she got lost. She'd been playing follow-the-leader, but Jacob got ahead of her and disappeared. Katie had called out for him, but he was teasing her that day and wouldn't come. She walked in circles, she grew tired and thirsty, and finally she lay down on her back on the ground. She squinted up between the slats of stalks and took comfort from the fact that this was the same old sun, the same old sky, the same familiar world she'd awakened in that morning. And eventually, feeling guilty, Jacob came and found her.

At the defense table, with a flurry of words hailing around her like a storm, Katie remembered that day in the corn.

Things had a way of working out for the best, when you let them run their course.

'The patient was brought into the ER with vaginal bleeding, and a urine pregnancy test was positive. She had a boggy uterus about twenty-four weeks' size, and an open cervical os,' said Dr Seaborn Blair. 'We started her on a drip of pitocin to stop the bleeding. A BSU confirmed that the patient was pregnant.'

'Was the defendant cooperative about treatment?' George asked.

'Not as I recall,' Dr Blair answered. 'She was very upset about having a pelvic done – although we do see that from time to time in young women from remote areas.'

'After you treated the defendant, did you have a chance to speak to her?'

'Yes. Naturally, my first question was about the baby. It was clear that Ms Fisher had recently delivered, yet she wasn't brought in with a neonate.'

'What was the defendant's explanation?'

Dr Blair looked at Katie. 'That she hadn't had a baby.'

'Ah,' George said. 'Which you knew to be medically inaccurate.'

'That's right.'

'Did you question her further?'

'Yes, but she wouldn't admit to the pregnancy. At that point, I suggested a psychiatric consult.'

'Did a psychiatrist ever examine the defendant at the hospital?'

'Not as far as I know,' the doctor said. 'The patient wouldn't permit it.'

'Thank you,' George finished. 'Your witness.'

Ellie drummed her fingers on the defense table for a moment, then stood. 'The boggy uterus, the positive BSU, the bleeding, the pelvic exam. Did these observations lead you to believe that Katie had had a baby?'

'Yes.'

'Did these observations lead you to believe that Katie had killed that baby?'

Dr Blair glanced, again, at Katie. 'No,' he said.

Dr Carl Edgerton had been the medical examiner in Lancaster County for over fifteen years and easily fit the role, with his tufted eyebrows and white hair waving back from a central part. He'd participated in hundreds of trials, and approached every one with the same slightly irritated look on his face, one that said he'd rather be back in his lab. 'Doctor,' the prosecutor said, 'can you tell us the results of the autopsy on Baby Fisher?'

'Yes. He was a premature liveborn male infant with no congenital abnormalities. There was evidence of acute chorioamnionitis, as well as some meconium aspiration and early pneumonia. There were various indications of perinatal asphyxia. Additionally, there were perioral ecchymoses and intraoral cotton fibers that matched the shirt the infant was found in.'

'Let's break that down a bit for those of us who didn't go to med school,' George said, smiling at the jury. 'When you say it was premature and liveborn, what does that mean?'

'The baby wasn't carried to term. Its skeletal age was consistent with a gestational age of thirty-two weeks.'

'And liveborn?'

'As opposed to stillborn. The lungs of the infant were pink and aerated. Representative samples of each lower lobe, with a control sample of liver, were suspended in water. The lung tissue floated, while the liver sank – which indicates that the infant was born and breathed air.'

'How about a lack of congenital abnormalities – why is that important?'

'The baby would have been born viable. There were also no chromosomal defects and no evidence of substance abuse – all significant negative findings.'

'And the chorioamnionitis?'

'Basically, it's an infection in the mother that led to premature delivery. Additional examination of the placenta ruled out the usual other common causes for premature labor. The cause of the chorioamnionitis was not identified because the fetal tissues and placenta were contaminated.'

'How did you know that?'

'Microbiological studies revealed diphtheroids – common contaminants – in the fetal tissues. The placenta is rarely sterile after vaginal birth, but this one had been sitting in a stable for some time before being retrieved, as well.'

George nodded. 'And what is asphyxia?'

'A lack of oxygen, which eventually led to death. Petechiae – small hemorrhages – were visible on the surface of the lungs, thymus, and pericardium. A small subarachnoid hemorrhage was found on the brain. In the liver were patchy zones of necrosis of hepatocytes. These findings sound very exotic, but are seen with asphyxia.'

'What about the ecchymoses and cotton fibers?'

'Ecchymoses are small bruises, in layman's terms. These were all approximately one to one-point-five centimeters in diameter, all surrounding the mouth. Scrapings of the oral cavity revealed fibers that matched the shirt.'

'What did these two observations lead you to believe?'

'That someone had stuffed the shirt in the infant's mouth and attempted to cut off his air supply.'

George let that sink in for a moment. 'Was the umbilical cord examined?'

'The attached portion of the umbilical cord was twenty centimeters in length, with no tie or clamp present on the cord, although the end was crushed as if a ligature had been present at some time. Fibers present on the cord stump were submitted to Trace Evidence for analysis and matched baling twine found in the barn. The cut surface of the cord was jagged, had bits of fiber on it, and indicated a small demarcation in the center.'

'Is that important?'

The doctor shrugged. 'It means that whatever was used to cut the cord, most likely scissors, had a notch in one of its blades and had been used to cut baling twine.'

'Doctor, based on all this, did you determine a cause of death for Baby Fisher?'

'Yes,' Edgerton said. 'Asphyxia, due to smothering.'

'Did you determine a manner of death?'

The medical examiner nodded. 'Murder.'

Ellie took a deep breath, stood, and approached the medical examiner. 'Dr Edgerton, are the ecchymoses around the mouth conclusive proof of smothering?'

'The proof of smothering is in the many organs that show signs of asphyxia.'

Ellie nodded. 'You mean, for example, the petechiae in the

lungs. But isn't it true that you cannot tell from an autopsy exactly when that asphyxia occurred? For example, if there was a problem with placental blood flow before or during birth, couldn't it cause a loss of oxygen in the fetus, which would show up in the autopsy?'

'Yes.'

'What if there was a problem with placental blood flow just after birth? Might that result in signs of asphyxia?'

'Yes.'

'How about if the mother were bleeding or having trouble breathing herself during the delivery?'

The medical examiner cleared his throat. 'That too.'

'What if the baby's lungs were immature, or if it were suffering from poor circulation or pneumonia – would that lead to evidence of asphyxia?'

'Yes, it would.'

'And if the baby choked on its own mucus?'

'Yes.'

'So asphyxia may be caused by many things other than homicidal smothering?'

'That's correct, Ms Hathaway,' the medical examiner said. 'It was the asphyxia, in conjunction with the bruises around the oral cavity and the fibers found within it, that led to my specific diagnosis.'

Ellie smiled. 'Let's talk about that. Does the evidence of a bruise prove that someone held a hand over the baby's mouth?'

'The bruise indicates that there was local pressure applied,' Dr Edgerton said. 'Make of it what you will.'

'Well, let's do just that. What if the baby was delivered precipitously, and landed on his face on the barn floor – might that have led to bruises?'

'It's possible.'

'How about if the mother grabbed for the infant as it was falling after that delivery?'

'Perhaps,' the doctor conceded.

'And the fibers in the oral cavity,' Ellie continued. 'Might they have come from the mother wiping mucus from the baby's air passages, to help it breathe?'

Edgerton inclined his head. 'Could be.'

'In any of those alternative scenarios, is the mother of the infant causing it harm?'

'No, she is not.'

Ellie crossed to the jury box. 'You mentioned that the cultures were contaminated?'

'Yes. The lapse of time between the birth and the recovery of the placental tissue made it a culture plate, picking up bacteria.'

'The fetal tissue was also contaminated?'

'That's correct,' Dr Edgerton said. 'By diphtheroids.'

'On what did you base your identification of these . . . diphtheroids?' Ellie asked.

'Colony and Gram's stain morphology of the placental and fetal cultures.'

'Did you do any biochemical studies to make sure they were diphtheroids?'

'No need to.' The doctor shrugged. 'Do you reread your textbooks before every case, Ms Hathaway? I've been doing this for fifteen years. Believe me, I know what diphtheroids look like.'

'You're a hundred percent sure these were diphtheroids?' Ellie pressed.

'Yes, I am.'

Ellie smiled slightly. 'You also mentioned that the placenta showed signs of acute chorioamnionitis. Isn't it true that chorioamnionitis can lead a fetus to aspirate infected amniotic fluid, and thus develop intra-uterine pneumonia – which in turn leads to septicemia and death?'

'Very, very rarely.'

'But it does happen?'

The medical examiner sighed. 'Yes, but it's a real stretch. It's far more realistic to point to the chorioamnionitis for premature delivery, rather than cause of death.'

'Yet by your own admission,' Ellie said, 'the autopsy revealed evidence of early pneumonia.'

'That's true, but not severe enough to lead to mortality.'

'According to the autopsy report, meconium was found in the air spaces in the lungs. Isn't that a sign of fetal distress?'

'Yes, in that the fetal stool – the meconium – was passed into the amniotic fluid and breathed into the lungs. It's very irritating and can compromise respiration.'

Ellie crossed toward the witness. 'You've just given us two additional reasons that this infant might have suffered from respiratory distress: early pneumonia, as well as aspirating fetal stool.'

'Yes.'

'By your own testimony, asphyxia was the cause of death for this infant.'

'Yes.'

'Isn't it true that pneumonia and meconium aspiration – both of which are due to natural causes – would have led to asphyxia?'

Dr Edgerton seemed amused, as if he knew exactly what Ellie was trying to do. 'Maybe, Ms Hathaway. If the smothering didn't do the job all by itself.'

Ellie had always found the concept of a vending machine that sold hot soup and coffee a little upsetting – how long did all that liquid sit around in its insides? How did it know to give you decaf, instead of chicken broth? She stood before one in the basement of the court, hands on hips, waiting for the small Styrofoam cup to shoot out, for the steam to curl and rise.

Nothing.

'Come on,' she muttered, kicking the bottom of the vending machine. She raised a fist and thumped it on the Plexiglas for good measure. 'That was fifty cents,' she said, more loudly.

A voice behind her stopped her in mid-tirade. 'Remind me to never owe you money,' Coop said, his hands cupping her shoulders, his lips falling on the violin curve of her neck.

'You'd think someone would keep these maintained,' Ellie

huffed, turning her back on the machine. As if that was all it took, it began to splash out hot coffee without a cup, spraying her shoes and her ankles.

'God*damn!*' she yelped, jumping out of the way, then surveying the brown stains on her light hose. 'Oh, great.'

Coop sat down on a metal bridge chair. 'When I was a kid my grandma used to try to make accidents happen. Knock over bottles of milk on purpose, trip over her own feet, splash her blouse with water.'

Blotting at her ankles, Ellie said, 'No wonder you went into mental health.'

'Makes perfect sense, actually, provided you're superstitious. If she had something important to do, she wanted to get the mishap out of the way. Then she'd be free and clear for the rest of the day.'

'You do know it doesn't work that way.'

'Are you so sure?' Coop crossed his legs. 'Wouldn't it be nice to know that now since this has happened, you can walk into that courtroom and do no wrong?'

Ellie sank down beside him and sighed. 'Do you know that she's shaking?' Folding the soiled napkin in half and then in half again, she set it down on the floor beside her chair. 'I can feel her trembling next to me, like she's a tuning fork.'

'Do you want me to talk to her?'

'I don't know,' Ellie said. 'I'm afraid that bringing it up might terrify her more.'

'Psychologically speaking—'

'But we're not, Coop. We're speaking legally. And the most important thing is to get her through this trial without her coming apart at the seams.'

'You're doing fine so far.'

'I haven't done anything at all!'

'Ah, now I get it. If Katie's this nervous just listening to testimony, what's she going to be like when you get her up as a witness?' He rubbed Ellie's back gently. 'You must have faced skittish clients before.'

'Sure.'

'You—' Coop broke off as another attorney entered the room, nodded, and stuffed a set of quarters into the coffee vending machine. 'Careful,' he warned. 'It's not toilet trained.'

Beside him, Ellie swallowed the bubble of a laugh. The attorney kicked the defective machine, cursed beneath his breath, and walked upstairs again. Ellie smiled up at Coop. 'Thanks. I needed that.'

'How about this?' Coop asked, leaning forward to kiss her.

'You don't want to kiss me.' Ellie held him at arm's length. 'I think I'm coming down with something.'

His eyes drifted shut. 'I'm in a gambling mood.'

'Oh, there you are.'

At Leda's voice, Ellie and Coop jerked away from each other. Standing on the staircase was Ellie's aunt, with Katie in tow. 'I told her you were coming right back,' Leda said, 'but she wasn't having any of it.'

Katie walked down the last few steps to stand in front of Ellie. 'I need to go home now.'

'Soon, Katie. Just hang on a little longer.'

'We need to be back for the afternoon milking, and if we leave now, we'll be able to do it. My Dat can't manage with Levi alone.'

'We're required to stay in court until it's adjourned,' Ellie explained.

'Hey, Katie,' Coop interjected, 'why don't you and I go somewhere and talk for a few minutes?' He cast Ellie a sidelong glance, urging her to be compassionate.

Even at a distance, it was possible to see the tremors that ran through Katie. She ignored Coop, staring directly at Ellie instead. 'Can't you make court adjourn?'

'That's up to the judge.' Ellie set her hand on the girl's shoulder. 'I know this is hard for you, and I – where are you going?'

'To talk to the judge. To ask her to adjourn,' Katie said stubbornly. 'I can't miss my chores.'

'You can't just go talk to the judge. It's not done.'

'Well, I'm gonna do it.'

'Get the judge angry,' Ellie warned, 'and you'll be missing your chores forever.'

Katie rounded on her. 'Then you ask.'

'This is a new one for me, counselor,' Judge Ledbetter said. She leaned over her desk, frowning. 'You're requesting that we wrap up early today so that your client can do her chores?'

Ellie straightened her spine, her expression impassive. 'Actually, Your Honor, I'm requesting that we adjourn at three P.M. every day this trial goes on.' Gritting her teeth, she added, 'Believe me, Judge. If this were not germane to my client's way of life, I wouldn't be suggesting it.'

'Court adjourns at four-thirty, Ms Hathaway.'

'I'm aware of that. I explained as much to my client.'

'I'm just dying to know what she had to say.'

'That the cows wouldn't wait till then.' Ellie risked a glance toward George, who was grinning like the cat who'd eaten the canary. And why shouldn't he be? Ellie was doing a splendid job digging her own grave without a single syllable's contribution from him. 'At issue, Your Honor, is the fact that in addition to my client, one of the sequestered witnesses is also a hired hand on the Fisher farm. For both of them to miss the afternoon milking would put undue strain on the economic affairs of the family.'

Judge Ledbetter turned toward the prosecutor. 'Mr Callahan, I assume you have something to say about this.'

'Yes, Your Honor. From what I understand the Amish don't abide by daylight saving time. It's one thing to run their own schedules when it doesn't affect anyone else, but in a court of law they ought to be required to adhere to our clock. For all I know, this is some plot of Ms Hathaway's to point out the glaring differences between the Amish and the rest of the world.'

'It's not a plot, George,' Ellie muttered. 'It's just lactation, pure and simple.'

'Furthermore,' the prosecutor continued, 'I have one witness remaining to be questioned, and postponing his testimony would be detrimental to my case. Since it's Friday, the jury wouldn't be able to hear it until Monday morning, and by then any momentum that's been building would be lost.'

'At the risk of being presumptuous, Your Honor, may I point out that in many trials I've participated in, schedules have been reworked at the last minute according to the whims of child care, doctor's visits, and other emergencies that come up in the lives of the attorneys and even judges? Why not bend the rules for the defendant as well?'

'Oh, she's done a fine job of that by herself,' George said dryly.

'Pipe down, you two,' Judge Ledbetter said. 'As tempting as it is to get out of here before Friday-night traffic settles in, I'm going to deny your request, Ms Hathaway, at least for as long as it takes the prosecution to present their case. When it's your turn, you're welcome to adjourn court at three P.M. if it suits you.' She turned to George. 'Mr Callahan, you may call your witness.'

'Imagine that you're a young girl,' said Dr Brian Riordan, the forensic psychiatric expert for the state. 'You find yourself involved in an illicit relationship with a boy your parents know nothing about. You sleep with the boy, although you know better. A few weeks later, you find out you're pregnant. You go about your daily routine, even though you're a little more tired these days. You think the problem will take care of itself. Every time the thought crosses your mind, you shove it aside, promising you'll deal with it tomorrow. In the meantime, you wear clothes that are a little looser; you make sure that no one embraces you too closely.

'Then one night you wake up in severe pain. You know what is happening to you, but all you care about is keeping your secret. You sneak out of the house so no one can hear you giving birth. In solitude, in silence, you deliver a baby that means nothing to you. Then the baby begins to cry. You cover its mouth with your hand, because it is going to wake everyone up. You press harder until the baby stops crying, until it is no longer moving. Then, knowing you have to get rid of it, you wrap it up in a nearby shirt and stuff it somewhere out of sight. You're exhausted, so you go up to your bedroom to sleep, telling yourself you'll deal with the rest tomorrow. When the police approach you the next day asking about a baby, you say you know nothing about it, just like you've been telling yourself all along.'

Mesmerized, the jury leaned forward, caught on the sharp, stiletto edges of the scene Riordan had crafted with words. 'What about maternal instincts?' George asked.

'Women who commit neonaticide are completely detached from the pregnancy,' Riordan explained. 'For them, giving birth packs all the emotional punch of passing a gallstone.'

'Do women who commit neonaticide feel badly about doing it?'

'Remorse, you mean.' Riordan pursed his lips. 'Yes, they do. But only because they're sorry their parents have seen them in such an unfavorable light – not because there's a dead baby.'

'Dr Riordan, how did you come to meet the defendant?'

'I was asked to evaluate her for this trial.'

'What did that entail?'

'Reading the discovery in this case, examining her responses to projective psychological tests like the Rorschach and objective tests like the MMPI, as well as meeting with the defendant personally.'

'Did you reach a conclusion as to a reasonable degree of psychiatric certainty?'

'Yes, at the time she killed the baby she knew right from wrong and was aware of her actions.' Riordan's eyes skimmed over Katie. 'This was a classic case of neonaticide. Everything about the defendant fit the profile of a woman who would murder her newborn – her upbringing, her actions, her lies.'

'How do you know she was lying?' George asked, playing

devil's advocate. 'Maybe she really didn't know that she was pregnant, or having a baby.'

'By her own statement, the defendant knew she was pregnant but made the voluntary decision to keep it secret. If you choose to act a certain way to protect yourself, it implies conscious knowledge of what you're doing. Thus, denial and guilt are linked. Moreover, once you lie, you're likely to lie again, which means that any of her statements about the pregnancy and birth are dubious at best. Her actions, however, tell a solid, consistent story,' Riordan said. 'During our interview, the defendant admitted to waking up with labor pains and intentionally leaving her room because she didn't want anyone to hear her. This suggests concealment. She chose the barn and went to an area that she knew had fresh hay placed in it. This suggests intent. She covered the bloody hay after the delivery, tried to keep the newborn from crying out – and the body of the newborn was found tucked beneath a stack of blankets. This suggests that she had something to hide. She got rid of the bloody nightgown she'd been wearing, got up and acted perfectly normal the next morning in front of her family, all to continue this hoax. Each of these things – acting in isolation, concealing the birth, cleaning up, pretending life is routine – indicates that the defendant knew very well what she was doing at the time she did it – and more importantly, knew what she was doing was wrong.'

'Did the defendant admit to murdering the newborn during your interview?'

'No, she says that she doesn't remember this.'

'Then how can you be sure she did?'

Riordan shrugged. 'Because amnesia is easily faked. And because, Mr Callahan, I've been here before. There is a specific pattern to the events of neonaticide, and the defendant meets every criteria: She denied the pregnancy. She claims she didn't realize she was in labor, when it first occurred. She gave birth alone. She said she didn't kill the baby, in spite of the truth of the dead body. She gradually admitted to certain holes in her story as time went on. All of these things are landmarks in every neonaticide case I've ever studied, and lead me to believe that she too committed neonaticide, even if there are patches in the story she cannot apparently yet recall.' He leaned forward on the stand. 'If I see something with feathers and a bill and webbed feet that quacks, I don't have to watch it swim to know it's a duck.'

The hardest part about changing defenses, for Ellie, had been losing Dr Polacci as a witness. However, there was no way she could give the psychiatrist's report to the prosecution, since it stated that Katie had killed her newborn, albeit without understanding the nature and quality of the act. This meant that any holes Ellie was going to poke in the prosecution's argument of neonaticide had to be made now, and preferably large enough to drive a tank through. 'How many women have you interviewed who've committed neonaticide?' Ellie asked, striding toward Dr Riordan.

'Ten.'

'Ten!' Ellie's eyes widened. 'But you're supposed to be an expert!'

'I am considered one. Everything's relative.'

'So – you come across one a year?'

Riordan inclined his head. 'That would be about right.'

'This profile of yours, and your claims about Katie – they're made on the extensive experience you've collected by interviewing all of . . . ten people?'

'Yes.'

Ellie raised her brows. 'In the *Journal of Forensic Sciences*, didn't you say that women who commit neonaticide are not malicious, Dr Riordan? That they don't necessarily want to do harm?'

'That's right. They're usually not thinking about it in those terms. They see the action only as something that will egocentrically help themselves.'

'Yet in the cases you've been involved in, you've recommended that women who commit neonaticide be incarcerated?'

'Yes. We need to send a message to society, that murderers don't go free.'

'I see. Isn't it true, Doctor, that women who commit neonaticide admit to killing their newborns?'

'Not at first.'

'But eventually, when faced with evidence or pressed to explain, they crumble. Right?'

'That's what I've seen, yes.'

'During your interview with Katie, did you ask her to hypothesize about what had happened to the baby?'

'Yes.'

'What was her response?'

'She came up with several.'

'Didn't she say, "Maybe it just died, and someone hid it."'

'Among other things, yes.'

'You said that when pressed, women who commit neonaticide crumble. Doesn't the fact that Katie offered up this hypothetical scenario, rather than breaking down and admitting to murder, mean that it might have been what actually happened?'

'It means she can lie well.'

'But did Katie ever admit that she killed her baby?'

'No. However, she didn't admit to her pregnancy at first, either.'

Ellie ignored his comment. 'What did Katie admit, exactly?'

'That she fell asleep, woke up, and the baby was gone. She didn't remember anything else.'

'And from this you inferred that she committed homicide?'

'It was the most likely explanation, given the overall set of behaviors.'

It was exactly the answer Ellie wanted. 'As an expert in the field, you must know what a dissociative state is.'

'Yes, I do.'

'Could you explain it for those of us who don't?'

'A dissociative state occurs when someone fractures off a piece of her consciousness to survive a traumatic situation.'

'Like an abused wife who mentally zones out while her husband's beating her?'

'That's correct,' Riordan answered.

'Is it true that people who go into a dissociative state experience memory lapses, yet manage to appear basically normal?'

'Yes.'

'A dissociative state is not a voluntary, conscious behavior?'

'Correct.'

'Isn't it true that extreme psychological stress can trigger a dissociative state?'

'Yes.'

'Might witnessing the death of a loved one cause extreme psychological stress?'

'Perhaps.'

'Let's step back. For a moment, let's assume Katie wanted her baby, desperately. She gave birth and, tragically, watched it die in spite of her best efforts to keep it breathing. Might the shock of the death cause a dissociative state?'

'It's possible,' Riordan agreed.

'If she then could not recall how the baby died, might her memory lapse be due to this dissociation?'

Riordan grinned indulgently. 'It might, if it were a reasonable scenario, Ms Hathaway, which it unfortunately is not. If you want to claim that the defendant went into a dissociative state that morning that subsequently led to her memory lapses, I'm happy to play along with you. But there's no way to prove that the stress of the baby's natural death put her into that state. It's equally possible that she dissociated due to the stress of labor. Or as a result of the highly stressful act of committing murder.

'You see, the fact of dissociation doesn't absolve Ms Fisher from committing neonaticide. Humans are able to perform complex meteoric actions even when the ability to recall these actions is impaired. You can drive your car while in a dissociative state, for example, and travel for hundreds of miles without remembering a single landmark. Likewise, in a dissociative state, you can deliver a baby, even if you can't recall the specifics. You can try to resuscitate a dying baby, and not recall the specifics. Or,' he said pointedly, 'you can kill a baby, and not recall the specifics.'

'Dr Riordan,' Ellie said, 'we're talking about a young Amish girl here, not some self-absorbed mall-rat teen. Put yourself into her shoes. Isn't it possible that Katie Fisher wanted that baby, that it died in her arms, that she became so upset about it her own mind unconsciously blocked out what had happened?'

But Riordan had been on the stand too many times to fall so neatly into an attorney's trap. 'If she wanted that baby so badly, Ms Hathaway,' he said, 'why did she lie about it for seven months?'

George was standing up before Ellie even made it back to the defense table. 'I'd like to redirect, Your Honor. Dr Riordan, in your expert opinion, was the defendant in a dissociative state on the morning of July tenth?'

'No.'

'Is that important to this case?'

'No.'

'Why not?'

Riordan shrugged. 'Her behavior is clear enough – there's no need to invoke this psychobabble. The defendant's subversive actions before the birth suggest that once the baby arrived, she'd do anything within her power to get rid of it.'

'Including murder?'

The psychiatrist nodded. 'Especially murder.'

'Recross,' Ellie said. 'Dr Riordan, as a forensic psychiatrist you must know that for a Murder One conviction, a person must be found guilty of killing with deliberation, willfulness, and premeditation.'

'Yes, that's true.'

'Women who commit neonaticide – do they kill willfully?'

'Absolutely.'

'Do they deliberate about the act?'

'Sometimes, in the way they'll pick a quiet place, or bring a blanket or bag to dispose of the baby – as the defendant did.'

'Do they plan the murder of the infant in advance?'

Riordan frowned. 'It's a reflexive act, stimulated by the newborn's arrival.'

'Reflexive act,' Ellie repeated. 'By that you mean an automatic, instinctive, unthinking behavior?'

'Yes.'

'Then neonaticide isn't really first-degree murder, is it?'

'Objection!'

'Withdrawn,' Ellie said. 'Nothing further.'

George turned to the judge. 'Your Honor,' he said, 'the prosecution rests.'

Sarah had held dinner for them, a spread of comfort food that offered no appeal for Ellie. She picked at her plate and felt the walls closing in on her, wondering why she hadn't taken Coop up on his suggestion to get a bite to eat at a restaurant in Lancaster.

'I brushed Nugget for you,' Sarah said, 'but there's still tack to be cleaned.'

'All right, Mam,' Katie answered. 'I'll go on out after supper. I'll get the dishes, too; you must be tired after helping out with the milking.'

From the opposite end of the table, Aaron belched loudly, smiling a compliment at his wife. '*Gut* meal,' he said. He hooked his thumbs beneath his suspenders and turned to his father. 'I'm thinking of heading to Lapp's auction on Monday.'

'You need some new horseflesh?' Elam said.

Aaron shrugged. 'Never hurts to see what's there.'

'I heard tell that Marcus King was getting set to sell that colt bred off his bay last spring.'

'*Ja?* He's a beauty.'

Sarah snorted. 'What are you gonna do with another horse?'

Ellie looked from one family member to another, as if she were following a tennis match. 'Excuse me,' she said softly, and one by one they turned to her. 'Are you all aware that your daughter is involved in a murder trial?'

'Ellie, don't—' Katie stretched out her hand, but Ellie shook her head.

'Are you all aware that in less than a week's time, your daughter could be found guilty of murder and taken directly from the courthouse to the prison in Muncy? Sitting here talking about horse auctions – doesn't anyone even care how the trial is going?'

'We care,' Aaron said stiffly.

'Hell of a way to show it,' Ellie muttered, balling up her napkin and tossing it onto the table before escaping upstairs to her room.

When Ellie opened her eyes again, it was fully dark, and Katie was sitting on the edge of the bed. She sat up immediately, pushing her hair back from her face and squinting at the little battery-powered clock on the nightstand. 'What time is it?'

'Just after ten,' Katie whispered. 'You fell asleep.'

'Yeah.' Ellie ran her tongue over her fuzzy teeth. 'Looks like.' She blinked her way back to consciousness, then reached over to turn up the gas lamp. 'Where did you go, anyway?'

'I did the dishes and cleaned the tack.' Katie busied herself around the room, pulling the shades for the night and sitting down to unwind her neat bun.

Ellie watched Katie run a brush through her long, honey hair, her eyes clear and wide. When Ellie had first arrived and seen that look on all the faces surrounding her, she'd mistaken it for blankness, for stupidity. It had taken months for her to realize that the gaze of the Amish was not vacant, but full – brimming with a quiet peace. Even now, after a difficult beginning to the trial that would have kept most people tossing and turning, Katie was at ease.

'I know they care,' Ellie heard herself murmur.

Katie turned her head. 'About the trial, you mean.'

'Yeah. My family used to yell a lot. Argue and spontaneously combust and then somehow get back together after the dust settled. This quiet – it's still a little strange.'

'Your family yelled at *you* a lot, didn't they?'

'Sometimes,' Ellie admitted. 'But at least all the noise let me know they were there.' She shook her head, clearing it of the memory. 'Anyway, I apologize for blowing up at dinner.' She sighed. 'I don't know what's wrong with me.'

Katie's brush stopped in the middle of a long stroke. 'You don't?'

'Well, no. I mean, I'm a little anxious about the trial, but if I were you I'd rather have me nervous than complacent.' She looked up at Katie, only to realize the girl's cheeks were burning.

'What are you hiding?' Ellie asked, her stomach sinking.

'Nothing! I'm not hiding a thing!'

Ellie closed her eyes. 'I'm too tired for this right now. Could you just save your confession until the morning?'

'Okay,' Katie said, too quickly.

'The hell with the morning. Tell me now.'

'You've been falling asleep early, like you did tonight. And you exploded at the dinner table.' Katie's eyes gleamed as she remembered something else. 'And remember this morning, in the bathroom at the court?'

'You're right. I can blame it all on this bug I've caught.'

Katie set down the hairbrush and smiled shyly. 'You're not sick, Ellie. You're pregnant.'

14

Ellie

'Clearly, it's wrong,' I said to Katie, holding out the stick from the pregnancy test kit.

Katie, squinting at the back of the box, shook her head. 'You waited five minutes. You watched the little line appear in the test window.'

I tossed the stick, with its little pink plus sign, onto the bed. 'I was supposed to pee for thirty seconds straight, and I only counted fifteen. So there you go. Human error.'

We both looked at the box, which contained a second stick. At the pharmacy the deal had been two for the price of one. All it would take for proof was one more trip to the bathroom, five more interminable minutes of destiny. But both Katie and I knew what the results would be.

Things like this did not happen to forty-year-old women. Accidents were for teenagers caught up in the moment, rolling around the backseat of their parents' cars. Accidents were for women who considered their bodies still new and surprising, rather than old, familiar friends. Accidents were for those who didn't know better.

But this didn't feel like an accident. It felt hard and hot, a nugget nestled beneath my palm, as if already I could feel the sonic waves of that tiny heart.

Katie looked into her lap. 'Congratulations,' she whispered.

In the past five years, I had wanted a baby so much I ached. I would wake up sometimes beside Stephen and feel my arms throb, as if I had been holding a newborn weight the whole night. I would see an infant in a stroller and feel my whole body react; I would mark my monthly period on the calendar with the sense that my life was passing me by. I wanted to grow something under my heart. I wanted to breathe, to eat, to blossom for someone else.

Stephen and I fought about children approximately twice a year, as if reproduction were a volcano that erupted every now and then on the island we'd created for ourselves. Once, I actually wore him down. 'All right,' he'd said. 'If it happens, it happens.' I threw away my birth control pills for six consecutive months, but we didn't manage to make a baby. It took me nearly half a year after that to understand why not: You can't create life in a place that's dying by degrees.

After that, I'd stopped asking Stephen. Instead, when I was feeling maternal, I went to the library and did research. I learned how many times the cells of a zygote divided before they were classified as an embryo. I saw on microfiche the pictures of a fetus sucking its thumb, veins running like roads beneath the orange glow of its skin. I learned that a six-week-old fetus was the size of a strawberry. I read about alpha-fetal protein and amniocentesis and rH factors. I became a scholar in an ivory tower, an expert with no hands-on experience.

So you see, I knew everything about this baby inside me – except why I wasn't overjoyed to discover its existence.

I didn't want anyone on the farm to know I was pregnant – at least not until I broke the news to Coop. The next morning, I slept late. I managed to make it out to a secluded spot behind the vegetable garden before I started dry heaving. When the smell of the horse grain made me dizzy, Katie wordlessly took over for me. I began to see her in a new light, amazed she had hidden her condition from so many people, for so long.

She came to join me outside the barn. 'So,' she asked briskly, 'you feeling poor, still?' She slid down beside me, our backs braced by the red wooden wall.

'Not anymore,' I lied. 'I think I'll be okay.'

'Till tomorrow morning, anyway.' Katie dug beneath the

waistband of her apron and pulled out two teabags. 'You'll be needing these, I figure.'

I sniffed at them. 'Will they settle my stomach?'

Katie blushed. 'You put them here,' she said, grazing her breasts with the tips of her fingers. 'When they're too sore to bear.' Assessing my naïveté, she added, 'You steep them, first.'

'Thank God I know someone who's already been through this—' Katie reared back as if I'd slapped her, and too late I realized what I'd said. 'I'm sorry.'

'It's okay,' she murmured.

'It's not okay. I know this can't be easy for you, especially in the middle of the trial. I could say that you'll have another baby of your own one day, but I remember how I felt every time one of my pregnant, married friends said something like that to me.'

'How did you feel?'

'Like I wanted to deck her.'

Katie smiled shyly. '*Ja*, that's about right.' She glanced at my stomach, then away. 'I'm happy for you, Ellie, I am. But that doesn't make it hurt any less. And I keep telling myself that my Mam lost three babies, four if you count Hannah.' She shrugged. 'You can be happy for someone else's good fortune, but that doesn't mean you forget your own bad luck.'

I had never been more aware than I was at that moment of the fact that Katie had wanted her baby. She may have put off having it, she may have procrastinated owning up to her pregnancy – but once the infant was born, there had never been any question in her mind about loving it. With no little amazement I stared at her, feeling the defense I'd prepared for her trial dovetail into the truth.

I squeezed her hand. 'It means a lot to me,' I said. 'Being able to share this secret with someone.'

'Soon you'll be able to tell Coop.'

'I guess.' I didn't know when or whether he'd be by this weekend. We hadn't made any official plans when he dropped us off at the farmhouse on Friday night. Still annoyed after my refusal to move in with him, he was keeping his distance.

Katie wrapped her shawl around her shoulders. 'You think he'll be happy?'

'I know he will.'

She looked up at me. 'Suppose you'll be getting married, then.'

'Well,' I said, 'I don't know about that.'

'I bet he'll want to marry you.'

I turned to her. 'It's not Coop who's holding back.'

I expected her to stare at me blankly, to wonder why on earth I'd shy away from the obvious, easy path. I had a man who loved me, who was the father of this child, who wanted this child. Even I didn't understand my reluctance.

'When I found out I was carrying,' Katie said softly, 'I thought about telling Adam. He'd gone away, sure, but I figured that I could have dug him up if I put my mind to it. And then I realized that I really didn't want to tell Adam. Not because he would have been upset – *ach*, no, the very opposite. I didn't want to tell him because then all the choices were gone. I'd know what I had to do, and I would have done it. But I was afraid that one day I'd look down at the baby, and I wouldn't be thinking, I love you . . .'

Her voice trailed off, and I turned to catch her gaze, to finish her words. 'I'd be thinking, how did I get here?'

Katie stared at the flat expanse of the pond in the distance. 'Exactly,' she said.

Sarah headed toward the chicken coop. 'You don't have to do this,' she told me for the third time.

But I was feeling guilty about having slept the morning away. 'It's no trouble at all,' I said. The Fishers kept twenty-four hens for laying. Tending to the chickens was something Katie and I did in the mornings; the chore involved feeding the birds and gathering the eggs. I had been pecked hard enough to bleed at first, but finally learned how to slide my hand under the warm bottom of a chicken without suffering injury. In fact, I was looking forward to showing Sarah that I already knew a thing or two.

Sarah, on the other hand, wanted to pepper me with questions about Katie's trial. With Aaron far out of earshot, she asked about the prosecutor, the witnesses, the judge. She asked whether Katie would have to speak out in court. Whether we would win.

That last question fell at the door to the coop. 'I don't know,' I admitted. 'I'm doing my best.'

Sarah's face stretched into a smile. 'Yes,' she said softly. 'You do that well.'

She pushed open the wooden door, sending feathers flying as the birds squawked and scattered. Something about a chicken coop reminded me of a batch of ladies gossiping at a hairdresser's salon, and I smiled as a high-strung hen flapped around my heels. Heading to the roost on the right, I began to search the beds for eggs.

'No,' Sarah instructed as I upended a russet-colored hen. 'She's still *gut*.' I watched her tuck a molting chicken beneath her arm like a football and press her fingers between the bones that protruded from its bottom. 'Ah, here's one that stopped laying,' she said, holding it out to me by the feet. 'Let me just grab another.'

The chicken was twisting like Houdini, intent on escaping. Completely baffled, I fisted my hand more tightly around its nubby legs as Sarah found another bird. She headed for the door of the coop, shooing hens. 'What about their eggs?' I asked.

Sarah looked back over her shoulder. 'They're not giving 'em anymore. That's why we'll be having them for dinner.'

I stopped in my tracks, looked down at the hen, and nearly let her go. 'Come along,' Sarah said, disappearing behind the coop.

There was a chopping block, an ax, and a steaming pail of hot water waiting. With grace Sarah lifted the ax, swung the bird onto the block and cut off its head. As she released its legs, the decapitated chicken somersaulted and danced a jitterbug in a pool of its own blood. With horror I watched Sarah reach for the chicken I was holding; I felt her pull it from my grip just before I fell to my knees and threw up.

After a moment Sarah's hand smoothed back my hair. '*Ach,* Ellie,' she said, 'I thought you knew.'

I shook my head, which made me feel sick again. 'I wouldn't have come.'

'Katie don't have the stomach for it either,' Sarah admitted. 'I asked you because it's so much easier than going back in there again after doing the first one.' She patted my arm; on the back of her wrist was a smear of blood. I closed my eyes.

I could hear Sarah moving behind me, dipping the limp bodies of the chickens into hot water. 'The dumpling stew,' I said hesitantly. 'The noodle soup . . . ?'

'Of course,' Sarah answered. 'Where did you think chickens came from?'

'Frank Perdue.'

'He does it the same way, believe me.'

I cradled my head in my hands, refusing to think about all the brisket and the hamburger meat we'd eaten, and of the little bull calves I'd seen born in the months I'd been on the farm. People only see what they want to see – look at Sarah turning a blind eye to Katie's pregnancy, or a jury hanging an acquittal on the testimony of a certain sympathetic witness, or even my own reluctance to admit that the connection between Coop and me went beyond the physical fact of creating a baby.

I glanced up to see Sarah stripping the feathers off one of the birds, her mouth set in a tight line. There were tufts of white fluff on her apron and skirt; a trail of red blood soaked into the hard-packed dirt before her. I swallowed the bile rising in my throat. 'How do you do it?'

'I do what I have to do,' she said matter-of-factly. 'You of all people should understand.'

I was hiding in the milk room when Coop found me that afternoon. 'El, you're not gonna believe this—' His eyes widened as he saw me, and he sprinted to my side, running his hands up and down my arms. 'How did this happen?'

He knew; God, all he'd had to do was look at me, and he knew about the baby. I swallowed and met his gaze. 'Pretty much the usual way, I guess.'

Coop's hand slid from my shoulder to my waist, and I waited for him to move lower still. But instead, his fingers plucked at my T-shirt, rubbing at the bright red streak that stained it. 'When was your last tetanus shot?'

He wasn't talking about the baby. *He wasn't talking about the baby.*

'Well, of course I am,' Coop said, making me realize I'd spoken aloud. 'But for God's sake, the stupid trial can wait. We'll get you stitched up first.'

I pushed Coop's hands away. 'I'm fine. This blood's not mine.'

Coop raised a brow. 'Have you been committing homicide again?'

'Very funny. I was helping kill chickens.'

'I'd save the pagan rituals until after you've presented your defense, but then—'

'Tell me about him, Coop,' I said firmly.

'He wants answers. After all, the man jumped on a plane the day after finding out he was a father – but he wants to see Katie and the baby.'

My jaw dropped. 'You didn't tell him—'

'No, I didn't. I'm a psychiatrist, Ellie. I'm not about to cause someone undue mental anguish unless I'm there, face to face, to help him deal with it.'

As Coop turned away, I put my hand on his shoulder. 'I would have done the same thing. Except my motive wouldn't have been kindness, but selfishness. I want him to testify, and if that works to get him here, so be it.'

'This isn't going to be easy for him,' Coop murmured.

'It was no picnic for Katie, either.' I straightened. 'Has he seen Jacob yet?'

'He just got off the plane. I picked him up in Philly.'

'So where is he now?'

'In the car, waiting.'

'In the car?' I sputtered. 'Here? Are you crazy?'

Coop grinned. 'I think I can tell you with some authority that I'm not.'

In no mood for his jokes, I was already walking through the barn. 'We've got to get him out of here, fast.'

Coop fell into step beside me. 'You may want to change first,' he said. 'Just a suggestion – but right now you look like you've stepped out of a Kevin Williamson film, and you know how important first impressions are.'

His words barely registered. I was too busy considering how many times that day I would be called upon to tell a man the one thing he least expected to hear.

'Why is she in trouble?' Adam Sinclair asked, leaning across the table at the diner. 'Is it because she wasn't married when she had the baby? God, if she'd just written to me, this wouldn't have happened.'

'She couldn't write to you,' I said gently. 'Jacob never forwarded your letters.'

'He didn't? That bastard—'

'—was doing what he thought was in the best interest of his sister,' I said. 'He didn't think she could bear the stigma of having to leave her faith, and that's what marrying you would have entailed.'

Adam pushed away his plate. 'Look. I appreciate you getting in touch with me and letting me know that Katie's in some kind of trouble. I appreciate the ride from the airport out here to East Paradise. I even appreciate the free lunch. But I'm sure that by now, Katie's back home with the baby, and I really need to go speak to her directly.'

I watched his hands play over the table and imagined them touching Katie, holding Katie. And with a great and sudden rage I hated this man whom I hardly knew, for unwittingly bringing Katie to this point. Who was he, to decide that his affection for Katie overruled everything she'd been brought up to believe? Who was he, to lead an eighteen-year-old girl down a path of seduction when he clearly knew better?

Something must have shown on my face, because beneath the table, Coop pressed his hand against my thigh in gentle warning. I blinked, and Adam came into clear focus: his bright eyes, his tapping foot, his sideways glance at every jingle of the bell over the door, as if he expected Katie and his son to come strolling in any minute.

'Adam,' I said, 'the baby didn't survive.'

He froze. With precision he folded his hands on the table, fingers gripped so tight the tips turned bloodlessly white. 'What . . .' he said softly, his voice breaking in the middle of the word. 'What happened?'

'We don't know. He was born prematurely and died shortly after delivery.'

Adam's head sagged. 'For the past three days, since you called, all I've been thinking of is that baby. Whether it's got her eyes, or my chin. Whether I'd know him in an instant. Jesus. If I'd been here, maybe I could have done something.'

I looked at Coop. 'We didn't think it was right to tell you over the phone.'

'No. No, of course not.' Adam looked up, quickly wiping his eyes. 'Katie must be devastated.'

'She is,' Coop said.

'Is that what you meant when you said she's in trouble? Did you need me to come because she's depressed?'

'We need you to stand up for her in court,' I said quietly. 'Katie's been charged with murdering the baby.'

He reeled back. 'She didn't.'

'No, I don't think so either.'

Pushing to his feet, Adam threw down his napkin. 'I have to see her. Now.'

'I'd rather you wait.' I stood in front of him, blocking his exit.

Adam loomed over me. 'Do you think I give a flying fuck what you want?'

'Katie doesn't even know you're here.'

'Then it's high time she found out.'

I put my hand on his arm. 'As Katie's lawyer, I believe that if the jury is given a front-row seat the first time she sees you again, they're going to be moved by her emotion. They're going to think that anyone who wears her heart on her sleeve like that couldn't be cold enough to kill her own infant.' I stepped away. 'If you want to see Katie now, Adam, I'll take you there. But think hard about that. Because the last time she needed you, you weren't here to help. This time, you can.'

Adam looked from me to Coop, and slowly sank back into his seat.

The moment Adam went to use the restroom, I told Coop we had to talk.

'I'm all ears.' Coop picked up a french fry from my plate and popped it into his mouth.

'In private.'

'My pleasure,' Coop said, 'but what do I do with my baby-sitting charge?'

'Keep him far away from mine.' I sighed, and considered keeping the news to myself until after the trial; this was a moment I should have been concentrating on Katie, after all, and not myself. But I had only to look as far as Adam Sinclair to see the grief that could come from remaining silent, even with the best of intentions.

Before I could puzzle out a solution, Adam provided me with one. Coming from the restroom with red-rimmed eyes and the smell of soap fresh about him, he stood awkwardly at the edge of the table. 'If it's not too much trouble,' he asked, 'could you take me to my son's grave?'

Coop parked beside the Amish cemetery. 'Take as long as you'd like,' he said. Adam stepped out of the back of the car, his shoulders hunched against the wind, as I got out of my own seat and led him through the small gate.

We kicked up small tornadoes of fallen leaves as we crossed to the new grave. The stone, chipped by Katie's hands, was the color of winter. Adam shoved his hands into his pockets and spoke without turning to me. 'The funeral . . . were you here?'

'Yes. It was lovely.'

'Was there a service? Flowers?'

I thought of the brief, uncomfortable prayer said by the bishop, of the Plain customs that did not allow for any adornment of the grave, neither flowers nor fancy headstones. 'It was lovely,' I repeated.

Adam nodded, then sat down on the ground beside the grave. He held out his hand, gently running one finger over the rounded edge of the headstone, the way a new father might reverently touch the soft curve of a newborn's cheek. Eyes stinging, I turned abruptly and walked back to Coop's car.

As I slid into the passenger seat, Coop watched Adam through the window. 'Poor guy. I can't even imagine.'

'Coop,' I said. 'I'm pregnant.'

He turned. 'You're what?'

I folded my hands over my abdomen. 'You heard right.'

The fact of this baby had tangled my thoughts. I had once left Coop for all the wrong reasons; I didn't want to stay with him for all the wrong reasons, either. I stared at his face, waiting; telling myself that his reaction wouldn't affect my decision about the future in the least; wondering why, then, I wanted to hear his response so badly. For the first time I could remember, I was unsure about Coop's commitment to me. Sure, he had asked me to move in with him, but this wasn't the same thing at all. Maybe he wanted to spend a lifetime together, but he might not have expected that lifetime to begin quite so suddenly or with such lasting consequences. He had never mentioned marriage. He had never mentioned children.

I'd provided Coop with the perfect reason to walk out of my

life and leave me the breathing room I'd always craved – but now I realized I didn't want him to go.

When he did not smile, or touch me, or do anything but sit frozen across from me, I began to panic. Maybe Katie had it right; maybe the best thing would have been to wait a few days, if not more. 'So,' I said, my voice shaking. 'What are you thinking?'

He reached across the seat and tugged my hand away from the place where it covered my stomach. He edged up the hem of my sweatshirt and leaned forward, and then I felt his kiss low against my belly.

The breath I did not realize I'd been holding rushed out in a great flood of relief. After a moment I cradled his head in my hands, sifting strands of his hair through my fingers, as Coop wrapped his arms around my hips and held tight to the two of us.

He insisted on walking me to the door of the Fishers' house. 'I'm not handicapped, Coop,' I argued. 'Just pregnant.' But the feminist in me rolled over, secretly thrilled to be treated like spun sugar.

At the porch, he took my hands and turned me to face him. 'I know this part is supposed to come before you actually make the baby, but I want you to know I love you. I've loved you so long I can't remember when it started.'

'I can. It was after the Kappa Alpha Theta San Juan Night party, somewhere between you diving into the grain alcohol and the naked blow pong tournament.'

Coop groaned. 'Let's not tell him how we met, okay?'

'What makes you so sure it's a *he*?'

Suddenly Coop stilled and held his hand up to his ear. 'Do you hear that?'

I strained, then shook my head. 'No. What?'

'Us,' he said, kissing me lightly. 'Sounding like parents.'

'Scary thought.'

He smiled, then cocked his head and stared at me. 'What?' I asked, self-conscious. 'Do I have spinach between my teeth?'

'No. It's just that I'm only going to get this moment once, and I want to remember it.'

'I think we can arrange for you to walk me into the house a few more times, if it's that important to you.'

'God, can't a guy get a break? Do all women talk this much, or is it just because you're an attorney?'

'Well, if I were you I'd say whatever it is you're going to say, because Adam's liable to get sick of waiting in the car and drive back to Philly without you.'

Coop cupped my face in his palms. 'You're a pain in the ass, El, but you're my pain in the ass.' His thumbs smoothed over my cheeks. 'Marry me,' he whispered.

I brought my hands up to grasp his wrists. Over his shoulder, the moon was rising, a ghost in the sky. I realized that Coop was right: I would remember this moment with the same level of detail and clarity that came to mind when I thought back to the last time Coop had asked me to share his life; the last time I'd told him no.

'Don't hate me,' I said.

His hands fell away. 'You are not doing this to me again. I won't let you.' A muscle jumped along his jaw as he struggled for control.

'I'm not saying no. I'm just not saying yes, either. Coop, I just found out about this. I'm still seeing how the word *mother* fits. I can't try on *wife* at the same time.'

'Millions of other women manage.'

'Not quite in this order.' I smoothed my hand over his chest, hoping to soothe. 'You told me a little while ago I could take a while to think. Does that still hold?'

Coop nodded, and slowly let the tension drain out of his shoulders. 'But this time, you won't be able to get rid of me so easily.' Then he splayed his hand over my abdomen, where part of him already was, and kissed me good-bye.

'You were gone for so long,' Katie whispered from her bed. 'Did you tell him?'

I stared up at the ceiling, at the small yellow stain that reminded me of Abraham Lincoln's profile. 'Yeah, I did.'

She came up on one elbow. 'And?'

'And he's happy. That's it.' I refused to let myself look at her. If I did, I would remember Adam's expression when he first heard about their baby, Adam's sorrow as he knelt at the grave. I couldn't trust myself to keep from Katie the news that Adam Sinclair was home again.

'I bet he couldn't stop smiling,' Katie said.

'Uh-huh.'

'I bet that he looked into your eyes.' Her voice grew more dreamy. 'I bet he told you that he loved you.'

'As a matter of fact—'

'And he put his arms around you,' Katie continued, 'and said that even if everyone else turned their backs, even if you never saw your friends or family again, a world with only you and him and the baby would feel downright crowded because of all the love that would be stuffed into it.'

I stared at Katie, at her eyes shining in the darkness, her mouth twisted in a half smile somewhere between rapture and remorse. 'Yes,' I said. 'It was just like that.'

15

Ellie might never have made it out the door on Monday morning, if not for the chamomile tea. She finally managed to get downstairs after a sleepless night and morning sickness, and found the steaming mug on her plate with a few saltines. By that time, the others had left the breakfast table; only Katie and Sarah remained in the kitchen cleaning the dishes. 'You understand we have to drive in with Leda today,' Ellie said, steeling herself against the smell of leftover food. 'Coop's meeting us at the courthouse.'

Katie nodded, but didn't turn around. Ellie glanced at the women's backs, thankful that Katie had known enough to spare her the sight of a platter heaped with eggs and bacon and sausage. She took a tentative sip of the tea, expecting her stomach to heave again, but curiously the nausea ebbed. By the time she finished, she felt better than she had all weekend.

She did not want to harp on the pregnancy, especially not today, but she felt duty-bound to acknowledge Katie's thoughtfulness. 'The tea,' Ellie whispered, as they climbed into the backseat of Leda's car twenty minutes later. 'It was just what I needed.'

'Don't thank me,' Katie whispered back. 'Mam made it for you.'

For the past months, Sarah had been piling her plate at mealtime as if she were a sow to be fattened up for the kill; the sudden change in menu seemed suspicious. 'Did you tell her I'm pregnant?' Ellie demanded.

'No. She made it for you because you're worried about the trial. She thinks chamomile settles your nerves.'

Relaxing, Ellie sat back. 'It settles your stomach, too.'

'*Ja*, I know,' Katie said. 'She used to make it for me.'

'When did she think you were worried?'

Katie shrugged. 'Back when *I* was carrying.'

Before she could say anything else, Leda got into the driver's seat and peered into the rearview mirror. 'You're okay with me at the wheel, Katie?'

'I figure the bishop's getting used to making exceptions to the rules for me.'

'Is Samuel coming with us today or what?' Ellie muttered, peering out the window. 'Being late on the first day of testimony doesn't usually sit well with judges.'

As if she had conjured him, Samuel came running from the field behind the barn. The jacket of his good Sunday suit hung open, his black hat sat askew on his head. Pulling it off, he ducked into the seat beside Leda. 'Sorry,' he muttered, twisting around as Leda began to drive. He handed a tiny, fading sprig of clover to Katie, the four leaves of its head lying limp in her palm. 'For luck,' Samuel said, smiling at her. 'For you.'

'You have a nice weekend?' George asked as they took their places in court.

'It was fine,' Ellie answered brusquely, arranging the defense table to her satisfaction.

'Sounds like someone's cranky. Must've gone to bed too late last night.' George grinned. 'Guess you were partying till the cows came home. What time do they come home, anyway?'

'Are you finished?' Ellie asked, staring at him with indifference.

'*All rise! The Honorable Philomena Ledbetter presiding!*'

The judge settled into her chair. 'Good morning, everyone,' she said, slipping on her half-glasses. 'I believe we left off on Friday with the prosecution resting its case, which means that today, Ms Hathaway, you're on. I trust you're ready to go?'

Ellie rose. 'Yes, Your Honor.'

'Excellent. You may call your first witness.'

'The defense calls Jacob Fisher to the stand.'

Katie watched as her brother entered the courtroom from the lobby, where he'd been sequestered as an upcoming witness. He winked at her as he was being sworn in. Ellie smiled at him, reassuring. 'Could you state your name and address?'

'Jacob Fisher. Two-fifty-five North Street, in State College, Pennsylvania.'

'What's your relationship to Katie?'

'I'm her older brother.'

'Yet you don't live at home with the Fishers?'

Jacob shook his head. 'I haven't for several years, now. I grew up Plain on my parents' farm and got baptized at eighteen, but then I left the church.'

'Why?'

Jacob looked at the jury. 'I truly believed I would be Plain my whole life, but then I discovered something that meant just as much to me as my faith, if not more.'

'What was that?'

'Learning. The Amish don't believe in schooling past eighth grade. It goes against the *Ordnung*, the rules of the church.'

'There are rules?'

'Yes. It's what most people associate with the Amish – the fact that you can't drive cars, or use tractors. The way you dress. The lack of electricity and telephones. All the things that make you recognizable as a group. When you're baptized, you vow to live by these conditions.' He cleared his throat. 'Anyway, I was working as a carpenter's apprentice, building bookshelves for a high school English teacher over in Gap. He caught me leafing through his books, and let me take some home. He planted the thought in my mind that I might want to further my studies. I hid my books for as long as I could from my family, but eventually, when I knew I would be applying to college, I realized that I could no longer be Plain.'

'At that point, what happened?'

'The Amish church gave me a choice: Give up on college, or leave the faith.'

'That sounds harsh.'

'It's not,' Jacob said. 'At any point – today, even – if I went back and confessed in front of the congregation, I'd be accepted back with open arms.'

'But you can't erase the things you've learned at college, can you?'

'That's not the point. It's that I'd agree to yield to a set of circumstances chosen by the group, instead of trailblazing my own.'

'What do you do today, Jacob?'

'I'm getting my master's degree in English at Penn State.'

'Your parents must be quite proud of you,' Ellie said.

Jacob smiled faintly. 'I don't know about that. You see, what commands praise in the English world is very different from what commands praise in the Plain world. In fact, you don't want to command praise if you're Plain. You want to blend in, to live a good Christian life without calling attention to yourself. So, no, Ms Hathaway, I wouldn't say my parents are proud of me. They're confused by the choice I've made.'

'Do you still see them?'

Jacob glanced at his sister. 'I saw my parents for the first time in six years just the other night. I went back to their farm even though my father had disowned me after I was excommunicated.'

Ellie raised her brows. 'If you leave the Amish church, you can't stay in touch with those who are Amish?'

'No, that's the exception rather than the rule. Sure, having someone around who's excommunicated can make things uncomfortable for everyone else, especially if you all live in the same house, because of the *Meidung* – shunning. One of those church rules I was talking about says that members of the church have to avoid those who've broken the rules. People who've sinned are put under the *bann* for a little while, and during that time, other Plain folks can't eat with them, or conduct business, or have sexual relations.'

'So a husband would have to shun his wife? A mother would have to shun her child?'

'Technically, yes. But then again, when I was Plain, I knew of a husband who owned a car and was put under the *bann*. He still lived with his wife, who was a member of the church – and even though she was supposed to be shunning him, they somehow managed to have seven children who all got baptized Amish when it came time. So basically, the distancing is up to the individuals involved.'

'Then why did your father disown you?' Ellie asked.

'I've thought a lot about that, Ms Hathaway. I'd have to say that he was doing it out of a sense of personal failure, as if it were his fault that I didn't want to follow in his footsteps. And I think he was terrified that if Katie continued to be exposed to me on a regular basis, I'd somehow corrupt her by introducing her to the English world.'

'Tell us about your relationship with your sister.'

Jacob grinned. 'Well, I don't imagine it's that much different than anyone else with a sibling. Sometimes she was my best buddy, and other times she was the world's greatest pain in the neck. She was younger than me by several years, so it became my responsibility to watch over her and teach her how to do certain things around the farm.'

'Were you close?'

'Very. When you're Amish, family is everything. You're not only together at every meal – you're working side-by-side to make a living.' He smiled at Katie. 'You come to know someone awfully well when you get up with them at four-thirty every morning to shovel cow manure.'

'I'm sure you do,' Ellie agreed. 'Were you two the only children?'

Jacob looked into his lap. 'For a while, we had a little sister. Hannah drowned when she was seven.'

'That must have been hard for all of you.'

'Very,' Jacob agreed. 'Katie and I were minding her at the

time, so we always felt the blame fell on our shoulders. If anything, that brought us even closer.'

Ellie nodded in sympathy. 'What happened after you were excommunicated?'

'It was like losing a sister all over again,' Jacob said. 'One day Katie was there to talk to, and the next she was completely beyond my reach. Those first few weeks at school, I missed the farm and my parents and my horse and courting buggy, but most of all, I missed Katie. Whenever anything had happened to me in the past, she was the one I'd share it with. And suddenly I was in a new world full of strange sights and sounds and customs, and I couldn't tell her about it.'

'What did you do?'

'Something very un-Amish: I fought back. I contacted my aunt, who'd left the church when she married a Mennonite. I knew she'd be able to get word to my mother and to Katie, without my father hearing about it. My mother couldn't come to see me – it wouldn't be right for her to go against her husband's wishes – but she sent Katie as a goodwill ambassador, about once a month for several years.'

'Are you telling me that she sneaked out of the house, lied to her father, and traveled hundreds of miles to stay with you in a college dormitory?'

Jacob nodded. 'Yes.'

'Come on now,' Ellie scoffed. 'Going to college is forbidden by the church – but behavior like Katie's is condoned?'

'At the time, she wasn't baptized yet – so she wasn't breaking any of the rules by eating with me, socializing with me, driving in my car. She was just staying connected to her brother. Yes, she hid her trips from my father – but my mother knew exactly where she was going, and supported it. I never saw it as Katie trying to lie and hurt our family; to me, she was doing the best she could to keep us together.'

'When she came to State College for these visits, did she become –' Ellie smiled at the jury. 'Well, for lack of a better term – a party animal?'

'Far from it. First off, she felt like she stood out like a sore thumb. She wanted to hole up in my apartment and have me read to her from the books I was studying. I could tell she was uncomfortable dressed Plain around all the college students, so one of the first things I did was buy her some ordinary English clothing. Jeans, a couple of shirts. Things like that.'

'But didn't you say that dressing a certain way is one of the rules of the church?'

'Yes. But, again, Katie hadn't been baptized Amish yet, so she wasn't breaking any rules. There's a certain level of experimentation that Plain folks expect from their children before they settle down to take the baptismal vow. A taste of what's out there. Teenagers who've been brought up Amish will dress in jeans, or hang out at a mall, go to a movie – maybe even drink a few beers.'

'*Amish* teens do this?'

Jacob nodded. 'When you're about fifteen or sixteen and you come into your running-around years, you join a gang of peers to socialize with. Believe me, many of those Plain kids take up stuff that's a lot riskier than the few things Katie experienced with me at Penn State. We weren't doing drugs, or getting drunk, or party hopping. I wasn't doing that myself, so I certainly wouldn't have been dragging my sister along. I worked very hard to get into college, and I made some wrenching decisions in order to go. My primary reason for being at Penn State was not to fool around, but to learn. Mostly, that's what Katie spent time doing with me.' He looked at his sister. 'When she came to see me, I considered it a privilege. It was a piece of home, brought all the way to where I was. The last thing I would have wanted to do was scare her away.'

'You sound like you care very much for her.'

'I do,' Jacob said. 'She's my sister.'

'Tell us about Katie.'

'She's sweet, kind, good. Considerate. Selfless. She does

what needs to be done. There is no doubt in my mind that she'll be a terrific wife, a wonderful mother.'

'Yet today she's on trial for murdering an infant.'

Jacob shook his head. 'It's crazy, is all. If you knew her, if you knew how she'd been brought up, you'd realize that the very thought of Katie murdering another living being is ridiculous. She used to catch spiders crawling up the walls in the house, and set them outside instead of just killing them.' He sighed. 'There's no way for me to make you understand what it means to be Plain, because most people can't see past the buggies and the funny clothes to the beliefs that really identify the Amish. But a murder charge – well, it's an English thing. In the Amish community there's no murder or violence, because the Amish know from the time they're babies that you turn the other cheek, like Christ did, rather than take vengeance into your own hands.'

Jacob leaned forward. 'There's this little acronym I was taught in grade school – it's J-O-Y. It's supposed to make Plain children remember that *Jesus* is first, *Others* come next, and *You* are last. The very first thing you learn as an Amish kid is that there's always a higher authority to yield to – whether it's your parents, the greater good of the community, or God.' Jacob stared at his sister. 'If Katie found herself with a hardship, she would have accepted it. She wouldn't have tried to save herself at the expense of another person. Katie's mind just wouldn't have gone there; wouldn't have even conjured up killing that baby as some kind of solution – because she doesn't know how to be that selfish.'

Ellie crossed her arms. 'Jacob, do you recognize the name Adam Sinclair?'

'Objection,' George said. 'Relevance?'

'Your Honor, may I approach?' Ellie asked. The judge motioned the two lawyers closer. 'If you give me a little leeway, Judge, this line of questioning will eventually make itself clear.'

'I'll allow it.'

Ellie posed the question a second time. 'He's my absentee

landlord,' Jacob answered. 'I rent a house from him in State College.'

'Did you have a personal relationship prior to your business relationship?'

'We were acquaintances.'

'What was your impression of Adam Sinclair?'

Jacob shrugged. 'I liked him a lot. He was older than most of the other students, because he was getting his doctorate. He's certainly brilliant. But what I really admired in him was the fact that – like me – he was at Penn State to work, rather than play.'

'Did Adam ever have the chance to meet your sister?'

'Yes, several times, before he left the country to do research.'

'Did he know that Katie is Amish?'

'Sure,' Jacob said.

'When was the last time you spoke to Adam Sinclair?'

'Almost a year ago. I send my rent checks to a property management company. As far as I know, Adam's still in the wilds of Scotland.'

Ellie smiled. 'Thank you, Jacob. Nothing further.'

George tucked his hands in his pockets and frowned at the open file on the prosecution's table. 'You're here today to help your sister, is that right?'

'Yes,' Jacob said.

'Any way you can?'

'Of course. I want the jury to hear the truth about her.'

'Even if it means lying to them?'

'I wouldn't lie, Mr Callahan.'

'Of course not,' George said expansively. 'Not like your sister did, anyway.'

'She didn't lie!'

George raised his brows. 'Seems to be a pattern in your family – you're not Amish, your sister's not acting Amish; you lied, she lied—'

'Objection,' Ellie said dispassionately. 'Is there a question in there?'

'Sustained.'

'You lied to your father before you were excommunicated, didn't you?'

'I hid the fact that I wanted to continue my schooling. I did it for his own peace of mind—'

'Did you tell your father you were reading Shakespeare in the loft of the barn?'

'Well, no, I—'

'Come on, Mr Fisher. What do you call a lie? Hiding something? Not being truthful? Lying by omission? None of this rings a bell for you?'

'Objection.' Ellie stood. 'Badgering the witness.'

'Sustained. Please watch yourself, counselor,' Judge Ledbetter warned.

'If it wasn't a lie, what was it?' George rephrased.

A muscle jumped in Jacob's jaw. 'I was doing what I had to do to study.'

George's eyes lit up. 'You were doing what you had to do. And you recently said that your sister, the defendant, was good at doing what needs to be done. Would you say that's an Amish trait?'

Jacob hesitated, trying to find the snake beneath the words, poised and ready to strike. 'The Amish are very practical people. They don't complain, they just take care of what needs taking care of.'

'You mean, for example, the cows have to get milked, so you get up before dawn to do it?'

'Yes.'

'The hay needs to be cut before the rain comes, so you work till you can barely stand up?'

'Exactly.'

'The baby's illegitimate, so you murder and dispose of it before anyone knows you made a mistake?'

'No,' Jacob said angrily. 'Not like that at all.'

'Mr Fisher, isn't it true that the saintly Amish are really no better than any of us – prone to the same flaws?'

'The Amish don't want to be saints. They're people, like anyone else. But the difference is that they try to lead a quiet, peaceful Christian life . . . when most of us' – he looked pointedly at the prosecutor – 'are already halfway down the road to hell.'

'Do you really expect us to believe that simply growing up among the Amish might make a person unable to entertain a thought of violence or revenge or trickery?'

'The Amish might entertain these thoughts, sir, but rarely. And they'd never act on them. It just goes against their nature.'

'A rabbit will chew off its leg if it's caught in a hunting trap, Mr Fisher, although no one would call it carnivorous. And although you were raised Amish, lying came quite naturally to you when you decided to continue your studies, right?'

'I hid my studies from my parents because I had no choice,' Jacob said tightly.

'You always have a choice. You could have remained Amish, and not gone to college. You chose to take what your father left you with – no family – in return for following your own selfish desires. This is true, isn't it, Mr Fisher?'

Jacob looked into his lap. He felt, rolling over him, the same wave of doubt that he'd struggled with for months after leaving East Paradise; the wave that he once thought he'd drown beneath. 'It's true,' he answered softly.

He could feel Ellie Hathaway's eyes on him, could hear her voice silently reminding him that whatever the prosecutor did, it was about Katie and not himself. With determination, he raised his chin and stared George Callahan down.

'Katie's been lying to your father for six years now?'

'She hasn't been lying.'

'Has she told your father she's been visiting you?'

'No.'

'Has she told your father that she's staying with your aunt?'

'Yes.'

'Has she indeed been staying with your aunt?'

'No.'

'And that's not a lie?'

'It's . . . misinformation.'

George snorted. 'Misinformation? That's a new one. Call it what you will, Mr Fisher. So the defendant *misinformed* your father. I assume she *misinformed* you too?'

'Never.'

'No? Did she tell you she was involved in a sexual relationship?'

'That wasn't something she—'

'Did she tell you she was pregnant?'

'I never asked. I'm not sure she admitted it to herself.'

George raised his brows. 'You're an expert psychiatrist now?'

'I'm an expert on my sister.'

The attorney shrugged, making it clear what he thought of that. 'Let's talk about these destructive Amish gangs. Your sister belonged to one of the faster gangs?'

Jacob laughed. 'Look, this isn't the Sharks and the Jets, with rumbles and territories. Just like English teenagers, most Amish kids are good kids. An Amish gang is simply a term for a group of friends. Katie belonged to the Sparkies.'

'The Sparkies?'

'Yes. They're not the most straitlaced gang in Lancaster County – that would be the Kirkwooders – but they're probably second or third.' He smiled at the prosecutor. 'The Ammies, the Shotguns, the Happy Jacks – those are the gangs that are, as you put it, more destructive. They tend to attract kids who get a lot of attention for acting out. But I don't think Katie even fraternizes with young people from any of those groups.'

'Is your sister still in a gang?'

'Technically, she could participate in their get-togethers until she's married. But most young people stop attending after they're baptized into the church.'

'Because then they can't drink alcohol or dance or go to movies?'

'That's right. Before baptism, the rules are bent, and that's okay. After baptism, you've chosen your path, and you'd better stick to it.'

'Katie tried beer for the first time when she came to visit you?'

Jacob nodded. 'Yes. At a frat party, where I was with her. But it wasn't substantially different from an experience she might have had with her gang.'

'It was perfectly okay under Amish rules?'

'Yes, because she wasn't baptized yet.'

'She went to some movies with you, too?' George asked.

'Yes.'

'Which, again, was something she might have even done with her gang?'

'That's right,' Jacob answered.

'And it was perfectly okay under church rules.'

'Yes, because she wasn't baptized.'

'How about dancing? Did you ever take her out dancing?'

'Once or twice.'

'But some gangs might have done a little dancing too.'

'Yes.'

'And it was perfectly okay under church rules.'

'Yes. Again, she wasn't baptized yet.'

'Sounds like you can test a lot of waters before you take the final plunge,' George said.

'That's the point.'

'So when did your sister get baptized?' George asked.

'September of last year.'

The prosecutor nodded thoughtfully. 'Then she got pregnant after she was baptized. Is sexual intercourse outside of marriage and having an illegitimate baby perfectly okay under church rules?'

Jacob, silent, turned red.

'I'd like an answer.'

'No, that wouldn't be all right.'

'Ah, yes. Because she was already baptized?'

'Among other things,' Jacob said.

'So let me sum up here,' George concluded. 'The defendant lied to your father, she lied to you, she got pregnant out of wedlock after taking baptismal vows – is this the truth about your sister you wanted the jury to understand?'

'No!'

'This is the "sweet, kind, good" girl you described in your testimony? We're talking about a real Girl Scout here, aren't we, Mr Fisher?'

'We are,' Jacob stiffly answered. 'You don't understand.'

'Sure I do. You explained it yourself far more eloquently than I ever could.' George crossed to the court reporter and pointed to a spot in the long loop of the trial's transcript. 'Could you read this back for me?'

The woman nodded. *'When you're Amish,'* she read, *'family is everything.'*

George smiled. 'Nothing further.'

Judge Ledbetter called for a coffee break after Jacob's testimony. The jury filed out, clutching their pads and pencils and studiously avoiding Ellie's gaze. Jacob, sprung from the witness chair, walked to Katie and took her hands into his. He bent his forehead against hers and whispered in Dietsch, saying something that made her laugh softly.

Then he stood up and turned to Ellie. 'Well?'

'You did fine,' she said, a smile pasted to her face.

This seemed to relax him. 'Does the jury think so, too?'

'Jacob, I stopped trying to figure out American juries around the same time Adam Sandler movies started raking in millions at the box office – people just don't act predictably. The woman with the blue hair, she didn't take her eyes off you the entire time. But the guy with the bad toupee was trying to pull a stray thread off his blazer cuff, and I doubt he heard a thing you said.'

'Still . . . it went well?'

'You're the first witness,' Ellie said gently. 'How about we just wait and see?'

He nodded. 'Can I take Katie to get a cup of coffee downstairs?'

'No. The cameras are no-holds-barred the minute she leaves this courtroom. If she wants coffee, bring it back here to her.'

The moment he left, Ellie turned to Katie. 'Did you see what George Callahan did to Jacob on the stand?'

'He tried to trip him up a little, but—'

'Do you have any idea how much worse it's going to be for you?'

Katie set her jaw. 'I'm going to make my things right, no matter what it takes.'

'I have a stronger case if I don't put you on the stand, Katie.'

'How? After all that talk about the truth, shouldn't they hear it from me?'

Ellie sighed. 'No one said I was going to tell them the truth!'

'You did, during that opening part—'

'It's an act, Katie. Seventy-five percent of being an attorney is being an Oscar-worthy performer. I'm going to tell them a story, that's all, and with any luck they'll like it better than the one George tells them.'

'You said that you would let me tell the truth.'

'I said that I wouldn't use an insanity defense. *You* said that you'd tell the truth. And if you recall, I basically said that we'd see.' She looked into Katie's eyes. 'If you step out there, George is going to cut you to ribbons. We'll be lucky if he doesn't destroy the thread of the defense while he's doing it. This is an English world, an English court, an English murder charge. You can't win if you play by Amish rules.'

'You have an Amish client, with an Amish upbringing, and Amish thoughts. The English rules don't apply,' Katie said quietly. 'So where does that leave us?'

'Just listen to what the prosecutor does and says, Katie. Right up till the minute you're supposed to get on the stand, you can change your mind.' Ellie gazed at her client. 'Even if you never speak a word in court, I can win.'

'If I never speak a word in court, Ellie, I'll be the liar that Mr Callahan says I am.'

Frustrated, Ellie turned away. What a catch-22: Katie wanting her to sacrifice this case on the altar of religious honesty; Ellie knowing that the last place honesty belonged was in court. It was like navigating a car in an ice storm – even if she'd been entirely sure of her own abilities, there were other parties on the road speeding by her, crossing lines, crashing.

Then again, Katie had never driven a car.

'You're not feeling well, are you?'

At the sound of Coop's voice, Ellie raised her face. 'I'm just fine, thanks.'

'You look awful.'

She smirked. 'Gee, I bet you have to beat girls off with a stick.'

He hunkered down beside her. 'I'm serious, Ellie,' he said, lowering his voice. 'I have a personal stake in your welfare, now. And if this trial is too much for you—'

'For God's sake, Coop, women used to give birth in the fields and then keep on picking corn after—'

'Cotton.'

'What?'

He shrugged. 'They were picking cotton.'

Ellie blinked at him. 'Were you there?'

'I was just making a point.'

'Yeah. A point. The point is that I'm fine. A-OK. Perfect and one hundred percent. I can win this trial; I can have this baby; I can do anything.' With horror, Ellie realized that tears were pricking the backs of her eyes. 'Now if you'll excuse me, I'm just going to end the war in Bosnia and stop hunger in a few Third World countries before court reconvenes.' Pushing to her feet, she shoved past Coop.

He stared after Ellie, then sank into the chair she'd vacated. Katie was rubbing her thumbnail over the top sheet of a legal pad. 'It's the baby,' she said. 'It can make you all *ferhoodled*.'

'Well.' He rubbed the back of his neck. 'I'm worried about her.'

Pressing deeper with her nail, she left a mark on the paper. 'I'm worried, too.'

Ellie slipped into the seat beside Katie just as the judge was coming back into the courtroom. Ellie's face was flushed and a little damp, as if she'd been splashing water on it. She would not look at Katie, not even when Katie touched her lightly on the hand beneath the defense table, just to make sure everything was all right.

Ellie murmured something then, something that sounded like 'Don't worry,' or 'I'm sorry,' although the latter didn't make any sense. Then she rose in one fluid stream, in the sleek, dramatic way that made Katie think of smoke curling from a chimney. 'The defense,' Ellie said, 'calls Adam Sinclair.'

Katie had heard wrong, surely. She sucked in her breath.

'Objection,' the prosecutor called out. 'This witness wasn't on my list.'

'Your Honor, he was out of the country. I discovered his whereabouts only days ago,' Ellie explained.

'That still doesn't tell me why Mr Sinclair didn't make it to your witness list,' Judge Ledbetter said.

Ellie hesitated. 'He represents some last-minute information I've found.'

'Your Honor, this is unconscionable. Ms Hathaway is twisting legal procedure to suit her own needs.'

'I beg your pardon, Judge,' Ellie countered, 'and I apologize to Mr Callahan for the short notice. This witness isn't going to win my case for me, but he will be able to provide an important piece of background that's been missing.'

'I want time to depose him first,' George said.

Katie did not hear the rest. All she knew was within moments, Adam was in the same room as her. She began to take short, shallow breaths; each one rustling, as if she might unwrap it to find the candy of his name. Adam placed his palm over the Bible and Katie pictured it, instead, pressed against the flat of her own belly.

And then he looked at her. There was a sorrow in his gaze that made Katie think anguish had risen within him like a sea, leaving a watermark that cut right across the blue of his eyes. He stared at her, kept staring at her, until the air went solid and her heart thudded in her chest, hard enough for there to be a recoil.

Katie bit her lip, pulling shame tight as a shawl. She had done this, she had brought them to this point. *I'm sorry.*

Don't worry.

She lifted shaking hands to cover her face, thinking like a child now: if she could not see Adam, surely she would be invisible.

'Ms Hathaway,' the judge said. 'Would you like to take a moment?'

'No,' Ellie answered. 'My client is fine.'

But Katie wasn't fine. She couldn't stop trembling, and the tears were coming harder, and for the life of her she couldn't look up and see Adam again. She could feel the stares of the jury members like so many tiny pinpricks, and she wondered why Ellie wouldn't do this one thing for her – let her run out of here, and never look back.

'Please,' she whispered to Ellie.

'Shh. Trust me.'

'Are you sure, counselor?' Judge Ledbetter asked.

Ellie glanced at the jury, at their open-mouthed expressions. 'Positive.'

At that moment, Katie thought she truly hated Ellie.

'Your Honor,' came his voice; oh, Lord, his sweet, deep voice, like the hum of a buggy running over the pavement. 'May I?' He picked up the box of tissues on the stand, and nodded in Katie's general direction.

'No, Mr Sinclair. You will stay where you are,' the judge ordered.

'I have to object to this, Your Honor,' the prosecutor insisted.

'Ms Hathaway put this witness on for purely dramatic value, and nothing of true import.'

'I haven't even questioned him yet, George,' Ellie said.

'Counsel – approach,' Judge Ledbetter said. She began to whisper angrily to Ellie and the county attorney, their voices rising in small spurts. Adam looked from the bench to Katie, who was still weeping. He picked up the box of tissues and opened the gate to the witness stand.

The bailiff stepped forward. 'Sir, I'm sorry, but—'

Adam pushed past him, his footsteps growing louder as he approached the defense table. Judge Ledbetter looked up and called out his name. When he kept walking, she banged her gavel. 'Mr Sinclair! You will stop now, or I'll hold you in contempt of court!'

But Adam did not stop. As the prosecutor's voice rose in outrage, wrapped around the angry warnings of the judge, Adam knelt beside Katie. She could smell him, could feel the heat coming off his body, and she thought: This is my Armageddon.

She felt the soft stroke of a tissue along her cheek.

The voices of the judge and lawyers faded, but Katie did not notice. Adam's thumb grazed her skin, and she closed her eyes.

In the background, George Callahan threw up his hands and began to argue again.

'Thank you,' Katie whispered, taking the tissue from Adam's hand.

He nodded, silent. The bailiff, following orders, grasped Adam's arm and wrenched him to his feet. Katie watched him being led back to the witness stand, every slow step a mile between them.

'I'm a ghost hunter,' Adam said, responding to Ellie's question. 'I search for and record paranormal phenomena.'

'Can you tell us what that entails?'

'Staying overnight in places that are assumed to be haunted;

trying to detect some change in the energy field either by dowsing or by a specialized type of photography.'

'Besides your Ph.D. from Penn State in parapsychology, do you hold any other degrees?'

'Yes. A bachelor's of science and a master's degree from MIT.'

'In what field, Mr Sinclair?'

'Physics.'

'Would you consider yourself a man of science, then?'

'Absolutely. It's why I know paranormal phenomena have to exist – any physicist will tell you that energy can't be lost, but only transformed.'

'How did you get to know Jacob Fisher?' Ellie asked.

'We met in a class at Penn State – I was a teaching assistant, he was an undergraduate. I was immediately attracted to his focus as a student.'

'Can you elaborate?'

'Well, obviously, given the field I'm in, I can't afford to make light of my work. I've found that the best way to go about my business is to put my nose to the grindstone and just do my research and not worry about what everyone else thinks. Jacob reminded me of myself, in that. For an undergraduate, he was far less interested in the social scene on campus than the academic side. When it came time to sublet my house, since I'd be traveling to do research, I approached him as a potential tenant.'

'When did you meet Jacob's sister?'

Adam's gaze moved from Ellie to Katie and softened. 'The first time was the day I got my Ph.D. Her brother introduced us.'

'Can you tell us about that?'

'She was beautiful and wide-eyed and shy. I knew she was Amish – I had learned that from Jacob some time back – but she wasn't dressed that way.' He hesitated, then lifted his palm. 'We shook hands. Perfectly ordinary. But I remember thinking that I didn't want to let go.'

'Did you have the opportunity to meet Katie again?'

'Yes, she visited her brother once a month. Jacob moved into my house a few months before I officially moved out, so I got to see Katie when she made her trips to State College.'

'Did your relationship progress?'

'We became friends very quickly. She was interested in my work, not in the *National Enquirer* hack way, but truly respectful of what I was trying to do. I found it very easy to talk to her, because she was so open and honest. To me, it was like she wasn't of this world – and in many ways I guess that was true.' He shifted in his seat. 'I was attracted to her. I knew better – God, I was ten years older than her, experienced, and clearly not Amish. But I couldn't stop thinking about her.'

'Did you become lovers?'

He watched Katie's cheeks bloom with color. 'Yes.'

'Had Katie ever slept with anyone before?'

'No.' Adam cleared his throat. 'She was a virgin.'

'Did you love her, Mr Sinclair?'

'I still do,' he said quietly.

'Then why weren't you here for her when she became pregnant?'

Adam shook his head. 'I didn't know about it. I'd postponed my research trip twice, to stay close to her. But that night after . . . after the conception, I left for Scotland.'

'Have you come back to the States between then and now?'

'No. If I had, I would have gone to see Katie. But I've been in remote villages, unreachable areas. Saturday was the first time I've been on American soil in a year.'

'If you had known about the baby, Mr Sinclair, what would you have done?'

'I would have married Katie in a heartbeat.'

'But you'd have to be Amish. Could you convert?'

'It's been done, I know, but I probably couldn't. My faith isn't strong enough.'

'So marriage wouldn't really have been an option. What else would you have done?' Ellie asked.

'Anything. I would have left her among family and friends, but hoped that I could still have some future with her.'

'What kind of future?'

'Whatever she was willing or able to give me,' Adam said.

'Correct me if I'm wrong,' Ellie continued, 'but a shared future between an Amish woman and a worldly man seems awfully unlikely.'

'A saguaro can fall for a snowman,' Adam mused softly, 'but where would they set up house?' He sighed. 'I didn't want to be a star-crossed lover. I would have been perfectly happy to find some corner of the universe where Katie and I could just be Katie and I. But if I loved her, I couldn't ask her to turn her back on everything and everyone else. That's why I took the coward's way out last year. I left, hoping that by the time I returned, things would have magically changed.'

'Had they?'

Adam grimaced. 'Yes, but not for the better.'

'When you came back on Saturday, what did you learn?'

He swallowed. 'Katie had given birth to my child. And the child had died.'

'That must have been very upsetting to hear.'

'It was,' Adam said. 'It still is.'

'What was your first reaction?'

'I wanted to go to Katie. I was certain she must have been as devastated as I was, if not more. I thought we could help each other.'

'At the time, did you know that Katie had been accused of murdering the baby?'

'Yes.'

'You heard that your baby was dead, and that Katie was the one suspected of killing him – yet you wanted to go to her to give and receive comfort?'

'Ms Hathaway,' Adam said, 'Katie didn't kill our baby.'

'How could you know for certain?'

Adam looked into his lap. 'Because I wrote a dissertation on it. Love's the strongest kind of energy. Katie and I loved each other. We couldn't love each other in my world, and we couldn't love each other in her world. But all that love, all that energy, it had to go somewhere. It went into that baby.' His voice broke. 'Even if we couldn't have each other, we would have both had him.'

'If you loved her so much,' George said midway through his cross-examination, 'why didn't you drop her a line every now and then?'

'I did. I wrote once a week,' Adam answered. From beneath his lashes, he watched Ellie Hathaway. She had warned him not to talk about the letters that had never found their way to Katie, because then it would come out that Jacob had not wanted his sister to have a future with Adam – a strike against the star-crossed lover defense.

'So during all this pen-pal time, she never told you she was pregnant?'

'As far I understand, she never told anyone.'

George raised a brow. 'Couldn't the reason she kept her pregnancy from you be because she didn't care as much about your relationship as you apparently did?'

'No, that wasn't—'

'Or perhaps she had gotten her wild ride and now intended to go back to her Amish boyfriend with no one the wiser.'

'You're wrong.'

'Maybe she didn't tell you because she planned to get rid of the baby.'

'She wouldn't have done that,' Adam said with conviction.

'Pardon me if I've misunderstood, but were you standing in the barn the night she gave birth?'

'You know I wasn't.'

'Then you can't say for certain what did or did not happen.'

'By the same logic, neither can you,' Adam pointed out. 'But there's one thing I do know that you don't. I know how Katie thinks and feels. I know she wouldn't murder our child. It doesn't matter whether I was there to witness the birth or not.'

'Oh, that's right. You're a . . . what did you call it? Ah, a *ghost hunter*. You don't have to see things to believe them.'

Adam's gaze locked onto the prosecutor's. 'Maybe you've got that backward,' he said. 'Maybe it's just that I believe things you can't see.'

Ellie gently closed the door of the conference room. 'Look,' she began with trepidation. 'I know what you're going to say. I had no right to spring him on you. As soon as I knew where Adam was, I should have told you. But Katie, the jury needed to know about the father of your baby in order to understand that the death was a tragedy. They needed to see how much it hurt you to watch Adam walk into the room. They needed to build up sympathy for you so that they'll want to acquit you, for whatever reason they can find.' She folded her arms. 'For whatever it's worth, I'm sorry.'

When Katie turned away, Ellie tried to make light of the situation. 'I said I was sorry. I thought if you confessed, you were forgiven and welcomed back to the fold.'

Katie looked up at her. 'This was mine,' she said quietly. 'This memory was the only thing I had left. And you gave it away.'

'I did it to save you.'

'Who said I wanted to be saved?'

Without another word, Ellie walked to the door again. 'I brought you something,' she said, and turned the knob.

Adam stood there hesitantly, his hands clenching and unclenching at his sides. Ellie nodded at him, then walked out, closing the door behind her.

Katie rose, blinking back tears. All he had to do was open his arms, and she would fall into them. All he had to do was open his arms, and they'd be back where they were before.

He took a step forward, and Katie flew to him. They whispered their questions into each other's skin, leaving marks as sure as scars. Katie wriggled closer, surprised to see she didn't quite fit, as if some small object was caught between their bodies. She glanced down to see what had pressed up between them, and found nothing except the invisible, hard fact of their baby.

Adam felt it too, she could tell by the way he shifted and held her at arm's length. 'I tried to write you. Your brother didn't give you my letters.'

'I would have told you,' she answered. 'I didn't know where you were.'

'We would have loved him,' Adam said fiercely, the tone as much a statement as it was a question.

'We would have.'

His hand stroked over her hair, catching at the edge of her *kapp*. 'What happened?' he whispered.

Katie stilled. 'I don't know. I fell asleep, and woke up, and the baby was gone.'

'I understand that's what you told your lawyer. And the police. But this is me, Katie. This is our son.'

'I'm telling you the truth. I don't remember.'

'You were there! You have to remember!'

'But I don't!' Katie cried.

'You have to,' Adam said thickly, 'because I wasn't there. And I need to know.'

Katie pressed her lips together and gave a tight little shake of her head. She sank down into a chair and curled forward, her arms crossed over her stomach.

Adam reached for her hand and kissed the knuckles. 'We'll figure this out,' he said. 'After the trial, somehow, it's all going to work out.'

She let his voice wash over her with the same spiritual cleansing that she'd felt at *Grossgemee*, communion services. How she wanted to believe him! Lifting her face to Adam's, she started to nod.

But something flickered in his eyes, the smallest dance of doubt, so brief that had Adam not turned away quickly, Katie might have put it from her mind. He had said he loved her. He had told a jury. He might not admit it in court, but here in private, he would allow himself to wonder if the reason Katie could not remember what had happened to their baby was because she'd done something unspeakable.

He kissed her gently, and she wondered how you could come so close to a person that there was not a breath of space between you, and still feel like a canyon had ripped the earth raw between your feet. 'We'll have other babies,' he said, the one thing Katie could not stand to hear.

She touched his cheeks and his jaw and the soft curve of his ears. 'I'm sorry,' she said, unsure for what she was apologizing.

'It wasn't your fault,' Adam murmured.

'Adam—'

Touching his finger to her lips, he shook his head. 'Don't say it. Not just yet.'

Her chest tightened, so that she could barely breathe. 'I wanted to tell you he looked like you,' she said, the words tumbling bright as a gift. 'I wanted to tell you he was beautiful.'

Adam stepped out of the bathroom stall and began to wash his hands. His head was still full of thoughts of Katie, of the trial, of their baby. He was only marginally aware when another man stepped up to wash at the sink beside him.

Their eyes met in the mirror. Adam regarded the man's broad-brimmed black hat, the simple trousers, the suspenders, the pale green shirt. Adam had never met him before, but he knew. He knew the same way that the blond giant who seemed unable to tear his eyes away from Adam knew.

This was the one she was with before me, Adam thought.

He had not been in the courtroom; Adam would have remembered him. Perhaps he was opposed to it for religious reasons. Perhaps he was sequestered, and would be on the witness stand later.

Perhaps, like the prosecutor had suggested, he had stepped in after Adam left to take care of Katie.

'Excuse me,' the blond man said in heavily accented English. He reached across Adam toward the soap dispenser.

Adam dried his hands on a paper towel. He nodded once – territorially, evenly – at the other man, and tossed the crumpled paper into the trash.

As Adam swung open the bathroom door to reveal the busy hallway, he looked back one last time. The Amish man was reaching for his own paper towel now, was standing in the very spot that Adam had been just a moment before.

Samuel's fingers fumbled on the doorknob as he entered the tiny conference room where Ellie had said he'd find Katie. She was there, yes, her head bent over the ugly plastic table like a dandelion wilting on its stem. He sat down across from her and set his elbows on the table. 'You okay?'

'*Ja.*' Katie sighed, rubbed her eyes. 'I'm okay.'

'That makes one of us.'

Katie smiled faintly. 'You're on the stand soon?'

'Ellie says so.' He hesitated. 'Ellie says she knows what she's doing.' Samuel got to his feet, feeling oversized and uncomfortable inside such cramped quarters. 'Ellie says I have to bring you back, now, too.'

'Well, we wouldn't want to disappoint Ellie,' Katie said sarcastically.

Samuel's brows drew together. 'Katie,' he said, that was all, and suddenly she felt small and mean.

'I shouldn't have said that,' she admitted. 'These days, I don't know myself.'

'Well, I do,' Samuel said, so perfectly serious that it made her grin.

'Thank goodness for that.' Katie did not like being in this courthouse, being so far away from her parents' farm, but knowing that Samuel was feeling just as out of place as she was somehow made it a little better.

He held out his hand and smiled. 'Come on now.'

Katie slipped her fingers into his. Samuel pulled her out of the chair and led her out of the conference room. They walked hand-in-hand down the hallway, through the double doors of the courtroom, toward the defense table; neither one of them ever thinking it would be all right, now, to let go.

16

Ellie

The night before testimony began for Katie's defense, I had a dream about putting Coop on the stand. I stood in front of him in a courtroom that was empty save for the two of us, the lemon-polished gallery stretching behind me like a dark desert. I opened up my mouth to ask him about Katie's treatment, and instead, a different question flew out of my mouth like a bird that had been trapped inside: *Will we be happy ten years from now?* Mortified, I pressed my lips together and waited for the witness to answer the question, but Coop just stared into his lap. 'I need a response, Dr Cooper,' I pressed; and I approached the witness stand to find Katie's dead infant stretched across his lap.

Questioning Coop as a witness rated high on my scale of discomfort – somewhere, say, between suffering a bikini wax and braving bamboo slivers under the nails. There was something about having a man locked in a box in front of me, at my mercy to answer any inquiry I threw at him – and yet to know that the questions I'd be asking were not the ones I truly needed answered. Plus, there was a new subtext between us, all the things that had not yet been said in the wake of this knowledge of pregnancy. It surrounded us like a sea, pale and distorting; so that when I saw Coop or listened to him speak, I could not trust my perception to be accurate.

He came up to me minutes before he was scheduled to take the stand. Hands in his pockets, painfully professional, he lifted his chin. 'I want Katie out of the courtroom while I testify.'

Katie was not sitting beside me; I'd sent Samuel to retrieve her. 'Why?'

'Because my first responsibility is to Katie as a patient, and after that last stunt you pulled with Adam, I think she's too fragile to hear me talk about what happened.'

I straightened the papers in front of me. 'That's too bad, because I need the jury to see her getting upset.'

His shock was a palpable thing. Well, good. Maybe this was the way to show him that I wasn't the woman he expected me to be. Turning a cool gaze on him, I added, 'The whole point is to gain sympathy for her.'

I expected him to argue with me, but Coop only stood there, staring at me for a moment, until I began to shift beneath his regard. 'You're not that tough, Ellie,' he said finally. 'You can stop pretending.'

'This isn't about me.'

'Of course it is.'

'Why are you doing this to me?' I cried, frustrated. 'It's not what I need now.'

'It's exactly what you need, El.' Coop reached out and straightened my lapel, gently smoothing it down, a gesture that suddenly made me want to cry.

I took a deep breath. 'Katie's staying, that's that. And now, if you'll excuse me, I need a few minutes by myself.'

'Those few minutes,' he said softly. 'They're adding up.'

'For God's sake, I'm in the middle of a trial! What do you expect?'

Coop let his hand trail off my shoulder, over my arm. 'That one day you'll look around,' he said, 'and you'll find out you've been alone for years.'

'Why were you called in to see Katie?'

Coop looked wonderful on the stand. Not that I was in the habit of judging my witnesses on the way they filled out a suit, but he was relaxed and calm and kept smiling at Katie, something the jury could not help but notice. 'To treat her,' he said. 'Not to evaluate her.'

'What's the difference?'

'Most of the professional psychiatrists who testify in court have been appointed to assess Katie's mind for the value of the trial. I'm not a forensic psychiatrist; I'm just a regular shrink. I was simply asked to help her.'

'If you're not a forensic psychiatrist, then why are you here today?'

'Because I've developed a relationship with Katie over the course of her treatment. As opposed to an expert who's only interviewed her once, I believe I know the workings of her mind more thoroughly. She's signed an agreement to allow me to testify, which I consider a strong mark of her trust in me.'

'What did your treatment of Katie involve?' I asked.

'Clinical interviews that grew more in-depth over a four-month period. I began by asking about her parents, her childhood, her expectations of pregnancy, history of depression or psychological trauma – your basic psychiatric interview, in effect.'

'What did you learn?'

He grinned. 'Katie's no run-of-the-mill teenager. Before I could really understand her, I needed to bone up on what it means to be Amish. As I'm sure everyone knows, the culture in which a child is raised dramatically impacts their actions as an adult.'

'We've heard a little about Amish culture. What, in particular, interested you as Katie's psychiatrist?'

'Our culture promotes individuality, while the Amish are deeply entrenched in community. To us, if someone stands out, it's no big deal because diversity is respected and expected. To the Amish, there's no room for deviation from the norm. It's important to fit in, because that similarity of identity is what defines the society. If you don't fit in, the consequences are psychologically tragic – you stand alone when all you've ever known is being part of the group.'

'How did this contribute to your understanding of Katie?'

'Well,' Coop said, 'in Katie's mind, difference is equated with shame, rejection, and failure. For Katie, the fear of being shunned is even more deeply rooted. She saw it happen to her brother, in a very extreme case, and absolutely did not want that to happen to herself. She wanted to get married, to have children . . . but she'd always assumed it would happen the way it happened to everyone else in her world. Discovering she was pregnant with an English man's child, and unwed – both glaringly against the Amish norm – well, it led right to being shunned, which was something her mind wasn't equipped to handle.'

I was hearing him speak of Katie, but thinking of myself. My hand crept inside the jacket of my suit, resting over my abdomen. 'What do you mean by that?'

'She had been brought up to believe that there was only one way to get from point A to point B,' he said. 'That if her life didn't march down that path or turn out as perfectly as she had expected, it was unacceptable.'

Coop's words wrapped so tightly around me that breathing became an effort. 'It wasn't her fault,' I managed.

'No,' Coop said softly. 'I've been trying to get her to see that for a while, now.'

The room narrowed, people falling away and sounds receding. 'It's hard to change the way you've always thought about things.'

'Yes, and that's why she didn't. Couldn't. That pregnancy,' Coop murmured, 'it turned her world upside down.'

I swallowed. 'What did she do?'

'She pretended it didn't matter, when it was the most important thing in the world. When it had the power to change her life.'

'Maybe . . . she was just afraid of taking that first step.'

A profound silence had blanketed the courtroom. I watched Coop's lips part, I waited for him to absolve me.

'Objection!' George said. 'Is this a direct examination, or *As the World Turns*?'

Shaken out of my reverie, I felt myself blush. 'Sustained,' Judge Ledbetter said. 'Ms Hathaway, could you flip the channel back to *The People's Court*?'

'Yes, Your Honor. Sorry.' I cleared my throat and deliberately turned away from Coop. 'When Katie found out that she was pregnant, what did she do?'

'Nothing. She shoved the idea out of her mind. She denied it. She procrastinated. You know how it is when you're a kid, and you close your eyes and think you're invisible? Well, the same principle was at work. If she didn't say out loud, "I'm pregnant" – she wasn't. Ultimately, if she admitted to herself that she was pregnant, she would have to admit it to her church, too – confess publicly to her sins and be shunned for a brief time, after which she'd be forgiven.'

'Ignoring her pregnancy – that sounds like a deliberate decision.'

'It's not, because she really didn't have a choice. In her mind it was the only sure way to keep from being excluded from her community.'

'She couldn't hide it when she went into labor. What happened then?'

'Quite obviously,' Coop said, 'that denial mechanism broke down, and her mind scrambled for some other way to keep herself from admitting to the pregnancy. When I first met Katie, she told me that she felt sick at dinner, went to bed early, and remembered nothing until she woke up. Of course, the facts indicate that sometime during those hours, she had a baby.'

'That was the new coping mechanism – a memory loss?'

'A memory gap, due to dissociation.'

'How do you know Katie wasn't dissociating from the minute she found out she was pregnant?'

'Because then she'd probably have multiple personality disorder. Anyone who fragments off her consciousness for that many months would develop another identity. However, it is possible to split off one's consciousness to survive brief periods of trauma, and for Katie, that's entirely consistent.' He hesitated. 'It's less important to understand which defense mechanism she used, and whether it was conscious or unconscious. For Katie, it's more crucial to understand why she felt a need to protect herself from the knowledge of pregnancy and birth, period.'

I nodded. 'Did she eventually recall what happened during and after the birth?'

'To a point,' Coop said. 'She remembers being afraid to get blood on the sheets of her bed. She remembers going to the barn to give birth, and being incredibly afraid. She remembers cutting the cord and tying it off. She knows that she picked up the infant and cuddled him. Quieted him.' He held up his pinkie. 'She remembers giving him her finger to suckle. She closed her eyes, because she was so tired, and when she woke up the infant was gone.'

'Based on your knowledge of Katie, what do you think happened to that infant?'

'Objection,' George said. 'This calls for speculation.'

'Your Honor, every witness the prosecutor put on speculated about this issue,' I pointed out. 'As Katie's psychiatrist, Dr Cooper is far more qualified than anyone else to comment on this.'

'Overruled, Mr Callahan. Dr Cooper, you may answer the question.'

'I believe that the baby died in her arms, for whatever medical reasons premature infants die. Then she hid the body – not well, because she was acting like a robot at the time.'

'What makes you believe this?'

'Again, it goes back to being Amish. To bring an illegitimate baby into the Amish community is upsetting, but not ultimately tragic. Katie would have been shunned for a brief time, and then accepted back into the fold, because children are treasured by the Amish. Eventually, after the stress of birth, Katie would have had to face the fact that she'd borne an illegitimate child, but I believe she'd have been able to handle it once the baby was alive and there and real to her – she loved children, she loved the baby's father, and she could have rationalized shunning on the grounds that something beautiful had come from her mistake.'

Coop shrugged. 'However, the baby died in her arms while she was passed out from exhaustion. She woke up, covered with blood from delivery and holding the dead newborn. In her mind, she blamed herself for the baby's death: he had died because he wasn't conceived in wedlock, within the Amish church.'

'Let me get this straight, Doctor. You don't believe Katie killed her baby?'

'No, I don't. Killing her own infant would have made it virtually impossible for Katie, in the long run, to be accepted back into the community. Although I'm no expert on pacifist societies, I think deliberately confessing to murder would most likely fall under that category. Since inclusion in the community was the foremost thought in her mind for the entire pregnancy, it was certainly with her at the moment of birth, as well. If she'd woken up to a live baby, I think she would have confessed to her sin in church, raised the baby with her parents, and gone on with her life. But as it was, that didn't happen. I think that she woke up, saw the dead infant, and panicked – she was going to be shunned for an illegitimate birth, and she didn't even have a child to sweeten that reproof. So her mind reflexively kicked into coping gear, and tried to remove the evidence that there had been either a birth or a death – in essence, so that there would be no reason to exclude her from her community.'

'Did she know she was hiding the body at the time she was doing it?'

'I assume Katie hid the baby's body while she was still in a dissociative state, because to this day she doesn't remember doing it. She can't let herself remember, because it's the only way she can live with her grief and her shame.'

That was the point at which Coop and I had planned to cut off the direct examination. But suddenly, on a hunch, I crossed my arms. 'Did she ever tell you what happened to the baby?'

'No,' Coop said guardedly.

'So this whole scenario – the baby's death and Katie's sleep-walking stint to hide the body – that's something you came up with entirely on your own.'

Coop blinked at me, confused, and with good reason.

'Well . . . not entirely. I based my conclusions on my conversations with Katie.'

'Yeah, okay,' I said dismissively. 'But since she didn't actually tell you what happened that night, isn't it possible that Katie murdered her baby in cold blood, and stuck it in the tack room afterward?'

I was leading, but I knew that George wouldn't have objected if his life depended on it. Coop sputtered, utterly confused. '*Possible* is a very big word,' he said slowly. 'If you're talking about the feasibility of certain—'

'Just answer the question, Dr Cooper.'

'Yes. It's possible. But not probable.'

'Is it possible that Katie gave birth, held her baby boy, swaddled her baby boy, and cried after discovering it had died in her arms?'

'Yes,' Coop said. 'Now, *that's* probable.'

'Is it possible that Katie fell asleep holding her live infant, and that a stranger came into the barn and smothered it, and hid it while she was unconscious?'

'Sure, it's possible. Unlikely, but possible.'

'Can you say for certain that Katie did not kill her baby?'
He hesitated. 'No.'

'Can you say for certain that Katie did kill her baby?'
'No.'

'Would it be fair to say that you have doubts about what happened that night?'

'Yes. Don't we all?'

I smiled at him. 'Nothing further.'

'Correct me if I'm wrong, Dr Cooper, but the defendant never actually said that her baby died of natural causes, right?'

Coop stared down the prosecutor, God bless him. 'No, but she never said she murdered him either.'

George considered this. 'And yet, you seem to think that's highly improbable.'

'If you knew Katie, you would, too.'

'By your own testimony, the foremost thought in Katie's mind was acceptance by her community.'

'Yes.'

'A murderer would be shunned by the Amish community – maybe even forever?'

'That's my assumption.'

'Well, then, if the defendant killed her baby, wouldn't it make sense for her to hide the evidence of the murder so that she wouldn't be excommunicated forever?'

'Gosh, I used to do this in seventh-grade math. If *x*, then *y*. If not *x*, then not *y*.'

'Dr Cooper,' George pressed.

'Well, I only brought it up because if the *if* part of that statement is false, the *then* part doesn't work either. Which is just a roundabout way of saying that Katie really couldn't have murdered her baby. That's a conscious act, with conscious reactive actions – and she was in a dissociative state at that point.'

'According to your theory, she dissociated when she gave birth – and was dissociating when she hid the body – but managed to be conscious and mentally present enough to understand that the baby had died of natural causes in the few minutes in between?'

Coop's face froze. 'Well,' he said, recovering, 'not quite. There's a distinction between knowing what's happening, and understanding it. It's possible that she was dissociating during the entire sequence.'

'If she was dissociating when she realized the baby had died in her arms, as you suggest, then she was not really aware of what was happening?'

Coop nodded. 'That's right.'

'Then why would she have felt such overwhelming grief and shame?'

He had Coop up against a tree, and we all knew it. 'Katie employed a variety of defense mechanisms to get through the birth. Any of these might have been at work at the moment she realized the infant had died.'

'How convenient,' George commented.

'Objection!' I called out.

'Sustained.'

'Doctor, you said that the first thing Katie recalled about the birth was that she didn't want to get blood on the sheets, so she headed to the barn to give birth?'

'Yes.'

'She didn't recall the baby itself.'

'The baby came after the labor, Mr Callahan.'

The prosecutor smiled. 'So my dad told me forty years ago. What I meant was that the defendant did not recall holding the baby, or bonding with it, isn't that right?'

'All that would happen after the birth. After the dissociation,' Coop said.

'Well, then, it seems awfully callous to be worrying about your sheets when you're apparently enraptured with the idea of having a child.'

'She wasn't enraptured at the time. She was terrified, and dissociating.'

'So she wasn't acting like herself?' George prodded.

'Exactly.'

'One might even say, then, that it was like the defendant's body was there, giving birth, feeling pain, although her mind was elsewhere?'

'Correct. You can function mechanically, even in a dissociative state.'

George nodded. 'Isn't it possible that the part of Katie Fisher that was physically present and mechanically able to give birth and cut the cord might also have been physically present and mechanically able to kill the baby?'

Coop was silent for a moment. 'There are a number of possibilities.'

'I'm gonna take that as a yes.' George started to walk back to the prosecution's table. 'Oh, one final question. How long have you known Ms Hathaway?'

I was on my feet before I even realized I had been rising. 'Objection!' I yelled. 'Relevance? Foundation?'

Surely everyone could see how red my face had become. A hush had fallen over the courtroom. On the stand, Coop looked like he wanted to sink through the floor.

Judge Ledbetter squinted at me. 'Approach,' she said. 'What does this have to do with anything, Mr Callahan?'

'I'd like to show that Ms Hathaway has had a working relationship with this witness for many years.'

Flattened on the polished surface of the judge's bench, my palms were sweating. 'We've never worked together in court before,' I said. 'Mr Callahan is trying to prejudice the jury simply by showing that Dr Cooper and I know each other personally as well as professionally.'

'Mr Callahan?' the judge asked.

'Your Honor, I believe there's a conflict of interest here, and I want the jury to know it.'

While the judge weighed our statements, I suddenly remembered the first time Katie had admitted to knowing the father of her baby. The moon had been full and white, pressed up against the window to eavesdrop; Katie's voice had smoothed at the edges when she said Adam's name out loud. And just ten minutes ago: *This memory was the only thing I had left, and you gave it away.*

If George Callahan did this, he'd be robbing me.

'All right,' the judge said. 'I'll allow you to proceed with your questioning.'

I crossed back to the defense table and took my seat beside Katie. Almost immediately, her hand reached for my own and squeezed. 'How long have you known the defense counsel?' George asked.

'Twenty years,' Coop said.

'Isn't it true that you two have more than a professional relationship?'

'We've been friends for a long time. I respect her immensely.'

George's gaze raked me from head to toe, and at that moment I had the profound urge to kick him in the teeth. 'Friends?' he pushed. 'Nothing more?'

'It's none of your business,' Coop said.

The prosecutor shrugged. 'That's what Katie thought, too, and look where it got her.'

'Objection!' I said, standing so quickly that I almost pulled Katie up too.

'Sustained.'

George smiled at me. 'Withdrawn.'

'Come on,' Coop said to me a little later, when he was released as a witness and the judge called for a coffee break. 'You need a walk.'

'I need to stay with Katie.'

'Jacob will baby-sit, won't you, Jacob?' Coop asked, clapping Katie's brother on the shoulder.

'Sure,' Jacob said, straightening a little in his seat.

'All right.' I followed Coop out of the courtroom, through a volley of quiet murmurs from the press reps who were still sitting in the gallery.

As soon as we reached the lobby, a camera flash exploded in my face. 'Is it true,' the accompanying reporter said, her face only inches from mine, 'that—'

'Can I just say something here?' Coop interrupted pleasantly. 'Do you know how tall I am?'

The reporter frowned. 'Six-two, six-three?'

'Just about. Do you know what I weigh?'

'One ninety.'

'Excellent guess. Do you know that I'm thinking really hard about taking that camera and throwing it on the ground?'

The reporter smirked. 'Guess you're a bodyguard in every sense of the word.'

I squeezed Coop's arm and pulled him off into a hallway, where I found an empty conference room. Coop stared at the closed door, as if contemplating going back after the reporter. 'It's not worth the publicity,' I said.

'But think about the psychological satisfaction.'

I sank into a chair. 'I can't believe that no one's tried to take a picture of Katie, but they came after me.'

Coop smiled. 'If they go after Katie, it makes them look bad – violating religious freedom and all that. But they still need something to run as a graphic with their stories. That leaves you and Callahan, and believe me, a camera's gonna love you more than it loves him.' He hesitated. 'You were fantastic in there.'

Shrugging, I curled my toes out of my pumps. 'You were awfully good yourself. The best witness we've had yet, I think—'

'Well, thanks—'

'—until George completely undermined your credibility.'

Coop came to stand behind me. 'Shit. He didn't nullify the whole testimony with that crap, did he?'

'Depends on how self-righteous the jury is, and how much they think we were taking them for a ride. Juries do not like to be fucked with.' I grimaced. 'Of course, now they'll think I'm screwing anyone I put on the stand.'

'You could recall me, so I could disabuse them of that idea.'

'Thanks, but no thanks.' Coop's fingers slid into my hair, began to massage my scalp. 'Oh, God. I ought to pay you for this.'

'Nah. It's one of the perks of sleeping with me to secure my testimony.'

'Well, then. It's worth it.' I tipped my head back and smiled. 'Hi,' I whispered.

He leaned forward to kiss me upside down. 'Hi.'

His mouth moved over mine, awkward at this angle, so that I found myself twisting around and kneeling on the chair to fit myself into Coop's arms. After a moment, he broke away from me and touched his forehead to mine. 'How's our kid?'

'Splendid,' I said, but my grin faltered.

'What?'

'I wish Katie had had some of this,' I said. 'A couple of moments, you know, with Adam, that made her believe it would all work out.'

Coop tilted his head. 'Will it, El?'

'This baby's going to be fine,' I said, more for myself than for Coop.

'This baby wasn't the party in question.' He took a deep breath. 'What you said in there during the direct – that line about taking the first step, did you mean it?'

I could have played coy; I could have told him I had no idea what he meant. Instead, I nodded.

Coop kissed me deeply, drawing my breath from me in a long, sweet ribbon. 'Perhaps I haven't mentioned it, but I'm an expert when it comes to first steps.'

'Are you,' I said. 'Then tell me how.'

'You close your eyes,' Coop answered, 'and jump.'

I took a deep breath and stood. 'The defense calls Samuel Stoltzfus.'

There were quiet titters and glances as Samuel appeared at the rear of the courtroom with a bailiff. A bull in a china shop, I thought, watching the big man lumber to the witness stand, his face chalky with fear and his hands nervously feeding the brim of his black hat round and round.

I knew, from Katie and Sarah and the conversations held over the supper table, what Samuel was sacrificing in order to be a witness in Katie's trial. Although the Amish community cooperated with the law, and would go to a courtroom if subpoenaed, they also forbid the voluntary filing of a lawsuit. Samuel, who had willingly offered his services as a character witness for Katie, was riding somewhere between the two extremes. Although his decision hadn't been called into question by church officials, there were members who looked less favorably upon him, certain that this deliberate brush with the English world was not for the best.

The clerk of the court, a pinch-faced man who smelled of bubble gum, approached Samuel with the customary Bible. 'Please raise your right hand.' He slid the battered book beneath Samuel's left palm. 'Do you swear to tell the truth, the whole truth, and nothing but the truth, so help you God?'

Samuel snatched his hand away from the Bible as if he'd been burned. 'No,' he said, horrified. 'I do not.'

A wave of disruption undulated across the gallery. The judge rapped her gavel twice. 'Mr Stoltzfus,' she said gently, 'I realize you're not familiar with a court of law. But this is a very customary procedure.'

Samuel belligerently shook his head, the blond strands flying. He looked up at me, beseeching.

Judge Ledbetter murmured something that might have been, 'Why me?' Then she beckoned me to the bench. 'Counsel, maybe you'd like a minute with the witness to explain this procedure.'

I walked over to Samuel and placed my hand on his arm, turning him away from the eyes of the gallery. He was trembling. 'Samuel, what's the problem?'

'We do not pray in public,' he whispered.

'It's only words. It doesn't really mean anything.'

His mouth dropped, as if I'd just turned into the devil right before his eyes. 'It's a promise to God – how can you say it means nothing? I cannot swear on the Bible, Ellie,' he said. 'I am sorry, but if that's what it takes, I can't do it.'

Nodding tightly, I went back to the judge. 'Swearing an oath on the Bible goes against his religion. Is it possible to make an exception?'

George jockeyed into position beside me. 'Your Honor, I'm sorry to sound like a broken record, but clearly Ms Hathaway has planned this performance to make the jury sympathetic to the Amish.'

'He's right, of course. And any minute now the troupe of thespians I've hired to reenact Katie's grief will come and take center stage.'

'You know,' Judge Ledbetter said thoughtfully, 'I had an Amish businessman as a witness in a trial some years back, and we ran into the same problem.'

I gaped at the judge, not because she was posing a solution, but because she'd actually had an Amishman in her courtroom before. 'Mr Stoltzfus,' she called out. 'Would you be willing to *affirm* on the Bible?'

I could see the gears turning in Samuel's head. And I knew that the literal-mindedness of the Amish would serve the judge well here. As long as the word she posed wasn't *swear* or *vow* or *promise*, Samuel would find the compromise acceptable.

He nodded. The clerk slipped the Bible beneath his hand again; I may have been the only one who noticed that Samuel's palm hovered a few millimeters above the leather-bound cover. 'Do you . . . uh, affirm to tell the truth, the whole truth, and nothing but the truth, so help you God?'

Samuel smiled at the little man. '*Ja,* all right.'

He took the stand, filling the whole box, his large hands balanced on his knees and his hat tucked beneath the chair. 'Could you state your name and address?'

He cleared his throat. 'Samuel Stoltzfus. Blossom Hill Road, East Paradise Township.' He hesitated, then added, 'Pennsylvania, U.S.A.'

'Thanks, Mr Stoltzfus.'

'Ellie,' he whispered loudly, 'you can call me Samuel.'

I grinned. 'Okay. Samuel. Are you a little bit nervous?'

'Yes.' The word came out on a guffaw of relief.

'I'll bet. Have you ever been in court before?'

'No.'

'Did you ever think you would be in court, one day?'

He shook his head. '*Ach,* no. We don't believe in the filing of lawsuits, so I never gave it a minute's thought.'

'By "we" you mean whom?'

'The People,' he said.

'The Amish?'

'Yes.'

'Were you asked to be a witness today?'

'No. I volunteered.'

'You willingly put yourself into an uncomfortable situation? Why?'

His clear, blue gaze locked on Katie. 'Because she didn't murder her baby.'

'How do you know?'

'I've known her my whole life. Since we were kids. I've seen her every single day for years. Now I work for Katie's father on the farm.'

'Really? What do you do there?'

'Anything Aaron tells me to do, pretty much. Mostly, I'm there to help with the planting and the harvesting. Oh, *ja*, and the milking. It's a dairy.'

'When is the milking done, Samuel?'

'Four-thirty A.M. and four-thirty P.M.'

'What does it entail?'

George raised a brow. 'Objection. Do we really need a lesson in farm management?'

'I'm laying foundation, Your Honor,' I argued.

'Overruled. Mr Stoltzfus, you may answer the question.'

Samuel nodded. 'Well, we start by mixing the feed. Then we shovel up behind the stanchions, and that goes into the manure pit. Aaron's got twenty cows, so this takes a while. Then we wipe down their teats and put on the milking pump, which runs on generator. Two cows get hooked up at a time, did I say that? The milk goes into a can that gets dumped into the bulk tank. And usually in the middle we have to stop and shovel up behind 'em again.'

'When does the milk company truck come to pick up the milk?'

'Every other day, save the Lord's Day. When it falls on a Sunday, it comes crazy times, like Saturdays at midnight.'

'Is the milk pasteurized before the truck takes it?'

'No, that happens after it leaves the farm.'

'Do the Fishers get their milk from the supermarket?'

Samuel grinned. 'That would be sort of silly, wouldn't it? Like buying bacon when you've just slaughtered a perfectly good pig. The Fishers drink their own fresh milk. I have to bring a pitcher in to Katie's mother twice a day.'

'So the milk the Fishers drink has not yet been pasteurized?'

'No, but it tastes just the same as the stuff you get in the white plastic jug. You've had it. Don't you think so?'

'Objection – could someone remind the witness that he's not supposed to be asking questions?' George said.

The judge leaned sideways. 'Mr Stoltzfus, I'm afraid the prosecutor's right.'

The big man reddened and looked into his lap. 'Samuel,' I said quickly, 'why do you feel that you know Katie so well?'

'I've seen her in so many situations I know how she acts – when she's sad, when she's happy. I was there when her sister drowned, when her brother got banned for good from the church. Two years ago, too, we started to go together.'

'You mean date?'

'*Ja.*'

'Were you dating when Katie had the baby?'

'Yes.'

'Were you there when she gave birth?'

'No, I wasn't,' Samuel said. 'I found out later.'

'Did you think at the time that it was your baby?'

'No.'

'Why not?'

He cleared his throat. 'We never slept together.'

'Did you know who the father of that baby was?'

'No. Katie wouldn't tell me.'

I softened my voice. 'How did that make you feel?'

'Pretty bad. She was my girl, you see. I didn't understand what had happened.'

For a moment, I simply let the jury look at Samuel. A strong, good-looking man dressed in clothes that seemed strange, speaking haltingly in his second language, trying to keep afloat in a situation that was completely unfamiliar to him. 'Samuel,' I said. 'Your girlfriend gets pregnant with someone else's baby – the baby's mysteriously found dead, although you're not there to see how it happens – you're nervous about being in a courtroom to testify – yet you've come here to tell us she *didn't* commit murder?'

'That's right.'

'Why are you sticking up for Katie, who, by all means, has wronged you?'

'Everything you said, Ellie, it's true. I should be very angry. I was, for a time, but now I'm not. Now I've gotten past my own selfishness to where I've got to help her. See, when you're Plain, you don't put yourself forward. You just don't do it, because that would be *Hochmut* – puffing yourself up – and the truth is there's always others more important than you. So Katie, when she hears others telling lies about her and this baby, she won't want to fight back, or stand up for herself. I am here to stand up for her.' As if listening to his own his words, he slowly got to his feet and stared at the jury. 'She did not do this. She could not do this.'

Every one of the twelve was arrested by the image of Samuel's face, set with quiet, fierce conviction. 'Samuel, do you still love her?'

He turned, his eyes sliding past me to light on Katie. 'Yes,' he said. 'Yes, I do.'

George tapped his forefinger against his lips. 'She was your girlfriend, but she was sleeping with some other guy?'

Samuel's eyes narrowed. 'Did you not just hear what I said?'

The prosecutor held up his hands. 'Just wondering about your feelings on that subject, that's all.'

'I didn't come here to talk about my feelings. I came here to talk about Katie. She's done nothing wrong.'

I covered my chuckle with a cough. For someone inexperienced, Samuel could be a hell of a mountain to move. 'Does your religion practice forgiveness, Mr Stoltzfus?' George asked.

'Samuel.'

'All right, then. Samuel. Does your religion practice forgiveness?'

'Yes. If a person humbles himself and confesses to his sin, he'll always be welcome back in the church.'

'After he admits to what he did.'

'After confessing, that's true.'

'Okay. Now let's forget about the church for a minute. Don't answer as an Amishman, just answer as a person. Aren't there some things you just can't excuse?'

Samuel's lips tightened. 'I cannot answer without thinking Plain, because it's who I am. And if I couldn't forgive someone, it wouldn't be their problem, but mine, because I wasn't being a true Christian.'

'In this particular case, you personally forgave Katie.'

'Yes.'

'But you just said that forgiveness implies the other party has already confessed to a sin.'

'Well . . . *ja*.'

'So if you forgave Katie, she must have done something wrong – in spite of the fact that you told us not five minutes ago she didn't.'

Samuel was silent for a moment. I held my breath, waiting for George to strike the killing blow. Then the Amishman looked up. 'I am not a smart man, Mr Callahan. I didn't go to college, like you. I don't really know what you're trying to ask me. Yes, I forgave Katie – but not for killing a baby. The only thing I had to forgive Katie for was breaking my heart.' He hesitated. 'And I don't think even you English can put her in jail for that.'

Owen Zeigler was apparently allergic to the courtroom. For the sixth time in as many minutes, he sneezed, covering his nose with a florid paisley handkerchief. 'Sorry. *Dermatophagoides pteronyssinus*.'

'I beg your pardon?' said Judge Ledbetter.

'Dust mites. Nasty little creatures. They live in pillows, mattresses – and, I'll bet, under the rugs here.' He sniffed a bit. 'They feed on the scales shed by human skin, and their waste products cause allergic symptoms. You know, if you monitored the humidity a little better in here, you might reduce the irritants.'

'I assume you're referring to the mites, and not the lawyers,' the judge said dryly.

Owen glanced dubiously at the air-conditioning vents overhead. 'You probably want to take a look at the mold spores, too.'

'Your Honor, I have allergies,' George said. 'Yet I've been perfectly comfortable in this courtroom.'

Owen looked aggrieved. 'I can't help my high level of sensitivity.'

'Dr Zeigler, do you feel that you'll be able to make it through your testimony? Shall I see about procuring another courtroom?'

'Or maybe a plastic bubble,' George muttered.

Owen sneezed again. 'I'll do my best.'

The judge kneaded her temples. 'You may continue, Ms Hathaway.'

'Dr Zeigler,' I said, 'did you examine the tissue samples from Baby Fisher?'

'Yes. The infant was a premature liveborn male with no congenital abnormalities. There was evidence of acute chorioamnionitis and infection in the baby. The cause of death was perinatal asphyxia.'

'Your findings, then, did not disagree with those of the medical examiner?'

Owen smiled. 'We agree on the cause of death. However, regarding the proximate causes of death – the events leading up to the asphyxia – our analyses are markedly different.'

'How so?'

'The medical examiner found the manner of death to be homicide. I believe the infant's asphyxia was due to natural causes.'

I let the jury absorb that for a moment. 'Natural causes? What do you mean?'

'Based on my findings, Ms Fisher did not have a hand in her newborn's death – it stopped breathing all by itself.'

'Let's walk through some of those findings, Doctor.'

'Well, the most puzzling was liver necrosis.'

'Can you elaborate?'

Owen nodded. 'Necrosis is cell death. Pure necrosis is usually caused either by congenital heart abnormalities, which this newborn didn't have, or by infection. When the ME saw the necrosis, he assumed it came part and parcel with the asphyxia, but the liver has a dual blood supply and is less susceptible to ischemia than other organs.'

'Ischemia?'

'Tissue hypoxia – lack of oxygen – caused by this loss of oxygen in the blood. Anyway, it's very unusual to find this sort of lesion in the liver. Add this to the chorioamnionitis, and I started to wonder if an infectious agent might have been at work here, after all.'

'Why would the medical examiner have overlooked this?'

'A couple of reasons,' Owen explained. 'First, the liver showed no signs of polys – white blood cells that respond to a bacterial infection. However, if the infection was very early, there wouldn't have been a poly response yet. The ME assumed there was no infection because there was no inflammatory response. But cell death can occur several hours before the body responds to it by mounting an inflammation – and I believe the infant died before this could happen. Second, his cultures showed no organism that would have been a likely cause of infection.'

'What did you do?'

'I got the paraffin blocks of tissue and did Gram's stains on the liver. That's when I found a large number of cocco-bacillary bacteria in the neonate. The ME chalked these up to contaminants – diphtheroids, which are rod-shaped bacteria. Now, cocco-bacilli are often misidentified as either rod-shaped bacteria, like diphtheroids; or cocci, like staph or strep. There were so many of these organisms I began to wonder if they were something other than mere contaminants – like perhaps an infectious agent. With the help of a microbiologist, I identified the organism as *Listeria monocytogenes*, a motile pleomorphic Gram-positive rod.'

I could see the eyes of the jury glazing, bogged down in scientific terms. 'You can say that again,' I joked.

Owen smiled. 'Let's just call it listeriosis. That's the infection caused by these bacteria.'

'Can you tell us about listeriosis?'

'It's an often unrecognized cause of preterm delivery and perinatal death,' Owen said. 'Infection in the second or third trimester usually leads to either stillbirth or preterm birth followed by pneumonia and neonatal sepsis.'

'Hang on a second,' I said. 'You're saying that Katie contracted some infection that may have compromised the health of her baby before it was even born?'

'That's exactly what I'm saying. Moreover, it's extremely difficult to diagnose in time to initiate therapy. The mother will exhibit flu-like symptoms – fever, aches, mild pain – only hours before the premature delivery takes place.'

'What is the effect on the newborn?'

'Perinatal depression, fever, and respiratory distress.' He paused. 'The mortality rate for the newborns, in case studies, is somewhere between thirty and fifty percent even after treatment.'

'An infant infected with listeria has a *fifty percent chance* of dying even if treated?'

'Correct.'

'How do you contract listeriosis?' I asked.

'From the studies I've seen, eating contaminated food is the most frequent mode of transmission. Particularly unpasteurized milk and cheese.'

'Unpasteurized milk,' I repeated.

'Yes. And people who are in contact with animals seem to be at particular risk.'

I put my hand on Katie's shoulder. 'Dr Zeigler, if I gave you the autopsy report for Katie's newborn, and then told you that Katie lived on a dairy farm, drank unpasteurized milk daily when she was pregnant, and was actively involved in the milking of the cows twice a day, what would you infer?'

'Based on her living conditions and potential exposure to *Listeria monocytogenes*, I'd say that she contracted this infection when she was pregnant.'

'Did Baby Fisher exhibit the symptoms of an infant infected with listeriosis?'

'Yes. He was born prematurely and suffered respiratory failure. He showed some signs of granulomatosis infantiseptica, including liver necrosis and pneumonia.'

'Could it have been fatal?'

'Absolutely. Either from the complications of perinatal asphyxia, or simply from the infection.'

'In your opinion, what caused Baby Fisher's death?' I asked.

'Asphyxia, due to premature delivery, because of chorio-amnionitis secondary to listeriosis.' He smiled. 'It's a mouthful, but it basically means that a chain of events led to death by natural causes. The baby was dying from the moment it was born.'

'In your opinion, was Katie Fisher responsible for her baby's death?'

'Yes, if you want to get technical about it,' Owen said. 'After all, it was her body that passed on the *Listeria monocytogenes* to her fetus. But the infection certainly wasn't intentional. You can't blame Ms Fisher any more than you'd blame a mother who unwittingly passes along the AIDS virus to her unborn child.' He looked at Katie, sitting with her head bowed. 'That's not homicide. It's just plain sad.'

To my delight, George was clearly rattled. It was exactly what I'd been counting on, actually – no prosecutor was going to dig up listeriosis on his own, and certainly it was nothing George had thought to ask about during the deposition. He stood up, smoothing his tie, and walked toward my witness.

'Listeria,' he said. 'Is this a common bacteria?'

'Actually, it's quite common,' Owen said. 'It's all over the place.'

'Then how come we're not all dropping like flies?'

'It's a very common bacteria, but a fairly uncommon disease. It affects one in twenty thousand pregnant women.'

'One in twenty thousand. And it hit the defendant full force, or so you said, because of her tendency to drink unpasteurized milk.'

'That's my assumption, yes.'

'Do you know for a fact that the defendant drank unpasteurized milk?'

'Well, I didn't personally ask her, but she does live on a dairy farm.'

George shook his head. 'That doesn't prove anything, Dr Zeigler. I could live on a chicken farm and be allergic to eggs. Do you know for a fact that every time the defendant reached for a pitcher at the dinner table, it contained milk – rather than orange juice, or water, or Coke?'

'No, I don't know.'

'Did anyone else in the household suffer the effects of listeriosis?'

'I wasn't asked to examine paraffin blocks of their tissue,' Owen said. 'I couldn't tell you for sure.'

'Let me help you out then. They didn't. No one else but the defendant exhibited signs of this mystery illness. Isn't it strange that a family drinking the same contaminated milk wouldn't all have the same physical reaction to the bacteria?'

'Not really. Pregnancy is a state of immunosuppression, and listeriosis flares up in immunocompromised patients. If someone in the household had cancer, or HIV infection, or was very old or very young – all of which would compromise the immune system – there might have been another response much like the one Ms Fisher apparently had.'

'*Apparently* had,' George repeated. 'Are you suggesting, Doctor, that she might not have suffered from this illness?'

'No, she definitely did. The placenta and the infant were infected, and the only way they could have contracted the bacteria is from the mother.'

'Is there any way to prove, conclusively, that the infant was suffering from listeriosis?'

Owen considered this. 'We know that he was infected with listeria, because of the immunostaining we did.'

'Can you prove that the infant died from complications due to listeriosis?'

'It's the listeria that's fatal,' Owen answered. 'It causes the infection in the liver, the lungs, brain, wherever. Depending on the pattern of involvement, the organ that causes death might be different from patient to patient. In the case of Baby Fisher, it was respiratory failure.'

'The baby's death was due to respiratory failure?'

'Yes,' Owen said. 'Respiratory failure, as caused by respiratory infection.'

'But isn't respiratory infection only one cause of respiratory failure?'

'Yes.'

'Is smothering another cause of respiratory failure?'

'Yes.'

'So isn't it possible that the baby might have been infected with listeria, might have had evidence of the bacteria in his body and lungs – but his actual death could have been caused by his mother suffocating him?'

Owen frowned. 'It's possible. There would be no way of knowing for sure.'

'Nothing further.'

I was up out of my seat to redirect before George made it back to his table. 'Dr Zeigler, if Katie's baby hadn't died of respiratory failure that morning, what would have happened to him?'

'Well, assuming that after the home birth the newborn wasn't whisked off to a hospital for diagnosis and treatment, the infection would have progressed. He might have died of pneumonia at two or three days of life . . . if not then, he would have died of meningitis within a couple of weeks. Once meningitis develops, the disease is fatal even if it's diagnosed and treatment is begun.'

'So unless the baby was taken to a neonatal care unit, he most likely would have died shortly after?'

'That's right.'

'Thank you, Doctor.'

I sat down just as George stood again. 'Recross, Your Honor. Dr Zeigler, you said the mortality rate for listeriosis is high, even with treatment?'

'Yes, nearly fifty out of a hundred babies will die from complications.'

'And you just hypothesized that Baby Fisher would have died within a few weeks, if not that first morning of life?'

'Yes.'

George raised his brows. 'How do you know, Dr Zeigler, that he wasn't one of the other fifty?'

For reasons I didn't understand, Katie retreated into her shell with each word of Owen's testimony. By all accounts, she should have been as pleased as I was. Even George's little dig at the end of his recross couldn't take away from the fact this fatal bacteria had been found in the baby's body. The jury, now, had to have a reasonable doubt – which was all that we needed for an acquittal.

'Katie,' I said, leaning close to her, 'are you feeling all right?'

'Please, Ellie. Can we go home now?'

She looked miserable. 'Are you sick?'

'*Please.*'

I glanced at my watch. It was three-thirty; a little early for milking, but Judge Ledbetter would never know that. 'Your Honor,' I said, getting to my feet, 'if it pleases the court, we'd like to adjourn for the afternoon.'

The judge peered at me over the edge of her glasses. 'Ah, yes. The milking.' She glanced at Owen Zeigler, now sitting in the gallery. 'Well, if I were you I'd make sure to wash my hands when I was done. Mr Callahan, do you have any objections to an early dismissal for farm chores?'

'No, Your Honor. My chickens will be thrilled to see me.' He shrugged. 'Oh, that's right. I don't have chickens.'

The judge frowned at him. 'No need to be a cosmopolitan

snob, counselor. All right, then. We'll reconvene tomorrow at ten A.M. Court is adjourned.'

Suddenly a wall of people surrounded us: Leda, Coop, Jacob, Samuel, and Adam Sinclair. Coop slid his arm around my waist and whispered, 'I hope she has your brains.'

I didn't answer. I watched Jacob trying to crack jokes that would make Katie smile; Samuel standing tight as a bowstring and careful not to let his shoulder brush against Adam's. For her part, Katie was attempting to keep up a good front, but her smile stretched across her face like a sheet pulled too tight. Was I the only one who noticed that she was about to fall apart?

'Katie,' Adam said, stepping forward, 'do you want to take a walk?'

'No, she does not,' Samuel answered.

Surprised, Adam turned. 'I think she can speak for herself.'

Katie pressed her fingers to her temples. 'Thank you, Adam, but I have plans with Ellie.'

This was news to me, but one look at the desperate plea in her eyes and I found myself nodding. 'We need to go over her testimony,' I said, although if I had my way there wasn't going to be any testimony from her at all. 'Leda will drive us back. Coop, can you manage to get everyone else home?'

We left the way we had on Friday: Leda drove to the rear of the court-house to pick Katie and me up at the food service loading dock. Then we circled to the exit at the front of the building, passing all the reporters who were still waiting for Katie to appear. 'Honey,' Leda said a few minutes later. 'That doctor you put on the stand was something else.'

I was looking into the little vanity mirror above the passenger seat, rubbing off circles of mascara beneath my eyes. Behind me, in the backseat, Katie turned to stare out the window. 'Owen's a good guy. And an even better pathologist.'

'That bacteria stuff . . . was it real?'

I smiled at her. 'He wouldn't be allowed to make it up. That's perjury.'

'Well, I bet you could win the case on that doctor's testimony alone.'

I glanced into the mirror again, trying to catch Katie's eye. 'You hear that?' I asked pointedly.

Her lips tightened; other than that, she gave no indication that she'd been listening. She kept her cheek pressed to the window, her eyes averted.

Suddenly Katie opened the car door, causing Leda to swerve off the road and come to a screeching stop. 'My stars!' she cried. 'Katie, honey, you don't do that when we're still moving!'

'I'm sorry. Aunt Leda, is it all right if Ellie and I walk the rest of the way?'

'But that's a good three miles!'

'I could use the fresh air. And Ellie and me, we have to talk.' Katie smiled fleetingly. 'We'll be okay.'

Leda looked to me for approval. I was wearing my black flats – not heels, granted, but still not my first choice for hiking shoes. Katie was already standing outside the car. 'Oh, all right,' I grumbled, tossing my briefcase into the seat. 'Can you drop this off in the mailbox?'

We watched her taillights disappear down the road, and then I turned to her, arms crossed. 'What's this about?'

Katie started walking. 'I just wanted to be alone for a bit.'

'Well, I'm not leaving—'

'I meant alone with you.' She stooped to pick a tall, curly fern growing along the side of the road. 'It's too hard, with the rest of them all needing a piece of me.'

'They care about you.' I watched Katie duck beneath an electric fence to walk through a field milling with heifers. 'Hey – we're trespassing.'

'This is Old John Lapp's place. He won't mind if we take a shortcut.'

I picked my way through the cow patties, watching the animals twitch their tails and blink sleepily at us as we marched across their turf. Katie bent down to pick tufted white dandelions and dried milkweed pods. 'You ought to marry Coop,' she said.

I burst out laughing. 'Is that why you wanted to talk to me alone? Why don't we worry about you first, and deal with my problems after the trial.'

'You have to. You just have to.'

'Katie, whether I'm married or not, I'll still have the baby.'

She flinched. 'That's not the point.'

'What is the point?'

'Once he's gone,' she said quietly, 'you don't get him back again.'

So that was what had her so upset – Adam. We walked in silence for a while, ducking out the other side of the pasture's electric fence. 'You could still make a life with Adam. Your parents aren't the same people they were six years ago, when Jacob left. Things could be different.'

'No, they couldn't.' She hesitated, trying to explain. 'Just because you love someone doesn't mean the Lord has it in His plan for you to be together.' All of a sudden we stopped walking, and I realized two things at once: that Katie had led me to the little Amish cemetery; and that her raw emotions had nothing to do with Adam at all. Her face was turned to the small, chipped headstone of her child, her hands clenching the posts of the picket fence. 'People I love,' she whispered, 'get taken from me all the time.'

She started crying in silence, wrapping her arms around her middle. Then she bent forward, keening in a way she had not the whole time I had known her: not when she was charged with murder, not when her infant was buried, not when she was shunned. 'I'm sorry,' she sobbed. 'I'm so sorry.'

'Don't, Katie.' I gently touched her shoulder, and she turned into my arms.

We stood in the lane, rocking back and forth in this embrace, my hands stroking her spine in comfort. The wild weeds Katie had gathered were strewn around our feet, an offering. 'I'm so sorry,' she repeated, choking on the words. 'I didn't mean to do it.'

My blood froze, my hands stilled on her back. 'Didn't mean to do what?'

Katie lifted her face. 'To kill him.'

17

By the time Katie ran up the driveway, a stitch in her side, the men were doing the milking. She could hear the sounds coming from the barn and she found herself drawn to them. Around the edge of the wide door she could see Levi pushing a wheelbarrow; Samuel stooping to attach the pump to the udders of one of the cows. A suck, a tug, and the thin white fluid began to move through the hose that led to the milk can.

Katie clapped her hand over her mouth and ran to the side of the barn, where she threw up until there was nothing left in her stomach.

She could hear Ellie calling out as she limped her way up the drive. Ellie couldn't run as fast as she could, and Katie had shamelessly used that advantage to escape.

Slinking along the side of the barn, Katie edged toward the nubby, harvested fields. They were not much use for camouflage now, but they would put distance between her and Ellie. Lifting her skirts, she ran to the pond and hid behind the big oak.

Katie held out her hand, examining her fingers and her wrist. Where was it now, this bacteria? Was there any left in her, or had she passed it all on to her baby?

She closed her eyes against the image of her newborn son, lying between her legs and crying for all he was worth. Even then, she'd known something was wrong. She hadn't wanted to say it out loud, but she had seen his whole chest and belly work with the effort to draw in air.

But she hadn't been able to do anything about it, just like

she hadn't been able to keep Hannah from going under, or Jacob from being sent away, or Adam from leaving.

Katie looked at the sky, etched with sharp detail around the naked branches of the oak. And she understood that these tragedies would keep coming until she confessed.

Ellie had defended guilty clients, even several who had patently lied to her, but somehow she could not recall ever feeling so betrayed. She fumed up the drive, furious at Katie for her deception, at Leda for leaving them three miles away, at her own sorry physical shape that left her breathless after a short jog.

This is not personal, she reminded herself. This is strictly business.

She found Katie at the pond. 'You want to tell me what you meant back there?' Ellie asked, bending down and breathing hard.

'You heard me,' Katie said sullenly.

'Tell me why you killed the baby, Katie.'

She shook her head. 'I don't want to make excuses anymore. I just want to tell the jury what I told you, so this can be over.'

'Tell the jury?' Ellie sputtered. 'Over my dead body.'

'No,' Katie said, paling. 'You have to let me.'

'There is no way in hell that I'm going to let you get up on that stand and tell the court you killed your baby.'

'You were willing to let me testify before!'

'Amazingly enough, your story was different then. You said you wanted to tell the truth, to tell everyone you didn't commit murder. It's one thing for me to put you on as a witness if you don't contradict everything else my strategy has built up; it's another thing entirely to put you on so that you can commit legal suicide.'

'Ellie,' Katie said desperately. 'I have to confess.'

'This is not your church!' Ellie cried. 'How many times do you need to hear that? We're not talking six weeks of suspension, here. We're talking years. A lifetime, maybe. In prison.'

She bit down on her anger and took a deep breath. 'It was one thing to let the jury see you, listen to your grief. To hear you say you were innocent. But what you told me just now . . .' Her voice trailed off; she looked away. 'To let you take the stand would be professionally irresponsible.'

'They can still see me and hear me and listen to my grief.'

'Yeah, all of which goes down the toilet when I ask you if you killed the baby.'

'Then don't ask me that question.'

'If I don't, George will. And once you get on the stand, you can't lie.' Ellie sighed. 'You can't lie – and you can't say outright that you killed that baby, either, or you've sealed your conviction.'

Katie looked down at her feet. 'Jacob told me that if I wanted to talk in court, you couldn't stop me.'

'I can get you acquitted without your testimony. Please, Katie. Don't do this to yourself.'

Katie turned to her with absolute calm. 'I will be a witness tomorrow. You may not like it, but that's what I want.'

'Who do you want to forgive you?' Ellie exploded. 'A jury? The judge? Because they won't. They'll just see you as a monster.'

'You don't, do you?'

Ellie shook her head, unable to answer.

'What is it?' Katie pressed. 'Tell me what you're thinking.'

'That it's one thing to lie to your lawyer, but it's another to lie to your friend.' Ellie got to her feet and dusted off her skirt. 'I'll write up a disclaimer for you to sign, that says I advised you against this course of action,' she said coolly, and walked away.

'I don't believe it,' Coop said, bringing together the corners of the quilt that he was folding with Ellie. It was a wedding ring pattern, the irony of which had not escaped him. Several other quilts, newly washed, flapped on clotheslines strung between trees, huge kaleidoscopic patterns of color against a darkening sky.

Ellie walked toward him, handing him the opposite ends of the quilt. 'Believe it.'

'Katie's not capable of murder.'

She took the bundle from his arms and vigorously halved it into a bulky square. 'Apparently, you're wrong.'

'I know her, Ellie. She's my client.'

'Yeah, and my roommate. Go figure.'

Coop reached for the clothespins securing the second quilt. 'How did she do it?'

'I didn't ask.'

This surprised Coop. 'You didn't?'

Ellie's fingers trailed over her abdomen. 'I couldn't,' she said, then briskly turned away.

In that moment, Coop wanted nothing more than to take her into his arms. 'The only explanation is that she's lying.'

'Haven't you been listening to me in court?' Ellie's lips twisted. 'The Amish don't lie.'

Coop ignored her. 'She's lying in order to be punished. For whatever reason, that's what she needs psychologically.'

'Sure, if you call life in prison therapeutic.' Ellie jerked up the opposite end of the fabric. 'She's not lying, Coop. I've probably seen as many liars as you have, in my line of work. Katie looked me in the eye and she told me she killed her baby. She meant it.' With abrupt movements, she yanked the quilt from Coop and folded it again, then slapped it on top of the first one. 'Katie Fisher is going down, and she's taking the rest of us with her.'

'If she's signed the disclaimer, you can't be held responsible.'

'Oh, no, of course not. It's just my name and my account-ability being trashed along with her case.'

'No matter what her reasoning, I doubt very much that Katie's doing this right now in order to spite you.'

'It doesn't matter why, Coop. She's going to get up there and make a public confession, and the jury won't give a damn about the rationale behind it. They'll convict her quicker than she can say "I did it."'

'Are you angry because she's ruining your case, or because you didn't see this coming?'

'I'm not angry. If she wants to throw her life away, it's no skin off my back.' Ellie grabbed for the quilt that Coop was holding but fumbled, so that it landed in a heap in the dirt. 'Dammit! Do you know how long it takes to wash these things? Do you?' She sank to the ground, the quilt a cloud behind her, and buried her face in her hands.

Coop wondered how a woman so willow-thin and delicate could bear the weight of someone else's salvation on her shoulders. He sat beside Ellie and gathered her close, her fingers digging into the fabric of his shirt. 'I could have saved her,' she whispered.

'I know, sweetheart. But maybe she wanted to save herself.'

'Hell of a way to go about it.'

'You're thinking like a lawyer again.' Coop tapped her temple. 'If you're afraid of everyone leaving you, what do you do?'

'Make them stay.'

'And if you can't do that, or don't know how to?'

Ellie shrugged. 'I don't know.'

'Yes, you do. In fact, you've done it. You leave first,' Coop said, 'so you don't have to watch them walk away.'

When Katie was little, she used to love when it rained, when she could skip out to the end of the driveway where the puddles, with their faint sheen of oil, turned into rainbows. The sky looked like that now, a royal purple marbled with orange and red and silver, like the gown of a fairy-tale queen. It settled over all these Plain folks' farms; each piece of land butting up against something lush and rich that seemed to go on forever.

She stood on the porch in the twilight, waiting. When the hum of a car's engine came from the west, she felt her heart creep up her throat, felt every muscle in her body strain forward to see if the vehicle would turn up the driveway. But seconds later, through the trees, the taillights ribboned by.

'He isn't coming.'

Katie whirled at the sound of the voice, followed by the heavy thumps of boots on the porch steps. 'Who?'

Samuel swallowed. '*Ach*, Katie. Are you gonna make me say his name, too?'

Katie rubbed her hands up and down her arms and faced the road again.

'He went into Philadelphia. He'll be back tomorrow, for the trial.'

'You came to tell me this?'

'No,' Samuel answered. 'I came to take you for a walk.'

She lowered her gaze. 'I don't figure I'd be very good company right now.'

He shrugged when Katie didn't answer. 'Well, I'm going, anyway,' Samuel said, and started down from the porch.

'Wait!' Katie cried, and she hurried to fall into step beside him.

They walked to a symphony of wind racing through trees and birds lighting on branches, of owls calling to mice and dew silvering the webs of spiders. Samuel's long strides made Katie nearly run to keep up. 'Where are we going?' she asked after several minutes, when they had just reached the small grove of apple trees.

He stopped abruptly and looked around. 'I have no idea.'

That made Katie grin, and Samuel smiled too, and then they were both laughing. Samuel sat, bracing his elbows on his knees, and Katie sank down beside him, her skirts rustling over the fallen leaves. Empire apples, bright as rubies, brushed the top of Katie's *kapp* and Samuel's brimmed hat. He thought suddenly of how Katie had once peeled an apple in one long string at a barn raising, had tossed the skin over her shoulder like the old wive's tale said to see who she would marry; how all their friends and family had laughed to see it land in the shape of the letter *S*.

Suddenly the silence was thick and heavy on Samuel's shoulders. 'You've sure got a good harvest here,' he said, removing his hat. 'Lot of applesauce to be put up.'

'It'll keep my mother busy, that's for certain.'

'And you?' he joked. 'You'll be in the barn with us, I suppose?'

'I don't know where I'll be.' Katie looked up at him, and cleared her throat. 'Samuel, there's something I have to tell you—'

He pressed his fingers against her mouth, her soft mouth, and let himself pretend for just a moment that this could have been a kiss. 'No talking.'

Katie nodded and looked into her lap.

'It's near November. Mary Esch, she's got a lot of celery growing,' Samuel said.

Katie's heart fell. The talk of November – the wedding month – and celery, which was used in most of the dishes at the wedding dinner, was too much to bear. She'd known about Mary and Samuel's kiss, but no one had said anything more to her in the time that had passed. It was Samuel's business, after all, and he had every right to go on with his life. To get married, next month, to Mary Esch.

'She's gonna marry Owen King, sure as the sunrise,' Samuel continued.

Katie blinked at him. 'She's not going to marry you?'

'I don't think the girl I want to marry is gonna look kindly on that.' Samuel blushed and glanced into his lap. 'You won't, will you?'

For a moment, Katie imagined that her life was like any other young Amish woman's; that her world had not gone so off course that this sweet proposition was unthinkable. 'Samuel,' she said, her voice wavering, 'I can't make you a promise now.'

He shook his head, but didn't lift his gaze. 'If it's not this November, it'll be next November. Or the November after that.'

'If I go away, it'll be forever.'

'You never know. Take me, for example.' Samuel traced his finger along the brim of his hat, a perfect black circle.

'There I was, so sure I was leaving you for good . . . and it turns out all that time I was just heading back to where I started.' He squeezed her hand. 'You will think about it?'

'Yes,' Katie said. 'I will.'

It was after midnight when Ellie silently crept upstairs to the bedroom. Katie was sleeping on her side, a band of moonlight sawing her into two like a magician's assistant. Ellie quietly dragged the quilt into her arms, then tiptoed toward the door.

'What are you doing?'

She turned to face Katie. 'Sleeping on the couch.'

Katie sat up, the covers falling away from her simple white nightgown. 'You don't have to do that.'

'I know.'

'It's bad for the baby.'

A muscle tightened along the column of Ellie's throat. 'Don't you tell me what's bad for my baby,' she said. 'You have no right.' She turned on her heel and walked down the stairs, hugging the bedding to her chest as if it were an armored shield, as if it were not too late to safeguard her heart.

Ellie stood in the judge's chambers, surveying the legal tracts and the woodwork, the thick carpet on the floor – anything but Judge Ledbetter herself, scanning the disclaimer that she'd just been given.

'Ms Hathaway,' she said after a moment. 'What's going on?'

'My client insists on taking the stand, although I've advised her against it.'

The judge stared at Ellie, as if she might be able to discern from her blank countenance the entire upheaval that had occurred last night. 'Is there a particular reason you advised her against it?'

'I believe that will make itself evident,' Ellie said.

George, looking suitably delighted, stood a little straighter.

'All right, then,' the judge sighed. 'Let's get this over with.'

*　　　*　　　*

You could not grow up Amish without knowing that eyes had weight, that stares had substance, that they could sometimes feel like a breath at your shoulder and other times like a spear right through your spine; but usually in Lancaster the glances came one on one – a tourist craning his neck to see her better, a child blinking up at her in the convenience store. Sitting on the witness stand, Katie felt paralyzed by the eyes boring into her. A hundred people were gawking at once, and why shouldn't they? It was not every day a Plain person confessed to murder.

She wiped her sweating palms on her apron and waited for Ellie to start asking her questions. She had hoped that when they came to this moment, Ellie would make it easier – maybe Katie would even have been able to pretend it was just the two of them, having a talk down by the pond. But Ellie had barely spoken a word to her all morning. She'd been sick in the bathroom, had a cup of chamomile tea, and told Katie it was time to go without ever meeting her gaze. No, Ellie would be giving her no quarter today.

Ellie buttoned her suit jacket and stood up. 'Katie,' she said gently, 'do you know why you're here today?'

Katie blinked. Her voice, her question – it was tender, full of sympathy. Relief washed over her, she started to smile – and then she looked into Ellie's eyes. They were just as hard and angry as they had been the night before. This compassion – it was all part of an act. Even now, Ellie was only trying to get her acquitted.

Katie took a deep breath. 'People think I killed my baby.'

'How does that make you feel?'

Once again, she saw that tiny comma of a body lying between her legs, slick with her own blood. 'Bad,' she whispered.

'You know that the evidence against you is strong.'

With a glance at the jury, Katie nodded. 'I've been trying to follow what's been said. I'm not sure I understand it all.'

'What don't you understand?'

'The way you English do things is very different than what I'm used to.'

'How so?'

She thought about this for a minute. The confession, that was the same, or she wouldn't be sitting up here now. But the English judged a person so that they'd be justified in casting her out. The Amish judged a person so that they'd be justified in welcoming her back. 'Where I'm from, if someone is accused of sinning, it's not so that others can place blame. It's so that the person can make amends and move on.'

'Did you sin when you conceived your child?'

Instinctively, Katie adopted a humble demeanor. 'Yes.'

'Why?'

'I wasn't married.'

'Did you love the man?'

From beneath lowered lashes, Katie scanned the gallery to find Adam. He was sitting on the edge of his seat with his head bowed, as if this was his confession as well. 'Very much,' Katie murmured.

'Were you accused of that sin by your community?'

'Yes. The deacon and the bishop, they came and asked me to make a kneeling confession at church.'

'After you confessed to conceiving a child out of wedlock, what happened?'

'I was put in the *bann* for a time, to think about what I'd done. After six weeks, I went back and promised to work with the church.' She smiled. 'They took me back.'

'Katie, did the deacon and minister ask you to confess to killing your child?'

'No.'

'Why not?'

Katie folded her hands in her lap. 'That charge wasn't laid against me.'

'So the people in your own community did not believe you guilty of the sin of murder?' Katie shrugged. 'I need a verbal response,' Ellie said.

'No, they didn't.'

Ellie walked back to the defense table, her heels clicking on the parquet floor. 'Do you remember what happened the night you gave birth, Katie?'

'Bits and pieces. It comes back a little at a time.'

'Why is that?'

'Dr Cooper says it's because my mind can't take too much too soon.' She worried her bottom lip. 'I kind of shut down after it happened.'

'After what happened?'

'After the baby came.'

Ellie nodded. 'We've heard from a number of different people, but I think the jury would like to hear you tell us about that night. Did you know you were pregnant?'

Katie suddenly felt herself tumble backward in her mind, until she could feel beneath her palms the hard, small swell of the baby inside. 'I couldn't believe I was,' she said softly. 'I didn't believe it, until I had to move the pins on my apron because I was getting bigger.'

'Did you tell anyone?'

'No. I pushed it out of my head, and concentrated on other things.'

'Why?'

'I was scared. I didn't want my parents to know what had happened.' She took a deep breath. 'I prayed that maybe I'd guessed wrong.'

'Do you remember delivering the baby?'

Katie cradled her hands around her abdomen, reliving the burning pains that burst from her back to her belly. 'Some of it,' she said. 'The pain, and the way the hay pricked the skin on my back . . . but there are blocks of time I can't picture anything at all.'

'How did you feel at the time?'

'Scared,' she whispered. 'Real scared.'

'Do you remember the baby?' Ellie asked.

This was the part she knew so well, it might have been engraved on the backs of her eyelids. That small, sweet body, not much bigger than her own hand, kicking and coughing and reaching out for her. 'He was beautiful. I picked him up. Held him. I rubbed his back. He had . . . the tiniest bones inside. His heart, it beat against my hand.'

'What were you planning to do with him?'

'I don't know. I would have taken him to my mother, I guess; found something to wrap him in and keep him warm . . . but I fell asleep before I could.'

'You passed out.'

'Ja.'

'Were you still holding the baby?'

'Oh, yes,' Katie said.

'What happened after that?'

'I woke up. And the baby was gone.'

Ellie raised her brows. 'Gone? What did you think?'

Katie wrung her hands together. 'That this had been a dream,' she admitted.

'Was there evidence to the contrary?'

'There was blood on my nightgown, and a little in the hay.'

'What did you do?'

'I went to the pond and washed off,' Katie said. 'Then I went back to my room.'

'Why didn't you wake anyone up, or go to a doctor, or try to find that baby?'

Her eyes brightened with tears. 'I don't know. I should have. I know that now.'

'When you woke up the next morning, what happened?'

She wiped her hand across her eyes. 'It was like nothing had changed,' she said brokenly. 'If everyone had looked a little different; if I'd felt poorly, maybe I wouldn't have . . .' Her voice trailed off, and she looked away. 'I thought that maybe I'd made it all up, that nothing had happened to me. I wanted to believe that, because then I wouldn't have to wonder about where the baby was.'

'Did you know where the baby was?'

'No.'

'You don't remember taking it anywhere?'

'No.'

'You don't remember waking up with the baby in your arms at any time?'

'No. After I woke up, he was already gone.'

Ellie nodded. 'Did you plan to get rid of the baby?'

'No.'

'Did you *want* to get rid of the baby?'

'Not once I'd seen him,' Katie said softly.

Ellie was now standing only a foot away. Katie waited for her question, waited to speak the words she had come here to say. But with a nearly imperceptible shake of her head, Ellie turned to the jury. 'Thank you,' she said. 'Nothing further.'

Frankly, George was baffled. He'd expected more flashes of brilliance from Ellie Hathaway in a direct examination of her client, but she hadn't done anything out of the ordinary. More importantly, neither had the witness. Katie Fisher had said what anyone would expect her to say – none of which added up to Ellie's disclaimer in chambers this morning.

He smiled at Katie. 'Good morning, Ms Fisher.'

'You can call me Katie.'

'Katie, then. Let's pick up where you just left off. You fell asleep holding the baby, and when you woke up, he was gone. You were the only eyewitness that night. So tell us – what happened to that baby?'

She squeezed her eyes shut, a tear leaking from one corner. 'I killed him.'

George stopped in his tracks. The gallery erupted in confusion, and the judge rapped her gavel for quiet. Turning to Ellie, George lifted his palms in question. She was sitting at the defense table, looking almost bored, and he realized this had not been a surprise to her. Meeting his gaze, she shrugged.

'You killed your baby?'

'Yes,' she murmured.

He stared at the girl on the stand, looking powerfully beaten as she curled into herself in misery. 'How did you do it?'

Katie shook her head.

'You must answer the question.'

She clenched her hands around her middle. 'I just want to make my things right.'

'Hang on now. You just confessed to killing your baby. Now I'm asking you to tell us how you killed him.'

'I'm sorry,' she choked out. 'I can't.'

George turned to Judge Ledbetter. 'Approach?'

The judge nodded, and Ellie walked up beside him to the bench. 'What the hell is going on?' he demanded.

'Ms Hathaway?'

Ellie raised a brow. 'Ever hear of the Fifth Amendment, George?'

'It's a little late,' the prosecutor said. 'She's already incriminated herself.'

'Not necessarily,' Ellie said coolly, although she and George both realized she was lying through her teeth.

'Mr Callahan, you know very well that the witness can take the Fifth whenever she chooses.' The judge turned to Ellie. 'However, she needs to ask for it by name.'

Ellie glanced at Katie. 'She doesn't know what it's called, Your Honor. She just knows she doesn't want to say anything else about this.'

'Your Honor, Ms Hathaway can't speak for the witness. If I don't hear the defendant officially plead the Fifth, I'm not buying it.'

Ellie rolled her eyes. 'May I have a moment with my client?' She walked to the witness stand. Katie was shaking like a leaf, and with no small degree of shame Ellie realized that was partly because she expected a tirade. 'Katie,' she said quietly. 'If you don't want to talk about the crime, all you have to do is say in English, "I take the Fifth."'

'What does that mean?'

'It's part of the Constitution. It means you have the right to remain silent, even though you're on the stand, so that your words can't be used against you. Understand?'

Katie nodded, and Ellie walked back to the defense table to sit down.

'Please tell us how you killed your baby,' George repeated.

Katie darted a glance at Ellie. 'I take the Fifth,' she said haltingly.

'What a surprise,' George muttered. 'All right, then. Let's go back to the beginning. You lied to your father so that you could see your brother at college. You did this from the time you were twelve?'

'Yes.'

'And you're eighteen now.'

'Yes, I am.'

'In six years' time did your father ever find out you were visiting your brother?'

'No.'

'You would have just kept lying, wouldn't you?'

'I didn't lie,' Katie said. 'He never asked.'

'In six years, he never asked how your weekend with your aunt went?'

'My father doesn't speak of my aunt.'

'How lucky. Then, you lied to your brother about sleeping with his roommate?'

'He—'

'No, let me guess. He never asked, right?'

Confused, Katie shook her head. 'No, he didn't.'

'You never told Adam Sinclair he'd fathered a child?'

'He'd gone overseas.'

'You never told your mother about your pregnancy, or anyone else for that matter?'

'No.'

'And when the police came the morning after you gave birth, you lied to them as well.'

'I wasn't sure it had actually happened,' Katie said, her voice small.

'Oh, please. You're eighteen years old. You'd had sex. You knew you were pregnant, even if you didn't want to admit it.

You've seen countless women in your community have babies. Are you trying to tell me you didn't know what had happened to you that night?'

Katie was crying silently again. 'I can't explain how my head was, except that it wasn't working like normal. I didn't know what was real and what wasn't. I didn't want to believe that it might not have been a dream.' She twisted the edge of her apron in her fists. 'I know I've done something wrong. I know that it's time for me to take responsibility for what happened.'

George leaned so close his words fell into her lap. 'Then tell us how you did it.'

'I can't talk about it.'

'Ah. That's right. Just like you figured that if you didn't talk about your pregnancy, it would disappear. And like you didn't tell people you murdered your baby, assuming they'd never find out. But that's not the way things work, is it, Katie? Even if you don't tell us how you killed your baby, he's still dead, isn't he?'

'Objection,' Ellie called out. 'He's badgering the witness.'

Katie hunched in the chair, sobbing openly. George's eyes flickered over her once; then he turned dismissively. 'Withdrawn. I'm through here.'

Judge Ledbetter sighed. 'Let's take fifteen. Ms Hathaway, why don't you take your client somewhere to compose herself?'

'Of course,' Ellie said, wondering how to help Katie pull herself together when she herself was falling apart.

The conference room was dark and dingy, with nonfunctioning fluorescent bulbs that spit and hissed and emitted no viable source of light. Ellie sat at an ugly wooden table, tracing a coffee stain that was likely as old as Katie. As for her client, she was standing near the chalkboard in the front of the room, weeping.

'I'd like to have some sympathy for you, Katie, but you asked for this.' Ellie pushed away from the table and turned her back. Maybe if she didn't look at Katie, the sobs wouldn't be quite so loud. Or upsetting.

'I wanted it to be over,' Katie stammered, her face swollen and red. 'But it wasn't like I expected.'

'Oh, no? What were you expecting – some movie-of-the-week where you break down and the jury breaks down right along with you?'

'I just wanted to be forgiven.'

'Well, it doesn't look like that's going to happen right now. You just kissed your freedom good-bye, sweetheart. Forget about forgiveness from your church. Forget about seeing your parents, or having a relationship with Adam.'

'Samuel asked me to marry him,' Katie whispered miserably.

Ellie snorted. 'You might want to let him know that conjugal visits are hard to come by in the state correctional facility.'

'I don't want conjugal visits. I don't want to have another baby. What if I—' Katie broke off suddenly and turned away.

'What if you *what*?' Ellie shot back. 'Smother it in a moment of weakness?'

'No!' Katie's eyes filled with tears again. 'It's that disease, that bacteria. What if it's still in me? What if I give it to all of my babies?'

Above Ellie's head, the bulb fizzed and popped. She slowly stared at Katie, from her obvious remorse to the way her fingers now clutched at the thick fabric of her bodice, as if this illness was something that might be scratched out of her. She thought of how Katie had once told her that you confessed to whatever the deacon charged you with. She thought of how a girl used to having others accuse her of sinning might hear the pathologist's testimony and take the blame for something that was, in truth, an accident.

She looked at Katie, and saw the way her mind worked.

Ellie walked across the room and grasped her shoulders. 'Tell me now,' she said. 'Tell me how you killed your baby.'

* * *

'Your Honor,' Ellie began, 'I'd like to redirect.'

She could feel George looking at her like she'd lost her mind, and for good reason: with a confession on the court record, there wasn't too much Ellie could do to erase all the damage that had been done. She watched Katie take the stand again and shift restlessly in the seat, nervous and pale. 'When the prosecutor asked you if you killed your baby, you said yes.'

'That's right,' Katie answered.

'When he asked you to explain the method of homicide, you didn't want to talk.'

'No.'

'I'm asking you now: Did you smother the baby?'

'No,' Katie murmured, her voice cracking wide open over the syllable.

'Did you intentionally end the baby's life?'

'No. Never.'

'How did you kill your baby, Katie?'

She took a deep, rattling breath. 'You heard the doctor. He said I killed him by having that infection, and passing it on. If I wasn't the baby's mother, he would have lived.'

'You murdered your baby by passing along listeria from your body?'

'Yes.'

'Is that what you meant when you told Mr Callahan you'd killed your baby?'

'Yes.'

'You told us before that in your church, if you sin, you have to confess in front of the other members.'

'*Ja.*'

'What's that like?'

Katie swallowed. 'Well, it's terrifying, that's what. First there's the whole Sunday service. After the sermon comes a song, and then all the nonmembers, they leave. The bishop calls your name, and you have to get up and sit right in front of the ministers and answer their questions loud enough that the entire congregation can hear you. The whole time, everyone's watching, and your heart is pounding so loud you can hardly hear the bishop talk.'

'What if you didn't sin?'

Katie looked up. 'What do you mean?'

'What if you're innocent?' Ellie thought back to the conversation they'd had months ago, praying that Katie remembered too. 'What if the deacon says you went skinny-dipping, and you didn't?'

Katie frowned. 'You confess anyway.'

'Even though you didn't do it?'

'Yes. If you don't show how sorry you are, if you try to make excuses, it just gets more embarrassing. It's hard enough walking up to the ministers with all your family and friends watching. You just want to get it over with, take the punishment, so that you can be forgiven and welcomed back.'

'So . . . in your church, you have to confess in order to be forgiven. Even if you didn't do it?'

'Well, it's not like people get accused of sinning for nothing. There's a reason for it, most of the time. Even if the story isn't quite right, usually you still did something wrong. And after you confess, the healing comes.'

'Answer the question, Katie,' Ellie said, smiling tightly. 'If your deacon came to you and said you'd sinned, and you hadn't, you'd confess anyway?'

'Yes.'

'I see. Now – why did you want to be a witness in your trial?'

Katie looked up. 'To confess to the sin that I've been accused of.'

'But that's murder,' Ellie pointed out. 'That means you intentionally killed your baby, that you wanted it dead. Is this true?'

'No,' Katie whispered.

'You had to know that coming here today and saying you killed your baby was going to make the jury believe you were guilty, Katie. Why would you do that?'

'The baby is dead, and it's because of me. It doesn't matter if I smothered him or not, he's still dead because of something I did. I should be punished.' She brought the hem of her apron up to wipe her eyes. 'I wanted everyone to see how sorry I am. I wanted to confess,' she said quietly, 'because that's the only way I can be forgiven.'

Ellie leaned on the edge of the witness box, blocking everyone else's view for a moment. 'I'll forgive you,' she said softly, for Katie's ears alone, 'if you forgive me.' Then she turned to the judge. 'Nothing further.'

'Okay, so this is all twisted around now,' George said. 'You killed the baby, but you didn't murder it. You want to be punished so that you can be forgiven for something you didn't mean to do in the first place.'

'Yes.' Katie nodded.

George hesitated for a moment, as if he was considering all this. Then he frowned. 'So what happened to the baby?'

'I made it sick, and it died.'

'You know, the pathologist said that the baby was infected, but he admitted there were several reasons it might have died. Did you see the baby stop breathing?'

'No. I was asleep. I don't remember anything until I woke up.'

'You never saw the baby after you woke up?'

'It was gone,' Katie said.

'And you want us to believe you had nothing to do with that?' George advanced on her. 'Did you wrap the baby's body in a blanket and hide it?'

'No.'

'Huh. I thought you said you don't remember anything after you fell asleep.'

'I don't!'

'Then technically, you can't tell me for certain that you didn't hide the baby.'

'I guess not,' Katie said slowly, puzzled.

George smiled, his grin as wide as a wolf's. 'And technically, you can't tell me for sure that you didn't smother the baby.'

'Objection!'

'Withdrawn,' George said. 'Nothing further.'

Ellie cursed beneath her breath. George's pointed statement was the last thing the jury would hear as part of testimony. 'The defense rests, Your Honor,' Ellie said. She watched Katie open the gate of the witness box and step down, crossing the room with studied caution, as if she now understood that something as stable as solid ground might at any moment tilt beneath her feet.

'You know,' Ellie said to the jury. 'I wish I could tell you exactly what happened in the early hours of the morning of July tenth, in the Fishers' barn, but I can't. I can't, because I wasn't there. Neither was Mr Callahan, and neither were any of the other experts you've seen paraded through here during the past few days.

'There's only one person who was actually there, who also spoke to you in this courtroom – and that's Katie Fisher. Katie, an Amish girl who can't remember exactly what happened that morning. Katie, who stood up here wracked with guilt and shame, convinced that the accidental transmission of a disease in utero to her fetus made her responsible for the baby's death. Katie, who is so upset over losing her child she thinks she deserves to be punished, even when she's innocent. Katie, who wants to be forgiven for something she did not intentionally do.'

Ellie trailed her hand along the rail of the jury box. 'And that lack of intention, ladies and gentlemen, is quite important. Because in order to find Katie guilty of murder in the first degree, the prosecution must convince you beyond a reasonable doubt that Katie killed her child with premeditation, willfulness, and deliberation. First, that means she planned this murder. Yet you've heard that no Amishman would ever consider such violence, no Amishman would choose an action that valued pride over humility or an individual decision over the society's rules. Second, it means that Katie wanted this baby dead. Yet you've witnessed the look on Katie's face when she first saw the father of her child again, when she told you that she loved him. Third, it means that she intentionally murdered her baby. Yet you've been shown proof that an infection transmitted during pregnancy could very well have caused the baby to die – a tragedy, but an accident all the same.

'It is the prosecution's job to prove to you that Katie Fisher's baby was killed. My job is to show you that there might be a viable, realistic, possible reason for the death of Katie's infant other than first-degree murder. If there's more than one way to look at what happened that morning, if there's even the slightest doubt in your mind, you have no choice but to acquit.'

Ellie walked toward Katie and stood behind her. 'I wish I could tell you what happened or did not happen the morning of July tenth,' she repeated, 'but I can't. And if I don't know for sure – how can you?'

'Ms Hathaway's right – but only about one thing. Katie Fisher doesn't know exactly what happened the morning she gave birth.' George surveyed the faces of the jury. 'She doesn't know, and she's admitted to that – as well as to killing her baby.'

He stood up, his hands locked behind his back. 'However, we don't need the defendant's recollections to piece together the truth, because in this case, the facts speak for themselves. We know that Katie Fisher lied for years to her family about her clandestine visits to the outside world. We know that she concealed her pregnancy, gave birth secretly, covered up the bloody hay, and hid the body of her infant. We can look at the autopsy report and see bruises around the baby's mouth due to smothering, the cotton fibers shoved deep in its throat, the medical examiner's diagnosis of homicide. We can see the forensic evidence – the DNA tests that place the defendant and the defendant alone at the scene of the crime. We can point to a psychological motive – Ms Fisher's fear of being shunned from her family forever, like her brother, for this transgression of giving birth out of wedlock. We can even replay the court record and listen to the defendant confess to killing her child – an admission made willingly, which the defense then desperately tried to twist to its advantage.'

George turned toward Ellie. 'Ms Hathaway wants you to think that because the defendant is Amish, this crime is unthinkable. But being Amish is a religion, not an excuse. I've seen pious Catholics, devout Jews, and faithful Muslims all convicted of vicious criminal acts. Ms Hathaway also would like you to believe that the infant died of natural causes. But then, why wrap up the body and hide it under a pile of blankets – actions that suggest a cover-up? The defense can't explain that; they can only offer a red-herring testimony about an obscure bacterial infection that may have led to respiratory failure in a newborn. I repeat: *may* have led. But then again, it may not have. It may just be a way of covering up the truth: that on July tenth, Katie Fisher went out to her parents' barn and willfully, premeditatedly, and deliberately smothered her infant.'

He glanced at Katie, then back at the jury. 'Ms Hathaway would also like you to believe one other falsehood – that Katie Fisher was the only eyewitness that morning. But this is not true. An infant was there, too; an infant who isn't here to speak for himself because he was silenced by his mother.' He let his gaze roam over the twelve men and women watching him. 'Speak up for that infant today,' he said.

George Callahan's father, who had won four consecutive terms as the district attorney in Bucks County a few decades ago, used to tell him that there was always one case in a man's legal career he could ride all the way into the sunset. It was the case that was always mentioned in conjunction with your name, whenever you did anything else noteworthy in your life.

For Wallace Callahan, it had been convicting three white college boys of the rape and murder of a little black girl, right in the middle of the civil rights protests. For George, it would be Katie Fisher.

He could feel it the same way he could feel snow coming a day ahead of its arrival, by a tightening in his muscles. The jury would find her guilty. Hell, she'd found herself guilty. Why, he wouldn't be surprised if the verdict came back before suppertime.

He shrugged into his trench coat, lifted his briefcase, and pushed out the doors of the courthouse. Immediately reporters and cameramen from local networks and national affiliates engulfed him. He grinned, turned his best side to the majority of the video cameras, and leaned in to the knot of microphones being shoved beneath his chin.

'Any comments about the case?'

'Do you have a sense of how the jury will find?'

George smiled and let the practiced sound bite roll off his tongue. 'Clearly, this will be a victory for the prosecution.'

'There's no question in my mind that this will be a victory for the defense,' Ellie said to the small group of media reps huddled in the parking lot of the superior court.

'Don't you think that Katie's confession might make it hard for the jury to acquit?' one reporter yelled out.

'Not at all.' Ellie smiled. 'Katie's confession had less to do with the legal ramifications of this case than the moral obligations of her religion.' She politely pushed forward, scattering the reporters like marbles.

Coop, who had been waiting for her impromptu press conference to finish, joined her as she made her way to Leda's blue sedan. 'I ought to just stick around,' she said. 'Chances are the jury will be back by the time we finish grabbing a bite.'

'If you stick around, Katie's going to be bombarded with people. You can't keep her locked in a conference room.'

Ellie nodded and unlocked the door of the car. By now,

Leda and Katie and Samuel would be waiting for her at the service entrance of the court.

'Well,' Coop said. 'Congratulations.'

She snorted. 'Don't congratulate me yet.'

'But you just said you're going to win.'

Ellie shook her head. 'I said it,' she admitted. 'But the truth is, Coop, I don't know that at all.'

18

Ellie

A full day later, the jury still had not returned a verdict. Because of my lack of proximity to a working phone, Judge Ledbetter ordered George to let me borrow his beeper. When the verdict came in, she would page me. In the meantime, we could all return home and go about our business.

I had been in situations before with a hung jury. It was unpleasant, not only because it automatically guaranteed that we'd have to go through the rigmarole of a second trial, but also because until the verdict came back, I became obsessed with second-guessing my defense. In the past, when it took some time for a jury to return, I'd try to distract myself with the other cases I was working on. I would go to the gym and pound on a Stairmaster until I could barely move, much less think. I'd sit down with Stephen, who would walk me through the case to see what I might have done differently.

Now, I was surrounded by the Fishers – all of whom had a vested interest in the verdict, and none of whom seemed to notice that it hadn't been returned yet. Katie continued doing her chores. I was expected to help Sarah in the kitchen, to make myself useful in the barn if Aaron needed me, to carry on with life even though we were anticipating a momentous decision.

Twenty-eight hours after we'd left the courthouse, Katie and I were washing windows for Annie King, an Amish woman who'd fallen and broken her hip. I watched Katie for a moment, tirelessly dipping her cloth in alcohol solution and scrubbing it over the glass, wondering how she could find the strength to help someone else when her own emotions had to be over-whelming right now. 'Isn't this bothering you?' I said finally.

'My back?' Katie asked. '*Ja,* a little. If it hurts you too much, you can rest a bit.'

'Not your back. The fact that you don't know the outcome of the trial.'

Katie let the cloth slip into the bucket and sank back on her heels. 'Worrying isn't going to make it happen any quicker.'

'Well, I can't stop thinking about it,' I admitted. 'If I was facing a murder conviction, I don't think I'd be washing someone else's windows.'

Katie turned to me, her eyes clear and filled with a peace that made it nearly impossible to turn away from her. 'Today Annie needs help.'

'Tomorrow, you might need it.'

She looked out the sparkling window, where women were busy hauling cleaning supplies from their buggies. 'Then tomorrow, all these people, they will be with me.'

I swallowed my doubts, hoping for her sake she was right. Then I stood up, leaving my rag draped over the bucket. 'I'll be right back.'

Katie hid her smile; the incredible number of times I went to the bathroom these days had become a running joke. But it wasn't funny moments later, when I sat on the toilet, when I looked down and realized that I was bleeding.

Sarah drove her buggy to the community hospital, the same one Katie had been brought to by ambulance the day she'd given birth. In the back, being jostled, I tried to tell myself that this was normal; that this happened all the time to pregnant women. I pressed my fist against the cramps that had started up in my abdomen while Katie and Sarah sat on the bench in the front, whispering in Dietsch.

I was taken into the ER, questions hammering at me from every direction. Was I pregnant? Did I know how far along I was? A nurse turned to Katie and Sarah, hovering uncomfortably at the edge of the curtain. 'Are you relatives?'

'No. Friends,' Katie answered.

'Then I'll have to ask you to wait outside.'

*   *   *

Sarah caught my eye before she turned away. 'You'll be all right.'

'Please,' I whispered. 'Get Coop.'

The doctor had pianist's hands, long white fingers so delicate that they seemed like flowers trailing over my skin. 'We're going to do some blood tests to confirm your pregnancy,' he said. 'Then we'll get you in for an ultrasound, to see what's going on.'

I hiked myself up on my elbows. 'What is going on?' I demanded, with more force than I thought I'd have. 'You have to have some idea.'

'Well, the bleeding is fairly heavy. Based on the date of your last period, you're most likely about ten weeks along. It's possible that this is an ectopic pregnancy, which is very dangerous. If it's not, your body may just have started to spontaneously abort.' He looked up at me. 'Miscarry.'

'You have to stop it,' I said evenly.

'We can't. If the bleeding slows or stops on its own, that's a good sign. If not . . . well.' He shrugged and looped his stethoscope around his neck. 'We'll know more in a little while. Just try to rest.'

I nodded, lying back, concentrating on not crying. Crying wouldn't do me any good. I stayed perfectly still, breathing shallowly. I could not lose this baby. I could not.

Coop's face was a ghostly white as the ultrasound technician swabbed gel on my belly and pressed what looked like a microphone against my skin. On the computer screen a wedge of static began to form into round balls that shifted and changed shape. 'There you go,' the technician said, marking with graphic arrows the tiniest circle.

'Well, the pregnancy isn't in a Fallopian tube,' the doctor said. 'Blow that up.'

The technician enlarged the area. It did not look like a baby; it did not look like much of anything but a grainy curl of white with a black dot in its middle. I turned to the doctor and the technician, but they were not saying a word. They were staring at the screen, at something that was apparently very wrong.

The technician pushed harder against my belly, rolling the wand back and forth. 'Ah,' she said finally.

The black dot was pulsing rhythmically. 'That's the heartbeat,' the doctor said.

Coop grasped my hand. 'That's good, right? That means everything is all right?'

'We don't know what makes someone miscarry, Dr Cooper, but nearly a third of early pregnancies do. Usually it's because the embryo isn't viable, so it's for the best. Your wife is still bleeding heavily. All we can do now is send her home and hope things turn around in the next few hours.'

'Send her home? You're just going to send her home?'

'Yes. You should stay off your feet. If the bleeding hasn't slowed by morning, or if the cramps intensify, come back in.'

I stared at the screen, frozen on that small white circle.

'But the heartbeat,' Coop pressed. 'That's a positive sign.'

'Yes. Unfortunately, the bleeding is a bad one.'

The doctor and technician left the room. Coop sank down on a chair beside the examination table and spread his fingers over my stomach. I covered his hand with my own. 'I'm not letting go of this baby,' I told him firmly. And then I let myself cry.

Coop wanted to take me to his apartment, but it was too far away. Instead, Sarah insisted we come back to the farmhouse where she could watch over me. 'Of course, you'll come too,' she told Coop, which was why he allowed the decision to be made.

He carried me up to the room I shared with Katie and set me gently on the bed. 'Here,' he said, arranging the pillows behind my head. 'How's that?'

'Fine.' I looked at him and tried to smile. He sat down on the edge of the bed and twined his fingers with mine. 'Maybe this is nothing at all.'

I nodded. Coop worried the edge of the quilt through his hands, looking at the nightstand, the window, the floor – anywhere but at me. 'Coop,' I said, 'do me a favor.'

'Anything.'

'I want you to call Judge Ledbetter. Let her know what's going on, just in case.'

'For God's sake, Ellie, you shouldn't even be thinking about that now.'

'Well, I am. And I need you to do this.'

Coop shook his head. 'I'm not leaving you.'

I touched his arm, whispering the words neither one of us wanted to hear. 'There is nothing you can do.'

I turned my head away, and a moment later I heard his footsteps as he left the room. But too quickly, the door opened again. Expecting Coop, I opened my eyes, and found Sarah pouring a glass of water from a pitcher.

'Oh,' I said. 'Thank you.'

She shrugged. 'I'm sorry this is happening, Ellie.'

I nodded. However she might have felt about having yet another unwed mother-to-be in her household, she was gracious enough to offer sympathy to me right now.

'I lost three babies between Katie and Hannah,' Sarah said matter-of-factly. 'I never did understand why they say it that way in English – lose a baby. You know right where she is, don't you? And you'd do anything to keep her there.'

I stared at her, this woman who understood what it was like to be at the mercy of your own body, what it was like to have no control over your own shortcomings. It was just like Katie had said – it didn't matter if it was accidental; you felt guilty all the same. 'She's real to me, already,' I whispered.

'Well, 'course she is,' Sarah agreed. 'And you're already willing to move heaven and earth for her.'

She bustled around the room. 'If you need anything, you just call, you hear?'

'Wait.'

Sarah paused at the door.

'How . . . ?' I was unable to form the question, but she understood me anyway.

'It's the Lord's will,' she said quietly. 'You get through it. You just never get over it.'

I must have fallen asleep, because the next thing I remembered, the sun was nearly setting and Coop was sprawled on Katie's bed across the room. As I stirred, he sat up and knelt beside me. 'How do you feel?'

'I'm okay. The cramps are gone.'

We looked at each other, afraid of what that might mean. 'I called the judge,' Coop said, quick to change the topic. 'She said the jury is still deliberating, and that if necessary she'd keep them sequestered until you were up and about.' He cleared his throat. 'She also said she's praying for us.'

'That's good,' I said evenly. 'We can take all the help we can get.'

'Can I ask you something?' Coop picked at a thread on the quilt. 'I know this isn't the time, and I know that I promised I wouldn't do this, but I want you to marry me. I'm not the lawyer here, so I don't have any fancy arguments to convince you. But when Katie called me today from the hospital, I couldn't breathe. I thought you were in an accident. And then she said it was the baby, and all I could think was, Thank God. Thank God it wasn't Ellie.

'I hate myself for that. I wonder if I deserve this, just because of what popped into my head. And now I've been imagining this baby, this gift that I didn't expect to have in the first place, getting taken away. If it happens, El, it's going to hurt so badly – but it's nothing compared to the way I'd feel if you were taken away. That . . .' he said, his voice breaking, 'that I wouldn't make it through.'

He brought my hand to his lips and kissed the knuckles. 'We'll have more babies. They won't be this one, but they'll be ours. We can have ten of them, one for every room in our house.' Coop raised his face. 'Just tell me that you want to.'

I had once left Coop because I wanted to see if I could be the best, if I could make my own way in the world. But living for months with the Fishers made me see the value of intrinsically knowing there was someone to help me up if I stumbled.

I had turned Coop down a second time because I was afraid that I'd only be saying yes out of responsibility, because of the baby. But there might not be a baby, now. There was only me, and Coop, and this terrible ache that only he could understand.

How many times would I throw this away, before I realized it was what I had been looking for all along?

'Twelve,' I answered.

'Twelve?'

'Twelve babies. I'm planning on a very large house.'

Coop's eyes lit up. 'A mansion,' he promised, and kissed me. 'God, I love you.'

'I love you too.' As he climbed onto the bed with me, I started to laugh. 'I'd love you more if you helped me into the bathroom.'

He grinned and looped his arms around me, carrying me down the hall. 'Can you do this yourself?'

'I've gotten very good at it after thirty-seven years.'

'You know that's not what I meant,' he said gently.

'I know.' We stared at each other for a moment, until I had to turn away from the sorrow in his eyes. 'I can handle it, Coop.' I closed the door behind myself and hiked up my nightgown, steeling myself for the sight of another heavily soiled sanitary napkin. When I glanced down, I started to cry.

With a crash, Coop burst into the bathroom, wild-eyed and frightened. 'What? What is it?'

The tears kept coming; unstoppable, overwhelming. 'Make that thirteen babies,' I said, a smile unraveling across my face. 'I think this one might be staying.'

19

It wasn't until George Callahan had gone through a bottle pack of Zantac that he realized this case was literally eating him alive. His sure thing, it turned out, was not necessarily so sure. He wondered which juror was hanging up the others – the fellow with the Claddagh tattoo? The mother of four? He wondered if he had enough time to run to the pharmacy after lunch, or if he'd be called in for the verdict the minute he got on the highway. He wondered if Ellie Hathaway had lost three nights of sleep, too.

'Well,' Lizzie Munro said, pushing away her plate. 'That's the first time I've ever packed away more than you have.'

George grimaced. 'Turns out my stomach's more delicate than I thought.'

'Well, if you'd asked – which I might point out you didn't – I could have told you that people around here would have trouble convicting someone Amish.'

'Why?'

Lizzie lifted one shoulder. 'They're sort of like angels-in-residence. If you admit that one of them's a murderer, the whole world's going to hell in a handbasket.'

'They're not acquitting her so quickly, either.' He blotted his mouth with a napkin. 'Ledbetter said the jury had requested the transcripts of the two psychiatrists.'

'Now, that's interesting. If they're quibbling over state of mind, it almost implies that they think she did something wrong.'

George snorted. 'I'm sure Ellie Hathaway would put a different spin on it.'

'Ellie Hathaway isn't spinning much of anything right now. Didn't you hear?'

'Hear what?'

'She's sick. Got taken into the hospital.' Lizzie shrugged. 'The news around the water cooler is that it had something to do with complications of pregnancy.'

'Pregnant? Ellie Hathaway's pregnant?' He shook his head. 'God, she's about as nurturing as a black widow spider.'

'Yeah,' Lizzie said. 'There's a lot of that going around.'

Ellie had been promoted from reclining in the bedroom to reclining on the living room couch. She had been allowed to walk only once, when Coop had taken her to the obstetrician to be given a clean but guarded bill of health. Now Coop was back at his office with a suicidal client, having left Sarah in charge to watch over her like a hawk. But Sarah had gone out to get a chicken for dinner – making Ellie, for the first time, happy about her status as an invalid.

Ellie closed her eyes, but she was certain that if she slept another hour she was going to go into a coma. She was trying to decide which argument to use on Coop to convince him that she should be allowed to be vertical – fetal circulation just slightly edging out bedsores – when Katie skulked by the doorway, trying not to be seen.

'Oh, no you don't. Get back here,' Ellie ordered.

Katie slipped into the room. 'Did you need something?'

'Yeah. I need you to break me out of here.'

Katie's eyes widened. 'But Dr Cooper—'

'—doesn't have a clue what it's like to be lying around for two entire days.' Ellie reached for her hand, and tugged so that Katie was sitting down beside her. 'I don't want to go climb Everest,' she begged. 'Just a little walk. Outside.'

Katie looked toward the kitchen.

'Your mom's at the chicken coop. Please.'

She nodded quickly, then helped Ellie from the couch. 'You sure you're okay?'

'I'm fine. Really. You can call my doctor and ask her.' Grinning, Ellie added, 'Well, you could if you had a phone.'

Katie slid her arm around Ellie's waist and took tentative steps with her through the kitchen and out the back door. Ellie quickened the pace as they passed the small patch of the vegetable garden, stepping over the pumpkin vines spread like the arms of an octopus. At the pond, she sank onto the bench beneath the oak tree, her cheeks flushed and her eyes bright, feeling better than she had in days.

'Can we go back now?' Katie asked miserably.

'I just got here. You want me to rest before I hike all the way home, don't you?'

She glanced toward the house. 'I want to get you back before anyone notices you're gone.'

'Don't worry. I won't tell anyone you brought me out here if you don't.'

'Not a soul,' Katie said.

Ellie tipped back her head and closed her eyes, letting the sun wash over her face and throat. 'Well, then, here we are. Partners in crime.'

'Partners in crime,' Katie echoed softly.

At the thin, sad note in her voice, Ellie blinked. 'Oh, Katie. I didn't mean—'

'Shhh.' Katie held up her hand, rising slowly off the seat as she stared at the pond. A flock of wood ducks, hidden among the dry marsh grass at the edges, suddenly startled and took to flight, sending up a spray of mist that illuminated the surface of the water. The late sun prismed through, and for a moment Katie could see her sister spinning in the midst of it, a hologram ballerina unaware of her audience.

This is what she would miss if she were put in jail. This home, this pond, this connection.

Hannah turned, and in her arms was a small package. She turned again, and the package shifted . . . so that a tiny pink arm slipped from the swaddling.

The mist settled, the nasal holler of the ducks receding in

the distance. Katie sat down beside Ellie, who suddenly looked much paler than she was before. 'Please,' Katie whispered. 'Don't let them send me away.'

Out of deference to Aaron, Jacob parked his car a half mile from his father's farm. He'd known guys who'd bought cars during their *Rumspringa*, fellows who'd parked them behind tobacco sheds while their dads pretended not to notice. Jacob, though, he'd never had a car. Not until he'd left for good.

Walking up the drive felt strange, too. He absently rubbed the scar on his chin that he'd gotten when he'd been roller-skating and had pitched over a rut in the pavement. The rut was still there. He'd bet that his roller skates were, too, up in the attic with whatever old clothes and hats had not been passed along to younger cousins.

His heart was so loud in his ears by the time he reached the barn door that he had to stop and breathe deeply just to get the courage to go further. The problem was, he'd become *Sod* so long ago that thinking Plain came less and less easily. It had taken Katie's trial – where he, of all people, was cast as the expert on Amish life – to make him realize that the Plain side of him had been there all along. Although he lived in a different world, he still saw it with the eyes of one who'd grown up separate and apart; he judged it with a set of values that had been ingrained long ago.

One of the first truths you learned when you were Plain was that actions spoke louder than words.

In the English world, people sent condolences and wrote e-mail and exchanged valentines. In the Amish world, sympathy came in the form of a visit, love was a look of satisfaction cast across the dinner table, help was hands-on. All this time, Jacob had been waiting for an apology from his father, when that wasn't his father's means of currency.

He slid open the heavy door of the barn and walked inside. Dust motes circled in the air, and the heady scent of hay and sweet grain was so familiar that Jacob froze for a moment and simply closed his eyes, remembering. The cows, chained at their stanchions, shuffled at his entrance and rolled their heavy heads in his direction.

It was milking time; Jacob had planned it that way. He walked into the central aisle of the barn. Levi was shoveling manure into a wheelbarrow, looking none too pleased about it. Samuel stood down at the far end, waiting for the feed to funnel down the chute from the silo. Elam and Aaron moved between the animals in tandem, checking the pumps and wiping down the teats of the next cow in line.

It was Elam who saw him first. Straightening slowly, the old man stared at Jacob and gradually smiled. Jacob nodded, then reached down into the bucket his grandfather held and ripped out a leaf of the old Yellow Pages. He took the spray bottle from Elam's hand to sanitize an udder just as his father came around the broad behind of the cow.

Aaron started. His shoulders tensed; the powerful muscles in his forearms locked up. Samuel and Levi watched the scene in silence; it even seemed that the cows had quieted, waiting to see what would happen.

Elam placed his hand on his son's shoulder. *'Es ist nix,'* he said. It's nothing.

Without saying a word, Jacob bent down and resumed his task. His palms slipped along the soft underskin of the cow. A moment later, he felt his father at his shoulder. The hands that had taught him how to do most everything gently pushed his out of the way, so that the milk pump could be attached.

Jacob stood up, toe to toe with his father. Aaron nodded slowly toward the next cow. 'Well,' he said in English. 'I'm waiting.'

George mounted the steps of the Fishers' front porch, unsure of what to expect. In a way, he'd figured a people so close to God would have managed to get lightning to strike him the minute he got out of his car, but so far so good. He straightened his jacket and tie and knocked firmly.

The defendant answered the door. Her friendly smile faltered, then completely withered. 'Yes?'

'I'm, uh, here to see Ellie.'

Katie crossed her arms. 'She's not taking visitors just now.'

From behind her, a voice yelled out, 'That's not true! I'll take anyone. If it's the UPS man, send him in!'

George raised his brows, and Katie pushed open the screen door to admit him. He followed her through a house that looked surprisingly like his own. In the living room, Ellie lay on a couch with an afghan tossed over her legs.

'Well,' he said. 'You look completely different in your pajamas. Softer.'

Ellie laughed. 'That's why I rarely wear them during litigation. Is this a social visit?'

'Not exactly.' George looked pointedly at Katie. She glanced at Ellie, and then went into another room. 'I've got a deal for you.'

'What a surprise,' Ellie said dryly. 'Has the jury got you running scared?'

'Why, no. In fact, I figured you're the one who's panicking, and I'm feeling chivalrous at the moment.'

'You're a regular Lancelot, George. All right, let's hear it.'

'She pleads guilty,' George said. 'We agree to four to seven years.'

'Not a chance.' Ellie bristled, but then thought of Katie, by the pond. 'I'll consider a *nolo*, and I'll take two to four as a capped plea, if you let me argue for less.'

George turned away, looking out the window. More than anything else, he wanted to win this case – it was what would buoy him through the next election. He had no grand desire to make Katie Fisher rot away in jail forever; and from what Lizzie had told him, he didn't think that would sit well with the community, either. With a *nolo contendere*, as Ellie was suggesting, a defendant didn't admit guilt, but still accepted a conviction. Basically, it meant saying that you didn't do it, but you understood that there was enough evidence to condemn you, so you accepted that verdict.

For Katie, it meant saving face and accepting punishment at the same time.

For Ellie, it meant erasing her client's unexpected courtroom confession from the record.

For George, it was still a guilty verdict.

He walked toward Ellie again. 'I need to think about it. If she does get convicted, she could be looking at a hell of a lot of time.'

'*If*, George. The jury's been out for five days. If they come back for us, Katie gets *nada*. As in *not a* thing.'

He crossed his arms. '*Nolo*. Three to six, capped.'

'Two and a half to five, and you've got yourself a deal.' She smiled. 'Of course, I'll have to run it by my client.'

'Get back to me.' George started out of the living room, pausing at the threshold of the doorway. 'Hey, Ellie,' he said. 'I was sorry to hear about what happened.'

She fisted the afghan in her hands. 'Well, it's all going to be fine now.'

'Yeah.' George nodded slowly. 'I think it is.'

Katie sat outside the judge's chambers, running her fingers over the smooth seams of the wooden bench. She'd flatten her palm against a spot, buff it with her apron, and then do it all over again. Although being here today was considerably less upsetting than being here for the trial, she was still counting the minutes until she could leave.

'I've been looking for you.'

Katie glanced up as Adam sat down beside her. 'Jacob told me about the plea.'

'Yes. And now it will be finished,' she said quietly, and both of them weighed the words, turned them over like stones, and set them down again.

'I'm going back to Scotland.' He hesitated. 'Katie, you could—'

'No, Adam.' She shook her head, interrupting him. 'I couldn't.'

Adam swallowed, nodded. 'I guess I knew that all along.' He touched the curve of her cheek. 'But I also know that these past months, you've been there with me.' When Katie looked up, puzzled, he continued. 'I find you, sometimes, at the foot of my bed, when I wake up. Or I notice your profile in the moorings of a castle wall. Sometimes, when the wind's right, it's like you're calling my name.' He took her hand, traced the outline of her fingers. 'I see you more clearly than I've ever seen any ghost.'

He lifted her palm, kissed the center, and closed her fingers around it. Then he pressed the fist tight to her belly. 'Remember me,' Adam said thickly; and for the second time in Katie's life, he left her behind.

'I'm glad to hear that you've come to an agreement,' Judge Ledbetter said. 'Now let's talk about time.'

George leaned forward. 'We agreed to a capped plea, Your Honor, two and a half to five years. But I think it's important to remember that whatever decision is reached here is going to send a message to society about neonaticide.'

'We agreed to a *nolo*,' Ellie specified. 'My client is not admitting to this crime. She has repeatedly stated that she doesn't know what happened that night, but for various reasons she's willing to accept a guilty verdict. However, we're not talking about a hardened felon. Katie has a commitment to the community, and she's not going to be a repeat offender. She shouldn't do a day of time, not even an hour. Sentencing her to a correctional facility sends the message that she's like any common criminal, when you can't even come close to comparing the two.'

'Something tells me, Ms Hathaway, that you have a solution in mind.'

'I do. I think Katie's a perfect candidate for the electronic monitoring program.'

Judge Ledbetter took off her half glasses and rubbed her eyes. 'Mr Callahan, we set an example for society by taking this case to trial and putting it in front of the press. I see no reason to shame the Amish community any more than the media attention already has, by sending one of their own into Muncy. The defendant will serve time – but in private. Which somehow seems like a little bit of poetic justice.' She scrawled her signature across the papers in front of her. 'I'm sentencing Ms Fisher to a year on the bracelet,' Judge Ledbetter said. 'Case closed.'

The plastic cuff went under her stockings, because she wouldn't be able to take it off for nearly eight months. It was three inches wide, implanted with a homing device. If Katie left Lancaster County, Ellie explained, it would beep, and the probation officer would find her in minutes. The probation officer might find her anyway, just for the heck of it, to make sure she was keeping herself out of trouble. Katie was officially a prisoner of the state, which means she had no rights to speak of.

But she got to stay on the farm, live her life, and go about her own business. Surely the sin of a small piece of jewelry could be overlooked when she was getting so much in exchange.

She and Ellie walked through the hallways, their shoes echoing in the silence. 'Thank you,' Katie said softly.

'My pleasure.' Ellie hesitated. 'This is a fair deal.'

'I know.'

'Even if it's a guilty verdict.'

'That never bothered me.'

'Yeah.' Ellie smiled. 'I suppose I'll get over it, in another decade or so.'

'Bishop Ephram says that this was a good thing for the community.'

'How so?'

'It keeps us humble,' Katie said. 'Too many English think we're saints, and this will remind them we're just people.'

They stepped outside together into the relative quiet of the afternoon. No reporters, no onlookers – it would be hours before the press got wind that the jury had been dismissed and the trial abruptly aborted, due to the plea bargain. Katie stopped at the top of the stairs, looking around. 'This isn't the way I pictured it.'

'What isn't?'

'*After.*' She shrugged. 'I thought that everything you talked about at the trial would help me understand what happened a little better.'

Ellie smiled. 'If I do my job right, then I tend to make things muddier.'

A breeze, threaded with the cold of winter, blew the strings of Katie's *kapp* across her face. 'I'm never going to know exactly how he died, am I?' she asked softly.

Ellie linked her arm through Katie's. 'You know how he didn't die,' she answered. 'That may have to be enough.'

20

Ellie

It's funny how you can accumulate so many things in such a small amount of time. I had come to East Paradise with a single suitcase, but now that it was time to pack up my things I could barely make them fit. Now, in addition to my clothes, there was my first and probably final attempt at a quilt, which would one day grace my child's crib. There was the straw hat I'd bought at Zimmermann's, a young boy's broad-brimmed hat, but one that managed to keep the sun off my face when I was working in the fields. There were smaller things: a perfectly flat stone I'd found in the creek, a matchbook from the restaurant where I'd first had dinner with Coop, that extra pregnancy test in the two-for-one kit. And finally, there were the things that were too grand in scope to fit the confines of any luggage: spirit, humility, peace.

Katie was outside, beating rugs with the long handle of a broom. She'd unrolled her stockings to show Sarah the bracelet, and I made sure to explain its limitations. Coop would be here any minute with his car, to take me home.

Home. It would take some getting used to. I wondered how many mornings I'd wake at 4:30 A.M., imagining the soft sounds of the men going to the barn for the milking. How many nights I'd forget to set an alarm, sure that the rooster would do the job.

I also wondered what it would be like to flip through the channels of a TV again. To sleep beside Coop every night, his arm slung over me like an anchor. I wondered who my next client would be, and if I would often think of Katie.

There was a soft knock at the door. 'Come on in.'

Sarah moved into the room, her hands tucked beneath her apron. 'I came to see if you need any help.' Looking at the empty pegs on the walls, she smiled. 'Guess you've pretty much taken care of it.'

'The packing wasn't so hard. It's *leaving* that's going to be a challenge.'

Sarah sank down onto Katie's bed, smoothing the quilt with one hand. 'I didn't want you here,' she said quietly. 'When Leda first suggested it in the courtroom that day, I told her no.' She lifted her face, eyes following me as I finished cleaning up. 'Not just because of Aaron, neither. I thought you might be one of those folks we get every now and then, looking to pretend they're one of us because they think peace is something a body can learn.'

Her hand picked at a small imperfection in the quilt. 'I figured out quick enough that you weren't like that at all. And I have to admit that we've learned more from you, I think, than you ever could have learned from us.'

Sitting down beside Sarah, I smiled. 'That would be debatable.'

'You kept my Katie here with me. For that, you'll always be special.'

Listening to this quiet, solemn woman, I felt a quick kinship. For a while, she had entrusted her daughter to me. More than ever, I understood that remarkable leap of faith.

'I lost Jacob, you see, and Hannah. I couldn't lose Katie. You know how a mother would do anything, if it meant saving her child.'

My hand stole over my belly. 'Yes, I do.' I touched her shoulder. 'You did the right thing, having me defend Katie in court. No matter what Aaron or the bishop or anyone else told you, you shouldn't doubt that.'

Sarah nodded, then pulled from beneath her apron a small packet wrapped in tissue paper. 'I wanted to give you these.'

'You didn't have to do this,' I said, embarrassed that I had not thought of giving a gift, too, in return for the Fishers' hospitality. I tore at the paper, and it fell away to reveal a pair of scissors.

They were heavy and silver, with a marked notch in one blade. They were polished clean, but a small loop of twine tied to the handle was dark and stiff with dried blood. 'I thought you could take these away,' Sarah said simply. 'I can't give them back to Aaron, now.'

My mind reeled back to the medical examiner's testimony, to the autopsy photos of the dead infant's umbilicus. 'Oh, Sarah,' I whispered.

I had based an entire legal defense on the fact that an Amish woman would not, could not, commit murder. And yet here was an Amish woman, holding out to me the evidence that incriminated her.

The light had been left on in the barn, because Sarah knew her daughter was pregnant all along. The scissors used to cut the cord, covered with blood, had been hidden. The baby had disappeared when Katie was asleep – and the reason she didn't remember wrapping and hiding his body was because she had not been the one to do it.

My mouth opened and closed around a question that never came.

'The sun, it came up so quick that morning. I had to get back to the house before Aaron woke for the milking. I thought I'd be able to come back later – but I had to go. I just had to.' Her eyes glistened with tears. 'I was the one who sent her out to the English world in the first place – and I could see how she was changing. No one else noticed – not even Samuel – but once he did, well, I knew what would happen. I only wanted Katie to have the kind of life she'd always imagined having – one here, among all of us.

'But Aaron had sent Jacob away, and for much less than this. He would never have accepted that baby . . . and Katie would have been sent away, too.' Sarah's eyes went to my abdomen, where my child lay safe. 'You understand now, Ellie, don't you? I couldn't save Hannah, and I couldn't save Jacob . . . I had one last chance. No matter what, someone was going to leave me. So I chose. I did what I thought I had to do, to keep my daughter.' She bowed her head. 'And I nearly lost her, all the same.'

Outside, a car horn sounded. I heard the door slam, and Coop's voice tangling with Katie's in the front yard. 'Well.' Sarah wiped her eyes and got to her feet. 'I don't want you carrying that suitcase. Let me.' She smiled as she lifted it, testing its weight. 'You bring that baby back so we can meet her, all right?' Sarah said, and setting down the suitcase, she put her arms around me.

I froze, unable to embrace her. I was an attorney; I was bound by the law. By duty, I needed to call the police, to tell the county attorney this information. And then Sarah would be tried for the same crime for which her daughter had been convicted.

Yet of their own volition, my hands came up to rest on Sarah's back, my thumb brushing the edge of one of the straight pins that held her apron in place. 'You take care,' I whispered, squeezing her tightly. Then I hurried down the stairs, outside to where the world was waiting.

If you enjoyed Plain Truth *read on for the first chapter of Jodi Picoult's latest novel,* My Sister's Keeper.

JODI PICOULT

My Sister's Keeper

In my first memory, I am three years old, and I am trying to kill my sister. Sometimes, the recollection is so clear I can remember the itch of the pillowcase under my hand, the sharp point of her nose pressing into my palm . . .

Anna is not sick, but she might as well be. By age thirteen, she has undergone countless surgeries, transfusions, and injections to help her sister, Kate, fight leukaemia. Anna was born for this purpose, her parents tell her, which is why they love her even more.

But now she can't help but long for respite from the constant flow of her own blood seeping into her sister's veins. And so she makes a decision that for most would be too difficult to bear, at any time or age, and sues her parents for rights to her own body.

'Compelling' *USA Today*

'The novelist displays an almost uncanny ability to enter the skins of her troubled young protagonists' *New York Times*

Hodder & Stoughton

Prologue

In my first memory, I am three years old and I am trying to kill my sister. Sometimes the recollection is so clear I can remember the itch of the pillowcase under my hand, the sharp point of her nose pressing into my palm. She didn't stand a chance against me, of course, but it still didn't work. My father walked by, tucking in the house for the night, and saved her. He led me back to my own bed. 'That,' he told me, 'never happened.'

As we got older, I didn't seem to exist, except in relation to her. I would watch her sleep across the room from me, one long shadow linking our beds, and I would count the ways. Poison, sprinkled on her cereal. A wicked undertow off the beach. Lightning striking.

In the end, though, I did not kill my sister. She did it all on her own.

Or at least this is what I tell myself.

I

Anna

When I was little, the great mystery to me wasn't *how* babies were made, but *why*. The mechanics I understood – my older brother Jesse had filled me in – although at the time I was sure he'd heard half of it wrong. Other kids my age were busy looking up the words *penis* and *vagina* in the classroom dictionary when the teacher had her back turned, but I paid attention to different details. Like why some mothers only had one child, while other families seemed to multiply before your eyes. Or how the new girl in school, Sedona, told anyone who'd listen that she was named for the place where her parents were vacationing when they made her (*'Good thing they weren't staying in Jersey City,'* my father used to say).

Now that I am thirteen, these distinctions are only more complicated: the eighth-grader who dropped out of school because she *got into trouble*; a neighbor who *got herself pregnant* in the hopes it would keep her husband from filing for divorce. I'm telling you, if aliens landed on earth today and took a good hard look at why babies get born, they'd conclude that most people have children by accident, or because they drink too much on a certain night, or because birth control isn't one hundred percent, or for a thousand other reasons that really aren't very flattering.

On the other hand, I was born for a very specific purpose. I wasn't the result of a cheap bottle of wine or a full moon or the heat of the moment. I was born because a scientist managed to hook up my mother's eggs and my father's sperm to create a specific combination of precious genetic material. In fact, when Jesse told me how babies get made and I, the great disbeliever, decided to ask my parents the truth, I got more than I bargained for. They sat me down and told me all the usual stuff, of course – but they also explained that they chose little embryonic me, specifically, because I could save my sister, Kate. 'We loved you even more,' my mother made sure to say, 'because we knew what exactly we were getting.'

It made me wonder, though, what would have happened if Kate had been healthy. Chances are, I'd still be floating up in Heaven or wherever, waiting to be attached to a body to spend some time on earth. Certainly I would not be part of this family. See, unlike the rest of the free world, I didn't get here by accident. And if your parents have you for a reason, then that reason better exist. Because once it's gone, so are you.

Pawnshops may be full of junk, but they're also a breeding ground for stories, if you ask me, not that you did. What happened to make a person trade in the Never Before Worn Diamond Solitaire? Who needed money so badly they'd sell a teddy bear missing an eye? As I walk up to the counter, I wonder if someone will look at the locket I'm about to give up, and ask these same questions.

The man at the cash register has a nose the shape of a turnip, and eyes sunk so deep I can't imagine how he sees well enough to go about his business. 'Need something?' he asks.

It's all I can do to not turn around and walk out the door, pretend I've come in by mistake. The only thing that keeps me steady is knowing I am not the first person to stand in front of this counter holding the one item in the world I never thought I'd part with.

'I have something to sell,' I tell him.

'Am I supposed to guess what it is?'

'Oh.' Swallowing, I pull the locket out of the pocket of my jeans. The heart falls on the glass counter in a pool of its own chain. 'It's fourteen-karat gold,' I pitch. 'Hardly ever worn.' This is a lie; until this morning, I haven't taken it off in seven years. My father gave it to me when I was six after the bone marrow harvest, because he said anyone who was giving her sister such a major present deserved one of her own. Seeing it there, on the counter, my neck feels shivery and naked.

The owner puts a loop up to his eye, which makes it seem almost normal size. 'I'll give you twenty.'

'Dollars?'

'No, pesos. What did you think?'

'It's worth five times that!' I'm guessing.

The owner shrugs. 'I'm not the one who needs the money.'

I pick up the locket, resigned to sealing the deal, and the strangest thing happens – my hand, it just clamps shut like the Jaws of Life. My face goes red with the effort to peel apart my fingers. It takes what seems like an hour for that locket to spill into the owner's outstretched palm. His eyes stay on my face, softer now. 'Tell them you lost it,' he offers, advice tossed in for free.

If Mr Webster had decided to put the word *freak* in his dictionary, *Anna Fitzgerald* would be the best definition he could give. It's more than just the way I look: refugee-skinny with absolutely no chest to speak of, hair the color of dirt, connect-the-dot freckles on my cheeks that, let me tell you, do not fade with lemon juice or sunscreen or even, sadly, sandpaper. No, God was obviously in some kind of mood on my birthday, because he added to this fabulous physical combination the bigger picture – the household into which I was born.

My parents tried to make things normal, but that's a relative term. The truth is, I was never really a kid. To be honest, neither were Kate and Jesse. I guess maybe my brother had his moment in the sun for the four years he was alive before Kate got diagnosed, but ever since then, we've been too busy looking over our shoulders to run headlong into growing up. You know how most little kids think they're like cartoon characters – if an anvil drops on their heads they can peel themselves off the sidewalk and keep going? Well, I never once believed that. How could I, when we practically set a place for Death at the dinner table?

Kate has acute promyelocytic leukemia. Actually, that's not quite true – right now she doesn't have it, but it's hibernating under her skin like a bear, until it decides to roar again. She was diagnosed when she was two; she's sixteen now. *Molecular relapse* and *granulocyte* and *portacath* – these words are part of my vocabulary, even though I'll never find them on any SAT. I'm an allogeneic donor – a perfect sibling match. When Kate needs leukocytes or stem cells or bone marrow to fool her body into thinking it's healthy, I'm the one who provides them. Nearly every time Kate's hospitalized, I wind up there, too.

None of which means anything, except that you shouldn't believe what you hear about me, least of all that which I tell you myself.

As I am coming up the stairs, my mother comes out of her room wearing another ball gown. 'Ah,' she says, turning her back to me. 'Just the girl I wanted to see.'

I zip it up and watch her twirl. My mother could be beautiful, if she were parachuted into someone else's life. She has long dark hair and the fine collarbones of a princess, but the corners of her mouth turn down, like she's swallowed bitter news. She doesn't have much free time, since a calendar is something that can change drastically if my sister develops a bruise or a nosebleed, but what she does have she spends at Bluefly.com, ordering ridiculously fancy evening dresses for places she is never going to go. 'What do you think?' she asks.

The gown is all the colors of a sunset, and made out of material that swishes when she moves. It's strapless, what a star might wear sashaying down a red carpet – totally not the dress code for a suburban house in Upper Darby, RI. My mother twists her hair into a knot and holds it in place. On her bed are three other dresses – one slinky and black, one bugle-beaded, one that seems impossibly small. 'You look . . .'

Tired. The word bubbles right under my lips.

My mother goes perfectly still, and I wonder if I've said it without meaning to. She holds up a hand, shushing me, her ear cocked to the open doorway. 'Did you hear that?'

'Hear what?'

'Kate.'

'I didn't hear anything.'

But she doesn't take my word for it, because when it comes to Kate she doesn't take anybody's word for it. She marches upstairs and opens up our bedroom door to find my sister hysterical on her bed, and just like that the world collapses again. My father, a closet astronomer, has tried to explain black holes to me, how they are so heavy they absorb every-thing, even light, right into their center. Moments like this are the same kind of vacuum; no matter what you cling to, you wind up being sucked in.

'Kate!' My mother sinks down to the floor, that stupid skirt a cloud around her. 'Kate, honey, what hurts?'

Kate hugs a pillow to her stomach, and tears keep streaming down her face. Her pale hair is stuck to her face in damp streaks; her breathing's too tight. I stand frozen in the doorway of my own room, waiting for instructions: *Call Daddy. Call 911. Call Dr Chance.* My mother goes so far as to shake a better explanation out of Kate. 'It's Preston,' she sobs. 'He's leaving Serena for good.'

That's when we notice the TV. On the screen, a blond hottie gives a longing look to a woman crying almost as hard as my sister, and then he slams the door. 'But what hurts?' my mother asks, certain there has to be more to it than this.

'Oh my *God*,' Kate says, sniffling. 'Do you have any idea how much Serena and Preston have been through? Do you?'

That fist inside me relaxes, now that I know it's all right. Normal, in our house, is like a blanket too short for a bed – sometimes it covers you just fine, and other times it leaves you cold and shaking; and worst of all, you never know which of the two it's going to be. I sit down on the end of Kate's bed. Although I'm only thirteen, I'm taller than her and every now and then people mistakenly assume I'm the older sister. At different times this summer she has been crazy for Callahan, Wyatt, and Liam, the male leads on this soap. Now, I guess, it's all about Preston. 'There was the kidnapping scare,' I volunteer. I actually followed that story line; Kate made me tape the show during her dialysis sessions.

'And the time she almost married his twin by mistake,' Kate adds.

'Don't forget when he died in the boat accident. For two months, anyway.' My mother joins the conversation, and I remember that she used to watch this soap, too, sitting with Kate in the hospital.

For the first time, Kate seems to notice my mother's outfit. 'What are you *wearing*?'

'Oh. Something I'm sending back.' She stands up in front of me so that I can undo her zipper. This mail-order compulsion, for any other mother, would be a wake-up call for therapy; for my mom, it would probably be considered a healthy break. I wonder if it's putting on someone else's skin for a while that she likes so much, or if it's the option of being able to send back a circumstance that just doesn't suit you. She looks at Kate, hard. 'You're sure nothing hurts?'

After my mother leaves, Kate sinks a little. That's the only way to describe it – how fast color drains from her face, how she disappears against the pillows. As she gets sicker, she fades a little more, until I am afraid one day I will wake up and not be able to see her at all. 'Move,' Kate orders. 'You're blocking the picture.'

So I go to sit on my own bed. 'It's only the coming attractions.'

'Well, if I die tonight I want to know what I'm missing.'

I fluff my pillows up under my head. Kate, as usual, has swapped so that she has all the funchy ones that don't feel like rocks under your neck. She's supposed to deserve this, because she's three years older than me or because she's sick or because the moon is in Aquarius – there's *always* a reason. I squint at the television, wishing I could flip through the stations, knowing

I don't have a prayer. 'Preston looks like he's made out of plastic.'

'Then why did I hear you whispering his name last night into your pillow?'

'Shut up,' I say.

'*You* shut up.' Then Kate smiles at me. 'He probably *is* gay, though. Quite a waste, considering the Fitzgerald sisters are—' Wincing, she breaks off mid-sentence, and I roll toward her.

'Kate?'

She rubs her lower back. 'It's nothing.'

It's her kidneys. 'Want me to get Mom?'

'Not yet.' She reaches between our beds, which are just far apart enough for us to touch each other if we both try. I hold out my hand, too. When we were little we'd make this bridge and try to see how many Barbies we could get to balance on it.

Lately, I have been having nightmares, where I'm cut into so many pieces that there isn't enough of me to be put back together.

My father says that a fire will burn itself out, unless you open a window and give it fuel. I suppose that's what I'm doing, when you get right down to it; but then again, my dad also says that when flames are licking at your heels you've got to break a wall or two if you want to escape. So when Kate falls asleep from her meds I take the leather binder I keep between my mattress and box spring and go into the bathroom for privacy. I know Kate's been snooping – I rigged up a red thread between the zipper's teeth to let me know who was prying into my stuff without my permission, but even though the thread's been torn there's nothing missing inside. I turn on the water in the bathtub so it sounds like I'm in there for a reason, and sit down on the floor to count.

If you add in the twenty dollars from the pawnshop, I have $136.87. It's not going to be enough, but there's got to be a way around that. Jesse didn't have $2,900 when he bought his beat-up Jeep, and the bank gave him some kind of loan. Of course, my parents had to sign the papers, too, and I doubt they're going to be willing to do that for me, given the circumstances. I count the money a second time, just in case the bills have miraculously reproduced, but math is math and the total stays the same. And then I read the newspaper clippings.

Campbell Alexander. It's a stupid name, in my opinion. It sounds like a bar drink that costs too much, or a brokerage firm. But you can't deny the man's track record.

To reach my brother's room, you actually have to leave the house, which is exactly the way he likes it. When Jesse turned sixteen he moved into the attic over the garage – a perfect arrangement, since he didn't want my parents to see what he was doing and my parents didn't really want to see. Blocking the stairs to his place are four snow tires, a small wall of cartons, and an oak desk tipped onto its side. Sometimes I think Jesse sets up these obstacles himself, just to make getting to him more of a challenge.

I crawl over the mess and up the stairs, which vibrate with the bass from Jesse's stereo. It takes nearly five whole minutes before he hears me knocking. 'What?' he snaps, opening the door a crack.

'Can I come in?'

He thinks twice, then steps back to let me enter. The room is a sea of dirty clothes and magazines and leftover Chinese take-out cartons; it smells like the sweaty tongue of a hockey skate. The only neat spot is the shelf where Jesse keeps his special collection – a Jaguar's silver mascot, a Mercedes symbol, a Mustang's horse – hood ornaments that he told me he just found lying around, although I'm not dumb enough to believe him.

Don't get me wrong – it isn't that my parents don't care about Jesse or whatever trouble he's gotten himself mixed up in. It's just that they don't really have time to care about it, because it's a problem somewhere lower on the totem pole.

Jesse ignores me, going back to whatever he was doing on the far side of the mess. My attention is caught by a Crock-Pot

– one that disappeared out of the kitchen a few months ago – which now sits on top of Jesse's TV with a copper tube threaded out of its lid and down through a plastic milk jug filled with ice, emptying into a glass Mason jar. Jesse may be a borderline delinquent, but he's brilliant. Just as I'm about to touch the contraption, Jesse turns around. 'Hey!' He fairly flies over the couch to knock my hand away. 'You'll screw up the condensing coil.'

'Is this what I think it is?'

A nasty grin itches over his face. 'Depends on what you think it is.' He jimmies out the Mason jar, so that liquid drips onto the carpet. 'Have a taste.'

For a still made out of spit and glue, it produces pretty potent moonshine whiskey. An inferno races so fast through my belly and legs I fall back onto the couch. 'Disgusting,' I gasp.

Jesse laughs and takes a swig, too, although for him it goes down easier. 'So what do you want from me?'

'How do you know I want something?'

'Because no one comes up here on a social call,' he says, sitting on the arm of the couch. 'And if it was something about Kate, you would've already told me.'

'It *is* about Kate. Sort of.' I press the newspaper clippings into my brother's hand; they'll do a better job explaining than I ever could. He scans them, then looks me right in the eye. His are the palest shade of silver, so surprising that sometimes when he stares at you, you can completely forget what you were planning to say.

'Don't mess with the system, Anna,' he says bitterly. 'We've all got our scripts down pat. Kate plays the Martyr. I'm the Lost Cause. And you, you're the Peacekeeper.'

He thinks he knows me, but that goes both ways – and when it comes to friction, Jesse is an addict. I look right at him. 'Says who?'

Jesse agrees to wait for me in the parking lot. It's one of the few times I can recall him doing anything I tell him to do. I walk around to the front of the building, which has two gargoyles guarding its entrance.

Campbell Alexander, Esquire's office is on the third floor. The walls are paneled with wood the color of a chestnut mare's coat, and when I step onto the thick Oriental rug on the floor, my sneakers sink an inch. The secretary is wearing black pumps so shiny I can see my own face in them. I glance down at my cutoffs and the Keds that I tattooed last week with Magic Markers when I was bored.

The secretary has perfect skin and perfect eyebrows and honeybee lips, and she's using them to scream bloody murder at whoever's on the other end of the phone. 'You cannot expect me to tell a judge that. Just because *you* don't want to hear Kleman rant and rave doesn't mean that *I* have to . . . no, actually, that raise was for the exceptional job I do and the crap I put up with on a daily basis, and as a matter of fact, while we're on—' She holds the phone away from her ear; I can make out the buzz of disconnection. 'Bastard,' she mutters, and then seems to realize I'm standing three feet away. 'Can I help you?'

She looks me over from head to toe, rating me on a general scale of first impressions, and finding me severely lacking. I lift my chin and pretend to be far more cool than I actually am. 'I have an appointment with Mr Alexander. At four o'clock.'

'Your voice,' she says. 'On the phone, you didn't sound quite so . . .'

Young?

She smiles uncomfortably. 'We don't try juvenile cases, as a rule. If you'd like I can offer you the names of some practicing attorneys who—'

I take a deep breath. 'Actually,' I interrupt, 'you're wrong. Smith v. Whately, Edmunds v. Womens and Infants Hospital, and Jerome v. the Diocese of Providence all involved litigants under the age of eighteen. All three resulted in verdicts for Mr Alexander's clients. And those were just in the past *year*.'

The secretary blinks at me. Then a slow smile toasts her

face, as if she's decided she just might like me after all. 'Come to think of it, why don't you just wait in his office?' she suggests, and she stands up to show me the way.

Even if I spend every minute of the rest of my life reading, I do not believe that I will ever manage to consume the sheer number of words routed high and low on the walls of Campbell Alexander, Esquire's office. I do the math – if there are 400 words or so on every page, and each of those legal books are 400 pages, and there are twenty on a shelf and six shelves per bookcase – why, you're pushing nineteen million words, and that's only partway across the room.

I'm alone in the office long enough to note that his desk is so neat, you could play Chinese football on the blotter; that there is not a single photo of a wife or a kid or even himself; and that in spite of the fact that the room is spotless, there's a mug full of water sitting on the floor.

I find myself making up explanations: it's a swimming pool for an army of ants. It's some kind of primitive humidifier. It's a mirage.

I've nearly convinced myself about that last one, and am leaning over to touch it to see if it's real, when the door bursts open. I practically fall out of my chair and that puts me eye to eye with an incoming German shepherd, which spears me with a look and then marches over to the mug and starts to drink.

Campbell Alexander comes in, too. He's got black hair and he's at least as tall as my dad – six feet – with a right-angle jaw and eyes that look frozen over. He shrugs out of a suit jacket and hangs it neatly on the back of the door, then yanks a file out of a cabinet before moving to his desk. He never makes eye contact with me, but he starts talking all the same. 'I don't want any Girl Scout cookies,' Campbell Alexander says. 'Although you do get Brownie points for tenacity. Ha.' He smiles at his own joke.

'I'm not selling anything.'

He glances at me curiously, then pushes a button on his

phone. 'Kerri,' he says when the secretary answers. 'What is this doing in my office?'

'I'm here to retain you,' I say.

The lawyer releases the intercom button. 'I don't think so.'

'You don't even know if I have a case.'

I take a step forward; so does the dog. For the first time I realize it's wearing one of those vests with a red cross on it, like a St Bernard that might carry rum up a snowy mountain. I automatically reach out to pet him. 'Don't,' Alexander says. 'Judge is a service dog.'

My hand goes back to my side. 'But you aren't blind.'

'Thank you for pointing that out to me.'

'So what's the matter with you?'

The minute I say it, I want to take it back. Haven't I watched Kate field this question from hundreds of rude people?

'I have an iron lung,' Campbell Alexander says curtly, 'and the dog keeps me from getting too close to magnets. Now, if you'd do me the exalted honor of leaving, my secretary can find you the name of someone who—'

But I can't go yet. 'Did you really sue God?' I take out all the newspaper clippings, smooth them on the bare desk.

A muscle tics in his cheek, and then he picks up the article lying on top. 'I sued the Diocese of Providence, on behalf of a kid in one of their orphanages who needed an experimental treatment involving fetal tissue, which they felt violated Vatican II. However, it makes a much better headline to say that a nine-year-old is suing God for being stuck with the short end of the straw in life.' I just stare at him. 'Dylan Jerome,' the lawyer admits, 'wanted to sue God for not caring enough about him.'

A rainbow might as well have cracked down the middle of that big mahogany desk. 'Mr Alexander,' I say, 'my sister has leukemia.'

'I'm sorry to hear that. But even if I were willing to litigate against God again, which I'm not, you can't bring a lawsuit on someone else's behalf.'

There is way too much to explain – my own blood seeping

into my sister's veins; the nurses holding me down to stick me for white cells Kate might borrow; the doctor saying they didn't get enough the first time around. The bruises and the deep bone ache after I gave up my marrow; the shots that sparked more stem cells in me, so that there'd be extra for my sister. The fact that I'm not sick, but I might as well be. The fact that the only reason I was born was as a harvest crop for Kate. The fact that even now, a major decision about me is being made, and no one's bothered to ask the one person who most deserves it to speak her opinion.

There's way too much to explain, and so I do the best I can. 'It's not God. Just my parents,' I say. 'I want to sue them for the rights to my own body.'

My Sister's Keeper *is available now in hardback from Hodder & Stoughton.*